ONE MUMMY
TO GO, *Please!*
BOOK 1

SHAWARMA WARRIOR KING

ONE MUMMY TO GO, Please!
BOOK 1

JM PAQUETTE AND BEAU LAKE

4 Horsemen
Publications, Inc.

One Mummy to Go, Please!
Copyright © 2024 JM Paquette & Beau Lake. All rights reserved.

Published By: 4 Horsemen Publications, Inc.

4 Horsemen Publications, Inc.
PO Box 417
Sylva, NC 28779
4horsemenpublications.com
info@4horsemenpublications.com

Cover Illustration by Oxford
Cover text & Typesetting by Autumn Skye
Edited by Laura Mita

All rights to the work within are reserved to the author and publisher. No part of this publication may be reproduced, stored in a retrieval system, or transmitted in any form or by any means, electronic, mechanical, photocopying, recording, scanning, or otherwise, except as permitted under Section 107 or 108 of the 1976 International Copyright Act, without prior written permission except in brief quotations embodied in critical articles and reviews. Please contact either the Publisher or Author to gain permission.

All characters, organizations, and events portrayed in this novel are either products of the author's imagination or are used fictitiously.

All brands, quotes, and cited work respectfully belongs to the original rights holders and bear no affiliation to the authors or publisher.

Library of Congress Control Number: 2024942257

Paperback ISBN-13: 979-8-8232-0615-0
Hardcover ISBN-13: 979-8-8232-0616-7
Audiobook ISBN-13: 979-8-8232-0618-1
Ebook ISBN-13: 979-8-8232-0617-4

BEAU

To Brendan Fraser and Rachel Weisz.
They know what they did.

JM

To Oded Fehr and Arnold Vosloo.
They also know what they did.

Acknowledgments

Beau: First, I want to thank J.M. Paquette for writing this with me (and encouraging silliness when the story called for it). Second, I want to thank Val for her encouragement when it came to outlining; she sat on countless calls with us while we complained about how much we *hated* outlining. And, as always, I must thank M. for being the most patient, encouraging partner a girl could ask for.

JM: First, thanks to Beau, for coming on this crazy adventure with me, and next to Val, whose outline was the best (only) way to organize a pantser like me (not to mention her creation of Teo, our favorite belly-dancing thief!). Writing this book was the most fun I've had (plus the gif game was on point in our Mummy Chat)! And finally smooches to Remi. He knows why.

# CONTENTS

ACKNOWLEDGMENTS VII
PROLOGUE XI

CHAPTER 1 1
CHAPTER 2 5
CHAPTER 3 10
CHAPTER 4 14
CHAPTER 5 18
CHAPTER 6 22
CHAPTER 7 26
CHAPTER 8 30
CHAPTER 9 34
CHAPTER 10 38
CHAPTER 11 42
CHAPTER 12 46
CHAPTER 13 50
CHAPTER 14 56
CHAPTER 15 62
CHAPTER 16. 67
CHAPTER 17 72
CHAPTER 18 77
CHAPTER 19 83
CHAPTER 20 88
CHAPTER 21 93
CHAPTER 22 98
CHAPTER 23 103
CHAPTER 24 108

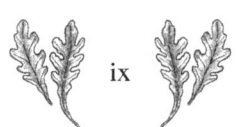

Chapter 25	113
Chapter 26	118
Chapter 27	124
Chapter 28	129
Chapter 29	134
Chapter 30	140
Chapter 31	144
Chapter 32	149
Chapter 33	154
Chapter 34	158
Chapter 35	163
Chapter 36	169
Chapter 37	173
Chapter 38	178
Chapter 39	187
Chapter 40	191
Chapter 41	196
Chapter 42	200
Chapter 43	204
Chapter 44	210
Chapter 45	220
Chapter 46	224
Chapter 47	230
Chapter 48	234
Chapter 49	239
Chapter 50	243
Chapter 51	247
Epilogue	251
Book Club Questions	255
Author Bios	257

Prologue

Kasmut tugged back the tapestry—adorned with an image of his Pharaoh hunting an oryx—and peered into the dark courtyard. Only one torch burned; the others had been doused by the wind, and no one was awake to tend them. It was quiet, save for the relentless trill of a nightjar roosting beneath a thorny shrub. *Perhaps it is calling its mate*, Kasmut thought bitterly. *If only I were a bird! I could fly far away from—*

"Well?" His Pharaoh's deep timbre seemed to shake the ground beneath Kasmut's feet. It was a voice that commanded an army thousands strong, but most importantly, it steered Kasmut. Milfonnos' voice preceded his every move, whether he liked it or not.

Kasmut sighed, releasing the tapestry. "It is quiet, Pharaoh. Not a soul in sight. Just a bird."

Resting his palms on the altar, Milfonnos squinted at the Book of Heka. He had been struggling to read since the tumors invaded his sinus cavity and compressed the optic nerve in his right eye.

Kasmut didn't bother to glance at the page—he couldn't read even with perfect eyesight. He would never say so out loud, but these days, his Pharaoh looked more like a man than the godhead. Once, Milfonnos was as muscular as an ox, but now he was as slight as a jackal, the sickness eating the meat off his bones. The ostentatious leopard pelt draped over his drooping shoulders made him look even smaller. They had killed the leopard together, riding side-by-side on camelback. Kasmut had pulled back his bow string first, but it was Milfonnos who cut the dying big cat's throat.

"Pharaoh?"

"Silence, Kas. I'm *reading*." Milfonnos reached for the ruby resting beside the book. It was the largest gem Kasmut had ever seen—as big as his palm and heavier than a gurma fruit. As Milfonnos held it up, the gem reflected the candlelight in a kaleidoscope of refracted pinpoints. "Once I start, no one may enter this room. Do you understand?"

Kasmut bit his lip, resting his hand on the scimitar at his hip. He hadn't minded the talk about the magical spell that could make his Pharaoh immortal, both curing his disease and making him invulnerable. But now that the book had been found and the day of the ceremony had arrived, Kasmut wasn't so sure. "Why must we start at all?"

"If we do not do something soon, there will be no reason to begin. Time is running out." Milfonnos sighed. He tapped the golden armbands on his thin upper arms, the bangles resting in the crook of his elbows. "Even these cannot protect me anymore." The Pharaoh turned to his loyal bodyguard, the fighter he had known since childhood. "You can wait outside, if you'd like." He gestured to the door, which they had blockaded with a wooden chair with legs carved to resemble a lion's. "You don't need to see this."

The thought made Kasmut even more uneasy. He didn't want Milfonnos to be alone, especially if he had to straddle the boundary between the Duat and the living world. "And leave you alone to traverse the lake of fire or scale the iron walls?" Kasmut snorted. "I'll stay. I am your faithful servant."

Milfonnos nodded, steeling himself for what was coming. The Pharaoh had researched the spell that would both restore his vitality and keep him safe, but he couldn't be certain that the magic would work. "Thank you, Kas," he said, before turning abruptly to the book resting on the altar, scanning the instructions he had memorized months ago.

He placed the gemstone back on the altar; as before, it caught the light, bands of crimson stretching across the rough-hewn worktop. Kasmut shuddered, thinking of the blood that would soon dampen the altar. Milfonnos' blood. "Once I start, you mustn't interfere," Milfonnos reminded him.

"I won't," Kasmut promised.

Milfonnos scoffed. "You blither like a woman if I so much as scrape a knee."

"Because it'll be *my* head if you're hurt," Kasmut grumbled.

Milfonnos clapped a hand on his bodyguard's shoulder. "No one is going to cut off your head, Kas. Not while I'm around."

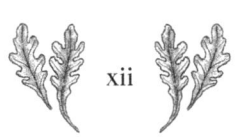

What if you perish?

Kasmut swallowed the question where it sat like a stone in his gullet. He mustn't doubt his Pharaoh, at least not aloud. He didn't doubt that Ra would rouse the sun come morning, or that Osiris would greet him when he closed his eyes for the last time, so he could not doubt Milfonnos.

Resigned, Milfonnos heaved a sigh. "Let's begin. Give me your scimitar."

Kasmut's hand flexed about the hilt. "I—"

Milfonnos shot him a dark look, baring his squarish teeth like an animal. "Now," he snarled. "Listen to your Pharaoh." This close, Kasmut could see the dark circles beneath Milfonnos' bloodshot eyes. When had he last slept?

Kasmut slowly drew the weapon from its scabbard, handing it over hilt-first. Milfonnos' face paled as he hefted it, but his expression remained impassive. "Will it be worth it?" Kasmut asked, the words spewing out of his mouth like vomit. If he kept the Pharaoh talking, perhaps the ritual could be delayed for one more minute, one more hour, one more night.

"If you could be impervious to a knife in the back, wouldn't you do it?" Milfonnos countered.

"If you keep your head on a swivel, there's no need to bring magic into it," Kasmut remarked.

Milfonnos chuckled. "I have too many enemies. Surely, my head can't spin fast enough."

Without another word, Milfonnos cut his palm open with the scimitar and muttered in a language Kasmut didn't understand. The words seemed to bounce off Milfonnos' tongue, the vowels no louder than an exhale.

Thick droplets of crimson speckled the book's page. Milfonnos swayed.

Suddenly, the door buckled inward, the chair skittering across the mud tiles. When it toppled over, Milfonnos' head snapped toward the sound. "No!" he cried as men in black robes and keffiyeh poured through the doorway. One raised a sword high, the sleeve pooling down his arm.

"The Amun Henet!" Kasmut shouted, recognizing the winged sigil burned onto the hand of the closest invader; they'd come for the ruby. He snatched his scimitar from his Pharaoh's hand to defend him. He knew he couldn't take on all five men, but he would try. For Milfonnos. "We have to go, Milfonnos!" He hadn't called him by his name since they were children.

Milfonnos picked up the ruby with his bleeding hand, holding it aloft. Not even the Amun Henet could stop him. Blood trickled down his arm, not unlike the Nile traversing the desert. He shouted in the strange language of magic as Kasmut's sword clashed with many.

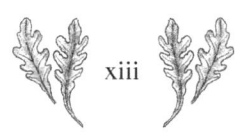

One Mummy to Go, Please!

"Stop him!" one of the men shouted, his voice familiar. Where did Kasmut know that voice? It brought to mind memories of long diatribes over roasted mutton and copious glasses of beer.

"The gemstone!" another cried. "He has stolen it from Amun-Ra's temple!"

Milfonnos had done nothing of the sort. It was Kasmut who had ridden into the temple complex at Karnak, his way lit only by the sliver of the moon. It was Kasmut who had subdued the priests who lived there, whispering apologies as he tied their hands and feet. It was Kasmut who had entered the chapel, prying the ruby out of the obelisk with his knife.

Kasmut parried a wildly swinging scimitar, elbowing the attacker in the face. His nose crunched. Before Kasmut could swing his weapon again, he was overpowered by three men and driven to his knees. Someone struck him in the temple with the hilt of their scimitar and his ears rang. Heat scored along his back, and then he fell forward, his body numb.

He caught one last glimpse of Milfonnos. Perhaps it was the concussion, but he swore the Pharaoh floated a few feet above the floor, the ruby embedded in the bleeding socket of his right eye. The gem glowed. As Kasmut's vision darkened, the Amun Henet surrounded the Pharaoh, their blades smeared with red.

Kasmut was dead, a growing pool of blood spreading beneath his prone corpse. Milfonnos was not sad, even though they had suckled at the breast of the same wet nurse and learned to walk while holding hands.

Milfonnos only felt euphoria.

The Amun Henet swarmed around him like ants on honey, but he was only dimly aware of the blade placed against his throat, dimpling the skin. When it sawed through his jugular, he felt no pain, only the warmth of blood soaking his leopard-spotted mantle. The static of magic raised the hair on his arms and scalp.

It worked.

He should be dead like poor Kasmut, but he felt only elation. He reached up, feeling the new skin of his throat. Blades plunged into his belly, but it was no more painful than a bee sting. He glanced down at the golden armbands encircling his upper arms, flexing his muscles and marveling at the return of his former body. He had always been aware of the dim thrum of

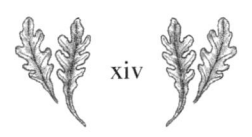

protection magic contained within the armbands, but now they were energized, their abilities amplified by the gemstone and the ritual.

"How are you doing this?" the apparent leader of the Amun Henet shouted in his face, spittle dappling the Pharaoh's cheeks. Milfonnos recognized him—Rahil, one of his supposedly devoted ministers. "What have you done?"

Milfonnos laughed, powerful magic crackling beneath his skin. "I have done what had to be done."

Rahil blanched, fear tingeing his eyes. "This is blasphemy—an affront to the gods. No one can escape death, not even you, Milfonnos." For a moment, Milfonnos could hear the honest concern in Rahil's voice. Even now, he feared for his Pharaoh's precious soul. A small part of him heard the words, felt the truth in them, but the rest of him knew that without this power, he was doomed. Besides, he was a Pharaoh—he deserved to live forever. Rahil could never understand.

"I *am* a god. Can't you see?" Milfonnos felt drunk and giddy. For months, he had been exhausted, too weak to do much more than slump upon his throne, waving away subjects asking for more, more, more. Now, he felt like he could traverse the unforgiving desert, as hardy as a camel. He gripped the hilt of one of the scimitars embedded in his belly, pulling it free. His blood coated the blade, glinting in the candlelight, and Milfonnos triumphantly held the blade aloft.

"You are no god," Rahil snarled. Quick as a snake, the Amun Henet leader dug his fingers into Milfonnos' eye socket. The gem shifted and Milfonnos dropped the sword to grab for Rahil's wrist. As soon as he touched Rahil's bare skin, his palm sizzled and blistered as though he'd grabbed a piece of hot coal.

Rahil's lip quirked. "Do you feel that? *That* is power endowed by the gods." He cupped the Pharaoh's cheek with his palm.

Blisters erupted on Milfonnos' face, the pustules bursting. He tried to open his mouth to speak—to scream—but his lips were melting.

Rahil's dexterous fingers attempted to pluck the ruby from Milfonnos' eye socket, and the gemstone cracked—Rahil holding a chunk aloft in triumph. Milfonnos' vision doubled, and the pain was immediate as the magic rebounded. As tumors filled his lungs, he found that he could not breathe. Milfonnos reached for the magical armbands he still wore, seeking the meager protection he had left.

The other Amun Henet quickly pinned the Pharaoh's arms as Rahil held the gem up, the ruby drenched in scarlet. Even with the echo of powerful

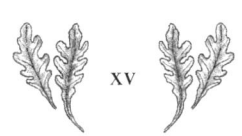

magic still coursing through his veins, Milfonnos could not escape their clutches. When Rahil struck again with his blade, the Pharaoh crumbled. Pain came like a rolling wave.

Chapter 1

"Get it together, Doctor Who," Jack Manning growled at the idiot studying the book on the far end of the burial chamber. "We don't have all day." Jack draped an arm over the rung of the ladder.

The wannabe archaeologist gave him a dirty look, then returned his attention to the battered tome resting on the stone slab in front of him. "You wouldn't understand any of this," Reese Eldin snapped. "You're just a hired thug. Ancient ritual magic is complicated. It takes time."

"We have time—just not a lot of it. You know we aren't supposed to be down here without the overseer." Jack listened for the telltale sound of footsteps above. No one seemed to notice their presence in the tomb—not yet anyway. "Besides, who said anything about performing ritual magic? You said you were making sure some artifacts were still down here." He snorted. "You worried the British Museum is going to steal 'em before you get the chance?"

"Tosh," the British man scoffed. "I'm only double-checking the contents of the tomb before tomorrow—making sure the contents match the official reports." He looked up at Jack, lingering too long on the fighter's athletic physique. Was that jealousy Jack saw in his eyes? Reese was younger than Jack by a few years, somewhere in his late-20s, but he was soft in the middle, the body of a man who never did actual labor. "And you've been hired to make sure nothing happens to me in the meantime. Do your job."

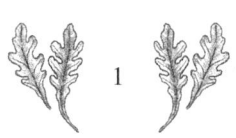

One Mummy to Go, Please!

Reese flipped a few pages with more force than Jack thought necessary, given the age of the book. *What do I know? As he said, I'm only the hired help.* Jack frowned, checking that both guns were within hands' reach. "I don't work for *you*, you little British goober. Shogun Security works for the dig site."

"And I'm running this site," Reese snapped, "so right now, you work for me. Stand there and let me do my job." His finger slid along the page he had open, clearly searching for something. Jack wondered if he could speed things up by offering to read some of it for him. His Hieratic was a little rusty, but he could still make sense of most of it. Staring at the odious man, Jack decided not to offer. The nerd would probably be offended at the idea that the "dumb" security guard actually had a brain and knew about more than just guns and strategy.

Also, it would serve the bastard right if they did get caught down here. Then Reese wouldn't be running anything any time soon. They took their dig sites seriously here in Cairo. He may be "running" the site, but he wasn't allowed down here to examine the artifacts without the overseer or some of the crew—just in case he decided to slide something small into a convenient backpack and sneak it back to England.

Sighing, Jack stretched, knowing that he wouldn't do anything except stand around and make sure nothing happened to the artifacts inside. He may wish ill on the Englishman, but he wouldn't say or do anything to jeopardize his position. He wasn't willing to risk this sweet gig for a few moments of satisfaction—no matter how annoying Reese could be.

Jack's jobs were normally more eventful—mercs in Africa, terrorists in the deep desert—but he went where the money was, and he kept people alive until he collected his paycheck. Babysitting a dig in Egypt was a cakewalk compared to his last three assignments. If it wasn't for the oppressive heat and uptight pricks like Reese Eldin, he might even be enjoying himself. The scenery wasn't bad, especially the woman running the food truck serving the dig.

And the extra paycheck from his secondary employer made everything a little bit easier. Both wanted the same thing—security for the artifacts on the site—so Jack didn't see a problem working for both at the same time. It wasn't like Shogun prohibited moonlighting.

Reese's voice drifted just above the pages, mumbling words in a language Jack didn't understand—which was odd because Jack knew a lot of languages. For a moment, he was sure something else was with them in the tomb, a presence that Jack didn't like.

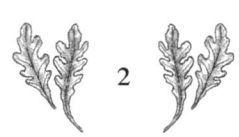

"Hey," Jack snapped. Startled, Reese yelped. "Don't go reading from ancient books while we're literally standing in a mummy's tomb. Honestly, have you never seen a movie before?"

Reese shook his head, closed the book, and tucked it beneath his arm. "You know nothing, foolish American. Just stand there with your muscles and your guns and let the grown-ups work."

Jack let the insult slide, though he wanted to ask where these proverbial grown-ups might be. He decided on a different tactic to speed things along.

"So some armbands and a ruby—that's what you're looking for?" Jack kept his voice casual. "You know that those little jars are worth way more, right?" He gestured at the alabaster canopic jars, each lid carved to resemble one of Horus' four sons. "You could get a cool million on the black market."

Reese's head jerked in his direction, guilt plastered on his features. He really needed to work on his poker face, or everyone would know what he'd been up to. Jack wasn't sure if his goal was straight theft or something else, but he would figure it out eventually. "H-h-how do you know about that?" Reese stammered.

Jack shrugged. "I pay attention. That's actually what they pay me for." He cocked his head, listening to the distant rumble of an approaching engine. When it backfired, Jack smirked. He recognized it as the food truck that camped out on the outskirts of the dig site, offering up pitas stuffed with meat and vegetables to the sweaty archeologists and laborers alike. The girl who ran it was a tiny thing with "fuck me" eyes. Jack would like to take her up on that.

"Speaking of, we are out of time." He gestured to the ladder leading to the ground above. "I hope you found what you were looking for."

"You wouldn't understand," Reese snapped condescendingly, but he obediently headed to the ladder, zipping the book up inside his windbreaker. Jack shook his head but said nothing. His employer wasn't particularly interested in the book—not yet anyway. If Reese wanted to keep it close, that was his business. Jack could always get it from him later—it wasn't as if the man could put up a fight against Jack Manning. Looking up at the exit, Jack saw that the Englishman was slow to climb the ladder, huffing like he'd just run a marathon.

Jack lingered in the tomb a moment longer, watching Reese's feet as they disappeared into the light above. There it was again: the feeling that Jack was being watched. A thorough scan of the excavated chamber assured him that he was alone, and he removed his hands from his guns.

He shook himself, letting the feeling go. Perhaps the heat was getting to him. As he climbed out of the tomb, his mind drifted back to the girl in the food truck. He could swear she'd been checking him out a few times over the last week, flirting just a little as he ordered his lunch.

I'll take her over a mummy any day, he thought.

Chapter 2

The truck was sweltering. The oscillating fan—which no longer oscillated—only offered a meager breeze, which did little to counteract the heat emanating from the sizzling cooktop. Eliza Cunningham, proud owner of the Shawarma Warrior King food truck, gathered her hair up in her fist to cool the back of her neck.

"Hey Duckling, hot enough for you?" Reese Eldin, Eliza's worst mistake, sidled up to the window, drumming his fingers on the countertop. He grinned, revealing a row of pearly white veneers. Despite spending the morning processing artifacts, his khaki outfit was pristine. He probably had the local laborers do all of his dirty work while he stood in the shade.

Eliza scowled at her old friend, if he could even be called that. Reese had been a nuisance since she was in primary school. He used to tug on her pigtails and snap her training bra, and his irritating behavior only escalated when they went to university. She hated the nickname "Duckling," but he refused to drop it—much like he refused to stop pursuing her despite her objections. "Are you ordering something or just here to bug me?"

"Don't be like that," Reese said. "I just wanted to say 'hello' to my best friend—that's all." He tugged down the brim of his baseball cap, shrouding the crow's feet that wrinkled the corners of his eyes.

"You're scaring away my customers," Eliza said, and she meant it. No one wanted to be around a know-it-all prat, a pompous ass, a—

One Mummy to Go, Please!

"Fine, I'll order," Reese huffed. "Lamb and tabbouleh on a pita. Extra tahini."

Eliza resisted the urge to roll her eyes. Reese ordered the same thing every day. "Coming right up," she said sweetly as she reached for her serrated knife. She cut a thin slice of lamb off of the rotating skewer, catching it in a folded pita, then scooped a spoonful of tabbouleh on top and grabbed the bottle of tahini. Before she could add her signature zigzag, a cloud of dust poured through the window, accompanied by the whirring of a helicopter's rotors.

Even though his lunch was now generously seasoned with dust, Reese beamed. "The investors!" he squealed, clapping his hands like an overstimulated toddler. He took off his hat and smoothed his sweat-dampened hair.

The laborers tried to throw tarps over the excavated artifacts, but the wind ripped them from their hands. *"Imshi!"* they shouted. *Go away.*

As the helicopter touched down, Eliza wiped the thin layer of dust off of the countertop with her fingertip. "Assholes," she grumbled.

Reese raised his eyebrows. "Have some respect, Duckling. These guys gave us millions of dollars."

"I'm sure they are going to turn a sarcophagus into a coffee table," Eliza mused. "They can sell it at West Elm."

"That's rich coming from you," Reese snickered. "Don't forget: you're making money because those investors gave you an exclusive contract—on *my* recommendation. Do you think you'd make as much money competing with the other food trucks in Maadi?"

How could she forget? He reminded her of that fact incessantly. She also wasn't too keen to go back to the city. Getting up at the crack of dawn for a prime spot on the curb had started taking its toll. It felt like each day blended into the next, separated only by a few restless hours of shut-eye.

The helicopter's rotors slowed, and two men in linen suits climbed out. One of the men wore a cream-colored Panama hat and boat shoes. As they strolled toward the dig site, Reese picked an imaginary piece of lint off of his shirtfront. "I'd better go," he said. "Time to turn up the charm."

You have the charm of a shit-covered pig.

As Reese trotted away, Eliza opened the lid of the trash can with her foot and dumped his lunch inside. She would have to throw all of the doners away and defrost a fresh batch. "Assholes," she grumbled again, resting her elbows on the countertop. Her fingers found the familiar red gemstone hanging around her neck, her mother's necklace a comfort as she fought her annoyance. She couldn't see the investors—or Reese—anymore; they

must be down in the pit. For the briefest of moments, a trench opened up in Eliza's stomach. She should be down there, covered in dust. Not in a rusty old Citreon … covered in dust.

No, she reminded herself, dropping the necklace and moving to wash her hands in the basin sink before skewering a half-frozen hunk of lamb onto the rotisserie. *You walked away from that life. Cooking is your calling.* She spun on her heel, facing the interior of the truck that was her life now.

She was lost in her work when a voice drifted in through the window. "Hey, sweetheart. Can I still get that lunch special, or did I miss my window?"

Eliza recognized the voice. She smiled as she turned to face the handsome security guard standing outside her truck. "I only have the packaged pitas left. That okay?"

"I missed the run on the fresh ones, huh? I guess I'll have to get here sooner if I want a proper taste of you…r food." He slid his sunglasses down and winked at her, the afternoon sunlight shining on his blond hair.

Eliza laughed, not missing the innuendo. "No need to hurry. I usually have more, but today's batch got ruined." She gestured behind him where the helicopter sat like a rotund sparrow, waiting for the return of the investors.

"Ah," the guard said, nodding in understanding as he hooked his sunglasses in his front breast pocket. His eyes were a bright blue. "The suits never seem to care about the mess they leave for everyone else."

"Truth," Eliza agreed. She cocked her head at him. "Though I didn't expect to hear that from one of their people."

"I'm my own person," the guard told her, leaning in to rest his muscular forearms on the small metal counter outside her window.

"I'm glad to hear it," she replied. "What are your own thoughts on tzatziki sauce?"

"Love it," the guard drawled, watching as she reached for the big knife and sliced chunks of meat into the pita in her hand. She made a show of zigzagging sauce across the top. "Veg?" she prompted, already reaching for the lettuce.

His hand shot out, reaching through the window to gently grab her wrist. "No," he said, letting his fingers linger on her skin for a moment. "Just like that."

"A plain man, I see," Eliza said as he released her. "Mysterious yet simple. Just the way I like them." She slid the pita into a wrapper, folded it in half, and handed it to him. "American dollars, I assume?"

"Do you take cards?" he asked.

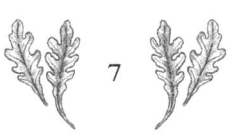

One Mummy to Go, Please!

Eliza put her hands on her hips, narrowing her eyes at him. "This may be Egypt, sir, but we are still civilized." She reached into her apron pocket and withdrew her phone with the small card reader plugged into the bottom.

"I know," he said, flipping his wallet open with one hand and pulling out a black card. "This is actually the cradle of civilization."

Eliza took the offering, surprised that he had an exclusive Black Card. She'd heard about them but had never actually seen one. She squinted, reading the name printed along the bottom. "'Jack Manning.'" She looked up at him. "Seriously?"

"That's me," he assured her.

"A plain man indeed," she murmured, still staring at the card. "And you're seriously using *this* to buy a pita?"

"Even plain people need to eat," he joked, taking a bite of the pita and closing his eyes in appreciation.

Eliza shook her head, then she ran the card. Of course, it went through without a hitch. She held out her phone to him. "Receipt?" she prompted, handing him back the card with her other hand.

He took the card first, sliding it back in his wallet with a one-handed grace she envied. Then he winked at her and tapped the screen a few times. "Done," he announced.

"Thanks," Eliza said, sliding the phone back into her pocket without looking at the screen. "It's been my pleasure... Jack."

"The pleasure is all mine," he replied, leaning on the counter. "Will you tell me your name?"

"Come back tomorrow," Eliza teased. "I'll have a fresh pita for you."

"But who will I ask for if you're not here?" he pressed, though his tone was easy-going.

"I'm the only one who is ever here," she assured him, gesturing to the truck around her. "This is my truck: Shawarma Warrior King."

Jack choked on the bite he had just taken. Hands on his knees, he spit into the sand. When he had regained his composure, he looked up with teary eyes. "Are you kidding me? That's the name of your truck?"

"Yes," she said, handing him a bottle of water. "Drink that before you die. I have a rule about not killing customers."

Jack accepted the bottle, downing half of it in one gulp. Eliza enjoyed watching his neck muscles work as he swallowed. With a tight t-shirt highlighting the line of his shoulders and his pants hugging his thick thighs, Jack Manning was a beautiful man.

He put the bottle down on the small aluminum counter then narrowed his eyes. "So you're looking for your warrior king?"

Eliza nodded. "Always."

"Do you have any rules about American security guards who hate vegetables?"

"Not yet," she retorted. "But I may have to develop some. You Americans can't be trusted."

"Nor can you Brits running around the desert," he said. "Either running to something or running away... I wonder which you are?"

"I'm just a girl with a food truck," Eliza replied casually then gave him a full smile. She wasn't about to tell him about her past—how she'd left university when her parents died, fleeing as far as the insurance money would take her. "I'm Eliza."

"Eliza," Jack repeated, nodding. "So British by birth as well as by upbringing."

She shrugged. He wasn't the first person to call her out for being a foreigner in Egypt, and he wouldn't be the last. "I've been here long enough to get used to the heat."

Jack snorted, gulping what remained in the water bottle. "I don't think I'll ever get used to it." He tossed the empty bottle into the garbage can a few feet away, sinking the shot without even looking. He retrieved his half-eaten pita off the counter. "Until tomorrow, then, Eliza."

"You too, Jack." Eliza watched him leave, waiting until he was a decent distance away before pulling out her phone to snap a few quick pictures of his ass. She had promised to send Poppy some visual evidence of the sexy security guard. Her last transaction was still on the screen.

Tip: $100.

Her stomach dropped. *Seriously?* Part of her was annoyed, feeling like he was trying to buy her off, but then the feeling passed. If sexy men wanted to give her money, she wasn't too proud to take it. It didn't mean she owed them anything more than she'd already given him—a few smiles and a warm meal. And maybe a tiny choking fit.

Jack Manning may not be a warrior king, but he was a damn fine man.

Chapter 3

As Jack unscrewed the cap of his canteen, the unforgiving sun beat down on the back of his neck. *The pit and its artifacts are protected with an awning, but fuck me, right?* He'd kill for even a sliver of shade. He would do worse things for a cold Budweiser in an icy glass.

His deodorant had worn off hours ago, no match for the unrelenting heat, and he caught a whiff of himself. Pungent. At least, on a dig site, everyone smelled horrible.

The water in his canteen was warm and tasted faintly metallic. It did little to soothe the 7000 grit sandpaper that was once his tongue. Jack longed for an oasis—a real one, not a Wile E. Coyote hallucination that turned into sand as soon as he swan-dived. *Is Ahm Schere a real place? I'll brave the pygmies for some cool water in the shade.*

Jack shifted his weight from foot to foot, the heels of his boots sinking into the sand. When he was a kid, he was terrified of the desert because he walked in on his parents watching some movie where the protagonist sank to his neck in quicksand. That little snot-nosed kid wouldn't be able to cope if he knew where he would eventually travel for work—scary places, shit-your-pants scary.

There was that one time in Kandahar when he ran headlong through a bush of crown-of-thorns because the alternative was getting shot in the head. The sticky sap stuck to every inch of exposed skin on his arms and legs

and burned like a son of a bitch. He had blisters for weeks and sorta-kinda wished the mercenaries had shot him instead.

There was that other time when he escorted an Exxon-Mobil exec with a target on his back through Jakarta. While Jack knew the guy was partially responsible for the razing of the rainforest, a buck was a buck. He would have escorted the Unabomber if it meant he would get paid afterward. Money talked and Jack listened.

Even though they'd checked into the hotel under a fake name—Ethan Hunt, after Jack's favorite action hero—they were rudely awakened by armed men in baklavas shouting in Javanese. Jack still had nightmares about being forced onto his knees on a stinking carpet, wearing only a pair of boxers. Though, sometimes, they were nice dreams where the hand that curled around his throat was soft and wore spade-shaped press-ons.

"*Menengo!*" *the men yelled, even though Jack hadn't said a word.*

The executive was crying pretty hard though, a snot bubble blooming beneath his nostril. He wore tighty-whities and an undershirt with yellow stains beneath the arms. Before they had been dragged from their twin beds, the man had been snoring like a chainsaw.

They had been forced into the back of a box truck with canvas bags over their heads. Jack's bag smelled like rotting potatoes. While the executive whimpered, Jack worked on the zip ties, glad he hadn't fallen asleep in the nude. Their kidnappers hadn't given them time to get dressed.

He knew there were armed men in the box truck with them, but he couldn't tell how many. There had been four men in their hotel room, but he wasn't sure how many were guarding them.

"*Anyone see any good movies lately?*" *Jack quipped. The potato sack tickled his nose, and he sneezed.*

"*Ora omong,*" *a man growled from directly across from him.* One.

"*Yeah, yeah, 'no talking,'*" *Jack grumbled. "I remember. What about books? I'm not much of a reader, but—*"

A rifle butt slammed into the side of his head. Jack saw stars. A tiny giggle escaped him. Two.

"*Tough crowd,*" *he managed, tasting blood in his mouth. Had he bitten his tongue? "If I'm going to get Stockholm syndrome and fall hopelessly in love, we've gotta get acquainted."*

"*Menengo, Amerikan,*" *the first man said, exasperated.*

Two guards. *Hopefully there wasn't some strong, silent type in here too. But Jack didn't have time to keep antagonizing them. If they got to wherever*

One Mummy to Go, Please!

they were going, the executive would be killed, and Jack wouldn't be paid. Worse, he'd probably be killed too.

Jack twisted his wrists and snapped the zip tie. He threw his shoulder into the man who'd hit him with the rifle, knocking him off-balance. As soon as he tugged the potato sack off of his head, the other man opened fire. Bullets ricocheted off the floor (plink, plink, plink!) and the blasts lit up the cargo hold. A searing pain lanced through Jack's shoulder—

"Are you okay?"

"Huh?" Jack was suddenly back in the desert, his shirt sticking to his back. "What did you say?"

He absently rubbed his shoulder and the knot of scar tissue beneath his shirt. He'd dug the bullet out in a bus station bathroom and puked in the rust-stained toilet afterward. He still got phantom pains sometimes. Maybe he'd missed a fragment or two.

The food truck girl—Eliza—looked up at him, a roll of toilet paper tucked under her arm. "You look like you've seen a ghost." Her British accent was like music to Jack's unsophisticated ears.

"Something like that." Jack slung the strap of his canteen over his shoulder, trying to look nonchalant. Truth was, that night in Jakarta made him persona non grata in the field for a long time. It's hard to book jobs after your client gets strung up in Menteng. The Exxon exec had been found by a group of yogis looking forward to an early morning sun salutation. A picture of the sign that had been pinned to his blood-soaked chest graced every newspaper. "No Peace For Big Oil."

Shogun Security hired him a year later. As Hak said during their first meeting via telephone, "There's nothing more deadly than a man with nothing to lose." And he was right. Jack took any job—no matter the odds. Whether he came home sitting in economy or in a body bag in the cargo hold, it made no difference to him.

"I'm alright," Jack assured Eliza. "It's just the heat."

"It's a hot one today." The corner of Eliza's lip quirked. *It's hot every day in the desert*, Jack thought. They may as well be commenting on the sky. *It's awful blue today, isn't it?* "If you want, you can come sit in the food truck. I have a fan."

"Does it help?" He couldn't help but imagine undressing her inside the cramped food truck, the oscillating fan cooling the sweat on their naked bodies. In his fantasy, he would press her back against the humming fridge and slip his hand between her quivering thighs. She'd taste like sweat.

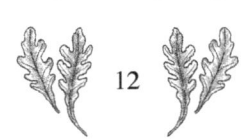

"Not really," she admitted. She tucked a strand of sweat-soaked hair behind her ear, revealing a tiny sterling silver earring shaped like a bumblebee. Jack would have never thought she was a bumblebee kind of girl. Maybe they were a gift from a boyfriend.

Jack rested his hand on the handle of his pistol. "I'm supposed to be watching the site anyway."

Eliza snickered. "What are you protecting it from? Camels?"

"I would never shoot a camel. I'm not a monster." Except, he was a monster, wasn't he? He tilted his chin toward her roll of toilet paper. "What's that for?"

"I'm too posh for the one-ply they keep in the porta-john." She laughed.

"My American ass is used to it," Jack joked.

"And on that note, I'll see you later," Eliza said, turning the roll of toilet paper in her hands. She flashed him a brilliant smile. "The offer stands. Though, I might put you to work."

"All I know how to make is scrambled eggs, but I'm a quick learner."

"I'm sure you are." Her teeth dimpled her plump lip. *Is she flirting with me?* "I'll see you later, Jack." Her fingers brushed against his arm as she passed. She was definitely flirting with him.

"Looking forward to it," he called over his shoulder.

Chapter 4

Even standing on her tiptoes, Eliza couldn't quite reach the pull cord that closed Shawarma Warrior King's awning. Each time her fingers made contact with the handle, it swung out of her reach. "Damn it," she hissed through clenched teeth.

"You look cute when you're angry," Reese said with his typical posh condescension, reaching over her shoulder to pull the awning down. He stood far too close, his hot breath tickling her earlobe.

"What did I tell you about calling me 'cute'?" Eliza turned on her heel to glare up into his smug face. While Reese may be handsome—in his own weaselly way—Eliza couldn't see it anymore. Not even the pinkish glow of the waning sun highlighting his high cheekbones could stir her heart. A half-liter of Bacardi? Maybe.

"I call it like I see it," Reese said with a shit-eating grin. "Do you need any help closing up? It'll be dark soon."

"I've got it," Eliza said testily.

"Suit yourself," Reese chuckled, gripping her shoulder. "Honestly, Beth, you are independent to a fault."

Eliza deftly ducked under his arm, not bothering to ask him yet again not to call her Beth. Her parents had called her Beth, and they had been dead for years. She was Eliza now. "It's grease trap night," she replied smoothly. "I can't imagine you'd want to get anything on those pristine khakis."

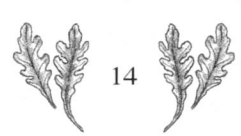

"What do you mean by that?" He scoffed but ran his hands over the ironed pleats in his slacks. The jab rattled him.

"That's why you don't dig anymore, right? Surely it's not because you're a corporate kiss-ass? You know, you used to have a little bit of dignity, back when we were…"

"Just friends!" Reese burst into Eliza's dorm room without knocking, dramatically draping his body over the overstuffed armchair she had rescued from the curb. He threw his arm over his head. "Can you believe that?"

Closing her battered copy of 'Salem's Lot, *Eliza took a measured sip of wine. "Don't you ever knock?" She had planned to have a quiet night in—emphasis on quiet. It was the last day before winter break, and she was using it as an excuse to eat and drink everything in her mini fridge. She had already tucked into a bag of crisps and a sleeve of Oreos.*

"The door was open." He pouted. "Can we focus? I was standing in line at Starbucks, and Winnie was right in front of me. I asked her out, and she fed me that old, tired line. Friends! I'll never be able to show my face in that Starbucks again."

"How ever will you cope? Imagine walking one more block for a macchiato! Winnie is too good for you anyway."

"Bitch!" Reese playfully tossed a throw pillow at her.

"Hey!" The pillow glanced off of Eliza's forearm and the Pinot Grigio sloshed, soaking her wrist. "You made me spill. You… you … brute!"

Reese sat up. "Elizabeth Cunningham, are you drunk?" His eyes flicked toward the nearly empty bottle of wine. "And you didn't invite me?"

"You were too busy flirting with other girls." She didn't intend for that to sound so possessive—so jealous. Was she jealous? No. No. She and Reese were just friends. He was like a very annoying cousin that ate all of the canapés at Christmas. In fact, he had done that very thing.

"I would cancel any plan for you," Reese said seriously. "You know that." He sat up in the chair, resting his elbows on his knees. "How are you feeling about the break?"

"Fine." The lie was easy. It was the same one she had told thousands of times since her parents' accident in April. I'm fine. *"Poppy's family is great." She tilted her chin toward Poppy's obnoxiously pink side of the dorm room. It was neat and tidy, the bed made and the pillows arranged just so. Eliza's side was a little more lived in. Her bed was unmade with a pillow on the floor and half of her laundry piled on top.*

That part was true. The Beuragards treated her like a long-lost daughter. They had turned their multipurpose room into her bedroom, complete with a new coat of olive green paint. Poppy's mother had even taken care of the funeral arrangements when Eliza couldn't stomach it. She picked out the most beautiful couple's headstone with a quote from Shakespeare: "Love comforteth like sunshine after rain."

"Are you sure you don't want to come to Kensington with me?" He plucked the wine glass from Eliza's hand and gulped down the last dregs. "You love my mom's Yorkshire puddings." He wiped his mouth. "Plus, there's a wine cellar. None of this boxed stuff from Tesco."

"I like the boxed stuff from Tesco. I'm fine, Reese. I just... this is the first Christmas without them." She swallowed the stubborn lump of emotion in her throat, swiping at her watery eyes. Pinot Grigio always made her emotional. "It all feels ... very lonely."

Reese carefully placed the empty wineglass on her desk and came to kneel before her, resting his hands upon her thighs. "Duckling, you aren't alone." He looked up at her with serious eyes. "I will always be here. Always."

She sniffled as he wiped the tears from her cheeks with his thumbs. It should be embarrassing—crying in front of him. He should be poking fun, like he always did. "Why are you being so nice to me?"

"I'm always nice to you," he countered, trying to look offended. The corner of his lip quirked, giving him away.

"You drank all my wine," she pouted.

"*You* drank all of *your* wine." He rose. "How about I go buy us another bottle? We can watch a movie."

When Eliza stood, the room seemed to tilt beneath her feet. She stumbled, and Reese deftly caught her by the elbow. They were so close she could smell his aftershave—sandalwood, vetiver, and a hint of spice. "Maybe you've had too much," Reese amended.

"The ground is just uneven, is all." Dizzy, she gripped his shirt front.

"Let me tuck you into bed," Reese urged. "C'mon, Cunningham." He led her to her bed, sweeping the pile of laundry onto the floor. "Honestly, you're a mess."

"Those are clean," she lamented. Still, Eliza let him guide her onto the mattress.

He pulled the sheets up to her chin and leaned close to kiss her forehead. "Sleep tight," he murmured with uncharacteristic softness. His breath commingled with hers. "The offer stands," he added, his rose-petal soft lips

brushing against hers as he spoke. Was it an accident? "Just say the word, and we'll do it. Christmas, I mean."

"Reese—" *The loneliness was unbearable; if she was left alone, she feared it would swallow her up. Was it so bad she wanted him to make her forget? She knew he wanted to. It was why he told her about all the girls that climbed into his bed. He didn't say the quiet part out loud, but she could hear it—plain as day.* I'd rather it was you.

"Hm?"

Her lips ensnared his, and he slid into bed without another word.

"I'm just looking out for you. It's going to be dark soon," Reese huffed, and Eliza could feel the years that stretched between that lonely night and her life now. Reese still didn't believe her when she insisted it would never happen again; he lingered in her life, hoping she'd let her guard down.

"I didn't know you were scared of the dark." Eliza climbed up into the truck and opened the cabinet beneath the sink, dragging out the enormous gray bin that collected grease and greywater.

"You don't have to be such a c—"

Eliza's head snapped up, and he wilted under her glare. "*Careful.* Go home, Reese."

Chapter 5

After sundown, the desert transformed into a new beast altogether. The wind tussled with the tarps, throwing menacing shadows across the site. Eliza's mind played tricks on her. Each shake of canvas was the wingbeat of an enormous vulture circling overhead. The squeak of an abandoned wheelbarrow's loose wheel became a disembodied voice. *I seeeee you*. There were other sounds too—sounds Eliza couldn't quite place nor explain away.

Eliza stuck close to the food truck, cursing her own lack of foresight. As always happened, emptying the grease trap made her look too closely at the floor, which meant she had to mop. A sparkly clean floor made her want a sparkly clean counter and cooktop, so she had to sprinkle a bit of Barkeeper's Friend on every surface. It got dark much more quickly than she had anticipated. One minute, the sky was a brilliant orange, and the next, she couldn't see her hand in front of her face. The site cleared out just as quickly; it was Friday, and payday besides. Most of the laborers and archeologists would be three drinks deep at a karaoke bar right about now.

A scorpion with a pearlescent exoskeleton skittered through the beam of Eliza's iPhone flashlight. Shrieking, Eliza hopped from foot to foot. The scorpion paid her no mind. "Almost done," Eliza muttered, rubbing away the gooseflesh on her arms. It seemed silly to talk to herself, but there was no one else to talk to.

Eliza

Wasn't there supposed to be someone on the dig site overnight? That hunk Jack with the gun, maybe? Eliza couldn't see anyone. She was the only person for miles.

The only task left was to put the trash can inside the truck. She pulled off the lid to tie off the bag, but a sudden gust of wind (where had *that* come from?) wrenched the lid from her grasp. When the aluminum edge struck the sand, it rolled, gained speed, and tumbled into the excavation pit.

A violent crash followed.

"Oh shit." Eliza nibbled on her fingernail, shining her meager light toward the rectangular trench. She inched closer, but there wasn't anything to see. The pit was three stories deep and darker than a black hole. It was so dark that the shadows seemed to take up space, as thick as spun wool.

She considered just leaving. It would be easy enough to climb up into the driver's seat and turn the key in the ignition. It would be even easier to drive the quiet two-lane road that would take her back to her apartment in Cairo. It would be downright simple to brew a cup of tea and tuck herself into bed. But that crash… She had to be sure that the artifacts were okay.

Even though she had dropped out of university, she was still an anthropologist at heart. It had been her first love, hadn't it? She could remember sitting at the kitchen table as a child, excavating plastic dinosaur bones from a brick of plaster of Paris. She did her history report on Tutankhamun that same year, wearing a bow tie and a pith helmet to look like Howard Carter. She couldn't live with herself if she had damaged a piece of history. And that was what it was—a tiny shard in the mosaic of human existence.

She tapped the call icon on her phone, pulling up Reese's profile. The photo was an old one, Oxford University's Radcliffe Camera in the background. He was smiling, revealing the snaggletooth he had recently hidden behind perfectly straight veneers.

Despite their spat, she knew he would come if she asked. She regretted being so abrasive, but he shouldn't act so entitled to her time, her kindness, and her body. Sure, he got her this job, but hadn't she paid him back tenfold? Sometimes, it felt like he did it just to trap her here with him in the middle of nowhere. He would lord it over her if she asked him for help.

She swiped away the app and edged closer to the pit. Her shuffling dislodged a clod of dirt, and it tumbled into the abyss. She didn't hear it land.

"Fuck." She stuffed her phone in the back pocket of her jeans. She'd need both hands for this. The ladder descending into the pit shifted as she tentatively stepped onto it. Eliza gripped the rails so hard that, later, she would find a perfect Phillips screw head imprinted on her palm, smack dab

in the center of her love line. She counted each rung for the first seven but lost her nerve; she still had to climb back up. Knowing would make it even more daunting. She would settle for "a lot."

Finally, her foot touched hard-packed dirt instead of metal. She reached for her phone, cursing her shaking hands. "This is the stupidest thing you've ever done," she muttered. "Ever."

As if on cue, her phone chimed. The sound was inordinately loud, and she dropped it. It landed face-up, dousing the flashlight.

She had gotten a text from Poppy.

[Poppy: Send me a pic of that security guard. For science.]

She punctuated the cheeky message with a peach emoji. Eliza snatched the phone, hurriedly typing with her thumbs.

[Eliza: Can't talk. I really fucked up].

She crept through the excavated catacombs, her phone's flashlight illuminating the tall, narrow passageway. She could see the trail left by the trash can lid, which had apparently landed on its rim and rolled deeper into the tomb. As she followed the divot, every fissure in the tightly packed dirt looked like a face; she couldn't shake the feeling of being watched.

The passage opened up into a cavernous room, flanked by eight partially excavated columns. Each column was decorated with carvings of papyrus, acanthus, and lotus leaves. Eliza leaned close to examine them, finding that she held her breath to avoid disturbing the thick layer of dust that coated the stone.

She cast the light around as she walked, admiring a relief of jackal-headed Anubis carved upon the wall. She didn't notice the canopic jar until she'd kicked it across the chamber.

"Oh no," she groaned, following it with her flashlight's beam. It came to a rest against her trash can lid, which was resting atop ... something. She crept closer, righted the canopic jar, and carefully shifted the trash can lid. It covered the corner of a human-sized container that was partially sunk into the floor. Something about it struck Eliza as odd, but at first, she couldn't quite figure out why.

Then, it hit her: it was plain, made of obsidian, with not a single hieroglyph to hint at what lay inside. She shivered, imagining the remains of

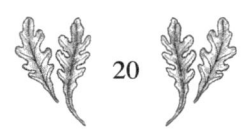

someone so awful their tomb was unmarked and abandoned in this site with other random artifacts collected over the years.

Her phone chimed.

[Poppy: How badly did you fuck up on a scale from 1 (a small grease fire) to 10 (fucking Reese Eldin)?]

She wouldn't dignify that with a response, nor could she. Maybe it was just the stagnant air getting to her, but she felt like she was being watched. Her heart hammering in her chest, she tucked the lid under her arm and turned back the way she came.

She was reminded, suddenly, of her childhood basement. It was dark and filled with junk that threw menacing shadows on the walls. Whenever she had to turn the light off and walk upstairs, she imagined a wraith grabbing her by the ankles. So, she ran, taking the steps two at a time.

Eliza speed-walked through the passage, trying to resist the urge to run. Her muscles spasmed, screaming at her to *go, go, go!* That was when she heard the voice, so soft that it may have just been her own harried exhale.

Rise, RISE.

Chapter 6

Eliza froze, the hairs on her arms standing upright as the whisper ran through her body. Looking around, she confirmed she was alone in the tomb—only artifacts surrounded her—but she could still hear voices echoing from somewhere deeper within. She almost said something but caught herself before the "Hello?" could escape. She'd seen enough horror movies to know better.

The whispering continued, "Rise! Rise! RISE!" She could feel it slithering over her skin, trying to pull her deeper into the tomb to investigate. The voice was familiar, and that was the most frightening thing of all—was she being pranked? She studied the open room she was in, sweeping the phone's flashlight around the edges, looking for hidden cameras or hiding crew members. Ancient statues and artwork peered back at her, but nothing moved. Only that odd chanting in the distance could be heard, sometimes louder than her ragged breathing, sometimes fading into a near echo. She couldn't tell if it was one voice multiplied by the angles of the corridors down here or if many people were chanting in an off rhythm.

"Who's there?" she called softy, giving in to her need for assurances. "This isn't funny!" Her voice echoed faintly off the stone walls, quickly buried under the chant as it grew louder again.

"From blight to might, rise!" the voice hissed, the vowels seeming to ping-pong off the excavated columns. "Do your master's bidding."

Eliza

Fuck that, she decided, gathering the lid to her side like a shield and turning to the passage that led to the exit. She took a step, and then something hot pierced her chest. With a shriek, she dropped the lid and her phone. Assuming that something horrible had crawled into her shirt and bitten her, she batted at her chest with both hands. In the sudden darkness, as her phone landed light side down, she could see a dim glow emanating from her chest.

Oh fuck, it's a magic scorpion! I'm so dead! The glow grew, a faint red light that was completely unnatural surrounding her, and her fingers finally located the heat source pressed against her skin. The metal chain holding the pendant was still cool, but the center grew progressively warmer as her fingers slid closer to the red gemstone.

Mum's necklace, she thought as she yanked it off. She held it out for a second, the broken ends of the chain swaying in the now bright red glow as the gemstone pulsed in time with the chanting voices, then hucked it into the tomb, not wanting to be nearby when that glowing gemstone reached its full potential and exploded—or whatever it was about to do.

The necklace hit something in the tomb with a loud thwack, and the entire room was suddenly bathed in a red glow. She squinted, trying to make sense of the sudden red wash of light, and both hands went up to shield her eyes. When the light steadied, her hands fell, and she stared as it seemed to engulf the entire black stone box in the far corner—which she now realized had to be some kind of sarcophagus. There were no markings to identify the person within, but Eliza knew enough about Egyptian customs to know that probably wasn't a good thing.

Oh, fuck. I'm in a mummy's tomb. Damn you, Reese! How could you not report there were remains down here?

She looked around, seeking the source of the red glow, trying to convince herself that it was coming from something other than a superheated gemstone. Seeing nothing, she finally admitted that it must be her necklace—much as it didn't make any sense.

Eliza took an awkward step back, hand swinging wildly to grab the lid, hoping she could hide behind it. She tripped over another one of the jars, this one new and seemingly pulled out of the sand by the magical glow. Eliza caught a glimpse of a stylized sword embossed on the front of the jar as she landed hard on her butt. For a moment, the new jar hovered in the air. Panicked at the idea of another magical item too close to her, Eliza kicked the jar, sending it across the room to shatter against the plain obsidian box. She watched, wide-eyed, as a person-shaped shadow emerged from the

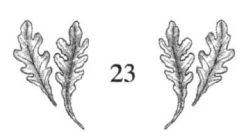

broken jar and seemed to merge with the bright red light still surrounding her necklace.

"I will RISE!" a voice whisper-shouted amid the magic. There was a flash, and Eliza's ears popped as both lights went out, seeming to disappear into the box.

Eliza sat in the dark, hearing nothing but her harsh breath and the pounding of her heart. She had no idea how much time passed, trying frantically to understand what she had just witnessed. As she returned to her senses, she could still hear that low whisper of voices from deeper in the tomb. "Rise, RISE!"

Do NOT rise, thank you very much!

Eliza patted around in the darkness for her phone. She winced as her fingers touched the sand, certain she would touch something unpleasant. She found her phone quickly, relieved that she hadn't stumbled on anything else in the darkness first, and flipped it over. Slowly, she aimed the flashlight beam in the direction of the sarcophagus.

What just happened...? Did I really just watch Mum's necklace ... explode? Her hand went to her chest, gently touching the skin just above her tank top, and she jerked her fingers away with a wince. Turning the beam at her body, Eliza could see the rising welt of burned skin where her necklace normally rested.

"No," she said, her voice inordinately loud, and she bent to pick up the lid. "No," she repeated, whispering now but feeling more firm about it. *My mum's necklace did not just float away and light up a tomb.* "Nope," she said once more, speed walking to the ladder.

At the ladder, she could see the brighter light of the night sky above. Peace settled over her frazzled nerves at the idea of freedom so close, and she took a deep reassuring breath. Starlight guided her as she slid her phone in her back pocket and tucked the lid under her armpit, holding it tight against her side as she climbed out.

A few moments later, she stepped onto the familiar sand of the desert. Glancing around to make sure she hadn't been seen, Eliza moved swiftly to her food truck, tossing the garbage can lid in the back to deal with later. The site seemed to be deserted, and Eliza let out a long breath, letting the warm night breeze soothe her as her sweat-dampened hair moved around her face. She closed her eyes, relishing the feeling for a minute before she pulled out her hair tie and smoothed her hair back into a neater ponytail. Feeling more situated, she opened her eyes.

I did not just see a magical light down there.

"Nope," she said one more time, peering at the entrance to the tomb again. Her hand went to her chest, where she could feel the ragged edge of a burn, and she shook her head. It wouldn't be the first time she had burned herself while cooking and not noticed until later.

Hopping into the driver's seat, Eliza started the truck and drove carefully away from the dig site, reminding herself not to touch the empty space where her mother's necklace should be.

Chapter 7

R ISE.
Milfonnos opened his eyes.

He expected to look up into Rahil's sneering face, but instead of the Amun Henet, he was surrounded by only darkness. He blinked, and his eyelashes brushed against something soft. Tentatively, Milfonnos touched his face and found that it had been shrouded in layers of thin linen. He could not discern the gauze's purpose, but he knew he needed to be free of it. He felt claustrophobic. He tore at the musty wrappings with his fingernails until his eyes and mouth were free.

Except, there was no fresh air. Only dust. It made him cough. He lurched up, striking his head on something hard and immovable. Red stars exploded in front of his eyes, the experience familiar though he couldn't explain why. It was almost a relief. Here it was: proof that he wasn't blind, at least not totally. Then, another frightening thought replaced the last: he was trapped. Cautious now, Milfonnos felt around to get some sense of his cell. It was no larger nor wider than his body. It may as well be a sarcophagus.

<Where …. am I?>

It was as though someone was talking at the opposite end of a long, long corridor. It wasn't so much a voice as it was a … feeling. Yes, that was what it was. A feeling. Was he finally being called home by the pantheon of gods

who made him Pharaoh? Yet, there was something familiar about the voice. Would a god use a voice he knew?

Perhaps this was some sort of purgatory, a transitory place that hadn't been given a name in their holy scriptures. The thought was not a comforting one. It meant he had failed, that he was not meant to be Milfonnos the Immortal. He was just a mortal man who had been felled like so many men before him.

<*Milfonnos?*>

"Kasmut?" Milfonnos' voice bounced around his cramped prison. "Where are you?" He pushed on the slab above him with all of his might. It shuddered but didn't budge.

<*I'm right here.*>

"Where's here?" Milfonnos planted his feet on the slab and pushed. He gritted his teeth, sweat beading on his brow. The added moisture made the gauze wrapped tightly around his head stink terribly. He certainly wasn't in the underworld, unless this was one of Osiris' many trials.

<*It's dark.*>

Milfonnos rolled his eyes. "Oh, is that so?" He drove his heels into the slab again, and this time, it shifted. A sliver of light poured into the small space.

<*Wait, a glimmer...*>

"That was me, you idiot. I did that." Milfonnos was not about to let someone else get credit for his hard work. "Kasmut, where are you? I can't see you."

Suddenly, Milfonnos' hand spasmed, the fingers spreading so far apart that his muscles cramped. <*I ... did that!*> Kasmut said, breathless.

Realization struck Milfonnos like a brick to the forehead.

"You can't be serious," Milfonnos grumbled. Such a cruel trick could only be the work of Set, the god of disorder. This was nothing else but disorderly: imagine a Pharaoh and his peon sharing a body. And Kas was still just a peon, even if they were childhood friends.

<*And I helped move that slab. You couldn't have done it without me.*> There was a smile in Kasmut's voice.

"I don't need you." Milfonnos planted his feet against the slab and pushed. It didn't budge. His calves ached.

<*You need me.*>

"Fine," Milfonnos spat. "Push."

Together, they pushed, and the slab moved. Soon, there was enough space for Milfonnos to slip out. He had only a moment to marvel at his own

body. It had been ages since he'd been able to stand without pain doubling him over and making him vomit.

Then, he saw where he was. It was a tomb but unlike any tomb he had ever seen. This one was dark with nary a torch in sight. Even the sconces that once held them were gone. The walls were filthy as if they hadn't been cleaned in millennia. "Where am I?"

<Where are we?> Kasmut corrected him.

A noise—no more than a sharp intake of breath—came from behind him. Milfonnos turned to find a man in strange clothes, holding a large book. The man was small, dwarfed by the tome in his hands. Milfonnos recognized the Book of Heka, stamped with hieroglyphics and bound in leather. "That's mine!" he snarled. "Give it to me."

The man's mouth hung open. He trembled with such violence Milfonnos wanted to laugh. "You're... you're..." the man babbled.

"I am your Pharaoh," Milfonnos huffed, stepping out of the casket. "Do you not recognize me? Kneel!"

Without another word, the man bolted down a corridor. Milfonnos was very sure the man was crying.

<He didn't recognize us.>

"There is no 'us,' Kasmut. There is only I, Milfonnos." His knee gave out, and he fell heavily to the floor.

<Us.> Kasmut insisted.

"Fine! You louse!"

<Where did that man go? He looked so pale—perhaps he was sick.>

"He was frightened. We frightened him. No wonder. We are not properly dressed." Milfonnos examined his hands, wrapped in the same dirty fabric he'd torn off his face. He tugged at a loose strip. His skin beneath wasn't skin at all but a scaly hide. He was a young man, but his hands looked downright wizened. "We're a leper! The gods have cursed us."

<The gods have cursed you.>

"You're the one stuck inside my head without a body," Milfonnos snarled. "It appears that we are both cursed."

Kasmut only sniffed. Milfonnos' pinky twitched.

"We must go to the palace. The Amun Henet dumped us here. This is a coup!"

<It wasn't a coup, Milfonnos. They wanted to stop the ritual.>

"Which I clearly didn't finish. Look at me—us. It was us against a dozen of them. You did fight bravely, Kasmut."

Warmth spread through Milfonnos' body as though he'd been pulled close in an intimate embrace. It made him uncomfortable. "Stop that!" he snapped.

The feeling dissipated. <*I tried to protect us. I am sorry that I failed.*>

Milfonnos sighed. "That is neither here nor there. We must find where the Amun Henet have hidden what we need to try again. And we must get that book from that tiny man."

<*You are stubborn.*>

"You are out of line." Milfonnos followed the sound of the man's frantic footsteps as they echoed down the corridor. He couldn't seem to lift his feet; his linen-wrapped toes dragged on the floor. His body felt stiff, but it felt good to shuffle along.

The corridor terminated at a wall and a ladder. With effort, Milfonnos craned his neck. There were thousands of stars in the sky above, glittering as if in glee. After all, their Pharaoh had triumphantly returned. But there was something strange about them—a faint red tinge.

Milfonnos went to rub his eyes, but his knuckles butted up against something hard. "The gemstone!" he cackled. "Those idiots left me with the gemstone!" It seemed different, smaller somehow, but that could just be his hands disobeying his wishes.

No prison could hold him—not with the gemstone's magic at his disposal. Though he had to admit, locking him in a tomb was poetic in a way. Even without completing his ritual, Milfonnos had defeated death.

"Let us go get our revenge," he said with a sneer.

With a shallow bend of his knees, he launched himself skyward. The wind whipped the loose bandages on his face, and for the first time in a long while, he took a deep, invigorating breath.

<Your *revenge*,> Kasmut corrected him, his voice small.

Chapter 8

Eliza had nearly driven out of the dig site when a flash of movement in her rearview mirror made her slow. Eyes wide, she stared into her side mirrors, trying to identify the blur as anything other than a gauze-wrapped human shape shooting out of the tomb opening.

No, she thought, determined not to be involved. Another flash of movement caught her attention, this time in front of her, and she slammed on the brakes, bringing the truck to a skidding halt just in time to avoid hitting a robed figure running across the road. With the heightened observational skills bestowed by a flood of adrenaline, she took in the designs on the robe, the image searing itself into her memory. The figure was small, and while she couldn't identify who it was, she did see the old book tucked beneath their arm.

Is someone stealing from the tomb?

None of my business, she reminded herself. *There's been too much supernatural stuff already.* Shaking her head, she glanced cautiously at both mirrors, and seeing no one, eased the truck back into motion. It had been the kind of day to make her want to go straight home and crawl into her bed, but she knew if she didn't stop and fill the truck with gas, she would lose half the day's business waiting in line tomorrow.

Eliza was all about progress, but not being able to fill her own gas tank was something she still struggled with. She supposed it was nice to relax

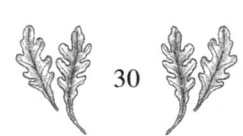

for a few minutes while the attendant filled the tank. Since she was in the habit of filling up on her way home, the night crew at Ali's Express knew her. Sometimes she brought them leftovers, but not today. That helicopter had ruined most of her food.

Eliza tried to make herself stop looking in her mirrors, scanning the night sky for a flying magical mummy who had been resurrected with her mother's necklace. Her hand pressed absently against her chest where the gemstone normally sat, and she winced, the burn still ragged.

Maybe I'll park and hang out for a few minutes after they fill me up, she decided. She could get some ointment for the burn and settle her nerves before she brought her crazy suspicions home with her. She knew she wouldn't be able to sleep anyway.

As she reached the gas station, Eliza's heart rate had settled to a normal rhythm, but her eyes still flicked across the sky while she pulled into the vacant pump at the end. "Hey, Yusef," she greeted the attendant as she hopped out of her truck. "I'm going inside for a bit, so no rush, okay?"

He gave her a thumbs up, then returned his attention to the line of cars at the neighboring pump. It wasn't the first time Eliza had lingered at the gas station, not eager to return to her empty apartment. She wasn't lonely, not really, but sometimes, she was tired of speaking to strangers all the time. Was it so much to ask for a conversation with someone who knew her name?

Reese knows your name.

Eliza grimaced, shaking away the reminder.

I know, I know. I make terrible choices.

As she walked inside the store, Eliza closed her eyes to savor the icy blast of the air conditioning as it cooled her sweat-dampened skin. Though the temperature had dropped with the sun, the humidity was still oppressive, and it had been a long time since the air conditioner in her truck worked properly.

She waved at Rana working at the front counter before strolling down to the cold case for a bottle of water before beginning the hunt for burn cream. The medical section in the store was small, but Eliza was in luck—plucking the tube from the little display box and heading to the front.

"Eliza!" Rana said, the young woman as pleasant as always. "How is it today?" she said in accented English. Rana enjoyed chatting with Eliza in English, practicing her small talk for a few minutes.

"Very well," Eliza replied, plunking the drink and burn cream on the counter.

Rana picked up the cream with a quizzical eye. "Everything okay?"

"It's fine," Eliza assured her. "Just a small burn."

"Do you need a bandage?" Rana asked. The mention of bandages made Eliza think of the human shape she had definitely NOT seen in the sky. A shiver caused the hairs to rise on her arms.

RISE.

Eliza shook her head, trying to forget the sound of the chanting, the weird color show—*everything*. "No, thanks," she told Rana. "It's not bad."

"You must be more careful," Rana told her, entering numbers on the register without looking at the keypad. "Take care, Eliza."

"I will," Eliza promised her, not eager to get into another conversation about her single status or being "all alone" in the country without even a family member to watch out for her. For all that Rana was progressive when it came to education, she was shocked at Eliza's casual freedom. Yusef, the attendant, was her brother, and he would never leave his sister alone if he wasn't just outside, nevermind traipsing across the countryside to dig sites filled with strange men.

I just need a distraction, Eliza thought, *something to get my mind off all this weirdness tonight.*

The bell above the door jangled, and Eliza turned toward the sound.

"Hey, is there—" Jack Manning began but stopped when he saw Eliza standing at the counter. "I thought it might be you!" He grinned. "The man outside told me to ask if there was a young lady inside."

Eliza nodded. "Yeah, why? Does Yusef need something?" She glanced through the glass window to where her truck sat next to the pump. The other lane was empty, the other customers fueled up and sent on their way, but a pickup truck was parked just behind her food truck.

Jack smiled apologetically. "He said you're all filled up," he told her, "and I should ask you to move your truck so that he can fill up mine." He shrugged. "I guess my truck doesn't fit in the regular lane?"

"Very American of you," Eliza said, "driving a large truck." She turned back to Rana, paying for her items with a few crumpled pounds.

"It's not an American truck," Jack insisted, and when she turned around, drink and burn cream in hand, he had a hand in his hair, his posture incredibly disarming and completely sexy. His shirt lifted just enough to reveal a line of tanned skin above his hips.

"It's the wheelbase," Eliza told him as he opened the door and gestured for her to step through. "It's still bigger than anything else around here." She flashed him a flirtatious smile, hoping he was picking up the vibe.

Jack Manning would be a delightful distraction.

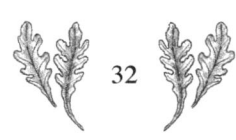

"Sorry to make you wait," she continued. "I'll get out of the way."

Jack walked beside her as she returned to the truck, then raised an eyebrow at the tube in her hand. "You okay?"

"Yeah," she assured him. "Just a burn. A hazard of the trade." She hoped he wouldn't pry. Though, he didn't seem the type to ask questions. She couldn't possibly make up an answer—much less one that stood up to an interrogation, well-intentioned or otherwise.

He gave her a sidelong glance, his eyes filled with promise. "You need some help with getting it on? I mean, if the burn is in an awkward spot..."

"I don't need help," Eliza told him curtly, "but I may accept an extra ... hand if you're willing." She hoped he could fill in the blanks as to what she wanted that hand to do.

She handed him the cream, then opened her driver's side door. The hinge squealed: the truck was older than she was. She tilted her chin toward the side of the building. "I'll go park over there. Find me when you get a free moment."

Jack nodded, standing by the door until she hopped up onto her seat. He glanced back into the dark interior of the kitchen area. "You know," he said casually, "I've never actually been on a food truck before. Perhaps after we get your burn taken care of, you can give me a tour."

Eliza smiled, tugging the door shut. "That sounds perfect," she told him through the open window. "I'd love to show you all the ways I have to contort to get things done back there."

Chapter 9

Inside, Ali Express seemed to hum. Jack strode down the aisle, sidestepping the teenagers who perused the magazine rack. Patrons chattered in Arabic and English, and Jack caught bits and pieces of conversation ("Al Ahly Sporting Club is going to trounce Zamalek. I'd put 500 pounds on it!"). He intended to only pay for his gas but found himself in a sizable line. Apparently, everyone and their mother needed a little pick-me-up for the road; it was, after all, the only gas station between Cairo and most anywhere else. The refrigerators full of sports drinks and bachelor meals buzzed noisily; someone had drawn a heart and their initials in the condensation. The panel lights above seemed to flicker in time with the percussion-heavy pop song crackling through the ancient speaker system. Nighttime in Egypt always felt inherently magical, but tonight felt even more so.

Jack grabbed a bag of paprika-flavored Tiger chips and a Pepsi but thought better of it and put both back. His meals often consisted of convenience store fare, but there was no reason to reveal that to Eliza. She was an honest-to-goodness gourmand and would undoubtedly laugh at him. He wasn't sure he could stomach being laughed at, especially after being bossed around by Reese Eldin.

Instead, he paid for his gas and went out to tip the young attendant. "Thanks, man," he said as he slipped him a few bills. "I appreciate it."

The attendant—Yusef, according to his embroidered work shirt—tucked the cash into his breast pocket. *"Shkran lak,"* he said. "You be nice to Eliza, sir," he added. "She is our best customer."

"Will do," Jack assured him. As he climbed into his truck, Jack marveled at Eliza's apparent hospitality. He had been coming to this same gas station since his contract started, but no one knew his name—he hadn't bothered to learn anyone else's either. He found that it was easier not to. There was no such thing as camaraderie while on contract. He did his job and moved on to the next. Friendships—relationships—were loose ends that couldn't be tied up.

He parked his truck next to Shawarma Warrior King and cut off the engine. Eliza stood in the truck's doorway; backlit, the flyaways that had escaped her ponytail seemed to glow. "What took you so long?" she asked.

"I couldn't decide whether you would laugh at my dinner selection," he admitted. "It's Friday, so I was going to splurge and get a Kinder egg for dessert. We don't have those in the U.S. It's a choking hazard, y'know."

Just as he expected, Eliza laughed. But it wasn't a mean-spirited one. "How about I whip you up something sweeter?" she asked. In the darkness, he couldn't quite see her face, but he imagined the way her teeth dimpled her lip at the dig site, her hands playing in her hair.

Jack mounted the steps. "Oh?" The corner of his lip twitched when she stepped backward. "What do you have in mind?"

Eliza's cheeks turned rosy. She reached blindly for the handle of her fridge. Jack wasn't sure if she was trying to steady herself or put the door between them. She was the one who started this little game of cat and mouse, hadn't she? "Well," she murmured, "I have a carton of mango ice cream from that place in Zamalek." She placed the carton on the stainless-steel counter and gave him a sidelong look. "You like mango, right?"

"Sure," Jack said good-naturedly. In truth, it wasn't his favorite. He was a Neapolitan man, though he often threw away the freezer-burnt strawberry after a few months.

Seemingly eager to have something to do, Eliza opened a drawer, pawing through the odds and ends. "I can never find anything in here," she muttered. "Hey, can you look for the ice cream scoop in that one ... over there?" She gestured to a drawer at his hip.

Jack did as he was told. He found the scoop beneath a spatula and an oven mitt. "Here," he said, handing it to her.

She grinned, showing all of her dazzling white teeth. "Thanks." Her cool fingers brushed against his. "Can I ask you something?"

They were standing very close; boxed in by counters and appliances, there was only a narrow aisle in which to maneuver. Jack was keenly aware of the smell of her sweat and shampoo. "Of course," he answered. He hoped she was going to ask him to rock her world, which he would happily oblige.

Eliza couldn't quite meet his eyes. "Did you notice anything odd ... at the dig site?" She wrung her hands.

"No. Unless you count that little prick who dresses like a guide on the Jungle Cruise."

He expected a laugh, but she pressed her lips together. "Never mind." She turned back to her task, scooping a generous serving of brightly colored ice cream into a porcelain ramekin. Even with the truck's oscillating fan, it was already melting. She pressed the bowl into Jack's hands.

She hadn't given him a spoon. "Are you okay?" Jack pressed.

"It's just been a long day," she said. The words seemed to tumble off her tongue. Jack wondered how often she used the same excuse. He may not have been a smart man, but he was an astute one. He knew a lie when he heard it. She dragged her fingertip around the lip of his ramekin and licked it clean. "I just want to ... forget about it."

Jack's cock stirred in his pants. Eliza swiped her finger in his bowl and held it up to his lips. "It's good," she prompted. "Try some."

She slid her finger into his mouth for him to suck. The ice cream tasted sweet and tart on his tongue, but he was hardly aware of it. He just wanted to taste her. His tongue swirled around her finger and her breath hitched.

"Jack—" she managed before he kissed her. Her fingers clawed at his belt buckle, threading it through the loops. He had fantasized about her plenty, but he never expected her to be so eager. It was as though she had been famished and he had promised to feed her. If Reese Eldin was her only option, perhaps she was starving.

Her hand slipped into the waistband of his pants and cupped his stiffening cock through his boxer briefs. Jack's teeth dimpled her lip as he cupped her breast through her thin cotton shirt. He closed his eyes as she rubbed him with her palm. She panted with desperate need.

Jack needed her too, if only to quiet his mind. When she touched him, he was able to forget who he was and how far he'd fallen. He was able to be in control again, rather than being some rich fuck's lapdog. "On your knees," he urged. "Please."

Eliza looked up at him through half-lidded eyes as she sank to her knees. She hooked her fingers in his waistband, pulling them down just enough to free his cock from its confines. He was as hard as a rock, pre-cum

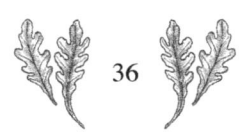

dribbling from its glistening head. "Wow," Eliza breathed, curling her hand around him.

God. Jack leaned back against the counter as she took him into her hot mouth, swirling her tongue around his vascular cock. Jack grasped a fistful of her hair, guiding her up and down his length.

Jack could dimly hear people walking past the truck, but he knew they couldn't see inside. The windows were heavily tinted and the awning was closed; it was as though he and Eliza were in their own little world, sticky-sweet mango on their tongues. Fearing he would cum, Jack urged her to her feet.

In one fell swoop, he lifted her onto the counter and tugged down her jean shorts. "I need to be inside you," he growled, slipping his hand between her legs. Her thighs quivered, and she bucked up against his palm.

"Yes," she breathed.

Jack pressed into her, groaning as her muscles tightened around him. She wrapped her arms around his neck and moaned as he buried his face between her breasts. She yelped as he brushed against the raw edges of her burned skin, and he jerked up, concerned eyes meeting her.

"Did I hurt you?" he asked.

"It's fine," she assured him. "Just a burn from earlier." She pushed his head back down, urging him on with her hips. "Don't stop!" Obeying her orders, he sucked the sensitive skin of her nipples between his teeth, delighting in the way it made her whimper. With a final thrust, he pulled out to cum on her thighs.

Eliza scooted to get off the counter, but he held her still. "We aren't done," he said. Getting on his knees, he leaned down to kiss her thighs, a trail of goosebumps guiding him toward his prize. She tasted even sweeter than any flavor of ice cream he'd ever tasted.

Chapter 10

Rafi Sabbagh remembered the very first time he had seen Eliza Cunningham, his beautiful neighbor a vision as she lugged two heavy suitcases up the stairs to the apartment above his. Being the gentleman he was, Rafi had immediately offered to help, lifting the heavy bag and trying to conceal the strain as he followed her up the narrow staircase and down the hall. They had been fast friends, and while Rafi longed for more, he would never burden Eliza with that knowledge, sensing that she had come to Egypt to get away from such things. Two years later, he now knew her reason for fleeing university and losing herself in the food truck, and while his feelings for her had only grown stronger, something always held him back. Staring at her across the table of their favorite breakfast cafe, Rafi wondered if this moment was what his soul had known was coming—the reason they could never be together.

"You think you saw a mummy?" he repeated. "As in, a cloth-wrapped reanimated corpse from the ancient world?"

Eliza speared another bite of pancake, raising an irritated eyebrow at him as she took a bite. She washed it down with more coffee, then leaned back in her seat. "I only told you because I need to know the legal ramifications here." At Rafi's expression, she added, "I was down inside the dig site. Unauthorized access to a government dig. What happens to me, to my visa, if anyone finds out I was there?"

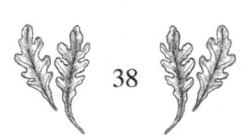

Rafi

Rafi took a sip of his own coffee, reviewing the laws he had memorized at the beginning of his education. "I would not concern yourself with that. While trespassing is a minor infraction, there are no cameras to record your presence. Besides, your visa is legal, and with your contract to service the site until it closes, your position here in Cairo is protected."

"But I touched things down there," she groaned. She looked down, clearly embarrassed. "I mean, I kicked a jar across the room into the sarcophagus." She buried her face in her hands, the anthropologist in her horrified at her disrespectful actions.

"You were frightened," he said soothingly. He never could bear to see her upset. She spread her hands, peering at him between two fingers.

"It was terrifying, Rafi," she admitted. "I don't know what I saw, but *something* was down there with me, and it wasn't just a bunch of artifacts."

"You said you heard chanting. Perhaps some of the locals decided to observe the old ways," he offered casually. "You know how we Egyptians can be about our ancient customs. A sarcophagus like that means royalty, perhaps even a pharaoh. They probably wanted to pay their respects." Eliza nodded, and something dark skittered across Rafi's soul.

He hated lying to her like this.

This is the reason, he reminded himself. *This is why you can never tell her how you feel. Because any time the Amun Henet is involved, you would have to lie just like this.*

Rafi had been born into the Amun Henet, raised with the expectation that along with his education in law, he would be entrusted with a sacred task: keeping the world safe from the supernatural echoes of the ancient days. Specifically, his job in Cairo was making sure no one dug up anything they weren't supposed to—and woke things best left sleeping. Rafi had worried that the dig might unearth a dangerous magical artifact, but he had never suspected it to be the resting place of Milfonnos' tomb. He had already excused himself under the pretense of using the restroom to send a text to his team. Now, he had only to reassure Eliza and convince her that she hadn't seen anything supernatural.

He could see the red line of the burn across her chest, her otherwise smooth skin slightly pebbled with perspiration. The fans were blowing in the crowded cafe, of course, but the heat was inevitable, coating everyone in a layer of damp. Rafi paused, wondering how to explain the physical wound.

Eliza had been wearing that necklace since they met, a family heirloom passed down from her mother. Rafi had never imagined the red stone was part of the same gemstone that the Amun Henet had been protecting for

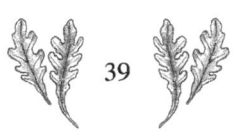

centuries. Rafi spun the gold ring on his middle finger, the red gemstone inlaid inside the Amun Henet's winged sigil.

We have been connected in this way, at least, he mused. Though his stone hadn't grown hot last night, nor had it seared his skin as the power of the mummy pulled the magic forth. He would have to find out why Eliza's stone had reacted—likely the proximity of Milfonnos the Blighted One's body and the remains of the original stone.

Perhaps there is hope for us after all. Rafi shook his head. He couldn't have distracting thoughts like this—he had a mission here. The Amun Henet was counting on him.

"It was an accident, Eliza," he told her again. "No one saw. No one knows. Best to forget about it."

"How do you know no one saw?" She peered at him, resting her elbows on the table. "And how do you know there are no cameras out there? This is 2023. There are cameras everywhere these days."

Because Shogun Security insisted on no cameras, Rafi thought, thinking of the company hired to provide security at the site. The still anonymous investor didn't want any knowledge of the tomb's contents leaking into the public sphere, going so far as taking the workers' phones when they arrived on site. Only a few people were allowed to keep their phones—Eliza among them—not that she knew about any of that. The Amun Henet had worked with Shogun Security before. Rafi knew his connection to them would help as they investigated what had happened at the site last night.

If the Blighted One has truly been released...

No, he decided, carefully choosing his words. *Until I know for certain, I can do nothing.*

"This is Egypt, Eliza," he reminded his worried friend. "No one here cares about dig sites anymore. So long as nothing valuable goes missing, no one will ask any questions." He gave her a hard look. "You didn't take anything from the tomb, did you?"

"Of course not!" she replied, offended at the thought. Her hand went to her neck, seeking the necklace, and she winced as she brushed her chest. "Oh shit! My necklace. I threw it at the tomb. It's probably still down there."

Rafi nodded, planning to send instructions to the team to retrieve it. "Probably. Do not worry. I can have someone get it for you."

"Who?" she asked, narrowing her eyes. "Who do you know at the site?"

Raf shrugged. "This is Cairo," he told her. "I know everyone. And everyone knows me."

Rafi

Eliza smiled at his bravado, and warmth filled his belly at the sight. She was so lovely when she was happy. Rafi liked seeing her so content.

"You're a lifesaver, Rafi," she told him, her hand catching his across the table. "Seriously. I don't know what I'd do without you." She frowned. "Even though you don't believe my mummy story."

"I believe you saw something, Eliza," he said. "I just don't know if it was a mummy flying into the sky."

"What do you think it was, then?" She gestured at her chest. "And this? How do you explain this?"

Rafi shrugged. "Some things cannot be explained," he said finally. "Some things just are."

"Spoken like an Egyptian," Eliza commented, reaching for her wallet in the back pocket of her shorts. "I got it this time."

Rafi thought about arguing, but they always took turns buying meals. He knew she was struggling, her food truck earning far less money than he had, but he also knew she was proud, and he allowed her to treat him. It was what friends did.

After she paid, they strolled leisurely back to the apartment, the sights and smells of the bustling city all around them as they fell into more familiar conversational topics: the price of fruit at the market, Rafi's "troubles" with his newest assistant at the office, the latest episode of *Hot Nights*—a supernatural drama they both watched on Thursday nights. When they reached the apartment, he left her at the bottom of the stairs, watching her ascend with a promise to see each other in a few days.

As he heard her apartment door close, Rafi took out his phone. If Eliza had awakened Milfonnos, she was in terrible danger. She would need more protection than Rafi himself could offer at the moment.

He scrolled through the recent numbers, then put the phone to his ear as he walked to his door. A few rings and then a curt voice answered, "What?"

"Get on a plane," Rafi said. "I need you here. She's in danger."

Chapter 11

Yong-Jin Hak saved the last swig of bourbon for the very moment when the wheels touched tarmac. It had been a turbulent flight, especially in a five-seater Cessna, and he wanted to celebrate his continued existence, even if he was on the way to risk his neck again.

As the plane slowed and the crew prepared to disembark, Hak shouldered his heavy leather backpack—a bag that he was careful not to take through security.

"Your ride is here," Sloan mumbled. He always spoke like he had marbles in his mouth as though he considered enunciating to be beneath him. That suited Hak just fine—the less he could understand, the better. Sloan's favorite topic of conversation was himself and what he could gain, whether that was muscles, money, or women. Hak had tired of hearing about his latest diet (100% elk meat) and his latest conquest (that bartender in Budapest) only twenty minutes into their three-hour flight. Hak knew it was all talk, of course. When he wasn't on assignment, Sloan was a devoted family man; he'd never disrespect his wife, but he also didn't want his team to think he was soft. So, he invented women and tales of bravado.

Hak sidestepped down the airplane's narrow aisle and ducked through the passenger door. He was immediately walloped by a wall of humidity.

"Woo-we, this is like Afghanistan all over again," Sloan hollered, slapping his massive paw onto Hak's shoulder.

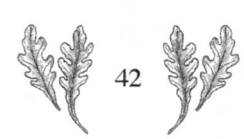

Hak winced. Another thing he despised about Sloan was his indiscretion. But Sloan had no need to be discreet; a tank certainly doesn't need anyone to move out of its way when it could just as easily roll over them.

But then, Hak saw it: a candy apple red Kawasaki sportbike parked on the runway. He hurried down the stairs and tightened the straps of his backpack. The Shogun Security insignia—a phoenix, its wings pointed skyward—was stamped on the gas tank. Beyond it, a Land Rover Defender idled, only the silhouette of a driver behind the tinted windshield.

"Beautiful," he murmured, his fingers trailing over the motorcycle's fender, the metal made hot from the sun.

"You gonna marry it?" Sloan chortled, elbowing him in the ribs. "Sticking your dick in that tailpipe is the only way you'd get laid."

Hak's jaw tightened as he fantasized about slipping a knife between Sloan's doughy ribs. *Be professional*, he reminded himself. *You are in control—act like it.* He slung his leg over the sportbike. "Do you have a status report?"

Sloan produced a small tablet from his pocket and tapped on the screen. He tipped it so that Hak could see, though it wasn't very clear with Sloan's greasy fingerprints all over it. "These ... were the last known coordinates of the asset."

Hak huffed. "I'm going to head out that way," he said, slipping on the helmet Sloan handed him. "See if I can get eyes on her."

"I'll see if I can find out anything from the locals," Sloan said. "You know, see if they saw a fucking Frankenstein or whatever. I'll be in touch."

In the long list of Sloan's faults, his stupidity was at the very top.

"Don't draw attention to yourself, Sloan. For once in your life, don't get overexcited. No one needs to die today."

"Maybe tomorrow." Sloan shrugged.

Hak grinned, though Sloan couldn't see it through the tinted visor. He revved the engine and peeled off toward the desert.

The sun slowly dipped below the horizon as he sped down El-Orouba. His shirt whipped as he drove. He should have put on a jacket—if he crashed, the asphalt would tear his skin up like a cheese grater—but he didn't want to be pouring sweat by the time he got to the coordinates. It was nice to drive. Sitting in the plane had been a lesson in discipline. He hated feeling impotent, at the mercy of a pilot who could fly them right into the side of a mountain. Not to mention the mercurial troposphere, where storms raged and the wind beat mercilessly on the fuselage.

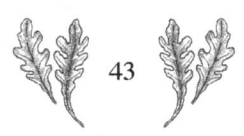

One Mummy to Go, Please!

The buildings in downtown Cairo varied, ranging from ornate to ramshackle. Tiny shops selling cheap wares butted up against veritable palaces, long abandoned by royalty. Hak cranked the throttle in front of the Said Halim Pasha Palace, admiring the wheat-colored marble while the sportbike purred. When he stopped at a red light beside a food cart selling batata, he considered pulling up to the curb; he hadn't eaten anything since he left Budapest the night before, and the bourbon sloshed in his belly in a particularly unsettling way.

Then, his phone rang. He answered it via the Bluetooth in his helmet. "Yeah?"

"Hey, Hak. Did you get to Cairo alright?"

"Yeah, Raf," Hak said. The light turned green. With a sigh, he pulled himself away from the sweet-smelling potatoes. "I'm almost to the apartment building."

"She isn't at the apartment. I heard the door open and close just a minute ago. If I know Eliza, she's going to the Osiris Pub over on Qasr El Nil."

Hak switched lanes so that he could do a U-turn. "Got it. I'll head over there." The tantalizing aroma of sweet potatoes followed him three blocks.

The Osiris Pub wasn't so much on Qasr El Nil street as it was off. Hak parked the bike at the curb and walked down a narrow alley, thick with bar goers. The air reeked of cigarette smoke and Drakkar Noir. Hak moved through them like a wraith, careful not to draw attention despite his very out of place backpack.

Inside, the Osiris Pub was dark and moody; the bar was made of mahogany and slick with Old English furniture polish. Most of its patrons hunched over the bar, sipping dark-colored drinks and eating handfuls of peanuts. A jukebox played a song by The 1975, the lyrics a love letter to cocaine and women. Hak found Eliza sitting at the end of the bar, chatting with the bartender. It was too loud to overhear their conversation, but her lips were upturned into a sweet smile. She twirled her blonde hair around her finger.

Hak sat at a small table and watched her. He was grateful to find a small bowl of peanuts on the tabletop, and he cracked the shells between his molars. He was patient and no stranger to a stakeout. When it came to stakeouts, this was luxurious compared to others he'd been on. Once, he'd laid on his belly in a bayou, being eaten alive by gnats.

After a few hours, Eliza gathered her things and made her way outside. He followed. In the alley, she stopped to say hello to a group of women who were taking turns checking their makeup in a small compact. Hak turned on his heel, heading in the opposite direction. He didn't need that many eyes on him, especially the wary eyes of women after dark. He resolved to circle the block and catch up with her on Qasr El Nil street.

As soon as he turned down a shadow-infested side street, someone grabbed his shirt collar, lifted him off his feet, and tossed him. His stomach flipped, and he slammed into the side of a dumpster. He may as well have been as light as a feather.

Hak landed in a stinking puddle, which he hoped was rainwater but was probably garbage sludge. He rolled away just before his much larger assailant could kick him.

"Why are you following her?" the man shouted in an ostensibly American accent. Texan, if Hak had to guess.

Hak hooked the toe of his boot behind the man's ankle and pulled. The man fell heavily onto his back. In a flash, Hak sat on his chest, pinning down his arms with his knees. Boiling hot anger coursed through his veins, and he punched the man in the face. His nose crunched.

Control.

Control yourself.

Hak took a deep breath. The fire in his belly extinguished, smoke pouring out of his mouth on the exhale. "Why are *you* following her?" Hak countered.

"I'm not!" the man snapped. "Not … in the way you're implying. I'm protecting her."

"From what?" He leaned close to the man's face. Even steeped in shadow, he could make out his ruggedly handsome features. He looked like a Hollywood cowboy—The Man With No Name with a better jawline. There was something familiar about him…

But Hak wasn't as in control as he thought he was. The man slammed his forehead into Hak's so hard that stars burst in front of his eyes. The alley spun, and suddenly, the ground rushed up.

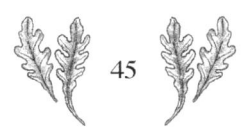

CHAPTER 12

Milfonnos flew.

This was not a means of travel he was accustomed to, but it came to him as naturally as putting one foot in front of the other. The unrelenting wind ripped at the bandages that concealed his nakedness, but he didn't mind. His desiccated skin felt too tight, and the cool nighttime air was a salve. Beneath him, his shadow slithered across the sand. Perhaps that was Kasmut, trailing behind him.

Milfonnos traveled north, guided by the star Polaris. He needed to visit the temple on Philae, to call upon Isis; surely, the goddess of rebirth would be able to provide the answers he sought. If it had been Isis who had awakened him — she had worn a beautiful face, so it must have been — she would have the tools that he needed to restore himself. He didn't have much time; his finger had fallen off just after he left the dig site, and he had lost a chunk of his lower jaw sometime later.

He had been to Isis' temple once before, during his coronation, a heavy leopard pelt slung over his tiny shoulders. He was only six years old, and his advisors told him that Isis would be his mother, that she would cuddle him against her bosom alongside her son Horus. This had pleased Milfonnos. He desperately wanted a mother — and a brother too. He was meant to walk down the hall with slow, measured steps, but he couldn't stand to wait another moment. His heart fluttered. *Mo-ther! Mo-ther! Mo-ther!* He ran,

the leopard pelt dragging in the dirt like a bridal train. Except, when he mounted the dais, there was no goddess. Just a statue in the shape of a woman, whose skin didn't yield when he hugged her.

Even now, doubt chewed at him. Would she appear now when he needed her most?

But what he found was worse. The island sequestered in the snaking Nile's churning whitewater was nowhere to be seen. Suddenly bone weary, Milfonnos landed on the river's bank. "It is gone," he rasped. "My mother…"

<*The air is different. The landscape… the river.*>

Kasmut's voice was soft, tempered by a swell of emotion. Milfonnos could feel his bodyguard's fear and grief itch at the back of his mind. He knelt, his fingers trailing in the cool water. "What is…?" He tugged at something strange mired in the sediment, lifting it into the moonlight. The object was unfamiliar—as translucent as a Nile jellyfish and as cylindrical as a viper. A bit of papyrus adhered to it said, E-V-I-A-N. "You are right, Kas. Everything is strange."

He leaped back into the sky, this time looking for his palace. Only wispy clouds were stretched across the sky, and he had a bird's eye view of the ground below. Suddenly, the desert was bisected by a gargantuan gray boa, a yellow stripe down its back. He had never seen a road before, at least, not like this one. <*It's not moving,*> Kas observed. <*Perhaps it is dead.*>

Milfonnos dipped low and found that the boa's skin was craggy and pockmarked. Indeed, it was not moving. He followed its serpentine path, interested to see what titan had killed it.

<*Look!*> Kasmut's shout echoed in Milfonnos' head, and starbursts burst before his eyes. It was as though Kas had violently shook him.

"Stop that!" he snapped, wishing he could punch Kas right in the nose. He'd done it before when they were teenagers. It was the only time he had managed to surprise Kas, who always thought him soft. *"Princes are so fragile that they must sit on pillows,"* he'd teased.

<*Look, damn you!*> Kasmut insisted.

Milfonnos looked and behold: a city lit by thousands of torches that did not seem to waver in the wind. The buildings were taller than he had ever seen and covered in silver. He landed upon the back of the boa—which he discovered was smashed flat as if run over by an enormous wagon wheel—and looked up at the buildings.

Suddenly, a hawk screamed and a bright light surrounded him. Milfonnos raised his arms to shield his face. A rumble—not unlike an earthquake—shook the ground beneath his bare feet.

One Mummy to Go, Please!

"Hey man, get out of the middle of the road!"

Milfonnos lowered his arms, squinting to see who had spoken. He couldn't understand the words, but he didn't like the implication. A man climbed out of a creature with wagon wheels for feet. "What is the fucking matter with you?" the man shouted. "You drunk?"

Milfonnos stared at the pale man with his straw-colored hair as he stormed closer. The man's face softened as he approached. "Yo, are you homeless? No offense, but you look like shit—smell like it too."

Milfonnos didn't like his tone, nor the way his nose wrinkled. "<Quiet! You will speak to me while on your knees.>"

"What language is that?" The man's brow furrowed. "I don't understand you. Just ... get out of the fucking road, okay?"

Milfonnos leaned close to the man. "<Your peasant tongue is incomprehensible. Though, this is the first time I've spoken to a peasant...>" A tickle trailed up Milfonnos' cheek, and he plucked a millipede off of his rotting face and flung it away.

The man paled and scurried backward. "Your face... What happened to your face?"

But Milfonnos wasn't listening, not that he could understand if he had. He was only aware of the fragrant aroma of the man's fear. It reminded him of roasted oxen, laid out on the feast table. He reached for the man, wondering what fear could taste like. "<You smell...>"

<Milfonnos, don't!>

Milfonnos' body spasmed, his joints popping like firecrackers. Kasmut was holding him back. "<Let go of me!>" Milfonnos growled. "<He smells so good. I'm so, so hungry.>"

He was famished. Starved. How long had it been since he had eaten? A year? One hundred? Millennia?

The peasant turned tail and scrambled toward the lights. The piquant scent of his fear dissipated. Suddenly, he stumbled and fell, letting out a pathetic yelp. Milfonnos reached toward him with his fingers outstretched and the peasant—

(Pop!)

—exploded. A rush of energy struck Milfonnos in the chest, and a soothing warmth spread through his limbs. When the smoke cleared, only a small pile of desert sand was left where the peasant once stood.

Milfonnos wasn't hungry anymore.

The palace was gone. In its place, a banquet hall stood, a pair of Golden Arches atop the signpost outside. It smelled like the grease his servants used to lubricate the wheels of his royal chariot. He stared at the building for some time, his anger washing over him like a wave; when it dissipated, grief replaced it. "<It's all gone,>" he whispered.

<It's all gone,> Kasmut echoed.

Milfonnos went inside. The bandage on his ankle came undone and fluttered behind him. His feet left dirty smears on the dark beige linoleum. He saw nothing that reminded him of his own glory. Even if he had been gone millennia, there should still be monuments to Milfonnos II, the Blighted One. At the very least, a relic!

A woman stood behind the counter, her eyes on a tiny obsidian slab. She tapped upon it with her thumbs. When he approached, she didn't bother to look up. "What can I get you?" she asked, but all Milfonnos heard was gibberish.

"<Kneel!>" he commanded. Her behavior irritated him more than the other peasant's had. At least the man had respected his prowess, like a rabbit respects a hawk.

She finally peeled her eyes away from the slab. "Wha—what the hell happened to you?"

"<I am Milfonnos, the greatest Pharaoh who ever lived! Kneel!>" The woman flinched as if he'd struck her.

<She doesn't know you,> Kasmut murmured. <We are strangers here.>
"<This is my kingdom!>" Milfonnos huffed. "<These are my subjects.>"

The woman backed away from the counter until her butt collided with a metal box. "Just… just take what you want and get out." Her lip trembled, fat tears trailing down her cheeks.

Milfonnos' stomach (did he have a stomach?) growled. Consuming the peasant had made him feel rejuvenated, but the feeling was quickly waning. He looked down at his hands, both just bone, bandage, and a frayed thread of tendon. "<I will do anything to be whole again,>" he said to Kasmut. "<Don't you want to be whole again too?>"

This time, Kasmut did not stop him when Milfonnos sucked the life force from his victim.

CHAPTER 13

Jack merged onto Qasr Al Nile and into stop-and-go traffic. When he approached a streetlight—an ornate beaux-art design, a holdover from the early twentieth century—he glanced at himself in the rearview mirror.

He was fairly certain his nose was broken, judging by the purple bruises forming beneath his eyes and the slight ten-degree angle on the bridge of his nose. His adversary had certainly gotten a good punch or three in. Before he could lose his nerve, Jack grasped his nose between his index and middle fingers and gave it a sharp tug. Stars burst in front of his eyes, and for one dizzying moment, he feared he might vomit.

Thankfully, the feeling passed just as traffic inched forward. Many of the vehicles were outfitted with an Uber sticker on the windshield, driving up and down the nightclub district in search of fares. That was just fine with Jack because it meant that Eliza was probably still waiting on the curb for an available ride. The sedan—which he'd "borrowed," never mind the circumstances—struck a pothole and his cargo bounced.

"Uff," the man from the alley groaned around the bandana stuffed in his mouth.

Jack glanced back, warily resting his hand on the pistol in the passenger seat. His captive laid on his side in the backseat, his knees drawn up to his chest. Jack had tied his wrists behind his back with a pair of jumper cables he'd found in the sedan's trunk.

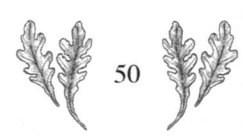

Jack

Suddenly, the passenger side door of his sedan swung open. A man stared at him. "Are you my ride? You don't look like your name is Husani." The man's bloodshot eyes settled on the pistol. "Whoa, whoa, sorry man, sorry!" He slammed the door and scampered away.

"Mhm mmm hm," the man in the backseat said.

"Shut up."

Finally, the sedan crept past the Osiris Pub, arriving just in time for Jack to spot Eliza as she climbed into a shiny black Escalade with her new friends. Jack waited for it to pull into traffic and followed.

"You seem awful interested in Elizabeth Cunningham," the man in the backseat observed. He'd managed to expel the damp bandana from his mouth with his tongue, at least enough to speak. He had a lisp, but Jack wasn't sure if it was from the gag or his swollen lip.

To Jack's untrained ear, there was something familiar about the man's voice and cadence, though he did not recognize his face. The man had coal black hair and expressive eyebrows that danced across his high forehead. While his face was somewhat round, his cheekbones were well-defined, giving him an elfin appearance. Unlike Jack, his nose was straight and narrow, the tip slightly upturned. While he was objectively handsome (even Jack could see that), there was something unsettling about him. It was his eyes—the irises so brown they were nearly black. A predator's eyes.

Jack scoffed. "I don't have any interest in talking to you."

The man wiggled like an inchworm, presumably trying to free himself from his restraints. He finally managed to spit out the rest of the gag. "Sure," the man relented. "But it seems silly to sit in silence for who-knows-how-long."

"If you think I'm going to take off those restraints, you've got another fucking thing coming," Jack grumbled, his eyes on the Escalade. Its windows were heavily tinted, and he couldn't see inside, which made him nervous. "Why are you following her?"

"Why are *you* following her?" his captive countered.

"I'm protecting her."

"What a funny coincidence. So am I."

"I've never seen you before," Jack said as the Escalade sped onto the bridge, flanked by two enormous stone lions. Even at this late hour, tourists took pictures beside the sculptures. "If you had been at the dig site, I would have noticed you."

The man struggled to sit up and managed to prop himself up against the door. With his arms behind him, he had to hunch in order to avoid sitting on

his own fingers. His disheveled hair fell into his eyes. "Now we're getting somewhere," he said. "You know her from the dig site."

"I didn't say that," Jack snapped as they sped over the Nile. The water looked pitch black, the moon's glow unable to penetrate the cloud cover. Jack could not help but think of a black hole. As a child, he had nightmares about stumbling into a black hole's orbit, floating in an inky black nothingness for an eternity.

Now, as an adult, he knew that it was truly a fear of the dark. As a child, he was left home alone while his mother went to get a case of beer at the gas station down the road. She often forgot to return until dawn, preferring to sit on the curb and shoot the shit with the other degenerates. For many years, he didn't blame her for it. She thought he was asleep, tucked safely in his bed. But he was wide awake inside the protective circle cast by his nightlight, too frightened to even walk down the hall to the bathroom.

"I think we got off on the wrong foot," the man said smoothly. "Let's take a step back. I'm Hak. What's your name?"

Startled, Jack veered out of his lane, and the bridge's concrete barrier sheared off his passenger side mirror. "Yong Jin-Hak?!" That was why he'd recognized the voice. Hak was his handler on the other side of the phone.

"That's me."

"It's me: Jack. Jack Manning."

Hak chuckled. "Coincidences on top of coincidences."

The bridge terminated, and the Escalade veered right down a narrow riverside street. The street ran parallel to a grimy warehouse district, the air thick with smoke that smelled like rotten eggs. The Escalade finally pulled into a crowded parking lot in front of a large, 3-story building that appeared abandoned with broken windows and graffiti painted over a sign reading BABYLON TEXTILES LIMITED. Jack pulled in too, parking several rows away from Eliza's ride.

"Are you going to untie me, Manning?" Hak asked.

"Shit! Yes." Jack climbed out of the car and opened the back door, leaning in to untie the jumper cables lashed around Hak's wrists. Once free, Hak rubbed his raw skin.

"You shouldn't have struggled."

"Well, you should have told me who you were."

Jack grabbed Hak's elbow and helped him out of the sedan. Hak winced.

"Well, if you hadn't thrown me into a dumpster, I might have." Hak leaned against the sedan, pressing his palm against his ribs. Jack wouldn't be surprised if he'd broken one.

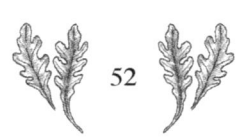

"You would have slit my throat otherwise. Remind me to give you back the knife you keep in your boot." Eliza's laughter turned his attention elsewhere, and Jack leaned between the cars to catch sight of her. She was walking toward the warehouse with her posse, her arm slung around a woman's waist as they giggled together.

"Can I have my knife back now?"

"No," Jack answered. "I'm not stupid. C'mon, we're about to lose sight of her."

The two men followed the group of women, careful to hang back in the crowd. They walked around the side of the building to a loading dock, where a line of people waited to be let inside. A large, broad-shouldered man stood in the doorway, checking IDs. Jack and Hak got in line a few people behind Eliza. "Do you have your ID?" Hak whispered.

"Of course, I don't," Jack huffed.

The line moved slowly. It was strange to see Eliza wearing anything other than shorts, a tee, and an apron. Tonight, she wore a shift dress that showed off her curves, the lace hem just barely reaching mid-thigh. Her blonde hair was loose and curled into waves. The back of the dress zipped from neck to hem, and Jack couldn't help but think of unzipping it achingly slowly, revealing inch after inch of soft, kissable skin.

The women passed through the bouncer's checkpoint with no more than cursory glances at their identification as did the people behind them. Finally, Jack and Hak reached him. The bouncer arched an eyebrow as he took in their disheveled and bloody appearance. "We have a dress code," he grunted.

Jack glanced back the way they came. No one else was waiting in line, though cars were still pulling into the lot. They only had a moment, if that. But before he could move, Hak punched the bouncer in the stomach. He doubled over, and Hak drove his knee into his nose. When he crumpled, Hak slipped past him and held the door open for Jack. "After you," he said.

It took some time for Hak and Jack to find Eliza. She was on the dance floor, dancing with a handsome man in an Armani suit coat and jeans. "What a douche," Jack said sourly, nursing an overpriced bottom-shelf bourbon.

Hak sucked a shot of Bacardi through a straw because his lips were far too swollen to properly drink out of a glass. "You seem jealous," he remarked.

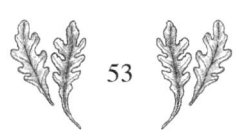

"I'm not jealous," Jack protested a little too quickly.

"You are supposed to be doing a job here," Hak reminded him. "That's why I sent you to Cairo."

"I did my job," Jack grumbled. "I'm doing my job. This is entirely separate from that."

"Do you really think I would travel all this way if this was irrelevant to the mission, Jack? My friend called me here to protect this girl, but I think this affects our mission too. I have a feeling she could compromise all of it." Hak's eyes flicked toward the door.

Jack looked too. The bouncer stood in the doorway, gripping the doorframe. Blood poured down his chin as he talked into a walkie talkie. "Do you think he's looking for us?"

"Wouldn't you be? We need to go before he does something stupid like call the police."

"I'm not leaving without Eliza." Jack slipped off his stool and walked purposefully through the crowd. The music was so loud that the floor trembled beneath his feet. Jack hated electronic music, especially the DJ who acted like pressing buttons made him a musician.

Eliza was still dancing with Mr. Armani. Her cheeks were rosy red, and she'd taken off her shoes. Armani pressed his crotch against her butt, his hands roving over her midsection. Jack clenched his teeth. "Can I cut in?" he asked, careful to keep his voice even and kind while inwardly he wanted to force the guy to swallow his own tongue.

Eliza grinned at him. "Jack! What are you doing here?" She was slurring her words a bit. "What happened to your face?"

Armani wrapped his arms around her. "Who's this, baby?"

Baby.

Tearing out his tongue and feeding it to him was starting to sound too nice. Eliza didn't seem to notice the endearment. "This is Jack. My Jack." She untangled herself from her dance partner and grabbed Jack's wrist. "We keep running into each other."

Hak appeared at Jack's shoulder. "Let's go," he urged breathlessly. "We have company." The crowd parted as the bouncer barreled through it, making a beeline straight for them. He was flanked by two other bouncers.

Eliza unabashedly looked Hak up and down, seeming not to notice the evidence of his recent beating. "Who are you?"

Jack gripped Eliza's elbow and steered her in the opposite direction. Armani tried to protest, but Hak gave him a stern look and pressed his finger to his lips.

Jack speed-walked toward a side door. Ignoring the "Alarm will sound if opened" sign, he pushed the bar and stepped out into the parking lot. The alarm didn't so much as chirp; the building didn't have power—the music and lights powered by a noisy generator. "Where are we going?" Eliza asked. "Ow!" She stopped to examine her bare heel. "I stepped on a rock."

Exasperated, Jack slung her over his shoulder. "We have to go. Right now."

Hak plucked the keys from Jack's pocket and trotted to the sedan. "I'll drive," he said. "I heard what happened in Burma."

Jack had flipped a car. *That's* what happened. But Jack didn't argue. He helped Eliza into the back just as the bouncers burst from the building and headed straight for them. Jack coolly slid into the backseat. "Let's go!"

Eliza dozed with her head in his lap until they reached her apartment building. When he shook her awake, she was bleary-eyed and a little grouchy. "You're home," Jack murmured. "I'll walk you up."

"We'll walk you up," Hak said cheerily.

Jack was surprised to find that he didn't mind the two flights of stairs to Eliza's rooftop apartment when she leaned against him as they ascended, body pressed against his in a way that made him wish violently that Hak wasn't with them. Her hands wandered along his arms, ass rubbing against him in invitation. When they reached the top, she lurched awkwardly to her door and began digging through her purse. "I can't ... find my ... keys," she grumbled.

"Let me help," Jack said, taking the bag from her. He found the keychain quickly and started trying various keys. *Not that one. No, not that one either. Maybe...*

"You're so handsome," Eliza crooned. Jack looked over his shoulder to see Eliza's arms slung around Hak's neck. "Even with that lip. So handsome." Her face inched closer as a wolfish grin spread across Hak's face.

Jack turned away before they kissed, hating the empty feeling in his stomach but hoping it would swallow him up like a black hole.

Chapter 14

R ISE.

Eliza jerked awake, her pillow soaked through with damp sweat. A headache pounded behind her eyes, courtesy of three glasses of white wine and an obscene amount of Jägermeister, judging by the taste of anise coating her tongue. With a groan, she pulled the comforter over her head, blocking out the midday sun beaming through her window. She had left the window cracked to let in a breeze; the smell of car exhaust trickled through the gap.

While the dream dissipated just as soon as she tried to recall it, she couldn't shake the fear. It burrowed behind her chest wall, squeezing her heart in its fist. She had clenched her fists in her sleep, and her nails left impressions shaped like half-moons on her palms. Her bed didn't feel like a safe harbor but a rocking ship on a turbulent ocean. She was sure if she thought about it a little too long, she would throw up.

She reached out of her cocoon for her phone charging on her end table. Her fingers walked over the cluttered surface, touching a tube of chapstick, her wallet, a tangle of cords, her Apple Watch, a pair of reading glasses (for fashion, not function), and finally her phone in its battered case. Despite the case, the phone sported a spiderweb of cracks on the screen.

When she woke the phone, the screen was so bright that it seared her retinas. Her headache intensified, a tremolo through her sinus cavity. It was just past noon, and she had a few texts from Poppy:

[Poppy: Someone got sloppy last night]

[Poppy: Hopefully not too sloppy. Drunk Eliza has very, very, VERY low standards]

And, later:

[Poppy: Did you get home okay?]

[Poppy: Hello?]

Eliza scrolled up to see the earlier part of the conversation. She'd sent Poppy a photo of her glass of wine on the mahogany bar top. If she zoomed in, she could just make out her reflection, partially hidden by her phone. After that photo, she'd sent a series of texts that grew increasingly incomprehensible:

[Eliza: Miss you, bitch]

[Eliza: The bartender is cute. Do you think he'd go on a date with me?]

[Eliza: I met the nicst girlssss, they invited me to a oartayyyy]

Then, a selfie, her thumb partially covering the lens. Her eyes were half-lidded, and her arm was slung around a slight Egyptian woman wearing a sequined mini dress. Eliza couldn't quite remember her name. Was it Aya or Eman?

Eliza sighed, placing the phone face down on her mattress. She'd met Aya/Eman and her friends outside of Osiris Pub, and as often happened when drunk women find one another, she was welcomed into the fold. Introductions were followed by an invitation to a house party in Mohandessin. Though it wasn't so much a house party as it was a warehouse party with a famous DJ. She'd danced with her new friends and had taken way too many shots. She wasn't entirely sure how she got home.

Reluctantly, Eliza slid out of her cocoon and stumbled to the bathroom. The floor seemed to tilt beneath her feet, but she wasn't sure whether that was the hangover or the shoddy construction. Her landlord had neglected repairs since she moved in, and the building was quite literally falling apart.

She had to wait eons for hot water, and the air conditioner seemed to only work two days out of every seven.

The bathroom was small and not well lit. She normally did her makeup sitting cross-legged on the floor in her bedroom, looking into a cracked full-length mirror she'd found sitting out on the curb. But today, she welcomed the low lighting. Her head didn't hurt as much in here. As she opened the medicine cabinet in search of Excedrin, she caught a glimpse of her reflection.

She looked like shit—her mascara smeared all over her eyelids and her lipstick blotchy. Her sleep-tousled hair stuck to her damp cheeks. While last night had been fun—what she could remember anyway—she would pay for it today. Eliza placed an Excedrin capsule on her dry tongue and cupped her hand beneath the tap to scoop water into her mouth. The water tasted like pennies, and she thought for sure the pill would come back up. Clutching the sink, she breathed through her nose until the feeling subsided.

In the bedroom, her phone chimed. Reluctantly, Eliza stumbled back into her bright bedroom and pawed through the sheets for it. It was another text from Poppy, this time a photo of her four children, all towheaded and wearing matching jumpers. They were sitting side-by-side on her mid-century couch. There was Paisley with her lopsided smile. The twins Paul and Peter, the latter with his finger in his nose. Only Portia was looking directly at the camera, but she was sitting with her leg slung over the arm of the couch. Eliza chuckled.

[Eliza: I miss them]

[Poppy: Oh look, someone's alive]

[Eliza: Barely]

She punctuated the message with three puking emojis. After a moment of Poppy's speech bubble waggling, letting Eliza know she was typing, she called instead. As soon as Eliza answered, she could hear the kids giggling and shouting in the background. "Can you hear me?" Poppy asked in her very posh accent.

"Yeah," Eliza answered, shuffling into the kitchen to make a pot of coffee. She put the phone on speaker and placed it on the chipped Formica countertop.

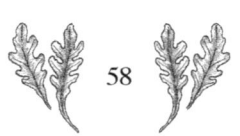

"We're at the park now. Chaz had an important phone call. Honestly, it's ghastly here. A bunch of screaming, snot-nosed kids with their nannies. Hold on."

Eliza scooped ground coffee into the machine while Poppy spoke to someone, her voice muffled. "Sorry, Peter needed me to wipe his nose. It looks like you're having fun in Cairo."

RISE. The memory came unbidden and Eliza touched the spot where her necklace had been. The burn ached, the skin there tight and shiny. "It's ... okay," she answered. "I miss you."

"I miss you, too. You sound weird."

The coffee machine whirred, and the room filled with the smell of medium roast. "What do I sound like?" Eliza asked as she opened the fridge and grabbed a carton of half-and-half. Her stomach flip-flopped, and she hesitated. *Dairy may not be a good idea right now.* She put the carton back. *I'll drink it black.*

"Just weird," Poppy replied. "Preoccupied."

"I'm hungover, Pops. I promise I'm fine." Guilt settled like a leaden weight in her stomach. But she already knew what Poppy would say if she told her the truth. *The hot sun has gotten to you. Shall I buy you a plane ticket home?* Eliza was worried that this time, she'd actually say yes. But Cairo had always been her dream, even if she wasn't excavating canopic jars and—

She pictured the canopic jar lying on its side in the tomb, a hairline crack running from its base to its jackal-headed lid. She should have put it back. At the very least, she should have placed it upright next to the unmarked sarcophagus. Leaving it that way was disrespectful.

Don't be silly, Eliza. They don't need it anymore. They're dead. Besides, what was once their stomach—if she could still remember which organ the jackal-headed god Duamutef's canopic jar contained—was now just a handful of ash.

I WILL RISE, the voice had said, her mother's ruby necklace floating in the darkness. She couldn't explain it, but she felt as though it could *see* her. When she was a child, she liked to hold the ruby up in front of her eye, turning it this way and that so that the prisms would catch the light. Whenever she heard the phrase "rose-colored glasses," she thought of that. Everything looked so beautiful with a cheery red hue.

"Eliza?" Poppy prompted.

"Sorry," Eliza managed, sinking down into her kitchen chair. "What were you saying?"

"Chaz is going on a business trip to Cyprus, and he's taking me with him! I will be just across the Mediterranean Sea from you. I looked it up: it's just a ninety-minute flight! Maybe I could come see you?"

Eliza pressed her lips together. She couldn't quite imagine Poppy in the desert nor in her tiny apartment. It was like trying to picture an elephant thriving in the Mariana Trench. "Maybe," she finally answered, non-committal.

"Oh my god, Peter just picked up a frog and is trying to lick it. Peter, put that down this instant! Eliza, I'm so sorry—I've got to go before he gets warts!" Before Eliza could say goodbye, the call abruptly ended.

A shower and a cup of coffee rejuvenated her. Eliza sat on her bedroom floor in her robe, leaning close to the mirror to apply a thick coat of mascara, hoping it would distract from the dark circles under her eyes. While she didn't feel entirely up to it, she wasn't sure how much more Egyptian soap opera she could take. When Rafi invited her out to Osiris Pub for a drink, she readily accepted.

Besides, a little hair of the dog might do her good.

Rafi knocked as he let himself into her apartment. "You ready?" he called from the living room.

"Almost!" she replied. She reached into her makeup bag for her eyeliner pencil.

He came to lean against the doorframe, crossing his arms over his broad chest. He looked handsome in a pair of pressed slacks and a button-down shirt that he'd left partially untucked. "How are you feeling?" he asked. The corner of his lip twitched as if he wanted to poke fun at her misfortune but thought better of it.

"Like I might die if I stand up," she admitted. "I overdid it last night."

"That's not like you," Rafi said. "You're stressed over what happened." It wasn't a question, per se, but it wasn't not one either.

Eliza focused on her reflection, tracing her eyeline with the kohl-colored pencil. "It's hard not to be."

"I told you: it wasn't your fault. Frankly, it was an act of God. The wind—"

"I know," Eliza interrupted, knowing she was in for an entire closing argument otherwise. "I just can't stop thinking about what I saw."

"It was dark," Rafi said gently. "You don't know that you saw anything."

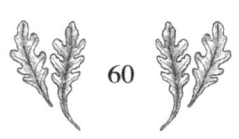

Eliza sighed, tossing the pencil back into her makeup bag. She rose, smoothing the skirt of her cotton maxi dress. "Let's go get fucked up," she said. "You're buying the first round."

Chapter 15

On Sunday during football season, the Osiris Pub was crowded. The flat-screen television mounted behind the bar played Egyptian Premier League football on mute; the inebriated fans provided their own commentary.

Eliza didn't care for sports, but she liked the ambiance. The bar was particularly popular with expats who appreciated the cheap beer and Eurocentric menu. It was the only place in Cairo where one could get fried tilapia with a side of chips while listening to an Ed Sheeran ballad (though "Shape of You" did often elicit a hearty jeer). It was a tiny piece of Britain folded into Egypt.

Eliza grabbed Rafi's hand as they wound their way through the milieu. Eliza was bumped by shoulders and elbows ("Sorry!" "*Asf!*"), and by the time they got to the bar, she desperately wanted to go home. Even her own anxiety didn't seem as troublesome as being social. She had forgotten there was football on, that the pub would be loud and made humid by bodies crushed together.

"What do you want to drink?" Rafi asked, leaning close so that she could hear him over the din. He smelled like sandalwood and mandarin orange. Eliza recognized the cologne. She'd seen the dark blue Sauvage bottle on his bathroom counter during their bi-weekly movie night and commented on it. He had found it funny she had snooped through his things, but she didn't think picking up something in plain sight counted as snooping. Still, after she remarked that it smelled nice, he started wearing it whenever they were together. Eliza had thought maybe he had a crush on her, but he'd never been anything more than friendly. In truth, she was relieved. It was nice to have someone steadfast whom she could talk to, who wasn't panting at the door, waiting to paw at her. Eliza unabashedly loved sex, but sex complicated things.

Sleeping with Jack Manning has complicated things, she thought.

"Vodka and grapefruit juice—only a little bit of vodka." She pushed down thoughts of Jack. It wasn't that she regretted it—she didn't—but it certainly wasn't her best idea. Though, it had been just what she needed at the moment.

"Coming right up," Rafi said, leaning his forearms on the bar. He'd rolled up his sleeves, and she admired the snake tattoo that stretched from elbow to wrist. She wouldn't have pegged him as the tattoo type. Did all lawyers have tattoos under their suits? Eliza chuckled as she pictured a barrister in a white powdered wig standing in the hallowed halls of Crown Court, sporting a full body tattoo beneath their robes.

Does Rafi have more tattoos hidden beneath his clothes? She wished they had occasion to go swimming. Seeing Rafi in swim trunks would definitely be worthwhile.

Eliza slid onto a barstool while he summoned the bartender. They spoke to one another in Arabic while she stared at her reflection in the mirrored barback. She looked pale and a little gaunt—probably because she hadn't eaten since the day before and thrown everything up besides.

"Can I get some chips?" she asked the bartender. "A big basket. Actually, make that two. A side of vinegar too."

The bartender raised his bushy eyebrows at Rafi. "Do you want me to put it on your tab, *sadiq?*"

"Yeah," Rafi said. "I've got it."

As the bartender went to make their drinks, Rafi took the stool next to her. "Someone is feeling better."

Eliza chuckled. "Watch it, or I won't share with you."

Rafi rapped his knuckles on the mahogany bar top, the ostentatious ring on his index finger catching the light, scattering crimson motes across the dark wood. Eliza had never considered him a jewelry person either, but he said it had been his father's. *"You can't put a family heirloom in a drawer,"* he'd joked. *"That's how you get cursed."*

He gave her a sidelong look. "How are you doing?" he asked. "I'm sure you are anxious about tomorrow."

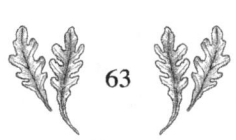

One Mummy to Go, Please!

Tomorrow. She had work tomorrow. She would have to drive to the dig site, set up, and wait for the laborers to discover the canopic jar. And, if she had actually seen what she thought she saw, there would be more to be found.

Like an unmarked sarcophagus with its lid cracked in half.

The bartender returned with their drinks and placed them on top of cocktail napkins. Eliza gulped hers, the ice cubes rattling. "What if they arrest me?" she moaned when she came up for air.

"On what evidence?" Rafi scoffed.

"I was there, Rafi!" Eliza anxiously tore up her damp napkin. "My fingerprints are on the ladder and—"

"You watch too much *Law & Order*. They aren't going to dust the ladder for fingerprints because no one has committed a crime."

Rafi slung an arm over her shoulders, pulling her into a friendly hug. She leaned her head on his warm, solid shoulder. "I'm just scared," she whispered. "I'm scared I'm going crazy." It felt good to utter her unspoken fear, though she worried that giving it breath meant it would grow legs. Fear was insidious that way. She imagined it crawling up her spine like a millipede.

"You aren't crazy," he assured her. "It was dark. Our eyes play tricks on us in the dark. Once, when I was a kid, a blanket on the floor looked so much like a crocodile that I called for my mother, certain one had crawled to our house from the Nile."

Eliza wasn't as confident as he was. She cast her eyes toward the television just as a man dressed in the red and white kit of the Zamalek SC kicked the ball into the goal. Behind her, the bar exploded with whoops and cheers. The bartender appeared with two steaming baskets of chips, setting them on the bar top before her. "Enjoy," he said. Eliza's stomach growled.

She plucked a crinkle-cut chip from the basket and popped it into her mouth. It was hot and scalded her tongue, but she was starving. She dunked her next fry into the malt vinegar. The salty-sour bite made her miss sitting on the curb outside of a chippy shop, unwrapping a greasy meal folded in newspaper. The tug toward London was so strong that tears welled in her eyes. She abruptly rose from her seat.

"Are you okay?" Rafi asked, his pint glass midway to his lips.

"Just going to the loo," she managed.

The bathrooms were in the rear of the bar. Eliza rushed through the crowd, desperate to be alone, if only for a moment. The dark, narrow hallway leading to the bathrooms was no better; it was humid, thanks to the kitchen

and the back door, which had been propped open with a cinderblock. A few line cooks, still wearing their dingy aprons, loitered just beyond the back door, smoking cigarettes. Eliza veered into the women's restroom.

She locked herself in a stall and leaned against the door. *What is wrong with me?* It had been two years in Cairo, and not once had she been so homesick. She had always known that Cairo was where her heart lay, especially after her parents' deaths. London had felt sad and gray and smothering ... after. Her hand moved to trace her mother's necklace, and another stab of longing filled her at the loss of her mother all over again.

After a few deep breaths, she reluctantly left the stall and made her way back to Rafi. But a familiar face stopped her dead in her tracks. "Jack?!"

He was almost unrecognizable without the layer of dust and sweat. That version of Jack elicited a feral lust, but this version made her want to make love. He'd combed his hair, and without a gun in his hands (replaced by a pint), he didn't seem so intimidating—just sexy and professional. Not that she had thought he was all that intimidating when he'd been inside her.

He had a black eye, a half-moon of purple swelling beneath his waterline. When he smiled, she noticed his lip had been split, closed up with one single stitch. She wanted to ask about it, but it was none of her business. The last seventy-two hours had confirmed that Eliza felt best when she was minding her business. If only she'd known that before she descended into the dig site, her flashlight beam bobbing.

"Eliza," he said, her name seeming to taste as sweet as honey on his tongue; he savored every syllable. Ee-lie-za. "I thought I saw you at the bar."

A cheer interrupted them—Zamalek scored another goal. Two men clinking glasses spilled beer on the floor.

Jack's eyes flicked toward her empty seat where Rafi was happily eating her chips. "Who's that?"

Is that a tinge of jealousy in his voice?

"A friend," Eliza said. She wasn't sure why she was being evasive. Normally, she would introduce her friends (Were she and Jack friends? Coworkers? Fuck buddies?), but a nagging feeling gave her pause. Part of her didn't want Jack to know she was talking to a lawyer. She thought it made her look a little ... guilty.

"A friend, huh?"

"Yeah. I'd better get back—my chips are getting cold."

Her apartment seemed inordinately quiet after the bar. Eliza was so exhausted that she undressed as soon as she closed and locked the door, desperate for her bed. But first, she needed a glass of water and a Tylenol.

She opened the fridge to grab the pitcher of filtered water, pouring it into a Yeti cup. She snapped the lid into place and turned—

—to see a gruesome face in the window, a red eye trained on her. Eliza shrieked and dropped her cup; the lid popped off and cold water soaked her bare feet. She glanced down at the mess and back up at the window.

There was no one there. It was only a trick of the light.

Chapter 16

On Monday morning, the dig site was overrun with men in suits and dark glasses. Jack recognized government officials when he saw them, but this was more than the usual shakedown for bribe money. His phone buzzed with constant messages from his employer, urging him to find out what had happened in the dig site over the weekend. His instructions were clear: make sure nothing was missing and, most importantly, assure the government that nothing was amiss. He needed them to leave fully reassured that everything was business as usual out here. If that meant greasing a few more palms, he could do that. His employer was certainly wealthy enough.

He watched another man in dark glasses enter the office to speak to Reese and the two men in pale suits who were ostensibly in charge. The official may look like a government stiff, but Jack knew the movement of a warrior when he saw it. These men may work for the Cairo office, as they claimed, but they weren't desk jockeys. These were soldiers, here to investigate something far more serious than a disturbed dig site. It was up to Jack to find out what.

His mind wandered back to his encounter with Eliza in her truck on Friday night. She had been flustered when he first saw her, but he had assumed that was her excitement at hooking up with him. Thinking of the mark across her chest—an odd place for a cooking-related burn, now that he thought about it—he wondered if she had seen something that night. Something that startled her enough that she fell eagerly into his arms.

Jack had had his share of flings in his life, and while he and Eliza were definitely flirting hot and heavy, he hadn't expected to have Eliza in his arms for another few days at least. Something had shifted in her—and now he wondered if it was more than just his charm.

He recalled his encounter with Hak over the weekend, both of them apparently watching over Eliza, though Jack's interest wasn't, at the moment, financially motivated. What had she gotten herself into?

His phone buzzed again, and he pulled it out of his pocket. The case was battered.

[Charles: Status?]

Dammit. Jack took a deep breath and headed for the office. The financiers and the government men had ordered Jack to stay outside, but that had been hours ago. It was time to get some answers. Besides, if that nerd Reese Eldin was allowed inside, he should be too. Using his build and height to his advantage, Jack strode to the door and walked right by the man standing outside. The guard made a pitiful excuse to stop him, raising a hand and starting to say something, but Jack gave him a withering look that crushed his confidence. Nodding sheepishly, the man invited Jack inside with a sweep of his hand.

Definitely one of the normal laborers, Jack thought, memorizing the man's face as he passed him by. One of the government guys would have put up a fight.

The cool air blasted as he entered, and Jack soaked it up while standing in the small alcove just inside. He knew it would only make going outside feel even hotter, but he would enjoy it while it lasted. Voices trickled out of the small conference room at the end of the tiny hallway, and Jack crept closer, not wanting to alert them to his presence just yet.

"...isn't a matter for the Cairo government to oversee!" That was Reese. Jack instantly recognized the entitlement in his voice.

"This is a minor misunderstanding." Jack thought that was one of the site bosses. There were two of them—Hayes and Swinton—and Jack could only tell them apart by their shoes. Hayes wore traditional brown penny loafers while Swinton wore open-toed sandals. He hadn't decided yet if Swinton wore the shoes because he was casual or if he wanted to kick them off and use his bare feet to fight. Jack had studied many forms of martial arts, and

he was always leery of men who wore sandals, especially after seeing one seemingly innocuous long-haired man in Laos take out an entire roomful of trained soldiers with deadly precision and kicks like concrete blocks. Jack didn't know their voices well enough to identify them through the plywood walls. He waited for the bribe he knew was coming. "I'm sure we can reach an accord," the voice continued, smooth and reassuring. "If the access fees are no longer sufficient, we will gladly—"

"This isn't about the fees," another voice interrupted—a new voice, serious with a clipped Egyptian accent. "Your dig threatens the local environment. Our people need to assess the effects before you continue."

"We're not actually digging," another smooth voice cut in—Hayes or Swinton? "The rooms were clear once we reached the entrance."

"We know," the Egyptian man continued. "We are merely affirming that the local ecosystem has not been disturbed by your activity underground."

"So… you want to do an inspection? Of rooms that have been this way for millennia?" Hayes/Swinton pressed. "And then what?"

"If nothing is amiss, you may continue your investigation," the Egyptian assured him.

"Oh," Hayes/Swinton said, clearly surprised by this.

"How long will this take?" Reese asked. "We're on a schedule here. We need to get all of this cataloged and packed up and sent overseas to be dated!"

"Of course," the Egyptian said calmly. Jack was surprised that there wasn't a hint of bitterness in his voice. Charles, Jack's employer, was taking the artifacts back to London for study—something the Egyptian authorities rarely allowed these days. Legally, that is. Jack could only imagine the amount of money that had exchanged hands. Given the exorbitant amount he was getting paid to stand guard over seemingly innocuous items in a tomb, it must be obscene.

For a moment, Jack wondered what Charles was looking for—and why it was worth so much to him. *Don't ask questions,* he reminded himself, his cardinal rule since Jakarta. *Do the job and get out alive.*

"Surely, you can spare a few hours to let us inspect the site?" the Egyptian continued. "After all, several witnesses mentioned an event on Friday night. Perhaps you can use this time to ask your staff if anyone saw anything suspicious as they packed up for the night?"

"Nothing happened Friday night!" Reese insisted, and Jack could hear the lie. He assumed the others probably saw through Reese as well; the Englishman was nothing if not slimy.

"Something happened," Hayes/Swinton disagreed, "and Mr. Sabbagh is correct: you should make sure nothing has been disturbed."

"I can't even get down there!" Reese exclaimed. "These government fo—"

"Then you should begin with the laborers," Hayes/Swinton interrupted, his tone severe. "Surely you have a list of employees? Ask them." Jack could picture Reese wilting. "Who else was here?"

"The hired security," Reese said. "And Eliza."

"Eliza?" Hayes/Swinton asked.

Jack took his cue to enter. "She works the food truck," he said, "and we both left at 7:30." Both Hayes and Swinton turned to face him, seemingly relieved for the respite. Reese Eldin may be in charge of the dig on-site, but they respected Jack. He would know what to do.

"Perhaps you should ask her what she saw," Hayes suggested, retrieving the Panama hat he had placed on the conference table. He covered his bald head with it, then glanced at Swinton, who was sitting casually in a chair, one foot propped on his knee, those sandals a quiet threat.

Swinton only had eyes for Jack. "Is she often here that late?"

Jack shook his head, but it was Reese who replied, "No, she was cleaning the grease trap."

"I see," Swinton said, but Jack wasn't looking at him. The Egyptian man he had heard looked down at his phone, his fingers moving swiftly across the screen as he typed a message, but when he looked up, Jack recognized him. Though he was dressed in a polished black suit with his hair perfectly curled, this was the man who had been sitting with Eliza at the bar last night. Jack steeled himself, forcing his expression to stay neutral as they assessed one another. He had watched the two of them at the bar, eating and drinking for a few hours, before quietly tailing them back to Eliza's apartment building—where they had both walked upstairs to Eliza's apartment.

Who is he? More importantly, he found himself wondering, *who is he to Eliza?*

"You must be Jack Manning," the Egyptian said, extending a hand in greeting. "I've heard good things. You come highly recommended from Shogun."

"Do I," Jack said flatly, accepting the handshake with a strong grip he couldn't prevent.

"Rafi Sabbagh," the Egyptian introduced himself. "Cairo Antiquities."

Jack nodded, releasing his hand. "Is the Office of Antiquities often involved in digs?"

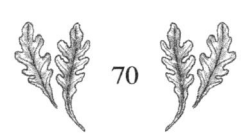

"Only when they are close to environmental resources," Rafi replied, turning to point at the map pinned to the wall of the conference room. His finger tapped the river just north of the site, nearly a kilometer away from the edge of the tomb. "We're just confirming nothing will interfere with the water—runoff and the like."

Jack narrowed his eyes, recalling everything he knew about environmental impact studies. It wasn't much, but he had briefly dated a girl studying environmental science, and he thought a kilometer was beyond the range of such investigations. Then again, that had been in the jungles of Rio—and this was the desert. Things could be different here.

But Jack knew Rafi and his men weren't here to check on the environment. They were here about whatever happened on Friday night—and Jack needed to know what it was just as much as they did. What had disturbed Eliza and sent her running into his arms? He tried not to wonder whether she would have done the same if she hadn't been so spooked.

"Of course," Jack said. He looked over his shoulder at Reese. "In the meantime, we can investigate the so-called event. Reese, you take the laborers." He turned back to face Rafi. "I can interview Eliza. See if she knows anything." Jack carefully watched Rafi's face as he said her name, wanting to know the nature of their relationship. The mercenary was surprised by the possessive wave that washed through him.

She was happy enough to fuck you, he reminded himself. *Is this guy another of her partners? Does she kiss him with those lips?* He recalled her drunken slur as she kissed Hak. *"You're cute."* He shook his head.

It wasn't like him to lose his head over a girl. Determined to get some answers, Jack left the room, heading straight for Shawarma Warrior King.

CHAPTER 17

Rafi watched Jack Manning leave the conference room, a slight smile playing on his lips. He knew that look—had seen it reflected on his own face when he caught himself in a mirror any time he was with Eliza.

How long? Clearly, the man already had feelings for Eliza, though Rafi doubted he would admit it. Americans were notoriously tight-lipped, and Rafi hadn't been lying when he mentioned Jack Manning's reputation with Shogun. The man was a machine.

Rafi's phone rang, and he glanced at the number. With a sigh, he shut the door to the small conference room, pulling a small carved scarab from his front pocket. Whispering a brief incantation to activate the artifact, he smiled at the pale white glow that warmed his palm. The magic ensured no one overheard him. He had acquired the artifact from another dig back when he was still in school, and its minor protective abilities had come in very handy over the years. Nodding at the small layer of magical protection, he answered the call.

"Yes, uncle," he said, his gut already tensing at the barrage he knew was coming.

"You had better have more for me than pleasantries, Rafi," his uncle said. "You should be assuring me that everything is under control."

Rafi took a deep breath, pushing thoughts of Eliza away as he remembered his purpose. "Everything is under control. We are interviewing

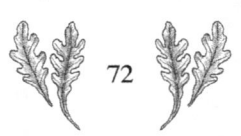

everyone at the site as we speak. If anyone saw anything, we'll deal with it—just like we always do."

"Excellent." There was a pause, and Rafi bit his lip, knowing what would come next. "Would you care to explain why you failed to inspect that site when it first opened?"

Rafi had his answer prepared for this, at least. "They only began a month ago, and no bodies were reported in the initial paperwork. It's been on the list for inspection of artifacts, but we thought we had more time—"

"*You* thought," his uncle corrected him.

"*I* thought," Rafi repeated, squaring his jaw. "Their license was fast-tracked but not through the normal channels. This Charles—the one pulling the strings from abroad—must be getting desperate." They had only recently gotten the investor's first name, though he covered the rest of his identity too well for even Rafi's agents to unearth.

"Any idea of what he's after yet?"

Rafi shook his head, the habit never gone despite being on the phone. He could picture his uncle sitting at the desk in the Cairo office, his suit perfectly pressed and hair styled. His Uncle Sarif never seemed to sweat in the heat, never appeared even slightly disheveled. Rafi glanced down at his own suit, slightly rumpled, and he ran a hand down the jacket, trying to smooth out the wrinkles. He tried to ignore the disappointment he imagined on his uncle's face. "No. But this site has jewelry and artwork, just like the last three, so it may be something decorative. You know how much foreigners love so-called 'exotic' decor."

"But you said there had been sightings of a mummy."

Rafi put a hand to his forehead, glad his uncle couldn't see him. "Only a whisper, and there isn't a sarcophagus at this site—at least, not on the official paperwork. We had no reason to rush the inspection. That said…"

"Yes?" Uncle Sarif prompted.

"The obsidian sarcophagus is here," he said, referring to the tomb in which Milfonnos the Blighted One had been buried. "Along with the canopic jars stamped with the sigil of a protector. We think it's … Kasmut."

"And the body?"

Rafi could feel his uncle's unease through the phone. "Gone." He cringed at his uncle's sharp intake of breath. "We can't tell if it's been gone for years or removed more recently. The lid is cracked in half, but it could have been that way for centuries. We suspect that both bodies were here for a time, but Kasmut's must have been moved elsewhere. His sarcophagus isn't here." Though the mad pharaoh and his bodyguard had been destroyed

for tampering with powers beyond their control, both had been laid to rest with all the proper rites and rituals befitting royalty.

"This makes no sense," his uncle complained, echoing Rafi's own thoughts. "The old tales swear his resting place is nearly 1000 kilometers from there, closer to what remains of the Siwa Oasis."

"I know," Rafi reminded him. He paused, waiting for the question he knew was coming. It was the Amun Henet's secret shame that they hadn't been able to secure the magical artifact—at least not in its entirety.

"And the ruby?"

While his ancestor Rahil had used his god-given abilities to snatch the magical gemstone from Milfonnos' eye, the gem had only fractured, part of it remaining wedged inside the pharaoh's skull. No amount of struggle could remove it, and finally, the Amun Henet had simply prepared the pharaoh's body with the gem intact, hoping that the magic had been destroyed when the gem shattered. The unmarked casket should have assured that no one disturbed Milfonnos's body. No one would have thought treasures hid within a plain black box.

"No sign," he reported. "We are scouring the site. Perhaps it is buried in the sand."

They had been foolishly naive, Rafi thought now, spinning the gold ring on his middle finger, the red gem glinting in the fluorescent lights. His family had been custodians of this portion of the gem for millennia now, his claim tracing back to Rahil himself, though unlike some of his ancestors, Rafi couldn't claim any divine powers. It was just a ring for him, though when he had a son one day, perhaps his tale would be different.

Eliza's necklace, Rafi thought. Another inert piece of the gemstone until she had gone into the tomb, bringing two pieces of the gem close together again. He assumed his ring would also burn him if he got too close to the mummy. He wondered again how her family had come by the stone, reminding himself to follow up with Jaxon to see what the man had unearthed about Eliza's family. He'd already done a basic background check on her when she first moved in—as he did with any new neighbor who posed a potential threat—but that hadn't unearthed anything that would connect her to the Amun Henet.

If it was more than just blind luck, Rafi needed to know. If the mummy was connected to Eliza in any way, he needed to know.

There was a long pause before his uncle spoke again. "Find out who saw what. Perhaps this is just another dead end."

"Yes, Uncle," he said, then ended the call. Neither man cared to swap pleasantries.

Sighing, he closed his eyes, the image of the map pinned to the wall still seared on the inside of his eyelids. *It's so far away from where it should be*, he thought again. *If we could be so wrong about Milfonnos, what else are we wrong about? Has the Book of Heka been found? And what of the magical bangles Milfonnos had once worn?* He knew the pharaoh had been buried with one of them, the other moved to a safe location, but perhaps they had been wrong to think separating the objects was enough. If the mummy had located the artifacts, his power would already be growing too fast for the woefully mortal Amun Henet to contain.

Rafi knew his ancestor had wielded divine magic, but that was a long time ago. Rafi's power these days came from his knowledge of the law and history, his connections to the government, and shadowy security firms like Shogun. He was no match for a resurrected mummy.

Rafi peered out the small window of the trailer and found Jack Manning casually leaning into the food truck. Eliza's shadow moved within, a flash of blonde hair there and gone. A brief surge of jealousy washed over him.

Eliza was her own woman, and she had never been his—she would *never* be his. She took her lovers as she found them. And Jack Manning was a solid choice—strong, focused—the merc would keep her safe if Milfonnos had indeed decided she was a target. So what if Rafi wondered what it would be like to be in Jack's position right now? He imagined leaning casually against the service counter, confident that she looked to him for something more than friendship, knowing the taste of her lips. He thought of her hand on his as they sat in the cafe, her desperate need for reassurance that he believed her.

And I lied to her, he reminded himself. *Like I will always have to do.*

Exhaling, he turned away from the window, knowing Jack would interview Eliza, likely with some heavy flirting and pointed questions about Rafi's connection to her. He would protect her. And where the mercenary fell short—as he would when his other employer had his own demands—Rafi's friend Hak would be there to pick up the slack. Eliza would be safe.

For a moment, he allowed himself to imagine that he was the one to hold her, promising her that she was safe, but he knew it was futile. Though he was expected to marry and have sons to carry on the tradition of the Amun Henet, Rafi's wife would be equally traditional, silently accepting of his mysterious work, not asking the questions he knew Eliza wouldn't be able to contain. In the past, the order had arranged marriages for the men in his

family. Though Rafi was higher in the Amun Henet than either his father or grandfather had been, he knew the time would come when the board members would introduce him to his future bride, a woman fully vetted and mind-numbingly acquiescent. He was thirty-three now—he expected they would announce his engagement to Naur Salem any time now. Though, if Milfonnos had truly returned, perhaps he would get a brief reprieve. No point in arranging marriages during a crisis.

He didn't want to admit it, but part of Rafi was relieved at the delay. He knew he would do his duty when the time came. It was what the men in his family did, what all the men in the order did.

Gazing once more out the window, he caught sight of Eliza stepping out of her truck, the sun shining on her golden hair and a broad smile on her lips. Rafi wondered what it would be like to smile like that. To be free.

Shaking his head, he pulled his phone from his pocket and dialed as he left the conference room and the small trailer behind.

Chapter 18

Eliza thought she had been jumpy that morning when she pulled her truck into its regular space west of the dig site's entrance. Traffic had been sparse for a Monday morning, but her nerves were twanging at the smallest movement; part of her worried she would see another swirl of fabric and red eyes whirling past only to disappear into the sky.

It was nothing, she told herself as she put the truck in park and pulled up the brake, twisting to climb into the back and start setting up. Before she stood, though, a movement of black material caught her eye. For a second, she thought it was the damn mummy, the creature taunting her even in daylight now, but as she squinted through the windshield, she saw that alongside the regular workers, clad in neutral tones to stay cool in the blazing sun, were men in dark suits and dark glasses.

She sat down hard in the seat, the strength flooding out of her legs.

Government officials, she thought, knowing the look of Cairo law enforcement. These men weren't the regular police. They were a step above—the people you called when something valuable had been stolen.

I didn't steal anything, she reminded herself. *I actually left something down there, but I didn't take anything. And I barely disturbed the place.* The image of the sarcophagus flashed in her mind, its lid cracked in half, the black stone reflecting the bouncing beam of her phone's flashlight as she climbed the ladder and fled. *Okay, so maybe I disturbed some things.*

Eliza took a deep breath, slowing her breaths to ease her racing heart. She recalled the chanting voices, goosebumps rising on her arms, and she closed her eyes, recalling her therapist's advice for these moments on the edge of a panic attack. *One thing I can feel*, she thought frantically, and her fingers scrambled for the battered seat beneath her, the buttery feel of the old leather, smooth and velvety against her fingers. *Two things I can hear*, she thought, moving through her grounding technique. She tried to listen, but for a terrifying moment, she could only hear her heart thumping in her ears along with a high-pitched ringing noise. *No*, she told herself. *There's noise. Listen.*

Another panicked moment passed, and then she could hear the normal sounds of the morning dig site—the workers speaking energetically and then quietly in turns. Eliza imagined they whispered when one of the G-Men walked too near. Even if one of them had seen her chase the garbage can lid into the site, she believed they wouldn't say anything. The laborers distrusted the government even more than they suspected foreigners. Eliza had been among them long enough to be accepted now. She was a worker at the site too—one of them.

The only person who knew she'd been down there was Rafi, and he wasn't here, not that he would ever tell on her. Rafi was her friend, though sometimes she wished he was more.

That left Jack Manning. She'd been curt with him at the pub, not wanting to think about how hooking up had affected their flirty dynamic. The last thing she needed was another Reese Eldin, though part of her was sure that Jack would never turn out like that. He was hot, and they'd definitely had a good time—an encounter she wouldn't mind repeating—but the possessive look on his face as he had glanced past her to see Rafi sitting at the bar had spooked her. Eliza enjoyed her freedom. She wasn't going to let some American, no matter how sexy, claim her for himself.

Still, she thought, opening her eyes as her body finally returned to normal, the only evidence a sheen of cold sweat on her exposed skin, *I need to be sure*. Swiveling in the seat, she scanned the crowd. She didn't see Jack anywhere.

Okay, she decided, standing up. She would open the truck, feed her morning customers, and keep an eye out for the security guard. When she spotted him, she would make sure he didn't say anything about her extracurricular activities. Eliza knew just how to persuade him.

Eliza

Jack Manning appeared at her window just after the lunch rush finished. She watched him exit the trailer that housed the dig site office, a popular building at the moment. She'd seen the two men in khaki heading in there that morning, surrounded by men in suits and loudly complaining about government oversight and jurisdiction. While she hadn't seen Jack go inside, she wasn't surprised that he would be in there; no doubt all of the stakeholders had been debating what had happened on Friday night and whether it would affect their shares.

Do they already know I was here late? she wondered, handing another pita to a worker before turning to make the next customer's order. *What did he tell them?*

Jack lingered at the edge of the small white canopy tent that shaded the area where the workers normally ate, obviously waiting for her to finish with her customers before approaching. Questions still peppered her mind, but her body knew what to do, filling orders and slapping sauces in the right places before serving the food with her usual smile. If she could feel the muscles in her cheeks aching today, they didn't need to know. As the last customer walked away, heading for the shade to eat, she let the smile fade as she turned away from the window, not wanting anyone to see her face as she massaged her jaw.

Do I always smile so much? She wondered if she was laying it on too thick. Jack was a trained security guard. She'd felt the scars on his body, short and long lines as well as raised round spots that must be bullet holes. He'd know if she lied to him. Eliza frowned then stood up straight, rubbing out a sudden kink in her shoulder.

I'll have to tell him the truth, then. As much as possible, anyway. The whole truth will make him think I'm a crazy person.

"Hey, sweetheart," Jack Manning said from just outside her window, "you want me to rub that for you?"

Eliza smiled, a genuine one this time, and turned to face him. "Maybe," she teased, resting her elbows on the small counter to show off her cleavage. To his credit, Jack's gaze didn't flick down to check out her chest, eyes fixed on hers. "Hardly enough room back here for you, though."

"That's not what you said last time," Jack replied, the heat apparent in his eyes as he watched her.

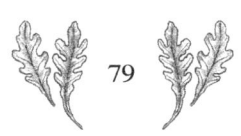

Eliza had a quick flash of Jack's body pressed against hers, arms tight around her back as he moved hard and sure. "Last time didn't involve a massage," she quipped. "That requires way more space."

"Next time?" Jack offered, and something in Eliza's core tightened at the question. "I have skills you haven't seen yet." She recalled just one of his skills, his face buried between her legs, and her cheeks pinked, the flush creeping up her chest despite the heat.

"I'd like that," she said, biting her lip. His eyes darted to her mouth, and Eliza knew she had him, at least a little bit. He wouldn't betray her—not yet anyway. Smiling, she nodded her head toward the trailer, still busy with people entering and leaving. "What's going on today? Some inspection?"

"Apparently something happened Friday night," he explained, then cocked his head. "Wait, you were here late. Did you see anything odd?" His voice was so natural. Eliza's fingers twisted together against the wall of the truck, hidden just below the lip of the window he stood beyond. She forced her face to stay just as neutral as his tone, thinking of his mouth pressed against hers—anything except colorful flashes of light and mummies.

"What do you mean, odd?" she asked. "Like what?"

He leaned closer, his body language friendly and mildly curious. "Like someone went into the tomb," he confided.

"Did they steal something?" she asked, knowing it was the question an innocent person would ask.

"They don't think so," he assured her, "but they're still cataloging everything." He gave her a calculating look. "Some things were ... disturbed."

She furrowed her brows, a hint of confusion. "Disturbed? Like ... moved around?" She frowned. "You think they were looking for something but didn't find it?"

"Did you see anyone near the entrance?" His voice was still charming, but the question was fast, direct, and Eliza couldn't help the furious shake of her head. It was true. She hadn't seen anyone near the entrance.

"No," she confirmed. "But I wasn't really paying attention. I had a minor issue with the grease trap, and I was on the floor in here cleaning."

"Did you hear anything?" he prompted.

Eliza pursed her lips, considering. Had she heard anything before the wind whipped the garbage can lid down into the tomb? After a moment, she shook her head again. "Nothing I can think of. It was windy, but that's not unusual."

She heard the whisper of the chanting in the tomb: Rise, RISE! Staring at Jack, she cocked her head, trying to recall any relevant detail.

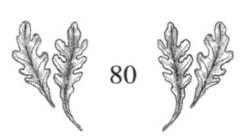

"How about when you left the site? Did you see anything as you were leaving? Anything suspicious?"

Again, Eliza paused, considering the question. She most certainly had seen someone run across the road on her way out. That seemed innocent enough to share. She could just leave out what she had seen after that.

"Actually," she began, "I did see something. A person ran across the road as I was leaving."

"What did they look like?" he asked.

She shrugged. "I'm not sure. It was dark, and it happened really fast. They were wearing black, so I didn't see much except the movement." She paused, then met his gaze. "You know, I think they might have been holding something, like a book. Or something book-sized and rectangular? They fumbled it as they dodged my truck." At his look, she quickly added, "I wasn't speeding or anything! I just really wanted to get out of there."

"Why such a hurry to leave?" he asked, charm again coating the words. "When we met at the gas station, you didn't seem to be in a rush at all."

"That's because I had a reason to linger," she replied primly. "Have you ever cleaned a grease trap, Jack?" When he shook his head, she added, "Great. When you have, ask me again why I would want to hurry home afterward."

"But you didn't go home," he reminded her again.

"I got ... distracted," she admitted. "I didn't think you minded."

Jack leaned back, that sense of interrogation fading, and he smiled at her. "I didn't mind," he told her. He paused, then seemed to decide something. "Yesterday, at the pub…"

Eliza grimaced. "I'm sorry," she apologized. "I was rude."

"Can I ask why?" Jack's face was open, vulnerable, and Eliza wanted to kiss the insecurity away.

"I didn't know if you would be … weird," she admitted. "Sometimes, people get … possessive. I seem to attract those types."

"You are not a possession, Eliza," Jack said quietly.

"I know that," she retorted. "But some people just…" She frowned, shrugging her shoulders.

"They do," he agreed after a moment. "I won't."

"What will you do?" she asked, not bothering to keep the suggestion from her tone.

"For starters, I'd like to see what I can do for that shoulder," he said, and Eliza smiled, reaching up to rub the sore muscle. "Maybe tonight?"

Eliza nodded. "I will require a proper bed," she said sternly, conjuring a grin from the security guard.

"I have a bed," he said, "but it's not one you'd appreciate." He frowned. "I have a very small room back in Cairo, but it's not fit for entertaining."

"Well, then I suppose you'll just have to come to my place," Eliza offered. "You can follow me there after we close today."

Jack nodded. "It's a date, sweetheart." He raised an eyebrow. "Though if you come out of there, maybe I can give you a preview of my skill set."

Eliza nodded, then stepped to the door and down the step to the dirt outside. Jack put a hand on her shoulder, fingers beginning to press her skin, but then movement at the dig site caught her attention and she turned. He glanced around, seeming to note the remaining people—laborers lingering near the entrance, clearly waiting to see if they would be granted access to the tomb today, a few men in suits standing at attention and waiting for orders. She saw both men in khaki appear from the tomb's entrance, followed by Reese, all three awkwardly climbing off the ladder. She couldn't hear their conversation, but they seemed much happier, nodding as another man in a suit approached from the trailer.

Something about the man seemed familiar, the back of his head filled with luscious black hair that touched his shoulders. He said something to the khaki-clad men, then turned to walk alongside them. As he approached, Eliza recognized Rafi.

What the hell?

Eliza finally tore his gaze away to find Jack Manning staring at her. "Friend of yours?" he asked, his voice neutral as his hand stilled on her shoulder.

"Yes," she answered, the confusion on her face completely genuine. "I have no idea what he's doing here."

"Does he work for the Egyptian government?"

Eliza shrugged. "I guess so?" She frowned. "He's a lawyer."

"Figures," Jack grumbled. Reese gestured in their direction, clearly calling Jack over, and the guard turned to Eliza. "Tonight?"

She nodded, still wondering what Rafi was doing at her dig site. "Yeah," she agreed. "Definitely."

As she watched Jack Manning head back to work, Eliza wondered if she actually wanted to know what was happening. Maybe it was better if she didn't know.

She climbed back into the truck and returned to the world she did.

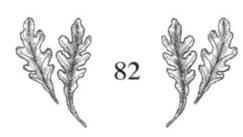

Chapter 19

The sportbike purred between Hak's thighs as he waited for Eliza to appear at her third floor window. She was a creature of habit, which put Hak on edge. It was absurdly easy to hurt someone when you knew where they'd be and when they'd be there.

Hak wasn't much for ghost stories. Nor mummy stories, for that matter. In truth, he wasn't sure that Rafi's anxiety was founded. People simply didn't come back to life, no matter how much a person prayed, or wept, or begged the devil for a fair trade. Dead was dead. There was nothing fantastical about it.

The fantastic had always been Rafi's thing. Before he buckled down in law school, Rafi's nose was always buried in some dusty occult text. He brandished that ostentatious ring as though it was anything more than costume jewelry, spouting on about honor and magic. In truth, Hak thought Rafi lost it a little after his dad died and he went to live with his uncle.

Rafi had been careful to bury the lede on the phone. "Get on a plane. I need you here. She's in danger."

"'She'?" Hak asked, breathless. He was midway through a ten mile jog and wasn't entirely sure what possessed him to answer. But something about Rafi's name on the caller ID got his hackles up; Rafi didn't call often, and when he did, it was often something capital-b Big. Like when he passed the Bar exam or learned he was betrothed to the very dull Naur Salem.

One Mummy to Go, Please!

"My neighbor," Rafi explained. "Eliza."

Hak wiped his brow and slowed to a walk. His calf muscle twinged. "The same Eliza you've been pining over for years?"

"It hasn't been years," Rafi huffed. "Listen: she told me that she was at the dig site and saw something strange."

"What, like a mummy?" Hak doubled over in laughter at his own joke. A passing runner shot him a sour look. It wasn't polite to stop in the middle of the track. Hak hurriedly veered into the grass.

But Rafi didn't laugh. He cleared his throat. "Yeah, a mummy."

"You're serious?" Hak sank down onto a park bench overlooking the Danube. A cool breeze ruffled his hair. "Please don't tell me you're serious."

"She saw it in the tomb. Her necklace, my ring... it's all connected. I should have known something was wrong. I felt it. Well, not just then—but in retrospect." He spoke so quickly that his words tumbled together. When he finished, he sucked in a huge breath.

Hak pressed his lips together. "Rafi, you're starting to sound crazy, my friend."

"Maybe I am. But there's one thing I'm certain of: she's in danger. You're the only one I trust. Please." And Hak got on a plane because, after all, Rafi had asked politely.

At 8:30 a.m., as always, Eliza snapped open the curtains, a velvet sleep mask pushed up onto her high forehead. She only wore an oversized t-shirt to bed, probably stolen from an ex-boyfriend, and the frayed hem barely touched her thighs. Sometimes, when she moved just right, Hak caught a glimpse of her lace panties. It wasn't gentlemanly to look, but Hak wasn't necessarily a gentleman. If he were, he wouldn't be in his line of work.

Her lips were always pulled down into a frown. She was clearly not a morning person. Or she suffered from a severe case of RBF. Hak didn't think it was the latter. He'd watched her long enough to know she spared a smile for most anyone, whether they were a friend or stranger.

Typically, Hak wouldn't see her again until approximately forty-five minutes later when she left the apartment building, a thermos of coffee in hand. Today, it was thirty. She'd showered, and her hair was still a little damp.

The food truck was parked several blocks away, and she walked the same route every morning with earbuds in her ears. *Stupid*. But today was different. Instead of walking toward the truck, she made a beeline for him. "Hey!" she shouted, pointing at him. "Why are you following me?"

She carried a hot pink canister of mace in her fist, her finger poised on the trigger. "You think I don't see you, but I do—sitting here with your

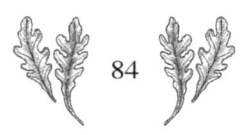

stupid fucking bike! The loudest fucking engine on the whole block, by the way!"

Hak snapped down his visor and put his feet on the pegs. With a twist of the throttle, he rocketed past her and down the block. She was still yelling, but he only caught one word. "Prick!"

"Hey, boss."

When Hak opened his eyes, he found Sloan's face only inches from his. Sloan wore a pair of boxer briefs that were too tight and left nothing to the imagination. Hak wouldn't describe his cohort as muscular so much as enormous—Sloan had the body of a linebacker. "It's 9 o'clock. You overslept."

Shit!

Hak rolled out of bed and pulled on his jeans, hopping to get his feet into their respective leg holes. He bumped into Sloan. "Why didn't you wake me earlier?"

"I didn't know I was your mother." Sloan rolled his eyes. "Besides, I'm not sure why we have to tail this girl day in and day out. I'm tired of sitting in the fucking car, staring at her building."

"Because Rafi asked us to," Hak snapped, pulling a V-neck t-shirt over his head.

"Rafi asked *you* to," Sloan reminded him—not for the first time. "He's playing you. That whole mummy story? It's the stupidest shit I've ever heard. Surely you see that, right? C'mon Hak. I'm missing my kid's birthday party for this job."

"Don't you think it's a little odd that this girl works at a Shogun-protected dig site? It seems awfully coincidental." Hak had come for Rafi, that was true, but he was starting to slowly tie the loose threads together. He also knew there was no such thing as coincidence, just men pulling strings. Who was really pulling his?

"Shogun works a lot of digs, but surely you know that, boss." He stretched out the last syllable so that it sounded like a hiss.

"Are you questioning my competency?" Hak slipped on his leather shoulder holster, the twin pistols bumping against his ribs.

"I'm just saying." Sloan brushed past him into their shared living space. He sat heavily upon the futon and reached for the pack of Cleopatra cigarettes on the coffee table. Or rather, the milk crates they used as a coffee table.

"You can go home, Sloan," Hak said as he slipped his feet into his favorite Doc Marten boots.

Sloan lit his cigarette, the spark reflected in his beady eyes. "Someone has to watch your six, Hak. Even if that someone thinks you're a fucking idiot."

"Jack is here to back me up."

"Jack Manning!" Sloan exclaimed. "Trust me, that prick isn't gonna back up nothin' but himself. Hell, he might even double-cross himself if someone threw a dollar at him. He's as trustworthy as a rabid dog."

"Is … that a saying in America?"

"No, it's called a metaphor. A rabid dog looks normal and cute 'til it starts foaming at the mouth and rips your arm off." He took a long drag of his cigarette, and purplish smoke poured out his nostrils.

"Sloan, you are a wordsmith. Don't let anyone tell you otherwise," Hak said dryly. He went into the kitchen to pour a cup of coffee but was disappointed to find that the coffee pot was empty. "You didn't put the coffee on?"

Sloan didn't answer. Instead, he turned on the television. Hak sighed and scooped grounds into a fresh filter.

"Hey, Hak!" Sloan called over the murmur of the television. "You'd better come out here, man!"

Hak pressed the button to brew his coffee. When he walked back into the living room, he found Sloan staring slack-jawed at the screen. The morning news was on, a correspondent standing in front of a McDonald's.

"—multiple sightings of what can only be described as a man wearing rags."

A blurry photo appeared on screen. It looked double-exposed; a dark figure stood in front of his own shadow, but the shadow seemed almost corporeal. The figure was wrapped in bandages and dressed in rags. It was impossible to make out any facial features or identifying characteristics, save for an expressionless red eye. *Wait,* Hak leaned close to the screen, *is that an eye?*

The reporter looked a little pale. "There have been sightings all over Cairo. Our other headline tonight: A rash of missing persons cases with one similarity between them. In their stead, a pile of sand. Law enforcement says…"

"That looks an awful lot like…" Sloan trailed off, his forgotten cigarette burning to the filter.

"A mummy," Hak finished for him. He grabbed his leather jacket and headed for the door.

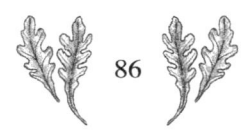

Hak

Hak sped through Cairo, veering around taxis and slow-moving box trucks. He disobeyed every traffic law, riding the center line and speeding through red lights. "Call Rafi!" he ordered his phone, wired into his helmet via Bluetooth. His helmet filled with the sounds of ringing, then Rafi's voicemail picked up. *Shit!* "Call Yasser and Salem."

"Yasser and Salem, how can I direct your call?"

"I need to speak to Rafi Sabbagh," Hak said. "It's an emergency."

"Mr. Sabbagh is in a meeting."

Hak clenched his teeth as he turned onto Eliza's street. He passed the lot where Shawarma Warrior King parked overnight, but it wasn't there. She wasn't here. Hak did a U-turn, the wheels squealing on the asphalt. "I need to speak to him immediately!" he shouted.

"I'm sorry, sir. That's just not possible."

Hak disconnected the call and headed toward the desert. He passed the gas station in record time, and while he desperately needed to stop for gas, he didn't dare.

As the land flattened and the only thing for miles was sand, the Kawasaki was shrouded in shadow. The mummy was keeping pace with him.

Their eyes met.

Chapter 20

The following morning, Eliza got to the dig site earlier than usual, the unhealthy rumbling of her truck on the bumpy road alerting him to her arrival. Jack excused himself from the laborers who were already working, moving up and down the ladder with various objects, each one carefully tagged and packed in plastic and foam and crates. He could see their excitement at Eliza's arrival, and he wanted to say good morning before the line formed.

As her truck pulled into its usual spot, he could see her through the windshield, and she flashed him a bright smile. He couldn't help the goofy grin he returned, feeling a terrifying lightness in his chest that he couldn't ignore. They'd had a wonderful evening at her apartment, and he'd wondered if she would be upset that he hadn't been able to spend the entire night, leaving in the wee hours of the morning to report in and shower before returning to the dig site. Exhaustion pulled at him, but he brushed it aside as his training demanded.

"Good morning," he called, walking over to slide up her window, pleased to see her grateful expression as she pulled out tubs of food to begin her day's work. "Did you sleep well?"

"Not enough," she admitted, wiping down the counter before popping the lid of a container. "But I think it was worth the sacrifice." She winked at him. "Maybe you should come over again, and we can actually sleep this time." She glanced over his shoulder, no doubt counting the laborers who had already started to linger in a sort-of line beneath the tent, waiting for her to open. "Maybe this weekend?"

Jack nodded. "Definitely." Smiling cheerfully, he walked away, letting her work. The morning passed in relative peace. Jack's interviews of the laborers had yielded nothing of interest—no one had seen the person in black, nor had Reese mentioned anything about a missing book. Jack wondered if perhaps the person had been Reese himself, but why would he run in front of a truck?

He still didn't know what actually happened last Friday, and he was beginning to think he never would. His employer hadn't asked him anything else about it, so Jack assumed he'd gotten the information he wanted from elsewhere. That was fine with Jack. Other than making sure no one died at the site, his job was simple. He had plenty of time to fantasize about his next encounter with the lovely Eliza.

Just before lunch, a black car arrived, and Jack sighed, squaring his shoulders and preparing to face yet another Cairo official. There had been fewer today, but a handful still lingered, watching the laborers and logging everything that came out of the site. It was mostly small items, Jack noted. Jewelry, he assumed, or perhaps those canopic jars everyone fussed over. There was a lot down there, but it wasn't anything new or earth-shattering. Even the black rectangular box he'd assumed held more of the same hadn't contained anything fabulous. No one had said anything about it, but Jack could see they had opened it, the lid now split into two pieces and pushed off to the side. Maybe they found more books, he mused.

I wonder if Reese ever found his armbands or gem? The ponce hadn't said anything to him about it, and Jack hadn't overheard the laborers gossiping—a very unusual trait at a dig site. They must be getting paid very well for their silence.

He stood at attention, wondering what, if anything, this new official would want from him. Swinton and Hayes weren't on site, so Jack assumed whoever this was would want to meet with Reese. He could lead the man down into the tomb where Eldin spent his days, or they could both wait above for Reese to climb out. Jack preferred that because he could keep an eye on Eliza.

The car parked and the driver got out to open the back door. A tall man climbed out, and Jack recognized Rafi Sabbagh, the lawyer and Eliza's neighbor. Jack still didn't know why her neighbor was involved in all this,

One Mummy to Go, Please!

but he knew it had something to do with Eliza ... and whatever had happened on Friday night.

Jack waited where he was and let Rafi make his way to him. The driver got back in the car and drove away. Apparently, Sabbagh wasn't leaving any time soon. He held out his hand to Jack. "Mr. Manning, a pleasure as always." The greeting was cheerful, but Rafi's smile didn't quite reach his eyes.

Jack nodded, accepting the handshake with a little more force than was necessary. After all, this man was only Eliza's neighbor, not her boyfriend or even an ex-lover—not that Jack knew anyway. He should be more gracious, but he couldn't help the part of him that saw Rafi as a threat.

"Quiet day?" Rafi asked, his back to the Shawarma Warrior King food truck. Jack wondered if it was intentional, or if he was too caught up in his work to remember her presence.

Jack would never forget her like that.

He nodded again. "Very quiet, sir. All proceeding as expected."

"Good," Rafi said. Then he paused, seemingly waiting for something.

"Can I help you with something?" Jack prompted. "If you're looking for the Panama twins, they aren't here."

Rafi chuckled, then immediately bit his lip to hide the reaction. "Actually, I came to speak to you." This time, he did glance over at Shawarma Warrior King. Eliza didn't have a line at the moment, and she was leaning against the counter inside. As Rafi turned, her head cocked in recognition, and she hopped out of the vehicle, walking swiftly across the sand toward them.

"Me?" Jack gestured at Eliza. "I think she wants a word with you."

Rafi nodded. "Of course. Can you find Reese Eldin? I'd like to have a word with him, too."

Jack nodded, turning to obey, hoping he could hide his smirk at the look on Eliza's approaching face. Rafi caught his arm. "And you, afterward," Rafi said. "There are things to be said."

"Very well," Jack agreed, then slowly trudged toward the ladder. He wasn't too far away to hear Eliza's opening question.

"Rafi, what the hell?"

Jack was underground when the screaming started. He had found Reese, the idiot insisting on finishing up whatever he was writing before coming up to see Rafi. Jack had been waiting nearly ten minutes for him to finish up, and it took everything in him not to tap his foot. He'd hoped retrieving the Brit would be quick, fast enough for him to catch the tail end of Eliza's conversation with Rafi, but no such luck. He should have known better.

He'd just have to ask her about it that weekend, preferably with his face between her thighs. He knew how to make his Eliza sing now. He was in the middle of a particularly vivid fantasy when he heard the first distant shout of alarm. Jack didn't wait, instincts reacting immediately, and he raced down the corridor, pushing a few laborers aside as he ran by. He scampered up the ladder at top speed, already pulling his guns as he reached solid ground. The wind was vicious, whipping sand into his face in a way that didn't make any sense. He'd seen sandstorms before, even been caught in one, but this was all wrong. The sand seemed to whirl in patterns that defied all reason or the laws of physics. He yanked his shirt up over his mouth, knowing he had to keep breathing, and scanned the site, looking for Eliza and Rafi.

His search was halted by what appeared to be an actual fucking mummy hovering a few feet above the ground. For a second, he faltered, his guns falling to his sides as he stared, mouth wide open in shock. Jack had seen some crazy shit in his day, including what may have been a reanimated corpse down in Haiti one very late night, but he never thought he'd be staring at a floating creature surrounded by whirling dervishes of sand.

The wraps fluttered in the harsh wind, but Jack could see the glowing red eyes, one shimmering. He followed the creature's gaze and found that he was staring directly at Rafi and Eliza. They huddled behind a car, Rafi shouting as he tried to put his body in front of hers.

Hell no, Jack thought as his senses returned. He lifted both guns and fired several shots. The mummy's body jerked as his bullets hit their mark, but the creature didn't even flinch. Instead, those red eyes turned slowly to assess Jack, and he was moving before thought; his instincts saved his life as a car smashed into the spot where he had been standing only a moment before. He rolled aside, holstering one gun in the process to use his hand, then skidded to a halt a few feet away. Looking up, he saw Eliza disappear into the food truck, Rafi running in the other direction, clearly hoping to draw the mummy's attention. Jack fired again, but he had little hope that his guns would do any real damage. He needed something stronger.

Why didn't I ask for a rocket launcher for this mission? Shogun certainly has one!

The mummy ignored him, following Rafi as he moved away from the truck. Suddenly, another security guard popped out from behind the trailer,

ONE MUMMY TO GO, Please!

brandishing a semi-automatic. The few rounds should have been louder, but Jack couldn't hear much above the roaring wind. As he watched, the man—Alan was his name—was picked up by the wind and tossed into the side of the food truck. Before his body could slide down to the ground in a boneless heap, Jack watched in horror as Alan began to shrink, his body desiccating until nothing remained but another pile of sand next to a fallen weapon.

"Oh fuck," Jack muttered, knowing he needed more firepower. Backup. He needed backup. His hand brushed the radio at his waist, but he knew it was useless. No one could hear him. Instead, he lay flat, hoping not to draw the mummy's attention for a second as he withdrew his phone and sent a quick text to Hak.

[Jack: We're fucked. Bring HUGE guns. Mummy.]

Flipping his phone shut, he looked up just in time to see Eliza's truck lifted into the air. He got to his feet, watching helplessly, knowing there was nothing he could do to save her.

Chapter 21

Eliza gripped the counter as Shawarma Warrior King rocked on its axles. The awning had come unmoored from its supports and flapped in the seemingly interminable wind. The truck was parked in the eye of a cyclone, and she could see little more than whirling sand and shadow. Someone shouted nearby, but she couldn't make out the words over the howling wind, nor could she tell whose voice it was.

"C'mon baby," she murmured. "Don't tip over. Don't tip over."

Gunfire echoed. Something hit the wall with a heavy *fwump*. The whole truck shuddered. What if that had been Jack? A tiny whimper escaped her before she could clamp down on the emotion. She shouldn't cry. She was safe. Well, as safe as could be.

Someone knocked on the truck's back door, and she rushed to open it. Reese grasped the doorframe, his face caked in a thick layer of dust. He pulled off his dirty wire-rimmed glasses, revealing wide, terrified eyes. "Duckling," he gasped. "Did you see it?"

She could only nod. She had seen the creature—the mummy—tear apart cars as though they were little more than tin cans. He had turned a man into sand with a casual flick of his wrist.

"This is … my… oh, I'm so sorry." Before he could clarify, a wall of sand erupted between them. Suddenly blind, Eliza reeled backward, clawing sand out of her mouth. Her saliva thickened it to mud, and it was hard to

breathe. She spit and gagged and, finally, vomited. She scrubbed at her burning eyes with her shirttail. When she could finally open them, the world was bleary, and Reese was gone. Eliza hoped he had done what he did best and crawled into some rat hole somewhere.

Slamming the door shut, Eliza sank down onto her butt in the narrow aisle, bracing against the cabinets and fridge door on either side. She tried not to think about what would happen if a hailstorm of food and cookware thundered down upon her.

The truck tilted, and for one terrifying moment, she feared it would tip over.

I'm going to die. The thought came to her unbidden as goosebumps trailed up her bare arms. *If I don't run, I'm going to die.* But she was too frightened to go back out into the sandstorm, especially without Jack's steady hand to guide her.

Crawling on her hands and knees, Eliza slowly inched her way toward the cab. She rose to pluck the key from under the visor and, with shaking fingers, slotted it into the ignition. With a practiced twist of her wrist, and a prayer to the gods of mechanical engineering (whomever they may be), she turned the truck on.

The engine sputtered but didn't turn over. "C'mon, baby!" she groaned as she sat in the driver's seat, the broken spring in the headrest jabbing her in the neck. "Not today. Please, not today," she begged. Eliza had purchased the truck for a steal at only E£140,000, and it reminded her of it every day. The engine overheated, she couldn't use both stovetop burners at once, and the air conditioner only offered two temperature settings: blow dryer and sauna. It desperately needed a mechanic, but she couldn't afford one.

Eliza turned the key again, and this time, the engine roared. Relief poured through her, and her body shook with grateful sobs. "That's my girl."

Eliza pulled her seatbelt on and sped toward the road, desperate to be anywhere but here. The cast iron skillet she'd left on the counter slid to the floor with a hollow clunk. The silverware drawer opened, the contents as deadly as shrapnel. A spoon bounced off the windshield, and a hairline crack crawled across the glass. "Really?" Eliza groaned. "That's going to cost so much to—"

The truck bucked like a bronco and veered sharply to the right. Bullets *plink-plink-plinked* across the passenger door. Eliza slammed her foot on the brake, but the truck continued to defy her. When she jerked the wheel to the left, the truck lurched skyward, and the buildings and people grew small.

"Fuck!" Eliza shouted, stepping on the accelerator and brake in turn. The engine roared and quieted, but she wasn't in control.

A shadow amid the whirling sand grew more corporeal as it moved closer. It was the mummy—the creature that had caused all this chaos. Except he looked different now. The bare skin peeking between the bandages was no longer necrotic. Their eyes met—hers fearful and his impassive. The stained gauze shrouding his face split apart as he grinned, revealing teeth that were much too sharp and numerous. As he flew closer, she white-knuckled the steering wheel.

"You," he hissed. His voice made the hair on the back of her neck prickle. "I'll ... keep you safe, little honeybee." Wordlessly, Eliza touched one of her bumblebee earrings, given to her by her parents when she turned sixteen.

He lifted his hand, and the food truck lifted with it. Eliza could only stare at him, her heart pummeling against her chest wall. The mummy twisted his wrist, and the truck drifted out of the sandstorm's grip. The blue sky with its cotton candy clouds looked particularly beautiful after the brown-beige of oblivion. The sun, blotted out by the cyclone, warmed her sand-burned skin. The mummy's ruby red eye glowed. "Who are you?" Eliza whispered.

A volley of gunfire popped all around them. A bullet struck the mummy in the shoulder, and his psychic grip on the truck faltered. Eliza's stomach jumped up into her throat as she—and the truck—plummeted toward the earth. The mummy reached out to her, but another bullet rocked his head back.

Eliza didn't have time to scream as the ground rushed up to meet her.

"Eliza? Eliza!"

Her ears were ringing. She cracked her eyes open. The sand had settled, and the wind had stilled. She found herself staring at a trailer that had been built upside down. *Typical corporate assholes*, she thought. *Can't even put a prefabbed building upright, but they think they can handle precious artifacts!* She giggled, more than a little punch-drunk.

The windshield had shattered, and the shards that remained in the frame glittered. They reminded her of the mummy's grotesque teeth. Why had he tried to save her?

One Mummy to Go, Please!

A pair of boots appeared in her line of sight, those upside down as well. No, they weren't upside down—she was upside down—lashed in place by her seatbelt. The air was hazy with smoke and sodium azide; the airbag had gone off.

"Eliza!" a familiar voice shouted. "Eliza, can you hear me?"

Jack.

"H-here!" she croaked. "I'm ... here." Her mouth tasted like copper and ash, and pain seared up her jaw. She gingerly touched her face, and her fingers slipped through a trail of blood.

Eliza fumbled for her seatbelt, but the button wouldn't release her. Jack knelt to peer through the windshield, or rather, what was left of it. "Are you okay?" he asked.

"I'm stuck," she managed, fighting against a swell of emotion. Her lip trembled.

"Don't worry," Jack said, carefully crawling into the cab; the glass crunched beneath him. "I've got you." He fished a pocket knife out of his pocket and went to work sawing at the seatbelt. He smelled like sweat, and his breath came shallow and fast.

"Is everyone okay?" Eliza asked. The blood had rushed to her head, and her extremities tingled uncomfortably. It was hard to think; her brain and mouth didn't quite work in tandem. Of course, everyone wasn't okay. Even if they all lived, surely some were hurt.

Jack's jaw tightened. "Let's focus on getting you out of here." His blade was small, and the polyester was tough, and it took several minutes to cut through the belt. Finally, it snapped, and Jack guided her to solid ground. "Go that way," Jack urged, gesturing toward the windshield.

Eliza crawled out into the sunlight, Jack following close behind. There was an eerie stillness, sand blanketing every conceivable surface. It reminded her of the quiet moment after a blizzard, the ground undisturbed by snow boots, skis, and tire treads. Eliza stumbled past a pile of sand with a rifle laying alongside. "That was one of my guys," Jack said. "Whatever that ... *thing* was ... killed him."

"Eliza!" Rafi rushed toward her, his arms outstretched. His shirt was ripped and his hair mussed.

As soon as he folded her in his arms, Eliza burst into tears. "The truck," she sobbed. "It's..." Her friend shushed her and rubbed her back in great, sweeping circles.

"The important thing is that you're okay. When the truck fell... I thought for sure that you were dead."

Eliza glanced back at the truck and immediately wished she hadn't. It had crumpled on impact, and its contents were spilled across the sand: pots and pans, the engine block, and even the kitchen sink. Not even the most skilled mechanic could salvage it.

"It was strange," Rafi continued. "Just before the mummy disappeared, and the sandstorm stopped, the truck slowed down."

Chapter 22

Hak ejected the empty magazine from his pistol and reloaded a fresh one. Even after the wind stilled, he remained behind cover—a cement barrier that had been used to guide traffic in and out of the dig site. He slowly rose just enough to survey the scene. A few shell-shocked laborers wandered aimlessly through the site. A man in a ripped suit jabbed at his phone screen, which didn't appear to be cooperating,

Hak looked at the halcyon sky, scanning the clouds for danger. But nothing was amiss—the mummy was gone. Hak was certain he'd managed to shoot the creature. Had he killed it?

A voice drew his attention back to earth. He'd recognize Rafi Sabbagh's voice anywhere. Hak warily came out from cover, tucking his gun in his waistband. Rafi stood facing away from him, his shoulders hunched. Jack Manning stood alongside him, his own weapon held loosely at his side.

"Raf!" Hak called. In the quiet of the decimated dig site, his voice sounded inordinately loud and seemed to echo. He strode toward his friend, relief slowing his pounding heart. He had looked for Rafi in the chaos but couldn't find him.

Rafi turned, his arms wrapped around Eliza Cunningham. She was red-faced, her slight body wracked with silent sobs. "Hak," Rafi breathed, "you're alright."

"I shot him," Hak said as he approached, giving his friend's shoulder an affectionate shake. He looked at Jack. "The mummy—I shot him with a huge gun. It didn't work."

Eliza swiped at her tears with her arm, smudging sand across her face. "I think it—he—was protecting me. There was gunfire after the truck turned. It would have gone straight through the windshield if—"

"You're overheated and tired," Jack interrupted. "Eliza, we all saw it. He was trying to kill you."

"He smiled at me," Eliza argued. "He pulled me out of the storm."

A phone rang. Jack reached into his breast pocket, pulling out a satellite phone. "Yeah?" After a moment, he ended the call. "I think it's best that we get Eliza home. There's nothing she can do here, and she's very clearly in shock."

"I can take her home," Hak offered. In truth, he was curious about the mummy's motives, and it seemed that she had some insight no one else had. He wanted to question her further, but Jack seemed very opposed to it. And no wonder. He'd just watched many men he knew die, if that was truly what happened when their bodies disintegrated into sand. Hak wasn't so sure about that either.

Eliza looked up at Hak with watery eyes. "Do you remember me?" he asked. After all, she'd been very drunk when they'd met. "We met the other day." *Does she remember the kiss?*

She nodded. "The party…" She could only recall bits and pieces of that night: dancing, hustling into the humid night air, a kiss with a stranger whose face she couldn't quite see…

"Are you comfortable coming with me?" Hak asked. "I'm friends with Rafi—we go way back."

She glanced at Rafi, who nodded in reassurance, letting her know that Hak could be trusted. Biting her lip, she looked back at him, then nodded again.

"I'll call you when we get there," Hak assured Rafi, who looked a little pained. "You have work to do, Sabbagh."

Rafi sighed and straightened his shoulders. If Hak knew Raf, his little secret society would be responsible for cleaning up this mess. Someone had to tell the laborers they hadn't seen what they thought they saw. Someone had to sweep up the remains of the men the mummy had reduced to sand.

Hak led Eliza to his motorcycle and handed her his helmet. She hesitated but put it on, flipping up the visor to squint up at him. "I've seen this bike before."

"Very perceptive." Hak grinned. "But perhaps we can discuss that later." He mounted the bike and offered her his arm so that she could climb on behind him. "Put your feet on those pegs," he instructed her. "And hold on to my waist."

She loosely wrapped her arms around his waist.

Hak turned the key, popped the clutch, and shifted gears with a practiced downward thrust of his left foot. Eliza's arms reflexively tightened. "Let's get you home," Hak shouted over the engine. "Hold on tight."

Eliza didn't ask how he knew where her apartment was. She didn't speak at all for the entire ride nor while they walked side-by-side up to the third floor. She unlocked the door and led him inside. "I need a shower," she mumbled. "Don't sit on the couch. You're all sandy."

Hak took that as an invitation to stay and sat on one of the wooden dining room chairs. He listened as she turned on the tap, and the pipes moaned. After twenty minutes, during which time he contacted Sloan to let him know what had happened ("It's already on the news—some worker called CBC. They're calling it a freak storm"), she returned with damp hair and skin that had been scrubbed red. She'd changed into pajama pants and the oversized t-shirt he'd seen in her window time and time before.

"You said the creature saved you," Hak prompted as she got two bottles of water from the fridge. She handed him one and sat in the chair opposite him.

"I know Jack doesn't believe me." She squared her shoulders as if expecting a fight.

"It just seems a little far-fetched is all." His grip tightened on the bottle, and the plastic crinkled in his hand. He had lost some good contractors today—good men with families. "We all saw the destruction it caused."

Eliza unscrewed the cap of her water bottle, gulping it down. She grimaced. "I don't think I'll ever get the taste of sand out of my mouth." She looked up at him through her eyelashes. "I recognize your bike, you know. I'm not stupid."

"I know you aren't stupid."

"Why were you following me?" she pressed.

"Because you're in danger. Wasn't that evident today?" He knew he was treading on dangerous ground. Rafi wouldn't want her to know it was

him that called. The Amun Henet worked because they were shrouded in shadow; they were so covert that they didn't exist even in conspiracy circles. "I'm a mercenary. It's my job to protect people in danger."

"It sure looked like a lot of people were in danger. I was in the least amount of danger out of anyone."

"It didn't look that way from where I was standing. Need I remind you that you were the only one who was dropped from hundreds of feet up?"

Her lips pressed together, the line of questioning forgotten. A tear trickled down her cheek. "My truck…"

Hak reached across the table and squeezed her hand. "Trucks can be fixed. Do you know how amazing it is that you survived with only a few bumps and bruises? That fall should have killed you."

"He slowed me down. Just before I hit the ground."

Hak gave her an incredulous look but didn't argue. She glared at him. "I'm so tired of men looking at me like that. I know what I felt." She rose and went to sit on the couch, tucking her legs beneath her. She turned on the television, clicking past the news so that she could watch a sitcom with an obnoxious laugh track. "You can use the shower if you want. Get all that sand off. There are fresh towels."

A shower sounded heavenly. He went to the bathroom, finding that she had left him a folded towel on the corner of the sink. There was also a pair of baggy flannel pajama pants. Hak turned on the shower—accompanied by the discordant clanging of the pipes—and stripped out of his soiled clothes.

He felt rejuvenated after the shower, and the pants fit well enough, though the waistband was a little tight, and the hem was a good inch and a half above his ankles. In the living room, he found Eliza asleep on the couch, her head pillowed on her arm. She still clutched the remote in her fist. Hak pulled a throw blanket off the back of the couch and draped it over her.

Eliza's phone chirped on the coffee table. Hak didn't intend to look at the screen, but he caught the message out of the corner of his eye.

[Poppy: Did you see that crazy shit on the news? A dig site got destroyed by a sandstorm—was it yours? I hope that sexy Jack Manning kept you safe. Call me.]

Hak scoffed and sat on the couch beside the sleeping woman. He thought about taking the remote but feared he would wake her. She looked so peaceful when she slept. Her frown lines had smoothed out, and her jaw

One Mummy to Go, Please!

had relaxed. He would kick himself if he inadvertently brought her back to the sad reality where her food truck was destroyed, and she was prey for an ancient evil, much as she denied it.

Chapter 23

Jack kicked the sand in the corridor of the tomb. He shouldn't be here, making sure nothing had been disturbed by the creature's attack.

He should be with Eliza, making sure she was safe.

Eliza isn't paying you, he reminded himself, pulling out his phone with a sigh. He reviewed the information he'd been sent, then flicked on the flashlight he held in his other hand. The night was dark overhead, but at least he was alone for the moment. Reese Eldin had, fortunately, inhaled quite a lot of sand during the storm, and he was currently receiving medical attention back in Cairo.

Jack was glad. He would find the items his employer wanted, make sure they were still intact, and get back to the office to make his report. Then he could go check on Eliza.

"Okay," he said, voice echoing in the empty space. "This isn't creepy at all."

At least the mummy who was down here is gone now, he reminded himself. *Not like he's going to come back and crawl back into his tomb.* His flashlight skimmed the walls, and he thought of the broken lid on what must have been a sarcophagus. *What awakened him?*

Clearly, Eliza had something to do with it. That's what she had seen on Friday night. He couldn't believe a mummy had been running around town for nearly a week, and this was the first they'd seen of it. Shaking his head,

he skimmed a finger across his phone screen to reread his list of artifacts. Charles was very specific about the items he wanted kept safe.

Face mask. He studied the attached picture, then moved deeper into the tomb where Reese had been when the mummy attacked. The mask was still sitting atop the stone slab where Reese had abandoned it, the clipboard with his detailed report leaning against the side, pages splayed against the sandy floor. Jack picked up the clipboard and laid it next to the mask, snapping a quick picture to send to his employer. He checked the list for the next item.

Limestone vase. Using the flashlight, he scanned the room, spotting the vase on a high shelf across the atrium. The shelf's items clearly hadn't been cataloged yet, so Jack snapped a picture of the entire line of items and sent it.

He worked for nearly an hour, following the same pattern. Locate item, make sure it hadn't been broken or lost, snap a photo, and send it. The final item, a small tiara, was in the same room as the tomb, sitting atop a short pillar clearly built to display it. After he sent the photo, Jack snapped his phone shut, then wandered over to examine the tomb. Now that he knew a person—a mummy—had been buried inside, he was curious to see more. It was big enough, he decided, staring down into the empty space. Sand had drifted in to coat the bottom, and he wondered if that was the result of the recent sandstorms above or if the mummy had been laid to rest on a bed of sand. Jack shifted, pulling his shirt away from his chest as he imagined how much it would itch after a while.

Not that the mummy would have minded, being dead.

Was he dead? He wondered. Or had he been alive down here, buried inside that sarcophagus for thousands of years? No wonder he'd come out throwing cars. Jack would be pissed too.

He was about to leave when a glimmer of light caught the beam of his flashlight. Moving closer, he skirted the edge of the tomb, aiming the beam between the edge and the wall. Something was back there, a glint of silver. Glancing around, Jack spied a scepter that looked thin enough to fit in the gap. Pushing it gently between the tomb and the wall, he slowly push-pulled the object toward him. The sand made the job tricky, and a few times he thought he had lost it beneath the tomb or under the wall, but eventually, his determination won out, and he lifted it.

It was a necklace, the silver shining in the glow of his flashlight. He recognized it, though when Eliza had worn it, there had been a red gem in the center of the setting. There was nothing there now but a dark smudge, as if the gem had been burned away. Jack thought of the burn on Eliza's chest, right where this necklace had been sitting.

Oh, Eliza, he thought. *What did you do?*

Jack sped almost the entire way to Eliza's apartment. It was late enough, and traffic was light, but he still felt like he was taking too long. His report at Shogun was brief, and he paused only long enough to shower and change his sandy clothing.

He knew that Eliza wasn't home alone—that Rafi or Hak or both would be there to watch over her—but he couldn't help himself. He kept seeing her truck lifting in the air as he stood by, helpless to save her. He knew that Eliza wasn't his, that theirs was a casual connection, and he tried to remember to check his possessive nature.

He'd promised her that he wouldn't be like those other people. Not guys, he recalled, slowing down to hunt for a parking spot along her street. People, she had said. He had a very sexy flash of Eliza with another woman and swallowed hard, lining the truck up with a spot on the next block over from her apartment. Truck situated until morning, Jack checked his appearance in the reflection of the driver's side window before heading to her door. He didn't bother with the code at the stairway door—the "security system" had stopped working long ago. Pushing the door open, he climbed the stairs quickly but quietly, so used to sneaking around that he never stomped anymore.

At the third floor, he turned left to Eliza's door, then paused to listen. He could hear the faint sounds of the TV inside. Straining, he listened harder, finally identifying the language as Korean. Hak must be watching something. Intrigued, he paused, translating the voices.

"Let us do as you said," a male voice said in Korean. "No touching."

"What do you think 'no touching' means?" a woman asked, annoyed exasperation in her voice.

A beat, then the male voice replied: "Living a happy and fun life."

Jack stifled a laugh, hand covering his mouth to catch the sound. Was Hak in there watching some kind of K-drama? It took a moment to reconcile the hardcore assassin with the romantic he must be. Maybe Eliza was watching the show, and he was humoring her?

He tapped gently on the door, then without waiting for a response, Jack turned the knob and let himself in. The scene within did not disappoint.

Hak sat on the couch, Eliza's head resting on his lap, and he was trying to move swiftly but without disturbing her sleeping body. His phone sat on

the edge of the coffee table before them, and as Hak tried to grab it, Jack snatched it, turning to stare at the TV with a quizzical eye.

It was a K-drama. Jack had seen enough advertisements to recognize the clothing, but he didn't know which one. The woman was in a lake, and the man was dragging her out. Jack thought that might be a recurring theme in those shows—people rescuing others from drowning. He tapped the phone in his hand, slowly pivoting to face Hak. A line of red was working its way up from beneath his collar to cover his neck.

Jack hadn't interacted with Hak a lot in person, but he knew a secret when he saw it.

"What's this?" he asked, then casually tossed the phone back to Hak, careful to aim for Hak's right side, away from where Eliza still slept. She grumbled something in her sleep as Hak caught the phone with a thunk then scowled as she opened one eye to glare balefully at Jack.

"What?" she snapped, clearly irritated.

"Nothing," Hak said, fingers quickly closing the show on his phone and ending the stream to the TV. The screen was quickly replaced with a slideshow of images—the first an ocean sunset with a pier. Jack thought it might be Santa Monica.

"Doesn't look like nothing," Jack said, not liking the way Eliza's head and hands were so familiar on Hak's lap. She was wearing pajamas, an oversized t-shirt that revealed a lot of thigh, and Hak wore a pair of obviously women's pajama pants—the blue and purple pattern ending at mid-calf on his long legs.

Did they...?

Jack's smile faded, and he latched on to the easiest target.

"Didn't peg you for a soap star fan?" he teased, knowing just how much his words would needle Hak. As employees of Shogun Security, they both withstood and dished out a fair amount of teasing with the other guards. "Wait 'til Sloan finds out..."

"You wouldn't," Hak snarled, generally pleasant face hardening as the repercussions dawned on him.

"This is too good not to," Jack told him, "and you know it."

"What are you talking about?" Eliza groaned, rolling over onto her back and lifting both hands up. Her left hand brushed against Hak's chest, and she left it there. Comfortable touching him.

Familiar.

"Hak's viewing preferences," Jack said.

She sighed. "*Mr. Queen*? Yeah, I told him it was good. I think he'll like it." Realizing the vibe in the room, she rolled onto one shoulder, then sat up, folding her legs beneath herself. "Wait." She glared at Jack. "Are you really giving him shit for watching K-dramas? What the hell did I wake up into?"

"So he was watching with you?" Jack asked.

Eliza shook her head. "I've been asleep for hours. You know, since I almost got killed by a freaking mummy today. I think a little K-drama is a fine way for Hak to unwind." She turned to Hak, clearly expecting him to appreciate her defense, but the guard was an even more alarming shade of red. She shook her head. "I don't get it."

"You wouldn't," Jack said, then immediately regretted it as Eliza's face turned angry, the same shade of red creeping up her neck. "I mean—"

"Oh I know what you mean," she snapped. She glanced at the clock on the wall, then frowned at him. "And why are you here anyway?"

"I came to check on you," Jack defended. "I wanted to make sure you were alright."

"And you do that by barging in here, waking me up, and shaming Hak?" She sighed. "Not too smooth, Manning." She reached for a glass of water on the table and took a sip, clearly calming herself. "Look, as you can see, I'm fine." She glanced at Hak, sliding her feet out to rest on his lap. "We're fine."

Hak, still red faced, lifted them off his lap, then got to his feet. "I should go."

"I was thinking—" Jack began, but he could see it was a lost cause.

"Oh, hell no," Eliza said then shook her head. "Nevermind. You know what? Both of you should go. I'm fine." She glanced at the door to her bedroom and the small bed within. "My bed is more comfortable anyway."

"You didn't even have the door locked!" Jack snapped.

"Because I was sleeping on a highly trained killer!" Eliza popped back. "I'm safe here." With a frustrated grunt, she got to her feet, gesturing both of them to the door. "Rafi is right downstairs. I'm sure you can stay with him, Hak!" She glanced at Jack. "As for you, I'm sure you have a bed somewhere."

"Sweetheart—" Jack tried.

"It's 4 a.m.," Eliza deadpanned. "I want my bed and sleep and quiet. Don't sweetheart me." She opened the door, ushering them both out. "I'll see you tomorrow."

She slammed the door shut, and Jack heard the lock click into place, and the chain slide home. He exchanged an awkward look with Hak.

"I'm not letting this go," Jack said, and Hak nodded, understanding exactly what Jack meant.

Chapter 24

<*Do you regret it?*>

Milfonnos loitered on the riverbank, staring out at the spot where he knew the temple of Isis once stood. He wasn't sure what compelled him to return; perhaps it was because it was the only place that looked a little like home, unmarred by car exhaust, garbage, and those infernal ... people.

The floodwater of the Nile had washed away any trace of their detritus. He imagined diving beneath the churning whitewater and swimming down, down, down until the water turned dark and still. He would glide between the crumbling pylons and admire the reliefs honoring long-dead Pharaohs and forgotten Gods. He would find the golden status of his goddess-mother Isis and kiss her cheeks. When his lungs seared, he would welcome it and—

<*Milfonnos, are you listening to me?*>

Milfonnos lurched back on shore, the reeds tickling his bandage-clad calves. "What did you say?" His voice sounded very small next to the Nile's interminable roar. He did not like to feel small.

<*I asked if you regretted it.*> Kasmut sounded miffed.

"Regretted what?" Milfonnos was a Pharaoh, and Pharaohs regretted nothing. After all, they were steered by gods. A god would never make a mistake. Kasmut's question made him feel testy. The bullets that punched through his shoulder and skimmed over his scalp didn't help his mood either. He absently scratched at the puckered bit of skin on his shoulder.

<Surely you feel some guilt. Why else would you have saved that girl?>

The girl. The priestess in the tomb when he first woke from his five thousand year nap.

When the ruby returned to him—for all pets return to their masters—it had been made warm by her skin. *Was it guilt that made me save her? No,* he decided. He did it because she had helped him be reborn. He was certain that she would lead him to the pieces that would make him whole. There was an invisible string stretching from his heart to hers, tied with magic that he didn't entirely understand.

Like all priestesses, she was a beautiful thing. Women in that esteemed position played the role of goddesses in ritual magic and read from the sacred texts in voices that dripped honey. Milfonnos had bedded many priestesses in his tenure as Pharaoh, and he couldn't help but wonder if she also wore the religious tattoos on her stomach. He'd very much like to run his tongue over the intricate designs, terminating just above her pubic bone. Or rather, he would if he had a tongue.

The reminder of his cursed body made him feel sour. And Kasmut's question made him feel worse. "Be quiet, Kas," Milfonnos snapped. Before they shared a body, Kasmut didn't talk so much. Milfonnos preferred him that way.

<I have never defied you, my Pharaoh. Not once. But I can't let you keep hurting innocent...>

"Bah!" Milfonnos scoffed. "They are not innocent. Our kingdom has been destroyed. Can't you see that? Where are the palaces? Even the tombs to great leaders are covered in garbage. People crawl inside them like they're playgrounds. It's disgusting. They found me—us—only because they were digging. Grave robbers, the lot of them!"

Milfonnos pulled up his sleeve and pinched a loose bit of gauze between his thumb and index finger. Peeling it away, he revealed a stretch of unblemished olive skin. "Besides, everyone is a means to an end. I am growing stronger. We ... are growing stronger!"

<At what cost?>

Milfonnos sorely wished he could cut Kasmut out of his head. "Never mind that," he snapped. "We must find the girl. She is a compass. Now be quiet, Kas. It is so hard to think with all of your yammering."

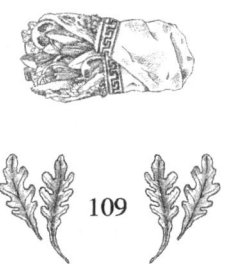

While Cairo was noisy at night, the air polluted with light and malodorous smells, the girl's street was quiet and dark. Milfonnos skimmed over the shadows, skirting around clotheslines. It was easy to find her. He merely tugged at the string between them, reaching hand-over-fist until he hovered outside her window. There was a small flower box on the windowsill, filled with cheery yellow daffodils.

<*This is a mistake,*> Kasmut cautioned.

"Quiet," Milfonnos hissed. He shoved Kasmut down into his subconscious, hoping he would take the hint and stay there.

Inside, Eliza Cunningham sat cross-legged on her couch, twisting her golden hair around her fingers as she watched a sitcom on television. A bottle of beer sweated on the coffee table. It was the first time he'd seen her unafraid, and he wanted to memorize the soft curve of her jaw and the way she smiled with her teeth. Her laugh was more like a guffaw, unabashed and loud.

Suddenly, there was a knock on the door. Eliza unfolded her legs and rose, stretching her arms above her head. Her back arched, revealing a sliver of pale skin once hidden by her shirttail. Milfonnos was disappointed to find that there were no tattoos there.

She padded, barefoot, into the foyer, adjusting her cotton shorts as she went.

Milfonnos inched the window up and slithered inside. He stood in her living room, inhaling the scent of vanilla and buttercream. The source of the smell was a candle burning on the kitchen counter, the flame licking the inside of its jar. Her home was modest, with not even a glimmer of gold. Milfonnos would never live in a palace without gold, sumptuous curtains, or servants ready to bend over backward at his whim.

As Eliza opened the door, Milfonnos shrouded himself in shadow. If she looked his way, her eyes would simply slide past him. But she wasn't looking at him at all—she only had eyes for the man in the doorway.

<*Milfonnos, is that..*> Kasmut shouted, making Milfonnos' ears ring. But the Pharaoh didn't admonish his bodyguard.

"Yes," he breathed. "It's..."

Rahil.

The leader of the Amun Henet wore his dark hair slicked back, coated in a strong-smelling oil. His face was unshaven, a few premature silver hairs threaded through his beard. He looked just like Milfonnos remembered, down to the snake tattoo on his forearm. Only his clothes were strange.

"Eliza," Rahil said, "I just wanted to check in."

Even his voice was the same—a deep, serious baritone. Milfonnos' breath became hot and thready. "Kas…"

Kasmut's anger crawled over the Pharaoh's skin, the sensation not unlike a thousand scorpions, their stingers poised to strike. Milfonnos knew that Kasmut would not stop him; this time, they would be perfectly in sync, and stronger for it. His fists clenched, his sharp fingernails digging into his palms.

"Do you want anything to drink, Rafi?" Eliza asked as she headed toward the fridge. "I just opened a beer. I have a few more."

Rahil (why had she called him Rafi?) hooked his thumbs in his pockets and strolled behind her. "Sure," he answered easily. "How are you doing?"

Eliza leaned into the fridge. "I wish you all would stop asking me that." She straightened, the cold making her cheeks pink, and handed him a bottle identical to her own. "I'm fine. I'm glad to have my apartment to myself. Though, your friend was very kind."

Rahil's lip quirked. "Hak is a good guy. We've known each other a long time, and he's gotten me out of a lot of trouble. I've gotten him out of some too."

"I can't imagine you getting into trouble." Eliza sat back on the couch, tucking her legs under her.

Rahil used his shirttail to twist off the bottle cap and took a sip. "We were kids—teenagers."

Rahil moved closer, and Milfonnos threw off his cloak made of shadow. He couldn't wait another moment. "Betrayer!" he howled.

Rahil flung his bottle at Milfonnos' chest, but the Pharaoh was not to be deterred. The bottle struck his sternum with a hollow thwonk, liquid gushing from its neck.

"Rahil Sabbagh, you treasonous rat!" He reached for Rahil's throat but met resistance. It was as though there was an invisible partition between them. Milfonnos slammed his fist against it, and the air shimmered.

<*A protection spell,*> Kasmut said, <*but we can claw through.*>

Before Milfonnos could try, Eliza leaped up and grabbed Rahil's hand. "Run!" she screamed.

Together, they skirted around the furniture, heading toward the door. Rahil made it into the hall first. Before Eliza could pass through the threshold, Milfonnos flicked his wrist; a gust of wind slammed the door shut. Eliza slammed into it, letting out a pitiful yelp.

Slowly, she turned, her back pressed against the door. The blood drained from her face. On the other side, Rahil pounded on the door, screaming her

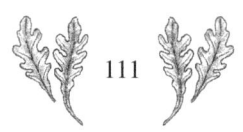

name. The doorknob turned, but no matter how hard he tried, Rahil could not disengage the latch.

"Priestess," Milfonnos hissed as he approached the frightened woman; her lip trembled. "I've been looking for you."

"L-l-leave me alone," Eliza blubbered. "Please." A tiny moan escaped her. "I won't tell anyone you were here, I promise."

Milfonnos leaned close. "You belong to me," he murmured. "You serve the gods, and I am your god."

Eliza's legs buckled, and she instinctively grasped his bony shoulders to keep from falling. She recoiled as if burned and hugged herself, tucking her hands into her armpits. "Please," she whimpered.

Milfonnos cupped the back of her neck. Her frightened eyes met his. His thumb found her carotid artery, jumping in time with her heartbeat.

Eliza's eyebrows furrowed at his gentle touch. "You saved me, didn't you?" With shaking hands, she touched his face. Her fingers slipped beneath the gauze, touching a cheek that was now smooth and whole.

"Come with me, Priestess," he murmured. "It is time to go." He threaded his fingers through hers. He took a step back and, transfixed, she followed.

He took another step, and another…

Suddenly, the door burst inward, the screws falling out of the hinges. Rahil held an ancient sword in his hand, one that Milfonnos recognized. After all, his belly had once been its scabbard. The sword slashed through the air, narrowly missing Milfonnos' outstretched arm. "Be gone, Milfonnos!"

Reluctantly, Milfonnos released Eliza and flew out of the open window. The warmth of her touch remained on his skin long after.

Chapter 25

"Worship me, Priestess."

Eliza shivered as the mummy's fingers trailed over her scalp. She was on her knees in the dark tomb, awash in the ruby-red glow of his gaze. Beyond them, there was only inky shadow; in truth, they could be anywhere, but Eliza knew where they were, just as she knew she was wearing her satin nightgown. Poppy had gifted it to her as a joke (*"Maybe Reese will like this the next time he gets those knickers off!"*), and Eliza had tossed it into her bottom drawer to languish amid the mothballs. The satin felt slippery and cool. She knew her suitor had picked it out for her.

Eliza looked up as the mummy hooked his finger beneath her chin. "I don't know how," she whispered, afraid that her voice would echo in such a cavernous space. She was embarrassed at the way her voice trembled, the final syllable plaintive and vulnerable. Eliza felt as though she had been flayed open, that those multifaceted red eyes could see straight through her.

The mummy grinned, the loose bandages splitting to reveal his sharp teeth and, to her surprise, full lips. "Let me show you," he crooned.

His thumb dragged over her lower lip, peeling it away from her teeth. "Show me your tongue, little honeybee," he prompted.

Obediently, Eliza opened her mouth, and her tongue lolled out. He grunted, clearly pleased. "Did you know that some Pharaohs had their tongues replaced with a gold-plated replica after death?"

Eliza shook her head. She felt silly with her tongue out, so she pulled it back into her mouth and pressed her lips together. What had gotten into her? She should be frightened, screaming, running. She was trembling, but not in fear.

"They thought it meant that they could talk to Osiris," the mummy continued, stroking her cheek with his knuckles. "That they could bargain with him in the afterlife. But gold is hard and cold. They made themselves mute."

He knelt so that they were eye-to-eye. "But I know better—a tongue must be able to sing, to beg, to undulate, to worship. I am dying to make your tongue do all of those things."

Eliza pressed her knees together, keenly aware of the heat pooling in her core. Hesitantly, she tugged at the gauze shrouding his face, desperate to see him—all of him. But his hand closed over her wrist.

"No," he growled. "I am not quite ... myself yet. Do I frighten you in this body?"

Eliza looked at his hand gripping hers. While his thumb and middle finger were still necrotic, the knob of bone visible at the knuckle, the other three were unremarkable with perfect fingernails. "A little," she admitted.

"When I was Pharaoh," he winced as if it pained him to say, "I was beautiful. Strong. I led armies and fucked princesses from neighboring kingdoms. At least, I was for a while. I only wish to be made whole again."

Eliza didn't know what to say. He rose while she sat back on her heels. From her vantage point, he reminded her of an ancient olive tree—tall, thin, and gnarled. She wanted to run her hands over his skin. Would it feel rough like bark?

"Enough talking, Priestess," he said. "We are in a holy place, and you are on your knees. Let us pray."

His growl seemed to rattle through her bones. He slipped his cloak off his shoulders, letting it pool around his feet. Eliza was surprised to find that beneath the tattered fabric was a body that looked startlingly ... alive.

His skin appeared almost golden, black tattoos swirling around his tapered hips. He wore a loincloth—a shendyt, she remembered—and she ran her fingers over the fabric. The mummy's breath hitched.

She glanced up at him as his fingers twined in her hair. His eyes were half-lidded, dousing much of the light in the chamber. The gauze circling his neck had come loose, and beneath it, she could just make out a knob of vertebrae peeking through his frayed flesh.

"You saved me," she whispered, "at the dig site—you saved me."

His eyes trained on her, turning her skin pink. "I did," he said slowly.

"Why?" She hated that the question made her sound like a child. But it gnawed at her. *Why me?* She was nobody—just the faceless girl who stuffed pitas. She wasn't important. At least, no more important than anyone else. Why was she spared and others weren't?

She'd seen the news coverage. The mummy had killed so many people, leaving only sand in his wake. There was nothing for their families to bury.

"Stop talking," the mummy commanded, though his voice was gentle. "Do you always talk so much?"

"Yes," she chuckled. "I used to get yelled at by my teachers, sent to detention—"

"Priestess, you must stop talking." His jaw clenched. "You are interrupting the ritual. How will the gods hear our passionate lovemaking if you are jabbering on?"

"Do we want the gods to hear?" She liked watching him squirm. His frustration made him twist his hand in her hair, the follicles tugging at her scalp.

"Oh yes," he said through gritted teeth. "They love to hear their followers scream. Now hurry, or I shall make you scream until you cannot breathe."

Eliza wasn't sure whether that was a threat or a promise, and she very badly wanted to ask if he meant in pain or in pleasure.

He was growing hard beneath the shendyt. Eliza carefully unlaced it, and the fabric dropped to the floor. She was secretly relieved to find that his cock resembled any other man's. It stood at full attention, pre-cum dribbling from the tip. The tattoos on his hips trailed down onto the shaft, terminating just above the lip of his foreskin.

Eliza wrapped her hand around him, finding his skin to be velvety and warm. This surprised her more than anything else. She had thought he would be cold to the touch, like the inside of the food truck's refrigerator.

At his prompting, she took him into her mouth. He shivered in delight as her lips brushed against his pubic bone. "Oh Priestess, you can't even possibly comprehend how long it has been."

Eliza lavished him with her tongue, and the mummy bucked his hips. His cock butted against her hard palate, and her eyes watered.

Abruptly, he dragged her to her feet. Eliza yelped, her knees protesting the sudden movement. The room spun. She found herself firmly pressed against his lean body.

Before she could take a breath, he kissed her. He gripped the back of her neck and walked her backward until the back of her knees connected with something hard and cold. She looked over her shoulder to see the

nondescript sarcophagus from which he had once emerged, its lid undamaged. She shivered.

The mummy pressed her down onto the sarcophagus' lid. The obsidian sapped the heat from her body, and her nipples hardened, straining against the satin. The mummy's hands—soft and rough all at once—slid up her thighs and beneath her nightgown.

"Tell me, Priestess," he murmured as his hands stilled, "do you hunger for me as I hunger for you?"

She arched her hips, silently begging him for more. He acquiesced, his thumbs skating across the hem of her panties. "Please," she gasped.

The mummy ripped at the gusset of her panties, the fabric tearing as easily as paper. She impulsively pressed her knees together. The mummy snickered, though she didn't get the impression he was laughing at her. "Are you ashamed?" he asked.

She shook her head. It wasn't shame—not really. It was the taboo of it. He had blood on his hands and cruelty in his heart. Besides, he wasn't quite human, was he? Not in the way she was.

"How could you be when sex is as important as food or drink? Let me taste you. I am certain that you are as succulent as roasted beef on a golden plate." His hands inched up her thighs, his thumb stroking her pubic mound.

Eliza's hips bucked. The mummy pressed two fingers inside her, his thumb finding the bundle of nerves just above her entrance. His glowing eyes were trained on her face, watching as she panted and squirmed. "I feel as though I must thank the gods that I've grown a tongue," he murmured. "Or maybe, the man I took it from."

While his words were horrifying, she could not immediately process them, not with his hand between her thighs. He expertly drove her close to orgasm. She teetered on the edge of it, but he wouldn't let her plummet over the cliff. Instead, he removed his hands.

"Please," she whimpered, pressing her legs together, desperate to cum.

He knelt between her legs and kissed the inside of her right thigh. Goosebumps prickled her skin, and a delicious shiver ran through her.

"Please!" she repeated.

"I want you to scream so loudly that Osiris, all the way in the underworld, can hear you." With that, his tongue trailed over her sex and circled her clit.

Eliza clawed at the smooth slab upon which she laid, desperate for something to hold on to. His tongue led her to the cliffside a second time, but before she could cum, he raised his head to look at her. "Once more, I think."

"Please," she gasped. "Please!"

He paid her no mind and positioned his body between her legs. When he pressed into her, he leaned close so that his lips brushed against her ear. "You will scream for me, won't you?" His breath was hot on her neck.

"Y-yes," she managed as he thrust harder.

He grasped her wrists and dragged them up over her head. The new position forced her back to arch, her satin-clad breasts pressing against his chest. "Promise," he crooned.

"I…"

"Promise," he insisted. "Or I shall make you start again."

Eliza could not take that particular brand of torture again. She felt as though every nerve ending was on fire as she teetered on the cliff's edge. "I … promise!"

"Good girl."

With that, his thrusts grew more forceful. She panted in time with his movements.

Finally, she came and unabashedly screamed. Her voice echoed in the chamber.

Beneath her, the sarcophagus' lid cracked.

Eliza woke with a gasp, gripping the sheets. As she sat up, the details of the dream dissipated so that only a flash of red remained. Her panties were damp, and goosebumps crawled up her arms. Whom had she been dreaming about?

In the living room, someone coughed. The guys had refused to leave her alone since the mummy had found her, taking turns lazing on her couch and eating the food in her fridge.

Keenly aware of the desperate throb between her thighs, she went to see who was babysitting her. Perhaps they could ease her discomfort.

Chapter 26

Hak loitered on the apartment's walkway, his elbows resting on the wrought iron railing. It was a beautiful night, and he could finally take a breath. The air felt less soupy, and the sweat that had soaked through his shirt had dried. Filtered through the haze of pollution, the stars were smudges. They reminded him of *Starry Night*, though he didn't imagine Van Gogh had painted it imagining Cairo.

He'd relieved Jack Manning only a few moments ago and started his shift with a quick walk around the apartment. Eliza had been asleep and didn't stir when the beam of his flashlight scoured the room for anything amiss. He checked all the window locks and even climbed up to the roof terrace to scan the sky for reanimated pharaohs harboring a grudge.

Jack had reported nothing of consequence.

"*We shared a large pepperoni from Pizza Hut and played a few rounds of dominos. She kicked my ass. No sign of that stiff.*" Hak had thought the mercenary had sounded relieved. He didn't blame him. None of them wanted to encounter the creature. After all, bullets had only slowed him down. Hak feared that they wouldn't be any match when it came down to it.

"*She's getting antsy,*" Jack warned as he gathered his keys and pistol off the kitchen counter. "*Asking a lot of questions I don't have answers for.*"

Hak

The scrape of a shoe on the stairs made Hak straighten and rest his hand on his gun. It was only an exhausted-looking Rafi. "Anything?" the lawyer asked, joining his friend at the rail.

"Nothing," Hak answered. "How is it going at the dig site?"

Rafi's shoulders slumped. "I am not sure the dig is going to resume anytime soon. The laborers have all been given their month's check early. Someone called the ENP, and they've been sniffing around, which has been a pain."

The police will certainly complicate things, Hak thought. It was bad enough that the site had to close, and artifacts had been destroyed. At least it had been easy to hide the body of his man—a dustbin and a broom was much simpler than a tarp and a shovel. "What did you tell them?"

"I told them the truth," Rafi replied. "There was a sudden dust storm. How has it been here?"

"Quiet. Jack did say that Eliza is asking a lot of questions. She isn't stupid, Raf. She is starting to make connections between you and me and me and Jack. She knows the mummy has her mother's necklace, and she's been staring at her old family photos, looking for anything tying her mother to Cairo." Hak chewed at his bottom lip, a bad habit from childhood.

"Do you think I should tell her?" Rafi asked. "About the Amun Henet, I mean."

Hak shrugged. "She's in danger, and it's best she knows who her friends are."

"Friends," Rafi repeated, mulling over the word. His jaw tightened. "I think she's sleeping with Jack Manning."

"He's handsome," Hak pointed out. "I wouldn't kick him out of bed as long as he kept his mouth shut."

Rafi just sighed and tapped his fingers on the railing. "I'm going to go to bed. I'll be up to relieve you in the morning. Maybe we can sit down and tell her … what we know."

Hak clapped his hand on his friend's shoulder, giving it an affectionate squeeze. "Get some sleep," he said. "We're all good here."

Hak watched *Friends* on mute so that he didn't wake Eliza. The closed captioning worked well enough, and he'd seen the episode a hundred times. There was one common denominator in every country he'd hunkered

down in, and that was *Friends*. Hak found comfort in knowing that wherever he was, if he clicked through enough channels, he could find Ross Geller standing in a cloud of baby powder, trying to wiggle into a pair of leather pants.

Yawning, Hak rested his sock-clad feet on the coffee table. His mother would have a conniption if she saw him. "Have some manners, *naekkeo*. I didn't raise you to act this way." But that didn't stop him from putting his feet up—it was the only comfortable position.

He missed sleeping in a comfortable bed. The Cairo safe house had a rock-hard mattress that he was certain was no less than thirty years old, and the room reeked of Sloan's obnoxious cologne. The frame of Eliza's futon was only covered by a thin piece of foam and a duvet.

He thought longingly of the hotel in Budapest with its plush mattress and clean sheets. Its atrium had overlooked the Danube, and he'd spent countless hours watching the flat-bottomed Zillen and luxury yachts while sipping espresso.

At some point, he must have drifted off because he woke to grayish twilight peeking through the blinds. The television had been turned off, the remote resting atop the coffee table. He could have sworn it had been on the couch's armrest before he'd closed his eyes.

Something clattered in the foyer, and Hak pulled his gun from its holster and disengaged the safety with a practiced thumb. He eased off the couch and tiptoed down the hall. The bathroom door was open, and a hand towel was wadded up on the sink, but Eliza's bedroom door was closed.

Someone was kneeling in the shadowy foyer, and for a moment, Hak feared it was the mummy. But it was only Eliza, struggling to put on her sneakers. She was dressed for the gym in bicycle shorts and a loose-fitting racerback tee which didn't leave much to the imagination. He could plainly see her black sports bra beneath the white shirt.

Eliza shrieked as his shadow fell over her. "Jesus, Hak! You scared me!"

Hak reengaged the safety. "What are you doing?" he asked, none too kindly. He was mostly angry at himself. He shouldn't have fallen asleep. It was a rookie move.

"I'm going for a run," she said, tying her shoe.

"Alone?" Hak slid his gun back into its shoulder holster, the metal cool against his ribs. "Are you serious?"

"Well, you were sleeping, and you don't really seem like the running type," Eliza said as she straightened up.

"Do you not remember the reanimated corpse trying to murder you?" Hak tried not to stare at Eliza's breasts, pushed up by the sports bra.

"He doesn't seem like the running type either," Eliza answered dryly. "I'm going whether you come or not. If I sit around here for one more minute, I'm going to scream."

"Fine," Hak grumbled. "Though, I don't have running shoes." He gestured at his steel-toed boots.

"Oh no," Eliza said, deadpan. "Perhaps you'll have to stay here."

"Fat chance," Hak snapped, slipping his feet into his boots, the supple leather molding to his feet. He'd broken them in, and it was like they were a second skin. Surely, he would be able to jog a few blocks in them.

"I think my feet are going to fall off," Hak panted as they entered the apartment. The sun had come up during their run, and sweat dripped down his back.

"I told you that you could stay here," Eliza reminded him. Hak couldn't help but notice how gorgeous she looked with a sheen of sweat on her chest. While his hair was damp and clung to his forehead, she wore hers in a high topknot; only a few flyaways at her hairline had escaped during their three-mile run.

Three. Miles. Hak's feet had started hurting in the first quarter-mile, and he thought for sure they were bleeding by mile two. He tried very hard to distract himself, asking Eliza inane questions about her time in Egypt, but she only offered a one- or two-word response. She had seemed irritated by him, and he didn't blame her. He slowed her down.

He followed Eliza into the kitchen, the air conditioning cooling his skin. "How often do you do that?" he asked, pulling off his soaked shirt. "Go for a run, I mean."

Eliza opened the fridge and pulled out the filtered water pitcher. She poured water into one of the recycled mason jars she liked to use as a cup and handed it to him. Hak chugged it gratefully, but not before he noticed that her eyes were on his bare chest. Perhaps it was the dragon tattoo that drew her eye there. It was a massive piece, stretching from his collarbone to his pubic bone.

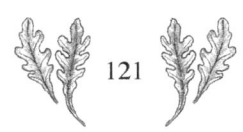

"It was after my parents died," she answered as she poured herself a glass. "I was too afraid to ride, and I needed to get out of my dorm—and out of my head."

"Ride?" Hak prompted, taking the pitcher from her hand so that he could pour himself another glass. He couldn't remember ever being so thirsty; his tongue felt like sandpaper.

"Horses," Eliza answered, leaning back against the counter. "I was an Olympic hopeful in show jumping, but after they died I just ... couldn't. They were so supportive and attended every show. It felt ... wrong to keep doing it without them. Plus, I was so anxious that I couldn't get back on my horse, Magnus. I sold him." She swallowed.

"I'm sorry," Hak murmured, his fingers brushing against the back of her hand. Her skin jumped at his touch.

Eliza placed her glass on the counter. "It was for the best," she said, her voice even. "I had already torn a ligament in my knee. I wasn't ever going to qualify for the Olympic team. I just kept training because I didn't want to fail them. They'd put so much time and money into it. It was their dream."

"And yet, you still outran me."

"Yeah well, I had on the proper shoes." She met his eyes, her teeth dimpling her bottom lip. "You can have a shower first."

"I need one," Hak chuckled. "I'll be quick."

"Take your time. I need to stretch." Hak lingered for a moment, sipping his water. Eliza paid him no attention, sitting on the floor in the living room to touch her toes.

Aching, Hak waddled into the bathroom and shut the door. Sitting on the toilet lid, he eased off his boots and winced as he peeled off his socks.

His feet were somehow sweatier than the rest of him, and a blister had developed on his right heel. He undressed and turned on the shower, stepping into the glass cubicle. The cool water was a shock to the system and he gasped. Still, he didn't turn the knob to a warmer temperature.

Suddenly, the frosted shower door opened, and Eliza stepped inside. She was naked, and her hair had been taken out of its bun.

Wordlessly, her hand found his and their fingers intertwined. Hak was keenly aware of his stirring cock. She stepped under the spray, and her pink nipples tightened. "God, it's cold!" she exclaimed.

She reached around him for the knob; warm water pounded against his back. Hak couldn't help but to imagine kissing the smooth plane between her breasts then pulling her nipple between his teeth. But—

—she was Rafi's girl. Rather, the girl Rafi pined for. Acting on his impulse would be a betrayal. "We can't," Hak whispered, giving her fingers a gentle squeeze. "I … can't."

Eliza stood on tiptoes to kiss him, her breasts pressed against his chest. Her tongue unabashedly pressed into his mouth. "Why not?"

Hak's hands hovered above her hips. He desperately wanted to touch her. "Rafi…"

"What about him?" Eliza's brow furrowed.

Hak pressed his lips together. It wasn't his place to tell her about Rafi's unrequited feelings. It was Rafi's fault for not telling her. He had every opportunity. "Nothing," Hak said. "Come here."

He groaned as her fingers wrapped around his hardening cock. He cupped her ass with both hands and lifted her off her feet. She gasped as her back pressed against the cool tile. Hak kissed her lips, her jaw, her neck as her fingers tangled in his hair.

Hak pumped his cock with one hand, desperate to be inside of her. Eliza mewled in need, a soft "please" reaching his ear over the cacophony of rushing water.

Hak pressed into her, and her fingernails bit into his arms. Eliza buried her face in his neck, her wet hair falling over his shoulder. Her legs tightened around him.

It was fast and hard, both of them needing a release after the strain of the last week. When Hak finally came inside of her, she sighed in satisfaction, her head dipping to his shoulder as she caught her breath. He paused there, savoring the moment before he slowly set her back on her feet. She reached for the body wash, intending to actually shower now that he'd satisfied her need, but he snatched the bottle out of her hand. "I've got it," he said, squeezing it into his palm. She started to protest, but he shushed her. "Close your eyes, Eliza."

She did what she was told, the corner of her lip downturned and her brow furrowed.

"Relax," he urged. He ran his soapy hands over her shoulders and down her breasts, tweaking the nipples between his thumb and forefinger. She gasped as his hand ventured lower.

When he made her cum again, the water ran cold.

Chapter 27

"Alright," Eliza demanded, staring at the three men in her apartment, "it's time to tell me what the hell is going on." She took a sip of her coffee, then gave each of them a long look. Jack sat on the couch with Hak, both men looking uneasily at one another before both looked at Rafi, who sat at her small dining table.

She stared at Hak for a second longer, recalling the feel of his hands on her body only an hour earlier, but that was a distraction, and she knew better than to hope for any loyalty there. The bodyguard was a good time, but he wasn't into her the way Jack Manning was.

Jack Manning, who wouldn't meet her eyes this morning.

"Oh, come on!" she whined. She moved her gaze to Rafi again, settling on him as the man in charge of … whatever the others didn't want her to know. "There's a freaking mummy after me. I'd like to know how you all magically managed to show up to protect me just in time."

Rafi nodded, took a final sip of his own coffee, then set the mug down on her table with a decisive thunk. "Eliza," her friend began, "how much do you know about secret societies?"

Eliza frowned. "What, like the Illuminati? Knights Templar or Skull and Bones stuff?"

Rafi nodded. "This land is ancient, and as such, it holds many secrets, dangerous knowledge that needs to be protected. Someone has to keep the world safe."

"Safe from mummies?" Eliza asked, not sure where he was going with this. "Is that in the secret society purview? That seems more like…" She trailed off, putting the details together. She stared at Rafi. "You're in a freaking secret society?" Her voice was quiet.

Her friend nodded, waiting for her to continue, knowing she would have questions.

She recalled their conversation at the cafe, his assurance that she couldn't have seen a mummy, that her mind was playing tricks on her. "You asshole," she breathed. "You lied to me. To my face."

Rafi nodded. "As we lie to anyone who gets close to the truth," he admitted. "As I would have continued to lie to you if you hadn't seen the creature with your own eyes."

Eliza shook her head, unbelieving, and turned to face Hak and Jack, silent on the couch. "And you two?" she asked. "You're part of this Knights Templar too?"

"It's not the Knights Templar," Rafi corrected gently. "They are east of Egypt."

"So what Knights are you then? Cairo Knights?" Eliza pressed.

"We are called the Amun Henet," Rafi said, and something slithered up Eliza's arms, the hair on her arms raising at the name. Something within whispered about the Amun Henet.

Betrayers!

She frowned, shaking the feeling away and focusing again on the men on the couch. "Amun Henet, then," she said. "You're part of that too?"

"Actually, no," Hak said, speaking casually. "We're with Shogun Security. We were hired to secure the dig site by the Amun Henet."

"Ah," Eliza said, trying to put it all together. She looked at Jack. "So you work for Rafi?"

Jack shook his head. "I'm actually private security on this one. The contract is through Shogun, but I have a different employer." He glanced at Rafi. "Not him. Not this time."

"But you all know one another," she said, "and no one thought to tell me?"

"It's not like we're best friends," Hak explained. He glanced at Jack. "We've worked together in the same circles over the years but never in person. We didn't even recognize one another at first." He paused, then added with a wink, "Technically, I'm his boss."

"But you were both here to protect me?" Eliza asked, confused now. She looked back at Jack. "You said you're working for someone else, doing security for the site." She paused. "So why are you here now?"

"I want you to be safe, sweetheart," Jack said, offering the first genuine smile she'd seen in a while. "Dig's shut down now, so I find myself with copious amounts of free time I can spend however I wish... with whomever I wish." He winked, and she had a brief flash of the last time they'd spent time together, him buried inside of her with her back against the bedroom wall, both struggling to be quiet with Rafi and Hak in the next room. Jack may not be thrilled about sharing her with anyone else, but he was definitely still down for a good time if the moment presented itself.

"Okay," she said slowly, turning to Hak. "But you... why are you here? Were you also working the dig?"

"No," Hak said with a quick glance at Rafi. The lawyer nodded, and Hak continued, "I'm here because he called me."

"Why?" she asked, turning to face Rafi again. "You're recruiting for your Amun Henet?"

Rafi shook his head. "Hak isn't part of the Amun Henet," he told her. "You have to be born into it, here, in Egypt."

"Oh," Eliza said, thinking of the men in dark suits who had flooded the dig site after the mummy awakened. "So it's like a government thing?" She had noticed that while political dynasties weren't uncommon back home in England—they still had a royal family, after all—the officials here in Cairo shared a handful of family names. Nepotism was alive and well in this city.

"Partly," Rafi admitted, "but it's mostly focused on guarding the people against ancient evils, like this mummy. We monitor dig sites to make sure nothing like this happens." He shook his head, failure weighing heavily on him. "We only missed this one because no sarcophagus was reported."

"It didn't look like a regular sarcophagus," Eliza said. She took another sip of her cooling coffee, remembering the smooth black stone slab—she had a flash of memory, a quick glimpse, of a man who could have been the mummy atop her, her body writhing in ecstasy. Heat flooded her stomach followed by a wash of fear.

A dream, she thought. *I remember fucking him on the slab...*

"Eliza?" Rafi said, and his voice brought her back from the memory of the dream, though she could still feel the desire in her body, the way the mummy had known exactly what she wanted.

"Huh?" she asked, distracted, then she finished her coffee and moved to the sink, putting her back to the room as she rinsed the mug.

"The sarcophagus?" Rafi prompted. "You interacted with it that night, didn't you?"

Eliza's shoulders slumped. She had told him most of what happened, but not everything. Not the way she could hear the voices chanting in the other room, or the way her necklace had burned her before exploding in a shower of white, or how she had kicked a jar into the magic and caused a bright flash of light before fleeing.

"Tell us," Rafi pleaded, his voice gentle behind her, "and this time, leave nothing out."

As she recounted the details of that night, Eliza found her mind filling in other gaps, particularly the dream she had had about being the mummy's priestess. She didn't share that part, not liking the look on the guys' faces as she recounted the magic she had seen.

"I didn't mean to do anything," she said defensively, settling on the couch between Hak and Jack. "I didn't know anything was down there."

"Your necklace," Rafi said. "It must be part of the gemstone."

"What gemstone?"

Rafi sighed, settling in for a long story. "Our mummy was once the Pharaoh Milfonnos. He was power-hungry and, by all accounts, dying of a disease, probably cancer, when he discovered the spell for immortality. He used a special ruby along with the incantation from an ancient book to upend the laws of nature. Though he was successful, the Amun Henet—including my ancestor Rahil—were able to subdue him. They cracked the gemstone and killed him, burying him in an unmarked tomb." He paused, adding, "He was known as Milfonnos the Blighted, and they didn't want anyone else to find his body and resurrect him."

"So much for that," Eliza snarked, and Jack put a hand on her leg, comforting her. "You said they cracked the gem?" She was thinking of the one red gleaming eye that haunted her. "What happened to it?"

Rafi held out his hand, the large ring on his finger catching the daylight. "Rahil kept part of it for his family. My family."

Eliza thought of the red glow exploding from her chest. "My mother..."

Rafi nodded. "Do you know where that necklace came from?"

Eliza frowned. "It was in my mother's family for generations," she said. "I don't know where it came from." She bit her lip, seeing her mom's face,

the pale skin and blonde hair her daughter had inherited. "But my mom's family isn't Egyptian. We're northern European, if you go back far enough, but we settled in England for over a hundred years. You think part of this gemstone made it that far?"

Rafi shrugged. "The Amun Henet wouldn't have wanted the gem pieces to be near one another, lest something happen. They would have sent it far away."

"Until I brought it back into the tomb where the mummy was also buried..." Eliza reasoned. "So that's what happened." She frowned. "I did bring him back. This is all my fault. All those people..."

"No," Hak said, "that's not on you. You didn't know, and besides, it seems like someone else was in the process of resurrecting the creature. You just brought something you didn't know they needed."

"I guess," Eliza agreed, but her heart was heavy. She recalled the pile of sand next to the weapon when she climbed free of her ruined truck. The mummy may have saved her life, but he was definitely taking others. "Why do you think he does it? Turns them into sand like that?"

"He's regenerating," Rafi explained. "Using their essence to fix his body. Soon he will be fully human again."

"Human—as in, vulnerable?" Hak asked, and Eliza could read his expression, the mercenary no doubt thinking of how the mummy hadn't been harmed by the many bullets in him.

"Perhaps," Rafi said, "but unlikely. The prophecies suggest that he will only grow more powerful the longer he remains here."

"But what happens now? Why is he ... following me?" Eliza asked, unable to hide the fear in her voice. She didn't know what she feared more: what the mummy would do to her when he came or what she would do if she had to face Milfonnos again.

"I don't know," Rafi admitted. "But I swear to you, Eliza, I will find out."

Chapter 28

"Hey, Eliza!" Jack called, cracking the bathroom door; steam poured into the hall. "Can you get me a towel?"

"It's in the cabinet!" Eliza had to shout to compete with the television. Rafi and Hak were playing *Street Fighter* on a PlayStation that had seemingly appeared out of nowhere. Jack had been evasive when she asked where he'd gotten it from.

"What?" Jack yelled. He leaned into the hall, his sopping wet hair dripping onto the linoleum.

With a sigh, Eliza rose. Hak and Rafi, both hunched over game controllers, paid her no attention. "I said," she snapped, pushing Jack aside so that she could reach the cabinet above the toilet, "the towels are in here!"

Eliza didn't intend to shout, but she was tired of sharing her apartment. She liked having her own space without the detritus of three men who couldn't seem to clean up after themselves. She liked using the bathroom without someone barging in. She liked opening a pint of ice cream without someone reaching for a spoon.

"I couldn't hear you." Jack took the proffered towel and slung it around his neck. He made no effort to cover up his nakedness nor to dry himself.

"You're dripping," Eliza said weakly. Her eyes drifted downward.

From the living room, Rafi whooped. "Take that, you… you… shithead!"

Hak snickered. "Shithead? Really? C'mon, pick up your controller. Let's go again."

"I don't think they'll notice," Jack whispered.

"Notice what?" Eliza watched a water droplet skate down his stomach, linger in the dip of his belly button, and then dive toward his cock.

Jack hooked a finger in the elastic waistband of her pajama pants, pulling her close. "I don't think they'll notice if we are gone for a few minutes."

Eliza squeaked. "You're getting me wet!"

"I'd like to," Jack growled. He pushed the door shut to punctuate his point, trapping them both inside the steamy room.

Eliza pressed her palms against his damp chest as his big hand slipped into her underwear. "We can't," she gasped.

Jack's hand stilled. "That's what you said last time. Are you sure?" He pressed his lips upon the top of her head, and she was very certain that she could feel the curve of his mouth. He was teasing her. "Because," he purred, "I can stop."

Eliza mewled. "Don't stop," she managed, pressing into his palm. Jack pressed two fingers inside of her, his calloused thumb finding her clit. Eliza rocked her hips with wild abandon, desperate to cum.

Suddenly, the door opened, and Hak took a step into the muggy room. He froze. "Oh." His eyes drifted lower. *"Oh."*

Eliza wrenched up her pants and stepped away from Jack, her face burning. She felt like she'd been caught with her hand in the cookie jar. Well, she amended, two cookie jars... and both had just found out about the other.

Jack covered himself up with his free hand. "Get out!"

Still, Hak lingered, eyes narrowing in speculation. "You can't leave the girl wanting, Manning. That is not the Shogun way."

Jack blanched. Eliza wondered whether it was the mention of his job—or Hak's position as his superior.

"I could come join you?" Hak raised a brow, his dark eyes meeting hers. "It wouldn't be the first time I've teamed up, so to speak." He leaned against the doorframe.

"What is going on over here?" Rafi appeared in the hall, his controller still in hand. Eliza could feel his eyes boring into the side of her head, but she had trouble meeting his gaze. Would he be disappointed in her? It was Rafi she cared about most of all—sweet Rafi, who was always just downstairs. When she finally gathered the courage to look, his lips were pressed together in a firm line, and he gripped the controller so hard his knuckles blanched. "I ... should go."

"No!" Eliza ducked under Hak's arm and rushed to him. "Rafi, please don't go. I want you to stay." She gripped his forearm.

"You seem awfully busy," he said softly.

"Rafi, you can't blame me for trying to find some release."

Rafi looked as though she'd slapped him. She hadn't intended to sound so flippant. Eliza let out a frustrated groan. "I'm scared, okay? There's an undead thing who wants to take me to god-knows-where. My best friend is a shadow agent for the Illuminati and—"

Rafi chuckled, despite himself. "The Amun Henet are much more civilized than the Illuminati, I promise you that."

"—this is all too much. I am looking for levity wherever I can find it. Jack and Hak have both been kind enough to give me some."

His face cycled through a wild series of emotions before he settled on a charming smile. Reaching out, he lifted her chin, meeting her eyes. "I understand. Believe me, I know. "

"Will you stay?" she asked, surprised at her boldness as her heart began to pound at the idea.

"If you wish it."

She swallowed, then took a step toward him. "Will you join us?"

Rafi raised an eyebrow, then shook his head slightly. "Not this time. Right now, I want to see what you like."

Hak clapped his hand on his friend's shoulder. "Are we okay, Raf?" His eyebrows knit together. "I should have talked to you first, before I... we..." Eliza was struck by how nervous the mercenary looked. When he'd faced Milfonnos, his face had been as impassive as a monk's.

"Yeah," Rafi assured him. "We're good, I promise."

Hak's features settled, and a smile loosened his jaw. "Good, because if I could never touch this woman again, I would be a miserable man."

With that, Hak slung Eliza over his shoulder. She squeaked in surprise. "Come on, Manning, let's show her what teamwork looks like."

It was dark in her bedroom, the curtains drawn. From the bed, she could only just make out Rafi sitting in her overstuffed armchair, his ankle resting on his knee. He slouched, looking for all the world like a bored prince. Eliza desperately wanted to crawl to him, to rest her head in his lap, but Hak drew her attention.

Standing bedside, he pulled off his shirt, tossing it onto the floor. His jeans were low-slung, revealing a tantalizing expanse of flesh beneath his belly button. The dragon tattoo on his abdomen seemed to slither in the half-darkness, but it must have been a trick of the eye. "Come here," he whispered.

Eliza moved on hands and knees across the mattress to him, keenly aware of three pairs of eyes crawling over every inch of her. Hak unbuttoned his jeans—an invitation. She pulled down the zipper, delighted to find him already growing hard.

Before she could wrap her hand around him, someone grabbed her hips. She recognized the hands, as big as oven mitts and rough like a farmhand's. What had Jack done to earn those calluses? He was evasive about his job. She only knew that his gun fit his hand like a glove, that he fired it with a bored detachment. He may as well have been brushing his teeth.

When he touched her, he was anything but detached. While her nose was inches from Hak's zipper, she pictured Jack's face during their last brief encounter. His eyes were dark and serious, and he held her gaze unabashedly. He may as well have said, "Look at me. Let me watch you moan." It had felt so much more intimate than a quick fuck in a quiet corner should have been.

Now, Jack Manning pulled down her pajama bottoms, cupping her asscheek. He made no move to remove her underwear, though his thumb drifted beneath the hem to stroke the spot where her thigh met her sex. Eliza arched her back in a silent plea.

"Focus, Eliza," Hak said gently. Eliza reached for him, her fingers drifting over his vascular length. When she took him in her mouth, he gathered up her hair in his fist, though he let her pick her own pace. She licked him lasciviously, the taste of pre-cum settling on her tongue.

As she sucked him, Eliza was also keenly aware of Jack's fingers creeping beneath her panties. He was slow and deliberate, his fingers dipping inside of her to stroke the sensitive walls therein. "You're so wet," he whispered. "You're loving this, aren't you?"

This was unlike any experience she'd ever had. Still, she wanted more. Eliza looked for Rafi in the dark, begging him with her eyes. *Please. Please.* But he only watched. His elbows rested on his knees now, but his face remained impassive. He may as well be watching a chess match.

As Jack freed his cock from his pants and, pushing her panties aside, eased into her, Hak thrust into her mouth with increasing frequency. They worked in tandem, though not a word passed between them. Each time Hak withdrew from her mouth, the head of his cock resting upon her lips, Jack thrust inside her. When Jack reared back, Hak's slippery cock butted up against her soft palate. Eliza's body thrummed with pleasure.

Abruptly, Jack pulled out and a splatter of warm cum graced her panties.

Hak joined Eliza on the bed, removed her panties, and pulled her onto his lap. When he slid into her, his cock slick with her saliva, she found herself looking over his shoulder at Rafi. Their eyes met, and he smiled.

Chapter 29

"If I have to stay in this apartment for one more second, I'm going to scream!" Eliza threw down the tea towel she'd been using to dry the dishes from dinner (Mediterranean takeout from a cafe with a mural of Santorini behind the counter, not that she'd gotten to see it) and let out an exaggerated groan.

It had been a week since the assault at the dig site, and she hadn't even been allowed to go to the laundromat on the bottom floor of her building. Jack had done the laundry instead and had consequently ruined a silk dress with a "dry clean only" tag.

"That's not possible," Hak reminded her, dipping a tea bag into the floral teacup with the chip in the handle. She had bought it in a tiny stall selling ceramic wares during her first week in Cairo, and it had chipped the very next day when she set it in the sink with just a little too much force. Still, she didn't have the heart to throw it away; it was hand-painted with tiny water lilies around the rim and a large blossom, with its petals unfurled, in the bottom. Hak had said the lilies reminded him of Seoul—of home. "It's funny," he'd said, pensive after one too many glasses of Riesling, "that the lotus is native to many countries, and we all see it as a symbol of creation. Maybe we aren't so different after all."

Eliza rolled her eyes. She hated when the guys treated her like a child. "What if we went somewhere public? Surely Milfonnos wouldn't show up

somewhere public." She whispered his name as though afraid she'd inadvertently summon him. Though, maybe inviting him into her dreams wouldn't be such a bad thing

"He showed up at the dig site. There have been sightings all over Cairo. He's not hiding." Hak sipped his tea and grimaced. "Can you hand me the creamer?"

Eliza retrieved the small carton from the fridge and handed it to him. "I'm not asking to go out alone. We would all go—together."

"Together?" Hak glanced into the living room, where Jack was lazing on the couch and Rafi was staring out the window. Eliza wondered whether Hak was thinking about the threesome the day before. None of them had talked about it. She and Rafi certainly hadn't.

"Just for an hour," Eliza assured him. "Please? We can have one drink and come right back."

Hak wrapped his hands around the teacup. His teeth dimpled his lip.

"Please?" Eliza wheedled. "One drink?"

"Fine," Hak relented. He had to raise his voice to compete with her excited whoop. "The first sign of trouble, we're leaving." He paused. "And you're convincing the others."

They went to an upscale bar tucked in the basement of the Ritz-Carlton across town. It was called Nox, and naturally, the ambiance was dark and moody. The music was so low that Eliza doubted she heard it at all. A melody would tickle her ears, but before she could place it, it was gone again. Even the barflies talked in hushed tones.

Eliza was underdressed. The patrons of the bar were tourists: impeccably dressed but sunburnt. Conversely, she was wearing leggings and an oversized button-up that might have belonged to an ex-boyfriend. True, the heels spruced up her look but not enough.

While no one would mistake them for locals—save for Rafi, that is—they also didn't look like people who stayed at the Ritz. Even the men in golf shirts, khakis, and sandals wore gold Cartier wristwatches and carried the latest iPhone.

Eliza didn't wear much jewelry, except for her honeybee earrings and her mother's necklace. She tenderly touched the spot above her sternum where it had once rested. Her chest tightened as it often did when she

thought about the necklace. For a moment, she feared she wouldn't be able to breathe, and she grabbed for Rafi's hand. He gave her a sidelong look, surprised by the touch.

"This place sucks," Jack remarked. His eyes glanced from her hand lingering against the empty skin of her neck to her other hand linked with Rafi's.

"It's out of the way," Rafi said, threading his fingers through hers. "Secluded. That's the whole point."

"That valet is going to cost an arm and a leg," Jack complained, seeming not to have heard him. "I swear if my car has an extra mile on it, I'll—"

"I think it's nice," Eliza offered, worried that Jack's grumbling would bring this whole excursion to an untimely end. "Rafi's right. No one would look for us here."

Jack huffed. "Hiding from the crypt keeper in a hotel bar!" Still, he stalked to the bar to order drinks from a man in a starched shirt and jaunty bow tie.

Hak gestured toward a small booth, and Eliza slid in. She found herself sitting next to Rafi with Hak sitting across from her. "Are you okay?" Rafi asked, his fingers brushing against her knee beneath the table.

"It just feels very strange," she admitted. "I thought I would be happy to be out—to be normal. But there's nothing normal about any of this."

Jack strolled up to the table awkwardly clutching four pint glasses. Foam sloshed over his knuckles as he walked, his brow furrowed with concentration. Despite herself, Eliza giggled. She'd never seen him look so serious, even while shooting at an undead pharaoh. "Hope everyone likes beer," he said. "The only other thing they had was a wine list."

"Take this swill back and get me a La Vieille Ferme Cotes du Ventoux," Hak insisted with a wolfish grin.

"Go fuck yourself," Jack said, with not a hint of humor. He placed the beers on the tabletop and scooted in next to Hak.

Wordlessly, Eliza took a sip. It was an ale—the malty flavor tempered by a fruity sweetness that made her feel a little sick. Or was that nerves? She was the one who insisted they come out, so she should have fun.

She took a gulp from the glass, the condensation making her palm slick. Hak and Rafi conversed easily, though Eliza only understood some of it; they often lapsed into a language known only to them, peppered with in-jokes and "you-had-to-be-theres."

Eliza wondered if that's how she and Poppy sounded when they got together, though their in-jokes related to ex-boyfriends and flings

(*"Remember when that guy stole your passport, and we were stuck in Barcelona for ages?"*).

Eliza drained her beer quickly, and another appeared before her as if by magic. Jack wordlessly raised his glass in a salute. She made it halfway through that pint before she had to pee. "Scoot," she urged Rafi. "I need to go to the ladies'."

Rafi gave her a quizzical look. "Alone?"

"Yes, alone. I'm not a toddler. Get up!"

Rafi slid out of the booth and ran his hand through his thick, pitch-dark hair. "Do you want me to come? I could stand outside."

"I'll be fine. If we're safe enough sitting here, I can go to the loo."

Before he could protest, Eliza set off through the maze of cocktail tables to the bar. The bartender rested his hands on the bar top to survey her. "What can I get you, sweetheart?"

"The bathroom—where is it?"

"Upstairs," he said. "Right off the lobby. You can't miss it."

Eliza glanced over at the table, worried that the guys would balk at the thought of her traipsing around the hotel, but she was bursting.

Eliza hustled out into the brightly lit hall. The carpet was ugly and multi-colored, the pattern so loud that it made her feel dizzy. The elevator looked to be up on the sixth floor, and she didn't want to wait. Instead, she took the stairs, cursing the heels she'd decided to wear. While they made her calves and butt look perky, they weren't good for walking, much less climbing stairs.

By the time she made it to the lobby, she thought the stilettos were destined for the dumpster. Her heel felt raw and unsettlingly damp—was she bleeding?

Finally, she found the bathroom and limped inside. After using the toilet, she lingered at the sink to fix her hair. The bathroom had inordinately high ceilings and everything echoed: the running tap, her footsteps, the groan of the stall door as it eased open.

Wait.

Goosebumps prickled up Eliza's arms. She was certain that she was the only one in the bathroom. There were three stalls, and she hadn't seen—nor heard—anyone else. No one came in after her either.

She bent to peer beneath the doors, but the stalls were empty. "Get it together, Cunningham," she whispered, turning back toward the mirror. She was getting paranoid and jumpy.

One Mummy to Go, Please!

Leaning close to her reflection, she wiped at her smudged eyeliner. Her hot breath fogged up the glass, and she wiped it away with her palm.

Her phone chimed from inside her purse, the leather muffling the sound. It was probably one of the guys, fretting because she'd been gone for longer than a minute.

With a sigh, she dug through her purse for it, tossing crinkled receipts and a tube of dried-out lip gloss onto the marble countertop. She was surprised to find that it was Poppy who had texted her, not one of her... what should she call them? Bodyguards? Babysitters? Fuck buddies?

[Poppy: Guess who is in Cyprus?]

She followed the question with a photo of herself in a floral dress and wide-brimmed hat, posing in front of Paphos Castle. Large, bug-eyed sunglasses overwhelmed her narrow face but could not hide her plump lips, courtesy of lip fillers and a beauty filter. Poppy had felt very unlike herself after her children were born, and she had started to overcompensate with mommy makeovers and shopping sprees. At least Chaz was fine with bankrolling the entire thing. "Happy wife, happy life? More like 'happy wife, nobody is sleeping on the couch,'" he had once said.

[Poppy: We're here for a few weeks. Please let me know when you're free and I'll jet to Cairo.]

Eliza wished she could be excited about a potential visit, but her stomach churned with worry. She couldn't, in good conscience, lead Poppy into danger. While Eliza felt entirely out of her depth, she knew that she had to keep Poppy afloat; she had children and a life to live. Eliza didn't have anything—no family, no possessions, and now, no job. Maybe she should have just let Milfonnos take her away.

For a second time, the stall door creaked on its hinges. A cool breeze ruffled Eliza's hair. *Is there a draft?* Her phone chimed again.

[Poppy: I'll even go to a stupid museum with you to look at a dusty old mummy.]

With a chuckle, Eliza slipped her phone back into her purse and tossed the wad of receipts in the trash can. If only Poppy knew how intimate she had been with a dusty old mummy—at least, in her dreams.

She reached for the bathroom door, but it only opened a crack before a sudden, stiff breeze wrenched the handle out of her grasp. The sudden friction made her palm burn. "What is going on with the air conditioning?" she mumbled.

In truth, she felt a little nervous and hoped speaking the most rational thought aloud would make it the truth.

The hair on the back of Eliza's neck stood on end, and she felt like she was being watched. It was as though she was the slender-necked gazelle standing in the tall grass, waiting for the lion to pounce.

She gave the bathroom a wary once-over: the row of stalls; the dappled marble counters with their shallow sink basins crowned by hands-free faucets; and a baby changing station, complete with complementary diaper cream and wet wipes. Despite herself, Eliza called, "Hello?"

For one queasy moment, she feared that someone would answer. After a moment, she tugged on the door handle again, but it didn't budge. She even tried pushing, in case the placard beneath the handle was lying.

"Priestessss…"

Eliza wrenched on the door handle. "No, no, nonono!" Her skin prickled beneath her arms, and sweat soaked her button-up.

She tried to dig her phone out of her purse, but the whole lot fell onto the floor. "Fuck!" Before she could scramble for it, a gust of wind slammed her against the door.

"Priestess." A hot breath tickled her ear, and a bony hand curled around her shoulder. "I've been looking for you…"

Chapter 30

The priestess smelled like ripe pomegranate, and saliva filled the Pharaoh's mouth. He had loved pomegranates when he was a boy. His earliest memories involved digging his fingers into the fleshy seed pod. His mouth and hands were perpetually stained purple. Kasmut would be right beside him, of course, his cheeks stuffed with seeds and pink drool dripping from his chin.

He had dreamt about the girl with the golden hair, though he couldn't remember sleeping. She haunted his every waking thought—perhaps that was the curse she laid upon him when she roused him from the tomb. He could feel the pull of it—manipulating his limbs like a marionette, shutting his eyes when even he couldn't handle the bloody work committed by his hands.

<*I am not your only passenger,*> Kasmut had warned him, hours after their waking. <*It is a dark shadow that comes and goes. I can't see their face, but I can feel their breath on my neck.*>

"Why did you wake me?" Milfonnos demanded, trapping the priestess between his body and the door. She shrank away from him, turning her head as if looking upon him was painful. "Tell me, Priestess!" He realized he was speaking in her language, the new sounds falling easily from his tongue. *More magic!*

"I didn't!" she managed through trembling lips, kohl-black tears staining her cheeks. Her palms pressed flat against his chest. He wondered if she longed to feel the beat of his heart, if the emptiness behind his chest wall frightened her.

"You were there when I was born anew!" Milfonnos boomed. "You were there, Priestess!"

"Please let me go," she whimpered. She shook with the violence of a flame just about to be snuffed out. The sweet scent of pomegranate dissipated, replaced by the acrid stench of sweat. "Please don't kill me."

Milfonnos leaned close, and a plaintive whine trickled out of her mouth. "You must be powerful to wield that magic."

"I... I'm not anybody," she argued. "I just run—ran—a food truck." Her fingers twitched at the mention of the truck, her nails snagging his robes. Despite himself, Milfonnos felt a pang of regret. He had dropped the truck, though it had been the fault of the man who had tried to lobotomize him with a bullet.

"Release your hold on me," Milfonnos growled. "You keep making me do things. No one makes Milfonnos the Blighted One do anything!" That was what made him the most indignant. Killing was killing, but being made to feel like a bug roasting beneath the magnifying glass was another thing altogether.

The girl slowly turned to look at him, though meeting his eyes seemed to cause her great pain. "I wasn't the one who brought you back. But I think I saw him. I ... almost hit him with my truck."

"A priest, of course!" In his excitement, Milfonnos shook her, and she winced. He didn't mean to hurt her. "Where can I find this priest?"

Her face contorted into an unsightly sob. "I ... don't know!" she hiccupped. "I didn't see his face. He was carrying a book."

A book. Of course, a book! His book. He had recognized it in the tomb. Milfonnos had spent years poring over the Book of Heka. It had been written by many hands and in many languages, including the oldest of all: ancient Sumerian. He had feverishly filled scrolls with notes even as the cancer chewed him up from the inside out, and his hands shook with tremors. Surely, that was the book! "Where is it?"

The priestess gulped. "I don't know."

<We are scaring her,> Kasmut observed.

"We are not," Milfonnos snapped, forgetting that the girl couldn't see or hear his passenger. He softened and took a step back.

The priestess crumpled, landing on her butt on the linoleum. "I'm sorry," she said, her chest heaving as she hyperventilated. "I'm sorry. I don't know. Please... please don't hurt me."

Milfonnos peered down at her. "I will not hurt you, Priestess." Though, he wasn't sure she believed him.

"I'm not... I'm not a priestess," she managed. "I'm just Eliza."

<Eliza.>

"Eliza," Milfonnos repeated. Her name felt pleasant on his tongue. There was a smile in the first syllable, a tap of the tongue the next, and finally, an exhale that smoothed the pinch between his shoulder blades. "I don't mean to frighten you." He knelt, tugging at the loose tail of gauze at his jawline. "Look upon me and know peace. I am no monster."

Her jaw tightened as he carefully unwrapped the gauze with slender fingers, revealing smooth, sun-burnished skin. Before his rebirth and the long illness that had preceded it, he had been handsome with sharp features and intense eyes surrounded by long lashes. Women—and men—found him equal parts intimidating and beguiling. He had regained that handsome exterior, though only the left eye had been restored. The right looked like it had been stained red, the color overwhelming the sclera and pupil. Except, it wasn't an eye at all, but a ruby nestled into his eye socket. It glowed with its own inner light, painting everything crimson.

The girl reached as if to touch him but thought better of it; her hand remained poised in the space between them. "You weren't like this when... my dream."

Milfonnos' fingertips brushed against hers. "In my dream," he said seriously, "you wore your hair down."

She jerked backward as if pushed, her cheeks a rosy red. "Your dream?"

"I dreamt of you," Milfonnos answered. "You knelt at my feet and said a prayer with your pretty tongue." In the dream, she wasn't afraid, and he had been so certain she was the one pulling his strings. At one point, with her eyes half-lidded and her lips pursed around his cock, he would have done anything she'd asked. He would have destroyed kingdoms.

Eliza averted her eyes.

"We are linked, you and I, even if you didn't cast the spell," Milfonnos said. "Why else would we have the same dream?"

"We don't know that it was the same," Eliza protested. She fiddled with the hem of her tunic.

"You are as red as the inside of a prickly pear." Milfonnos chuckled. "We had the very same dream."

<*I could only watch,*> Kasmut lamented.

Milfonnos wouldn't have minded if Kasmut had joined, if he were able. It wouldn't have been the first time they'd lain together, a woman sandwiched between them. Sometimes, they did without the woman altogether.

"The book." Milfonnos pointedly steered them back to the topic at hand. "I must find it. Whoever is controlling me has that book."

"Controlling you?" Eliza looked up at him with glassy doe eyes, her lips pressed into a thin line.

"Someone is moving me, like a knight on a chess board. Not all of the time, but their magic is strong. It overpowers even my own will."

Suddenly, the bathroom doorknob jittered. "Eliza?" a voice called. "Are you in there?"

Another voice followed: "C'mon, we need you. I feel like I'm on a date with Hak!"

Milfonnos quirked a brow. "I do not like to be interrupted. I will kill them."

"No!" Eliza exclaimed, grasping his arm. "Those are my friends. I need to go. But I'll look for the book. I know people. I have … resources."

"Fine," Milfonnos said.

"How will I find you, if I discover anything?"

"Just look for me in your dreams," Milfonnos murmured, helping her to her feet. His hand settled on the small of her back for a moment. "I will come when you call."

Before she could take a breath, he pressed his lips to hers and stepped back into the shadows.

Chapter 31

"Eliza!" Rafi pulled on the door of the ladies' restroom with all of his might, his knuckles blanching. Despite his growing panic, he was careful to keep his voice down and his back to the lobby; they didn't need any undue attention from passing patrons.

The door shuddered on its hinges but didn't budge. He imagined the deadbolt holding it in place. How much force would it take to rip the metal in two? He tried very hard to remember the magic the Amun Henet could wield with enough study and discipline. Unfortunately, he wasn't studious when it came to magic; the law felt more tangible and, well, real. He could only recall fragments of spells, mostly party tricks—water into wine and the like.

It was said that his ancestor Rahil Sabbagh could get through any door, whether he was welcome or not. He would have only had to breathe on this one to enter while Rafi could only pull and pull and pull and—

"Maybe you need to push," Jack offered. The mercenary crossed his arms as if to accentuate his bulging forearms. "Some doors are push doors, y'know."

"You are being too calm about this, Manning. The front desk clerk saw her walk in here ages ago. She isn't picking up her phone."

The front desk clerk was a sleepy-looking teenager who gladly took 1500E£ in exchange for information—and a little discretion.

"You're looking for the blonde with the tits?" he'd asked.

Rafi bristled, but Jack leaned against the counter. "Yeah, that's the one," he said congenially. He winked. "And I should know."

Rafi gritted his teeth.

"She went in the bathroom about fifteen minutes ago. I didn't see her come out, but I'm working." He gestured at an invoice on a clipboard; he'd drawn crude stick figures in the margins, many sporting enormous penises that curved, looped, and zigzagged.

"Did anyone else go in?" Jack asked.

"Not that I saw. Yo, your friend had better not be doing blow in there. This is the Ritz, not a hostel."

Just as Rafi weighed whether a flying kick would do them any good, a breeze trickled through the seam. It was so strong that it rustled his hair. A moment later, the lock turned and the door opened.

Eliza looked as though she had been crying. Her eyes were red-rimmed and puffy, and her nostrils were inflamed. She carried her purse by the strap, the bag dragging on the floor. She nearly walked right into them. "Oh."

"Are you okay?" Rafi asked, grabbing her shoulders. "We've been calling you."

Jack slid past them to peer into the bathroom. "Clear."

"Why weren't you opening the door?" Panic peppered Rafi's tone; he didn't mean to sound so irritated. He wasn't angry; he was frightened. Sometimes those didn't sound all that different.

Eliza swiped at her damp eyes with the heel of her hand. "I don't want to talk about it in the lobby." While her voice was even, it was apparent that she was rattled.

After the bright lobby, the bar seemed pitch dark. Rafi lingered in the doorway as Eliza and Jack made their way back to the table, rejoining Hak who guarded their beer glasses like a mother dragon guarding her eggs.

Rafi leaned back out into the hall. He couldn't shake the feeling that something had slithered behind them, though they had been alone. They hadn't even seen the front desk clerk on their way back to the stairwell. He was probably on a smoke break and chatting with the valets, Rafi decided.

Gooseflesh prickled the back of his neck. Something wasn't right. Eliza and Jack didn't seem to notice anything was amiss. Maybe it was all in his head.

"Trust yourself," Uncle Sarif had told him time and time again. "Even if you aren't adept, your body knows the score."

His body was telling him that they were being hunted, that Eliza had been marked like a tree meant to be felled, that they were standing on the edge of a very deep ... something.

As quickly as it came, the feeling of foreboding dissipated. Rafi hurried to the table and slid in beside Eliza, taking a gulp of his beer. It was lukewarm now, the effervescence little more than a tingle on the back of his tongue. "What happened?"

Eliza wrapped her hands around her glass. "The mummy—Milfonnos—appeared. He thought I brought him back. He wanted me to stop controlling him."

"Controlling him how?" Jack asked.

"He said someone was making him move—using magic."

Persuasion was a skill and manipulation an art; control was another beast altogether, especially when magic was concerned. Milfonnos had only been awake for a matter of days. There had been no time for his master to subjugate him in the more traditional manner; he hadn't been starved, beaten, gaslit, tortured. Instead, he had to have been reborn with the collar already tightened around his neck and no knowledge of the leash keeping him at heel.

"Obviously, I told him it wasn't me," Eliza continued. "And I told him about the man in the road."

"'The man in the road,'" Jack repeated slowly, shredding a cocktail napkin between his calloused fingers. "Wait, the man you nailed with your car?"

Eliza scoffed. "I did not hit him. I said I almost hit him."

At Hak's slack-jawed stare, she clarified. "After Milfonnos woke up, I left the dig site in a hurry. Just before I went through the security gate, someone ran across the road, carrying a book. They didn't look where they were going, and I had to slam on the brakes to avoid them."

Jack littered the sticky tabletop with tiny bits of napkin. His jaw worked, like a cow chewing its cud. "I didn't make this connection 'til now, but I did see a book at the dig site. It was old and full o' hieroglyphs and that squarish writing—cuneiform, I think it's called."

At their apparent surprise, Jack curled his lip. "What? I can speak a handful of languages, at least well enough to ask for a drink and a place to shit. Is it such a surprise I can read 'em, too?"

"Where did you see the book?" Rafi pressed. Jack's busy hands made him uneasy. Why hadn't Jack told them about this before?

"In the hands of our old slimy friend, Reese Eldin."

"Reese?" Eliza wrinkled her nose. "Are you sure?"

"As sure as I am of anything," Jack said. "He made me take him down in the tomb before the whole mess started, something about cataloging artifacts. But then he started droning on about ritual magic and jewelry. I thought he was trying to take a little overhead, if you know what I'm saying."

Rafi didn't know what he was saying, but Hak gave the handsome mercenary a knowing nod. Rafi felt, not for the first time, that he was the odd one out here. Hak and Jack were ropy with muscle, though they carried it differently. Jack was broad-shouldered while Hak was rangy. Rafi was thin and slouchy, a man who was well-read, not well-suited for battle. While Shogun Security crawled through the muck with a dagger clutched between their jaws, the Amun Henet stood in penthouses made of glass and metal, their only weapon a checkbook and a ballpoint pen.

"What do you mean?" Eliza pressed. "Do you think Reese was stealing?"

"It wouldn't surprise me." Jack shrugged.

Eliza's eyebrows knit together. "Reese is a lot of things, but he's not a thief. He adores his job. He wouldn't risk it."

"Some people need money more," Hak said gently. "Do you know of any debts?"

"The Eldin family is wealthy—summer and winter homes wealthy. He wasn't hurting for money, unless something happened that he didn't tell me about."

"Maybe Mommy and Daddy cut him off," Jack said dryly.

"Still," Eliza rested her elbows on the table, "I don't think he would steal. The 'ritual magic' angle is odd too. He doesn't believe in any of that stuff."

Rafi touched her hand. "Do you know where we can find him? The book is our only lead."

"Is it?" Jack looked unsure. "It's a lead we got from a dead guy. Maybe it's a trap."

"It's not," Eliza said, wearing her confidence like armor. She took a swig of her beer and wiped at her mouth with the back of her hand. "He could have killed me, but he didn't. He's scared, I think."

"Scared?" It was Rafi's turn to burst her bubble. "Eliza, Cairo is scared." While Rafi adored her empathy, it was misplaced; Milfonnos deserved a bullet to the brain, not a pat on the back. "I think the creature is trying to manipulate you."

"I'm not anybody," Eliza argued. "What does it matter if I think he's deserving of mercy?"

"It matters more than you think," Rafi murmured. "I'm going to go pay the tab."

Rafi drove back to the apartment, the lights of the Cairo Tower painting a latticework on the windscreen. The ride home had been largely silent, save for the ringing of the telephone.

Eliza slouched in the passenger seat, the light of her phone screen turning her pupils into pinpoints. As the ringing gave way to Reese's voicemail ("This is Reese Eldin. You know what to do"), she leaned her head back against the headrest with an audible thump. "He always answers me," she murmured.

It was the third time she'd said it, but no one dared to point that out. Her anxiety was almost corporeal, stalking around the sedan with its teeth bared. "Maybe we should drive by his place?" she suggested.

"And say what?" Jack asked from the backseat. "'Oh hey, sorry to drop in, but do you happen to have what is likely a priceless artifact in your apartment?'"

"It's late," Hak said soothingly. "Let's get some sleep, and we can try to call him again in the morning."

Eliza just tapped on her phone, the woosh of a sent text filling the cabin. Followed by another. And another.

Chapter 32

Eliza was sitting on the couch when Reese finally returned her call.

"Duckling!" Jack could hear the delighted voice from where he sat across the room. The ponce sounded legitimately happy to speak to her. "I never thought you cared so much, to keep checking up on me like this."

Eliza smirked, and Jack winked at her, both of them knowing that Reese assumed she was worried about him after the sandstorm and his brief hospital stay. "I just want to make sure you're okay," she told him, eyes rolling as she kept her voice light. "Can't have my friends dying on me, now can I?"

Hak had gone out, presumably to make some phone calls of his own. Apparently, Shogun Security still needed someone to make decisions and oversee things while the boss was on assignment protecting a friend's girl from a mummy. Rafi was also gone, presumably to check in with the Amun Henet. Jack had Eliza all to himself for the moment, so of course, the idiot had to choose now to return her phone calls.

Jack tried to keep his face impassive, openly listening to Reese on speakerphone as the man detailed his condition and treatment. *Yada, yada, yada*, he mouthed to Eliza, who nodded at him, clearly used to her old friend's mannerisms.

"That's awful," Eliza commiserated at the right moment. "I'm glad to hear you're on the mend now!"

Reese went on for a few more minutes, explaining his troubles now that the site had been shut down due to the freak weather conditions. Eliza made the right noises to show she was listening and completely on his side, but her face showed her boredom.

The book, Jack mouthed, miming holding a large tome and then clutching it to his chest.

I know, Eliza mouthed back, waiting for an appropriate pause in Reese's yammering to chime in. "Oh yes, I was so sorry to hear about the delay! Are you still able to work on the artifacts you already retrieved?"

"Well, yes, some," Reese admitted, annoyance clear in his tone that anyone would dare interrupt his work. "There was a lovely stock of jewelry and artwork that we've been documenting."

"That's great!" Eliza sounded honestly excited, and Jack marveled at her ability to lie so convincingly. He was starting to wonder if she ever did that to him when she finally broached the topic he'd been waiting for. "I know there were a lot of books in there—did you get those out?"

Reese hesitated a second, then he continued, voice a bit more subdued but still talking eagerly. "Some of them, yes."

"Well, if you need any help with the translations, you know I'm around," she offered casually.

"Since when do you translate books?" Reese asked, suspicious now.

But Eliza was too prepared, too smooth for him. "Since my truck was destroyed and I now have no job," she replied quickly. "Besides," she added, voice slightly husky, "maybe it would be nice to work together with you again, like the old days."

"You missing your dear old Reese?" he asked, and Eliza scowled at the phone, but her voice didn't change at all.

"Of course!" she insisted. "We had some good times together, didn't we?"

Jack's eyebrow raised at that, her words confirming his suspicions. Eliza scrunched her nose, clearly dismissing the history she had mentioned.

"We did indeed," Reese said, his voice lower now, nearly sexy if he could do such a thing.

"Do you have anything in…" Eliza paused, seeming to think about it, "ancient Sumerian, maybe? I'm still fluent."

"I'll have a look, Duckling." A pause, then he continued. "Perhaps we can discuss your renewed interest in antiquities over dinner?"

Eliza frowned, clearly debating how to answer this one. "Sure!" she replied, not missing a beat, though her face was unhappy. "Maybe later this week? I know you must be so busy with everything. Your new workspace is the Cairo Museum, right?"

"Actually, we have a private donor now, so we're able to work in our own space. I'll show you when we meet for dinner. You'll love it. We have all the toys you appreciate, Duckling."

"I bet," Eliza gushed. "A new donor, huh? Where is this fancy place?"

"I said I'll show you," Reese repeated, a hint of annoyance in his tone, and Eliza backed off, knowing a fight was lost.

"Just trying to make dinner convenient for you," she explained. "Is it near the Cairo Museum or the dig site or what?"

"Oh," Reese's voice was relaxed again, soothed by her seeming concern, "it's near the museum. We won't need to walk far."

"Well, let me know when is convenient for you," she said, pushing the conversation to the end. "When you're all better, of course."

"Of course," Reese agreed, then promised to call her in a day or so.

Eliza ended the call, then looked at Jack. "You get all that?"

Jack nodded. "You think he has the book?"

"I don't know," Eliza answered, and Jack believed her, despite having seen her deceptive skills only moments before. "I guess I'll have to meet him and convince him to take me back to wherever their new site is."

"Convince him?" Jack echoed, knowing exactly how Eliza would probably manage to maneuver Reese where she wanted him.

Eliza tilted her head, then slowly stood up, crossing the distance to where he sat on the old kitchen chair. "You have a problem, Jack?" she asked bluntly. "Something you want to talk about?"

She lifted a leg, then sat easily astride his lap, body fitting perfectly around his. His cock throbbed in his pants, eager to be closer to her heat. He wrapped his arms around her back, hands sliding up to tangle in her hair. "Maybe I do have a problem," he purred, tugging her hair so her head tipped back, baring her throat to him.

Eliza moaned, teeth biting her lower lip as she arched her body into his chest, clearly eager for more. He slowly released her hair, and she slid her hands over his face, one settling below his chin as she stared down at him, forcing him to look at her. "What problem is that?" she asked, voice husky with desire.

"I want you," he said, kissing her hard.

"I want you," she said, the words lost inside his mouth. "That's not a problem, Jack."

"Sweetheart," he said, pushing her away enough to unzip his pants and free his cock. He was glad she wore a sundress today, easy access as he slid her panties aside and pulled her down onto his shaft, her warmth enveloping him completely. "My problem isn't the wanting. It's wanting only you."

"I'm here," she panted, moving slowly up and down, eyes never leaving his.

"I want you all to myself," he admitted, eyes closing as he said the last part, feeling her tighten around him as he spoke.

Her voice was hard when she replied. "Look at me," she demanded, and Jack obeyed, staring into her eyes, connecting with her as he hadn't with anyone else in his life. "You get this," she told him, "right now, this moment." She moved faster, pushing him closer while her words made his heart ache. "I can't promise you anything else." Just as he was about to crash over the edge, she stopped, leaving him lingering in agony. "I like you, Jack, I do, but you aren't the only one for me, and you need to know that."

"I know that," he admitted, body singing with the need for release.

"Good," she said. "Then fuck me, Jack. Fuck me like you're the only man in the world."

At her words, something broke free inside, some hope long hidden away, and he stood, easily lifting her and twisted so he could lay her on the floor, wanting the hardness beneath them both. He tore her panties free, then used one hand to pin both her hands above her head, plunging into her hard and fast. He bit her shoulder, wanting to mark her as his own, and Eliza shrieked, her hips moving just as hard and fast as his own, meeting him stroke for stroke.

Moments later, they lay together on the floor, Jack collapsed atop her, and he could feel her rapid heartbeat against his chest as she caught her breath.

"Yeah," she managed between gasps, "I'm not willing to give that up any time soon." Jack smiled, lifting up on his arms to peer down at her smiling face. She cupped his cheek. "You gonna stick around, Manning?"

"Oh, sweetheart," Jack said, "nothing could drag me away."

A polite cough caught their attention, and they both turned to see Hak standing in the doorway. Jack scooted back and let Eliza sit up.

"Good times, I see?" Hak asked with a smirk. "Sorry I missed the festivities."

"Next time," Jack said, and Eliza smiled at him as she righted her clothing. Jack buttoned his pants, then helped her to her feet. He turned to the guard. "What's up?"

"He's killed another," Hak said.

"More sand?" Jack asked.

"Not this time," Hak said. "There's actually a body."

"What?" Eliza asked. "Does Rafi know? What did he say?"

Hak sighed, looking at Eliza. "He said to pick him up on the way to Samir's office. He said you'd know where."

"Who is Samir?" Jack asked. "Another friend?"

Eliza rolled her eyes at him. "Yes, a friend. One old enough to be my dad. We all do our laundry at the same place. He's a mortician."

"Oh," Jack said.

"I'm waiting for a daddy joke," Hak said, "but I'm sensing the time isn't quite right." He paused, cocking his head as Eliza and Jack walked through the door ahead of him. "At least a dead body joke?"

Chapter 33

"Is this it?" Jack asked as he pulled onto the shoulder in front of a squat, beige building.

"Yeah, that's the place," Rafi answered. The morgue was an unremarkable stucco building surrounded by chain-link fencing. Most passersby would never give it a second look; it was identical to most of the government buildings citywide and would only remind them of tedium. While Cairo bustled around them, the parking lot was deserted, save for a decommissioned orange ambulance with a missing headlight. It was Samir's daily car, bought for a steal at an auction. He joked that he kept the lawyers busy while the real ambulances got their work done.

Jack turned off the engine just outside of the unmanned security gate. "We're walking," he announced. "No use waiting for a gate that won't open."

Standing on the asphalt, Rafi felt as though he was baking. If he stood still long enough, he was certain that the rubber soles of his sneakers would melt. "You sure this guy is cool?" Jack asked, tucking a gun into the back of his pants. Rafi stared at his own reflection in the mercenary's mirrored sunglasses. He nodded. "He's cool. Eccentric, but maybe we need a little of that."

"Really? You'd think we'd already have enough," Jack quipped.

"It's like a horror movie," Eliza breathed as they ducked under the barrier arm of the security gate. Rafi caught a glimpse of a half-empty bottle of water and an adult magazine in the unoccupied cubicle.

"It's just a place, like any other place," Rafi said soothingly. "I mean, Samir comes here nearly every day."

Eliza pressed her lips together and focused on navigating the pockmarked asphalt, marred by potholes. Her sneaker was untied, but she didn't stop to tie it; it was so unsettlingly quiet that Rafi could hear the aglet skip upon the pavement.

He couldn't help but watch her out of the corner of his eye. She hadn't been sleeping well, and her somber eyes were dark and puffy despite the collagen patches she slapped on before bed. She'd braided her hair away from her face, piling the rest in a heap on top of her head. Despite the heat, Eliza chose a pair of black wide-legged pants and a boat-neck tee. A black chiffon scarf fluttered around her neck, which could be fashioned into a hijab if need be. He wasn't accustomed to seeing her in all black—it looked like she was on her way to a funeral, and in one sense, they were.

The reality of the situation fell upon Rafi's shoulders. This wasn't a social call, much as he tried to think of it that way; they were on their way to view a body. Rafi had seen bodies before, but they were done up in the trappings of a funeral rite. Their hair had been smoothed, their cheeks made lively with blush, and all of the unpleasantness tucked inside plastic inside church clothes. Here, there would be none of that.

At the entrance, Jack took the lead. The bell above the door tinkled merrily. The foyer was abandoned, but pleasantly cool.

Eliza leaned over the front desk. "The calendar is on yesterday's date," she murmured.

Suddenly, a shriek came from down the hall, ping-ponging off the walls. Jack coolly reached for his gun. "That sounded like Samir," Rafi said, glancing at Eliza, "didn't it?"

The room at the end of the hall smelled strongly of bleach and formaldehyde. Where Rafi had expected clinical neatness, there was disorder. It was as though the room had been vigorously shaken by a pair of gargantuan hands. The floor was sopping wet, soaking the hem of Eliza's slacks and invading their shoes. The spilt chemicals burnt Rafi's nose, and his eyes watered. Something crunched beneath their shoes; Rafi thought it was broken glass, but it was sand as if tracked in from a beach.

The doors of the stacked freezers bulged outward, their macabre contents in danger of spilling out. Eliza grimaced at her reflection in the polished

One Mummy to Go, Please!

metal. Jack accidentally kicked one of the empty jugs, and it skittered across the floor.

"Min hadha?!" A rotund man lurched up from behind an overturned embalming table, wielding a chair leg like a sword. He gave it a hearty swing, but with no enemies within hitting distance, he only succeeded in spinning himself around.

"Samir, brother!" Rafi said. "It's me: Rafi Sabbagh—Eliza is here too."

Samir's face softened, and he dropped his makeshift weapon. *"Alhamdulillah,"* he breathed. "Saved by my favorite girl."

Rafi chuckled. Samir doted on Eliza like she was his daughter. Perhaps it was because he missed his own daughter, who had moved to Perth with her new husband last spring. Every time they ran into him at the laundromat, Samir would offer her a butterscotch candy he had stashed in his pocket.

"What happened?" Eliza asked. She stood on her tiptoes to keep her pants dry, but she was starting to sway like a palm frond. Rafi grasped her elbow to steady her.

"Ach," Samir grunted, dropping his makeshift weapon. "You wouldn't believe me if I told you."

"Un-fucking-likely," Jack muttered, patrolling the perimeter of the room, opening closed doors, most of which were unmarked and empty—or rather, didn't contain mummies.

"Who're you?" Samir asked suspiciously.

"I'm Jack," the mercenary answered. Satisfied that no one was lurking, he put his gun away. Samir watched him warily.

Rafi righted a chair and patted the seat. "Come sit down, Sammy. Tell us what happened."

Samir stepped over an overturned hydraulic body lift, nearly snaring his ankle in the straps. Finally, he collapsed onto the chair and wiped at his damp face. "I wasn't supposed to be in today, but I had to do some inventory—government oversight, you know. I think I must have dozed off because I fell out of my chair. Then someone was leaning over me, their face was... was... wasn't human. He wanted to know where the John Doe was, but I didn't know which he was talking about. We have a handful at any given time, as unfortunate as that is. Suddenly, the room was filled with wind and sand." He shook his head, the memory overwhelming him. "The windstorm—Allah, what am I saying?—was too strong and I had to close my eyes, but he was here for several minutes more. When it stopped and I dared to uncover my head, he was gone."

Samir abruptly jerked his finger up at the corner of the room. For one nauseating second, Rafi thought Milfonnos had materialized, but Samir was only pointing at a security camera. "He may be on video."

"Can we see the tape?" Eliza asked. "It's important."

"I'm … not supposed to let anyone see the tapes. For the decedents' privacy. But no one was on the table today. For you, dear Elizabeth, I'll bend the rules."

The tape was preceded by a cup of tea, which seemed to bolster Samir's nerve. His hands steadied as he poured the boiling water into his mug and then portioned it into tiny Dixie cups meant for swishing mouthwash. Rafi found the tea to be too weak but sipped from his miniature cup politely.

"Ah, here we are." Samir clicked on a video thumbnail on his laptop. Eliza, Jack, and Rafi all leaned close to watch. Eliza's hand settled on Rafi's knee.

The video was fuzzy and monochrome; dead pixels danced around the screen. But the man puttering around on the screen was clearly Samir, bald head and all. He laid out boxes of eye caps on the embalming table, stacking them in neat rows. Then, he counted them, recording the number on a piece of paper with a #2 pencil. He hummed to himself as he worked.

"What song is that?" Jack asked.

"Alanis Morrissette," Samir answered. "'Jagged Little Pill.' Do you not know Alanis?"

"I know Alanis," Jack huffed. "I'm just surprised that you know Alanis."

Samir shrugged. "People contain multitudes. D'you know who said that?"

"Alanis?" Jack sounded unsure.

"Walt Whitman."

Suddenly, a loud crash on video made the laptop's speakers pop. Samir turned down the volume. "Here he comes," he announced, though Milfonnos needed no introduction.

Chapter 34

Milfonnos opened his eyes on the muddy bank of the Ain-el Sira, the smell of sulfur filling his nostrils. He didn't know how he got there. One moment, he was looking into Eliza's face and the next he was here. Time had passed. His last memory was of nighttime, but now the westerly sun warmed his skin; he'd lost most of the day. "Kas?" Milfonnos called, apprehensive. Had Kasmut been sleepwalking too?

<*It happened again, Pharaoh. The shadow crept up and swallowed us whole.*> Not even Kas could look upon the shadow—he may not have been nebulous at all. He was merely a hot breath on the back of the neck, a knife blade dimpling the throat. That was the most troubling of all. No one had ever snuck up on Kasmut before.

"What do you remember?" Milfonnos pressed.

<*Nothing.*>

Milfonnos floated toward the road, his toes skimming on the uneven ground. He was careful to remain out of sight of passing motorists, cloaking himself in shadow. At worse, he would appear as a pareidolia—a trick of the eye. He tried not to think about how tightly he had to hold the magic in place, how beads of sweat trickled down his brow.

He approached a large complex, the largest building's peaked roof casting a pyramid-shaped shadow on the ground. Vehicles topped with cherry-colored lights crowded the entrance, men in matching uniforms milling

around. Outside of the police cordon, vans topped with satellite dishes idled. Cameramen set up tripods while reporters preened, napkins tucked into their collars.

Milfonnos would have passed the scene by with nary a thought, but Kasmut tugged at him. <*Was this us?*>

Us. Us! This was Milfonnos' body, and if he had done anything, he had done it alone. Kasmut was just a voice, impotent in every other regard.

Suddenly, a clear voice rang out. A reporter with impossibly shiny black hair spoke into a microphone, his lips pressed into a serious line. "News out of Misr al-Qadima. This morning, at approximately 7:25 a.m., the National Museum of Egyptian Civilization was robbed. An artifact was stolen, though authorities have not revealed what exactly was taken."

<*If this was us, where have we been since? It is nearly dusk.*>

"Quiet, Kasmut, I must think." In truth, Milfonnos was troubled, but he couldn't let his bodyguard known that. A Pharaoh must be confident and poised. If he showed fear, he was fallible, and gods were not errant. Never.

The sky was a dusky purple when he reached the city proper. The night owls were out, their bodies doused in oils and their plumage stiff with hairspray. The air smelt of nicotine. Milfonnos found night life fascinating; he was no stranger to the bacchanal, but this was flashier than he was accustomed to.

"Hey handsome," a man called, dropping a cigarette butt on the pavement and extinguishing it with a twist of his heel. "Where's the costume party?" The man was handsome with sandy hair that reminded the Pharaoh of Eliza. The top three buttons of his shirt were unbuttoned, revealing a tattoo of the eye of Horus—a symbol of protection.

"Costume?" Milfonnos asked.

"Your robes!" The man chuckled, sidling closer. He walked with the liquidity of the very drunk, his limbs loose. He smelled like bergamot and beer.

"It is the clothing of a Pharaoh!" Milfonnos answered indignantly.

The man's eyes brazenly crawled over him. "Can I buy you a drink, Pharaoh?" His lip quirked, revealing a chipped canine tooth.

Milfonnos allowed himself to be led into the bar, amused at the man's audaciousness. Or perhaps it was stupidity—most had the sense to be

frightened of him. It was instinctual, much like a gazelle could sense a crocodile lingering in the murky water.

<*We do not look frightening anymore,*> Kasmut pointed out.

"Get out of my head," Milfonnos muttered.

"Did you say something?" the man asked. His fingers brushed against the back of Milfonnos' hand as they walked, and his groin tightened.

The bar back was mirrored, and Milfonnos stared at his reflection. He did look whole again; his skin was no longer leathery and gray, and there was nary an exposed bone in sight. Even the bugs had stopped tickling his insides. Only his red eye gave him away, though his companion didn't seem to notice. Perhaps it was the low lighting—or the booze.

"What would you like to drink?" the man asked. "It's on me."

"Shedeh," Milfonnos answered, thinking of the strong red wine that had once warmed his belly. It had been his favorite, and it pleased him that it was so prominently used in ritual. For Milfonnos, every meal was a ritual, an offering to a body blessed by the gods.

"Never heard of it. Is it a craft beer?"

The man ordered him something called an Ei Pea Ay. It came in a chilly glass, a thick layer of foam topping the amber-colored liquid. The bubbles tickled Milfonnos' nose, and he was disappointed to find that it was just beer. The man—whose name turned out to be Mahmoud—gabbed about his job at a local bank and took every opportunity to touch his captive audience. Milfonnos responded with noncommittal grunts, distracted by the life force emanating from him. There was an aroma to it, and his mouth watered. The hunger clawed at his belly. "Do you want to get out of here?" Milfonnos asked abruptly.

"I thought you'd never ask."

Mahmoud's apartment was just down the street from the bar. It was as small as a shoebox, the walls so thin that they could hear the neighbor's snoring. They barely made it through the threshold before the two men were intertwined. Milfonnos craved touch. It had been too unbearably long. He fumbled with Mahmoud's zipper but couldn't figure out how to undo it. Mahmoud did it for him. As soon as his pants were around his knees, Milfonnos pushed him down onto the bed and descended upon him.

Kasmut's desire welled up inside him, and Milfonnos was certain his cock had never been so hard. Gods.

His tongue pressed into Mahmoud's mouth as he worked his turgid cock with his hand. "You're so good at that," Mahmoud whimpered, his voice muffled by Milfonnos' lips. "There's lube on the nightstand."

Milfonnos sat up on his knees to grab the bottle while Mahmoud rolled beneath him. The lube was cold and made Milfonnos' hands slippery. He applied it, pressing his finger into Mahmoud's tightness. When he finally allowed himself to press his cock inside, he was keenly aware of Kasmut's panting, the weight of his hand on his shoulder. Together, the Pharaoh and his bodyguard pushed Mahmoud to orgasm.

Afterward, Milfonnos' hunger returned. Perhaps it was just desire, but it was a physical pain he could ignore no longer. Except, when he raised his hand to turn him to steal his soul, the man was not reduced to sand. Instead, Mahmoud's eyes bulged and blood poured from his mouth. He gurgled and lurched up from the bed, stumbling toward the bathroom. Before he could reach it, his knees gave out and he fell, clunking his head on the dresser.

The snoring stopped and someone knocked on the wall. "Mahmoud, are you alright? Mahmoud." When no answer came, Milfonnos heard a door slam and the voice from the hall. "Hello, yes. I think my friend has had an emergency. Please send help…"

Milfonnos expected gold, jewels, and tapestries; he found stainless steel, plastic eye caps, and sterile chuck pads.

<This is how they care for their dead? This is barbaric.> Kasmut was rattled, but Milfonnos couldn't blame him; he was unnerved too.

The cold, windowless room felt very lonely. In his time, women would be enlisted to cry, wail, and tear their clothes. They would drape their bodies over the sarcophagus, leaving smudges of kohl behind.

The only mourner in this tomb was a barrel-shaped man who counted aloud in Arabic, stacking boxes atop a wheeled table. Perhaps it was a meditation, a prayer, but Milfonnos didn't think so.

The Pharaoh padded across the room, keenly aware of the slap of his bare feet upon the linoleum. Since he'd tried—and failed—to consume the man, he'd felt leaden and exhausted.

<Pharaoh, we should talk about what..>

"Not now, Kas."

At his voice, the mourner turned. He was a jowly man with dark, deep-set eyes that reminded Milfonnos of overripe blackberries. Before the man could utter a word, Milfonnos raised his hand and the man rose with it. The man pinwheeled his arms and legs and let out a pitiful yip, but the sound was swallowed up by the howl of Milfonnos' sandstorm. With the man occupied, Milfonnos searched the room for the sarcophagus.

<*There are handles on the wall.*>

Kasmut was right: twelve handles placed equidistance apart on a shiny, silver wall. Milfonnos reached for the first, and pulled out an empty metal slab. The next drawer contained a body shrouded in white linen. "Not even clothing for the afterlife," Milfonnos scoffed as he peeled back the sheet. "He's just meant to be naked?"

<*Is that him?*>

In death, Mahmoud looked pallid and drawn, his skin pulled tight around his skull. Someone had cut him open from shoulder to sternum to groin and stitched him up again; the skin puckered beneath the slipshod stitches. But it was him. Milfonnos recognized the tattoo on his collarbone.

The irony! Milfonnos had been undone by a symbol of protection, manifested by his own god! What did this man know of Horus? If Isis had been Milfonnos' mother, Horus was his brother. *Perhaps it was jealousy then*, Milfonnos mused. Surely, he was a much better son than Horus could ever be!

"It is him," Milfonnos answered.

<*Why isn't he dust?*>

Milfonnos touched the man's face, trailing his fingers over his cold skin. "I have felt different since. Can't you feel it too?"

<*Our power...*>

"My power," Milfonnos softly corrected him.

<*...it used to make my fingers and toes tingle. My hair stood on end. It was effortless. Not anymore.*>

Maintaining the windstorm made Milfonnos' hands shake with effort. He gripped the edge of the drawer to keep himself upright, and dark motes danced in the corners of his vision. With every passing second, the cyclone slowed and its howl quieted.

He knew. It came to him with such crushing clarity that he cried out. "No! No, no, no!" He shoved the drawer closed and he was dimly aware of the body's thump-thump inside.

Milfonnos ran his hands over his body, his fragile, ostensibly human body. He was not a god at all. Not anymore.

Chapter 35

"What do you think he was doing there?" Jack asked as they rode back to Eliza's apartment. "He was looking for something."

Eliza recalled the video, the blurry image of her mummy opening doors until he pulled out a man and studied the body for a long silent moment. He said something too softly for the video to pick up, paused as he stroked a gentle hand across the dead man's cheek, then spoke again. Eliza thought she was watching one half of a conversation.

Perhaps he was speaking to the dead man? She pursed her lips, picturing the mummy as she had seen him in the bathroom, a handsome man with burnished copper skin and dark shaggy hair, one eye gleaming red. He spoke again, and something in the way he held himself struck Eliza and filled her with pity. He seemed genuinely sad—she assumed it was for the dead man he touched so tenderly. He stayed there for another moment, then stepped away, covering the man and sliding the body back inside the drawer. Two steps more and he faded into the shadows of the room.

"Perhaps he didn't kill the man intentionally," Hak offered from the back seat. "Maybe he was there to see what killed him." He turned to Rafi in the passenger seat. "If he is regenerated, can he be killed?"

Rafi frowned. "Perhaps. His body may be human, but he still possesses the ruby, and even with only one bangle, the magic protecting him is very strong. Only something equally magical has the power to affect him." He

gave Eliza a long, assessing look, hand jiggling something in his pocket, but then he shook his head, pulling his hand free and glancing out the window at the darkening sky.

"Magic weapon," Jack scoffed, turning onto Eliza's street and slowly hunting for parking space. "What is this—some kind of heroic quest? Who's going into the dungeon to slay the dragon and rescue the princess?"

Rafi glanced quickly back at Eliza then turned to face him. "I will do whatever is necessary to keep her safe," he said boldly, "no matter how many dragons or magic weapons it requires."

Hak snorted. "Why does everyone assume the dragon is the villain?"

Later that evening, the guys were glued to the PlayStation and Eliza wandered to the shower, needing some quiet space to clear her whirling thoughts. She couldn't get the image of the mummy out of her mind, the utter devastation she felt.

I should check on him, she thought then chuckled, the still-warm water spraying her mouth. *Yeah, because the mummy has a phone. Just send him a hug GIF. I'm sure he'll be fine.* She closed her eyes, lathering the shampoo in her hair.

"Priestess…" A voice whispered in her ear, and suddenly, there was a warm body pressed against her back, hands sliding up her arms to cover her hands, fingers pressing into her scalp.

"You!" she exclaimed, whirling around to see who had joined her in the shower. The naked mummy stood before her, no trace of the creature he had been in the man before her. His hands were still outstretched, now at his sides as he peered down at her, eyes narrowed in curiosity. His dark hair was getting wet in the spray, slowly flattening against his head.

"I," he affirmed, a slow smile crossing his lips as his gaze took in her naked form.

"What are you doing here?" she asked, tearing her gaze away from his perfect abs to look at his face, the arrogant expression of a man who knew he was handsome staring back at her.

"You called me," he said, as if that explained everything.

"No," she argued. "How could I do that?"

His hands moved forward to slide up her arms, making her shiver despite the warm water. "I hear you, Priestess," he whispered, leaning close to her ear. "I know what you yearn for."

She closed her eyes at his touch but opened them again at his words. Her hands reached out to press flat against his chest. "You think I yearn for you?" she asked, pushing him back. The mummy let himself be moved, taking a step back to lean against the wall, a smug smile in place on his gorgeous face.

"You want to worship me," he told her, "like in our dream."

Eliza raised an eyebrow. The dream had been hot, no doubt about it, but she wasn't going to worship him, not the way he was thinking. "Maybe it's time you worshiped me," she suggested.

"Of course, Priestess." He put his hands on her waist, leaning down to kiss her neck, but she stopped him. "I am generous."

"Eliza," she corrected, a hand on his chin. "We may have some kind of mystical connection since I accidentally was part of waking you, but I'm no priestess." She gave him a soft kiss. "And I don't need your generosity," she reminded him. She gestured over her shoulder to the room beyond and the three men in her apartment. "I have more than enough as it is."

The mummy seemed to pause for a moment as if listening to some internal voice, then he said, somewhat annoyed, "Yes, she is strong-willed. That is what draws me to her."

Eliza looked around, making sure they were alone in the shower and in the bathroom. "Hey," she said, frowning at him, "something you want to share, big guy?"

The mummy lifted an eyebrow, considering her. "I am Milfonnos, the Blighted One. I am Pharaoh."

Milf, Eliza thought immediately, the nickname sticking. Like "Mummy I'd Like to Fuck." *Definitely better.*

Eliza shook her head. "Yeah, not the best title, honestly." She ran a hand over his cheek, then down his neck to his chest. "Blight is not sexy."

Milfonnos looked offended, then he glanced down at where her hand pressed against his chest. "We are sexy," he declared.

Eliza tilted her head. "Is this some kind of royal 'we'? Or is someone here I just can't see?"

Milfonnos hesitated, seeming to have another of those one-sided conversations, then scowled. "I was not always thus." Eliza slid her hands up his muscled arms, fingers pausing at the ornate bangle encasing his upper left bicep. It was the only thing the pharaoh wore, and while it was

lovely, Eliza was far more interested in the rest of him. "When you called me forth—"

"Not me," she reminded him again. "Pretty sure it was the book that called you forth … and some magic."

He nodded, dismissing her words as unimportant. "We are drawn to one another by magic," he said, adding, "The magic of desire."

Eliza glanced down, seeing the evidence before her. Her hands left his arms, finding his hips and stroking along his length. "Of course there's desire," she said. "You're perfect." She gave him a few long, lazy strokes, and he closed his eyes. "You remember the dream?" she purred, leaning close so her breath tickled his ear as she continued to move her hands on him. "We were alone," she murmured, recalling the feel of his hands on her body, his mouth warm on her skin, "or were we?" She tried to pull the memory, trying to pinpoint just how many hands had been on her body at one time. "What is this?"

When she looked at him, Milfonnos was staring at her, a small smile still playing on his lips. "Clever priestess," he said, reaching down to cup her cheek. His other hand traced a line down the center of her chest, and her nipples tightened. "Greedy priestess," he said, moving so that he pressed her against the wall instead. "Perhaps we are enough to satisfy you." He bent down to kiss her, mouth starting off gentle enough, exploring one another slowly. One hand reached down to cup the swell of her ass and pull him to her.

"Maybe," she whispered, a little breathless. The pharaoh certainly could kiss.

"You are worthy of a Pharaoh," he told her, bending down to suck on her nipple, and she held onto his shoulders. "But you also desire the warrior." There was a pause, a shift, and then he was kissing her again, but this time, his mouth was determined, forceful, and Eliza's legs quivered at the change.

Kasmut.

She heard the whisper in her mind, the not-so-gentle demand of another, and she let herself be swept away in the sensation. When the mummy knelt before her, mouth finding her clit with practiced ease, she lost herself, letting him hold her upright as she dissolved into pleasure. "Milf!" she moaned.

"Next time," Milfonnos said, "I shall lay you down properly on an altar."

"Not an altar," Eliza managed, catching her breath as the mummy got to his feet. "A bed works perfectly fine." Another few gasps and her heart was starting to calm down. "Altars are for marriage or sacrifice, and I'm not into either."

"No," Milfonnos agreed, lifting her easily and walking so they both stood under the shower again, the water cooling Eliza's hot skin. "There will be no sacrifice tonight." Eliza wrapped her legs around his hips, sliding onto his hard length with a sigh. "Tonight, there shall be only worship," the mummy said, kissing her again as she moved slowly up and down. They started out soft, easy, a careless rhythm that didn't hurry, just enjoyed each sensation as it came, but as the moment built, Eliza sensed a shift, and someone far more physical took over, pressing her against the wall and pounding into her, swallowing her moans of pleasure as he devoured her mouth. When she came again, this time Eliza saw stars, and for a split second, she could see two men: one the mummy she recognized and the other also dark-skinned with longer hair, hugely muscled and powerful, with sharp eyes that never stopped scanning their surroundings.

"Kasmut," she said, but the name was lost in his kiss.

Eliza lost the next few moments, but then she was standing under the water, Milfonnos behind her, one hand holding her steady as the other washed her body, worshiping her as she had asked. "Wow," she managed, "that was fascinating." She glanced over her shoulder. "It's like there are two of you."

"There *are* two of us," Milfonnos said, and Eliza turned around, peering at him.

"What do you mean?"

"When you woke me—"

"I didn't—"

"Yes, yes," he said, hands soaping her breasts and gently rubbing her nipples. "When we woke, I wasn't alone." He gestured with one hand at his head. "In here, Kas is with me."

"And Kas is...?" Eliza asked, taking the soap and lathering his chest.

"My bodyguard," Milfonnos said. Then added, "My friend."

"The jar?" Eliza asked, recalling the jar she had kicked into the magical explosion. "Did I do that?"

Milfonnos shrugged under her touch, and she moved lower. He twitched as she touched his length, but he didn't get hard again immediately. Apparently, even pharaohs had refractory periods.

"Where is his body then?" she asked, making Milfonnos turn around so she could wash his back.

"We don't know," Milfonnos said, shoulders slumping.

"Is that what you've been doing then?" she prompted. "Looking for it?"

"No," Milfonnos said, turning back to face her. "We haven't had the chance."

"But," she began, cocking her head, "you've been running all over Egypt, breaking into museums."

Milfonnos shook his head. "Not me. Not us." He looked away as if hating to admit it. "We are … missing time."

Eliza nodded. "Someone is controlling you," she said, "with the book."

The pharaoh sighed. "It would seem so."

"So," Eliza said, not wanting to ruin the pleasant post-coital mood but needing to know, "when you turned those people into sand…?"

The pharaoh turned his dark eye on her, the ruby glowing softly in the steamy air of the shower. "I did what was necessary," he said coldly, and a shiver ran down Eliza's spine. "Sometimes sacrifice is necessary."

Eliza stepped away from him. "And the man in the morgue?"

Milfonnos looked ashamed for a second, then the haughty mask was back. "A mere human," he dismissed.

"I am a mere human," she reminded him. "Would you sacrifice me?"

"Not tonight," he said, "my little honeybee." He caressed her face, and despite herself, Eliza felt heat beginning to pool in her belly again. "You are mine."

Get in line, she thought, staring at him. *What is wrong with me? He's a villain!* Studying his beautiful body and that angelic face, Eliza couldn't help her attraction. *Yeah, I'm definitely into bad boys.*

Milfonnos' expression shifted then, and he sighed, shoulders slumping as he reached out to her. "Will you free me, Priestess?" he asked. "Will you bind me to you alone?"

"Eliza," she repeated. "And I can try." She frowned, reaching out to turn off the water. "I don't know about bindings, but no more sacrifices. Not if you can help it."

He smiled at her. "As my priestess wishes," he agreed.

Chapter 36

Eliza combed her fingers through her dripping wet hair. The steam fogged the bathroom mirror, and her reflection reminded Milfonnos of a post-Impressionist painting—beige and pink paint daubs arranged in the hourglass shape of a woman.

Milfonnos found her pinkness surprising—her lips, her cheeks, her nipples, the secret spot between her legs that he found with his tongue. It distracted him from asking the more important question: how did he know what post-Impressionism was, never mind what it looked like?

But Kasmut grasped for the thought and shook it loose. The memories beneath it floated in the air like dust: a painting in an ornate frame, a placard with "Renoir" written in precise block letters, red velvet stanchions, and a flashlight beam strafing across stained glass.

Before he could delve any further, Eliza's voice punched through the haze. "The guys can help," Eliza insisted. "Once they realize—"

"This is a bad idea," Milfonnos said softly, careful to keep his voice low. He could hear the murmur of voices in the other room—his priestess's other lovers. "They will not help me."

"They are good guys." Eliza pulled on the clothes she'd left folded on the corner of the sink.

"I am not a good guy," Milfonnos reminded her. "And neither is Kasmut."

<I am a man of honor.> Kasmut huffed. *<Anything I have done was to serve my Pharaoh. I am but a sword, and you are the mouthpiece!>*

Milfonnos wished he could excise Kasmut like a tumor and throw him into a waste bin. His voice had only grown louder since they took Eliza together. It was growing harder and harder to ignore him.

Eliza's damp hair left a dark patch on her white t-shirt, revealing the tantalizing curve of her breast. Milfonnos couldn't help himself: his fingers trailed down her sternum, cupping her breast through the fabric. She hadn't put on a bra, and he stroked her nipple with his thumb. Her eyelids drooped and a shuddering gasp escaped her. He could sense her resolve wavering. Perhaps he could keep her in here after all.

Suddenly, someone banged on the bathroom door. "Hey, you done in there? I have to take a leak." The vowels seemed to melt into one another, forming a puddle in the middle of the word 'the-ah.' It was not an accent that Milfonnos had ever heard before, and he'd heard plenty when traders came in from Nubia and Rome.

Before Milfonnos could protest, Eliza threw open the door. The man on the other side was broad and wore a University of Texas t-shirt that may have once been black but had faded to gray. The sleeves had been cut off and rolled up to reveal thick muscle. Catching sight of him, clad only in robes made of shifting shadow, the man let out a shout. "Behind you!" he roared, grabbing Eliza's wrist and pulling her against his sturdy chest. Eliza's breath rocketed out of her with a whoosh.

<He is one of the men from the dig site,> Kasmut observed coolly. *<He stinks.>*

"Shut up, Kas," Milfonnos hissed through clenched teeth, raising his hands to show the man with the strange accent that he had no weapons. It was a useless gesture—they had all seen what he could do with his bare hands.

At the man's shout, two others burst into the hallway, one shirtless and the other wearing the face of Rahil, the leader of the Amun Henet. It was too narrow for them to run shoulder-to-shoulder, and they scrambled over each other. It would have been amusing if not for the gun in the shirtless man's hand. "What the fuck?" he exclaimed. "Cover your ears so that I can shoot him."

"No," Eliza said, her voice muffled against Jack's chest. "Milfonnos came to me for help." Disentangling herself, she stepped into the middle of the fray. "Put down the gun, Hak."

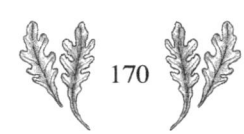

"I shouldn't have to remind you that this ... thing killed a whole lot of people," Hak snarled. "My men."

Milfonnos could not help but stare at the winged serpent tattooed on the man's chest. He knew the story of Apopis, an agent of chaos who tried to swallow the sun god Ra. Did the man think he could wield the same power?

"Which men were yours?" Milfonnos asked. "The ones who could not hit me with their puny bullets or the ones who ran?"

<You are not helping,> Kasmut groaned.

"Eliza, cover your ears," Hak insisted. He disengaged the gun's safety with his thumb, his finger curling around the trigger.

Eliza's hands remained at her sides. "Please," she begged. "Listen to him—listen to me. He's being controlled by someone else. He and Kasmut haven't done anything of their own free will."

"Who the fuck is Kasmut?!" Rahil's doppelgänger asked.

"Milfonnos' bodyguard," Eliza said patiently. "He's trapped inside Milf's head. Please, believe me, Rafi."

"Milf!" Jack scoffed. "He has a nickname now? Next, you'll be telling me he's taking you out for a candlelit dinner."

Milfonnos would have been pleased to do it. He imagined Eliza's face in the firelight, her hair shimmering like gold and sparks reflected in her dark eyes. He was also very adept at finding his way in the dark after the wick burnt down and drowned in the wax. His tongue would lead him home.

Eliza's cheeks colored. "I..."

"I did not ask to wake up," Milfonnos said evenly. "And Eliza is correct: there are moments when I am not in control. I blink, and it has been hours."

"So it wasn't you who turned those innocent people to sand?" Hak asked.

Milfonnos hesitated. "I was hungry. I felt as though I hadn't eaten in centuries. It was like I was being chewed up from the inside. I—"

"You ate them?!" Jack's disgust was palpable; his spittle flecked Milfonnos' cheeks. He wondered if Eliza would mind if he snapped Jack's neck. Surely, this one was only tolerated. Milfonnos knew many men like him: brutes, sword fodder, nothing more.

"Their essence, yes." He felt the distinction was important. It was less violent than tearing, ripping, chewing. He thought—hoped—his victims felt very little pain. "With each meal, I grow more human, but my powers are ... weaker."

Tentatively, Eliza's fingers settled on the gun's barrel, pushing it downward. "Hak, put the gun away," she whispered. "He's not going to hurt us."

One Mummy to Go, Please!

Hak's lips pressed together so firmly that they blanched. Finally, he relented, re-engaging the safety and tucking the weapon into his waistband. The handle rested against his taut stomach. "One wrong move, and I'm blowing his brains out. If he's human, he can be killed."

"I did not say I was entirely human," Milfonnos snarled. "Surely, you saw what I did in the morgue. It only took the power in one measly finger."

<Liar,> Kasmut chuckled. <You were shaking.>

"So what?" Jack scoffed. "You made a mess like a child having a tantrum."

"Can we please focus?" Eliza groaned. "We should go sit down."

The hallway was narrow and crowded; it may as well have been a cattle chute, bringing them to slaughter. Though, who would hold the bolt gun was yet to be determined. As they argued, the temperature rose in the airless anteroom and a sheen of sweat coated Hak's chest. Eliza's hair was frizzy. Rafi's mauve dress shirt looked black beneath his arms. Jack swiped at his brow with the back of his hand.

Only Milfonnos didn't sweat.

"What if this is all a lie?" Hak blurted.

"What good would that do?" Milfonnos snarled, growing exasperated. These men were not "good guys," as Eliza claimed. They were dim-witted, weak, and above all else, tiresome. What were they good for?

"I believe him," Eliza argued.

"Why?" It had been the first time the man who looked so much like his archenemy had spoken in some time. His forehead creased as his bushy eyebrows drew together.

Eliza let out a shuddering breath. "I've been… We've been … getting close." Her skin burned pink. "Rafi, I care about him. Just like I care about all of you." His lip curled in disgust, and Eliza winced as if he'd slapped her.

Chapter 37

Rafi slammed the door and the whole apartment shook. A framed photo on the wall wobbled and slid askew. It was of Eliza and Poppy in Barcelona, a man in sunglasses and a baseball cap sandwiched between them. The cap had "Wine Mom" embroidered just above the brim. Eliza couldn't remember the man's name, but she could recall how he threw her legs over his shoulders.

Eliza squeezed between Milfonnos and Jack to follow Rafi. "Please don't kill each other," she called over her shoulder. "I'll—we'll—be right back." Without waiting for assurance, she darted out the door, realizing, far too late, that she hadn't put on any shoes.

The walkway had been baking in the sunshine, and she had to hop from foot-to-foot to keep from burning her feet. Still, by the time she reached the stairwell, she could feel a blister forming on her insole. "Rafi!" she shouted down the stairs. "Please, come back!" While she couldn't see him, shouting felt good; the searing of her vocal cords felt like a punishment.

The door nearest the stairwell cracked open as far as the security chain would allow. While Eliza could only make out a hazel eye drooping with the weight of edema and a hawkish nose, she recognized the woman inside as one of the *jadda*—grandmothers—who spent their time gossiping in the courtyard. "Some of us are trying to nap, yi!" she exclaimed.

"I'm so sorry," Eliza said, clambering up onto the rail to avoid burning her feet. The rail, covered in flaky rust, wasn't any less hot. "My friend... I think I really hurt his feelings." Tears sprang into her eyes. "I forgot my shoes." Eliza's chest tightened. She missed her mother. She would know just what to say, even in an entirely novel situation like this one.

For one, she would tell her not to juggle four men. Especially if one of them was undead.

After a pregnant moment, the *jadda* threw a pair of slippers out onto the walkway. They were simple terrycloth slides, emblazoned with the logo of a local spa. "Go get your *habib* and be quiet!" While she said the words with as much venom as she could muster, Eliza caught a glimpse of her thin-lipped grin just before the door closed.

Eliza slipped her feet into the slippers and raced down the stairs. They were far too small and her toes hung over the edge, but she was grateful all the same. Rafi's apartment door was closed, and when she knocked, no one answered. "Rafi!" she called, trying the knob. "Rafi, please let me in." She rested her forehead against the door. "I'm sorry," she whispered. He must feel so rejected. She'd practically rubbed his face in her trysts; for god's sake, he'd had to sit and watch.

Rafi didn't have to, she reminded herself. He'd wanted to.

Afterward, when Hak and Jack went to clean up, Rafi stayed behind. His chocolate-colored eyes looked black in the darkness; Eliza couldn't read his expression. Gooseflesh prickled on her naked flesh, and she shivered. As she reached for a blanket, he shook his head.

"Come here," he murmured, patting his knee. He looked roguishly handsome, his hair disheveled from his fingers combing through it. It was an anxious habit; even when he gelled his hair back for work, he left the courthouse with his hair standing on end. Eliza preferred it that way because he looked more like the Rafi that sat on the dryer in the laundromat, kicking his heels against the drum. It was five o'clock shadow, t-shirt, and sweatpants Rafi.

Eliza rose, keenly aware of her nakedness and the kiss marks adorning her breasts. "I meant what I said," Rafi purred as she walked toward him. "I do just want to watch. Except..." Rafi pulled her onto his lap, his hands gentle.

One hand rested heavily on her leg, his thumb drawing lazy circles on her inner thigh. She looked into his eyes, and he licked his lips. "There's one thing I'd like to do," he continued.

Eliza swallowed, fearing that her voice would shake when she spoke. "What's that?" she finally asked.

His thumb stilled.

Rafi leaned close and kissed her. Their first kiss was soft and chaste, not unlike a stolen schoolyard smooch beneath the bleachers. Eliza's heart pounded, just like it had when she'd kissed Tad Phillips in the sixth grade. This was like her first kiss all over again. Their second kiss was less subdued. When his tongue twined with hers, she was surprised to find he tasted like tobacco.

"What are you doing?"

Eliza whirled to find Rafi standing in the courtyard, a hand-rolled cigarette dangling between his fingers. "I've been knocking," she said, inwardly cringing at the hurt she couldn't seem to squeeze out of her voice.

"I went for a walk," he said. "I had to think."

"I thought you said you only smoked on occasion."

Rafi dropped the cigarette on the cement and doused it with his heel. "I did."

"It doesn't seem like it," Eliza snorted.

"This seems like as good of an occasion as any." He shrugged.

"I'm not blind, you know."

Rafi scoffed. "Neither am I. The others may not be so quick on the uptake, but I knew what you did as soon as I saw your face. Your nose gets all scrunched up when you're uncomfortable."

Eliza crossed her arms. "You didn't judge me when it was Jack. Or Hak."

He had acted as though watching her was thrilling. When she came to sit on his lap afterward, he'd been impossibly hard, his cock tenting his slacks.

"I don't own you, Elizabeth. You can do whatever—or whomever—you'd like. But I don't think you're seeing the full picture here. This is Milfonnos the Blighted One. Even in life, he was not a good person. He didn't care about his people or even his kingdom, just power. He was more of a treasure hunter than a pharaoh. Except he sent his underlings into booby-trapped temples and catacombs to retrieve the artifacts he sought. He was delusional; he believed that he could be immortal and that he, alone, deserved it. There's a natural order to things, and he broke it."

"Does the Amun Henet get to decide what's 'natural'?" she shot back, forgetting she was supposed to be groveling.

"No." Rafi brushed past her to unlock his apartment door. "I don't trust the mummy, nor do I trust your judgment when it comes to him." He gave

her a long look, unspoken words hanging heavy in the air. "What I do know is that we all have the same goal right now—to find out why he's here."

Rafi went inside but left the door yawning open. Eliza wavered in the doorway, the air conditioning ruffling her hair. She should go back upstairs. Clearly, Rafi didn't want to talk to her. But then, he whooped. "I found it!"

Eliza rushed inside, his apartment the mirror image of her own. Its layout always confused her. She veered left into what she thought was his bedroom but found that it was a coat closet. His coats smelled like mothballs; they weren't used often in Cairo. She finally found Rafi sitting on his bed, a stack of pamphlets in his hands.

"My mom was a docent at the textiles museum, and she kept pamphlets from every museum we ever visited—and we visited a lot. After she died, I started doing the same, though I went to very few. Once you've seen one mummy, you've seen them all." Rafi looked at Eliza through his eyelashes. "But that's not the point. The point is there's only one book that could bring Milfonnos back from the dead: the Book of Heka."

Eliza wordlessly sat on the bed beside him. The mattress was soft and sank down, forcing their hips to touch. Rafi didn't seem to notice, back in business mode, and Eliza tried to ignore the sensation of his thigh pressed against hers. "There are two copies, Eliza. One was in the National Museum, which was stolen. The other is in a private collection." Rafi unfolded a dog-eared pamphlet and tapped on a black-and-white photo of a nondescript book. Beneath the photo, the caption read:

THE BOOK OF HEKA, located in the west atrium. Special thanks to the Valdano family for lending one of two copies to the museum.

"Valdano? Who is that?"

"Giuseppe Valdano owns Lair of Isis, a belly dancing club out on El Nil Street. It's super hard to get into—people wait in line all day only to get turned away by the bouncer. Valdano is an expat who made a name for himself here in Cairo for all of the wrong reasons. He's the leader of a crime syndicate and a collector of rare antiquities. He usually donates things when the cops are sniffing around. You can't arrest a patron of history."

"Does that mean you'll help?" Eliza asked hopefully. "You'll help Milfonnos?"

"I'll do it for you," Rafi answered, and that, Eliza conceded, was good enough.

Together, they walked up to her apartment, the pamphlet tucked into Rafi's pocket. Each time their hands inadvertently touched, Eliza hoped he would grab hold, but he didn't. She was too frightened to take his hand, fearing that he would shake her off. The rejection would hurt more than she'd care to admit.

Her apartment was unsettlingly quiet. They found Hak and Jack lounging on the couch, playing *Call of Duty*. Milfonnos sat cross-legged on the floor, holding a PlayStation controller upside down. The sight was so bizarre that Eliza doubled over with laughter.

"Who can get us into Lair of Isis tonight?" Rafi asked, tossing the pamphlet onto the coffee table.

Chapter 38

That afternoon Rafi wandered alone to the rooftop terrace. He was leaning against the railing, surveying the city below, wondering how exactly they were going to convince Giuseppe Valdano to let them borrow the Book of Heka, if the gangster even had the book in his possession anymore. Getting into Lair of Isis was a good start, but they needed more than that if they were to acquire the book and thereby control the creature.

Milfonnos, he corrected himself. *Eliza calls him Milf. A nickname for another lover.*

He bit his lip, cock stirring at the memory of his girl lost in ecstasy between Hak and Jack. Next time, he decided, she should have her mouth free. He wanted to hear every noise she made as she came.

As someone else makes her come, he reminded himself. Though they had shared several kisses afterward in the stolen moments they were alone, Rafi was fairly certain his knee jerk reaction to her confession about adding Milf to her stable of lovers had ruined any chance of Eliza ever falling into his embrace.

I'm a fool, he told himself yet again. *I finally don't have to lie to her—about anything—and I go and ruin it in an instant.* He hadn't meant to judge her. He knew Eliza's sexual appetite would be well served by the addition of the mummy and his dark passenger. But his face had revealed his true feelings—disgusted that he wasn't good enough to be with her. That she would never choose him.

She asked you to join her, a small voice reminded him. *She wants you.*

He sighed, running a hand through his hair. The thick strands were loose and wavy around his face, still slightly damp from his shower, and he hadn't yet greased them properly into place. They still had hours before they needed to head to Lair of Isis tonight. Rafi needed a better plan than the current one: show up and pray Valdano was feeling generous.

Hak and Jack were still down in Eliza's apartment, no doubt teaching Milfonnos how to play *Call of Duty*. He could hear the quiet murmur of voices blending with the television from below, the sound meshing with the afternoon sounds of the city, and Rafi closed his eyes, taking in the moment, letting his home calm him. He needed to clear his mind if they were going to succeed.

"Rafi?"

He opened his eyes but didn't turn around, surprised that he hadn't heard Eliza's approach. Sloppy. The kind of sloppy that Hak would berate him for. Rafi wasn't a warrior like Hak or Jack, but he had enough training that no one should be able to sneak up on him like that.

Then again, Rafi always had a blind spot for Eliza Cunningham.

"Eliza." He said her name softly, gently, loving the feel on his tongue, the syllables popping, and he recalled the taste of her kiss.

"Can we … talk?" she asked, voice hesitant. Rafi still hadn't turned to face her. He couldn't, not yet, not when everything in him screamed to gather her into his arms and make her his own—even if only for a brief moment.

"Always," he promised her, taking a deep breath and steeling himself to face her, knowing the sight of her face would gut him as it always did. "What is it?"

She chuckled, and he did turn, taking in her floral-patterned dress, the hem landing just above her knees—a conservative dress for her, no doubt another older article of clothing pulled from the back of her closet. Since the mummy's appearance, they hadn't paused to do much laundry, especially after Jack ruined her dress that first time. Rafi's own wardrobe was running low. Plus, Eliza wasn't working anymore, so she wasn't limited to clothing that would possibly get stained by food. She looked comfortable, adorable, and he couldn't help the smile he gave her.

"That's my question, actually," she said. "'What is it?'" she repeated. At what must be his confused expression, she moved closer, her sandals making no sound on the smooth rooftop. Her hand reached out to press

against his chest. He could feel the warmth of her palm through his thin shirt. She pinned him with her gaze. "What is it between us?"

"I am your friend, Eliza," Rafi said. "I will always be here for you." He didn't know where she was going with this. They had spent hours below in her apartment, discussing all the ways they could free the mummy as she wished, but they hadn't spoken of their relationship at all, not even after he kissed her.

She stepped forward. "Just a friend?" she pressed, her other hand reaching out to take his hand and press it to her chest. He could feel her heart beating rapidly. His Eliza was nervous. Excited.

Rafi reached down to cover her hand with his free one, feeling her heart slow as he took calming breaths and her body followed his lead. "I am whatever you have need of, Elizabeth. I am here. Always."

"Will you?" she asked, and Rafi thought there was a hint of tears in her eyes.

"Where is this coming from?" he asked, leaning down to tug her close, folding her into his embrace. She trembled in his arms. "I'm not going anywhere."

She took a few settling breaths, calming, but then she looked up at him, bright blue eyes watery with unshed tears. "They were talking after you left … about Valdano. He's so dangerous, Rafi. And you're not…" Her voice trailed off.

"I'm not what?" he prompted, though he could finish her thought easily enough.

Not a warrior.

Not dangerous.

Not worthy.

Her arms tightened around him. "I just don't want you to get hurt."

He nodded, kissing the top of her head, smelling the shampoo he loved. Eliza always smelled so good, despite the sweltering heat. He waited a moment, gathering his thoughts, then pushed her away enough so she could look at him.

"I am Amun Henet," he reminded her. "I may not be a bodyguard like your Jack or an assassin like your Hak… or even magic like your Milf, but I have my own skills. You need not worry for me."

"But … a gangster…"

"Should I be less brave than you facing a reanimated mummy who seemed intent on killing you?"

"Milf was never…" She paused, shaking her head. "I don't want to talk about him. Or anyone else. This is about you, Rafi." She narrowed her eyes at him, hand snaking up to poke his chest. "You're my best friend. They are fun—but they are temporary. When all this is over, I want to know that you will still be here. With me."

"I am always with you, Eliza," he promised. "You have my oath on that."

"Good," she said, leaning hard into him again, "because we have three episodes of *Hot Nights* to catch up on."

"Of course," he agreed, savoring the feel of her body so close.

"Can I ask you something?" she asked, quiet now.

"Anything," he replied, soul surging at the freedom in his response, knowing he didn't have any secrets from his Eliza anymore.

"Do you … want me?"

Rafi froze, eyes closing as her words caused his cock to stir. "From the very first moment I laid eyes on you," he said, the words out before he could stop them.

"Then why didn't you make a move?" she pressed, face still resting on his shoulder, neither looking at the other.

"You seem … occupied," he managed. He recalled the feel of her mouth against his, her naked body still flushed with spent pleasure in his arms, and his cock stirred again. He adjusted his hips, knowing that Eliza must be able to feel him as she stood tucked against him.

"Recently," she agreed, "but we've been friends for years now, Rafi. Why didn't you say something?"

He put some space between them again, just enough that he could look at her when he answered. "I am Amun Henet," he repeated.

"And?"

"And I have obligations," he explained. "There are things I could not tell you. I couldn't court you knowing I could never be honest with you."

"And now?"

He smiled, a finger lifting her chin slightly. "Now you know all my secrets," he said.

Eliza scoffed, reaching up to press his hand against her face. "Hardly," she said. "But it's a start at least."

"Ask me anything," Rafi breathed, peering into those bright blue eyes that so enchanted him. "I will tell you the truth." *Ask me*, he pleaded.

"You'd better," she snapped. "You're my best friend. Friends tell each other the truth."

Now it was Rafi's turn to lean closer, face only inches away from hers. "Is that all I am to you, Elizabeth?"

Eliza cocked her eyebrow, nose scrunching the way he loved. "What if I want more?" she whispered.

"Why now?" he asked, needing her to say it.

She sighed. "I know it's been a crazy few weeks with the mummy and magic and everything, but I've always wanted you, Rafi. I just assumed you weren't into me." She paused. "Honestly, I wondered if you were gay."

Rafi chuckled. "A man shows a little bit of restraint, and he's not interested in women? Eliza, you do make some hasty generalizations."

"Well, you said you only wanted to watch Hak and Jack… so I wondered if that meant you just wanted to see them…"

Rafi smiled, cock hardening even more as the doubt played across her face. He knew she was remembering their kiss afterward, when he had barely restrained himself from throwing her on the bed and claiming her for himself. "Men are lovely, but nothing compares to you, Eliza," he said, then leaned closer, lips pressing against her. Soft at first, a question, then more urgently as she responded, a hand snaking around his neck and holding him close. He twisted, lifting her slightly to sit on the edge of the stone railing, hands holding her tight to him. Her legs wrapped around his waist, pressing herself against the bulge of his cock, but Rafi wasn't about to hurry things along. He took his time, kissing her slowly, teasing her tongue, learning what she liked. Slowly, one hand drifted down the length of her body, finding the bare skin of her thigh and slipping beneath her dress, delighted to find she wore nothing beneath it.

"So wet," he whispered against her lips. "Is that for me, Eliza?"

"You know it is," she groaned, pressing close as his hand moved, slow and steady pressure building. He had seen her lose herself in the gradual buildup between Hak and Jack. Now he wanted to hear her.

"Tell me what you like," Rafi purred, leaning down to kiss her neck, pushing the dress down off one shoulder enough to reveal one full breast. He sucked the nipple into his mouth, feeling it harden immediately, hand never ceasing his slow rhythm between her legs.

"Yes," she moaned. "That. I like that."

"What do you want, Eliza?" he pushed, breathing on her nipple, hand solid against her lower back to keep her steady on the wall.

"I want you," she whispered, eyes closing as she arched her back, close now.

"Look at me, Eliza," he demanded, voice quiet but powerful, and she obeyed, body tightening as she came. "So beautiful," he said. "How do you want me, Eliza?" he asked after a moment.

Eliza's eyes were dark, her chest and neck flushed with desire. "I want you inside me."

"Soon," he promised, then glanced behind her at the horizon. The sun wasn't close to setting yet. They had time. "Until then, tell me what you want."

Eliza bit her lip, eyes hooded, and she raised an eyebrow at him. "Kiss me," she demanded.

"Always," Rafi said, falling to his knees before her. He set both hands on his thighs, sliding her dress up to reveal her bare sex. "I need to know what you taste like."

Eliza shuddered as he settled his grip on her hips, holding her steady as he set to work, savoring each sound she made as he learned the lines of her body. When her quivering legs gave out, he helped her slide down atop him, and when she leaned down to take him in her mouth, he leaned back, letting her yank his pants free.

"I need to feel you, Eliza," he groaned, lifting her up. He tugged the dress over her head in a swift movement, not caring if anyone saw them. The rooftop was public, but no one came up here but he and Eliza. The stone was hot, though, after a day in the sun. He laid Eliza's dress down, then took off his shirt and made a bigger barrier between her skin and the hot roof. Satisfied that she would be protected, he rolled her to the side, enjoying her wide eyes as he laid her on her back.

"How traditional," she said with a grin, and he climbed between her legs, a hand under her head to hold her tight.

"I'm Egyptian," he reminded her, sheathing himself in one stroke. Her body was tight and warm, and he nearly lost himself in sensation. Taking a deep breath, he pulled away from the edge, wanting to satisfy her in every possible way. "We have many traditions," he said between kisses.

Eliza's eyes fluttered closed as he found a rhythm, and her hand wrapped around his back, nails digging in as he shifted his hips. "There is something to be said about tradition," she gasped, legs wrapping around his hips and dragging him close, body demanding more.

"At least for the first time," he agreed, claiming her mouth with more insistence this time. She made delightful squeaks and squeals as he moved, and Rafi enjoyed finding new ways to elicit different sounds. When she opened her eyes, hand gripping the back of his head, and bit his lip, he let himself go, finally claiming his Eliza at long last.

Later, they lay on the rooftop together, the sun no longer baking them from above but the roof still warm beneath the layer of discarded clothing. Eliza rested at Rafi's side, her head cradled on his chest, and he played idly with her hair, letting the sound of the city settling down for the evening wash over them both.

Eliza grunted, then shifted her body, lifting her hip and reaching beneath her to drag out what ended up being Rafi's pants. "What is in here?" she asked, tossing them across his thighs. "It's been digging into my hip."

Rafi laughed, then reached down to pull the object free from his pocket. It was the magical totem, the scarab, except he'd had it made into a bracelet, the links just big enough for Eliza's wrist. He had imagined her wearing it, the protection just enough to keep her safe, but he couldn't find the right time to give it to her.

Or explain what it meant if she chose to wear it.

"Rafi, why do you have a bracelet in your pocket?" Eliza lifted it, holding the length out so it dangled above his chest. "Too small for your wrist." She twisted her head, raising an eyebrow. "Something you want to tell me?"

Rafi sat up on his elbows, moving Eliza as he did so, and she sat next to him, the bracelet still trailing from her fingers. "The scarab is for protection," he began. "The one who wears it is safe from those who would harm them." He took an end of the bracelet, then met her eye as he pulled her hand forward. "Would you wear it?"

"I'll take any protection I can get," Eliza said, tilting her head, "but I think there's more to it than that." She released her end of the bracelet, watching as Rafi sat the rest of the way up. "What does this mean … to you?"

Rafi held it up, the silver links catching the last of the afternoon sun. He pointed to the small circle next to the scarab. "This circle is empty." He paused, taking a deep breath, then continued, baring himself to her. "For now. If someday you wanted … more, I would attach another link here … to a ring. But this bracelet is a promise, perhaps, a consideration of something more. A possibility."

Eliza's face was very still. "Rafi, are you fucking asking me to marry you?"

Would it be so bad? He didn't say the words aloud, her expression telling him everything he needed to know about what her response to that would be. "I know I am not the only one for you, Elizabeth," he said carefully. "I would not ask you to give anything up. I am asking that you consider me for something more than a good time."

She narrowed her eyes at him, skeptical now. "How long have you had this?"

"I've had the scarab for years. It has kept me safe many times."

"And the bracelet?" she pushed.

"Recently," he admitted. "I knew it was always for you, and when you asked me to stay, I thought maybe there was a chance you might…"

"Might what?" she demanded.

"Might want me," he finished lamely.

Eliza shook her head, then ran both hands through her disheveled hair. "Obviously I want you," she told him. "I haven't come so hard in days—and never from missionary. You are full of surprises, Rafi Sabbagh." She took the bracelet from him, studying it. "So if you're not proposing, then this is … what? A promise bracelet?"

Rafi nodded.

"Does it have a name?"

Rafi grimaced, but he wasn't going to lie to her. Not anymore. "As is, it's a bracelet. With the ring, it's sometimes called a slave bracelet."

Eliza scoffed. "That's a terrible name."

"It's also called a harem bracelet," Rafi added quickly, thinking of her other men.

"Now that seems more appropriate," Eliza said, then held her wrist out to him, one finger holding the end of the bracelet. "Put it on me, Rafi."

Rafi's heart thudded hard in his chest. "You are accepting me?"

Eliza nodded. "I'm accepting the promise of you," she corrected. She leaned in to give him a quick kiss, which Rafi turned into a long kiss. "Besides," she said when he released her, "I want you to stick around when all of this is over. You're still my best friend, and now my lover. You're not getting rid of me that easily."

Rafi smiled at her, heart soaring, then quickly clasped the bracelet in place.

Eliza stared at it, then gave him a brilliant smile. "Thank you," she said. "For the protection, and the promise," her chest reddened as her gaze flicked down to his cock lying soft against his belly, "and the multiple orgasms."

"I look forward to many more," Rafi said, wishing violently that they didn't have to go anywhere tonight, that he could carry her over his shoulder like Hak had, throw her on the small bed, and watch as all three men made love to her like the goddess she was. Eliza's eyes flitted again to his lips, and he wondered if she had the same idea.

He sighed, crouching forward to tug her dress out from beneath his back. If they didn't leave now, he wouldn't have the strength to later. Besides, the sex had done him more than just the wonder of Eliza's body. His mind was clear, and the start of a plan for the evening was forming. He helped Eliza to her feet, watching as the dress covered her naked curves, then stepped into his pants. He tugged on his shirt and attempted to straighten his hair, and gave up to follow her down the steep stairs back to her apartment.

The bracelet jangled softly on her wrist as she walked.

Now, Rafi thought, *I just have to figure out how to explain to Naur Salem that I gave her engagement gift to another woman.*

A problem for another day.

Chapter 39

Jack Manning sat in Rafi's modest four-door sedan, staring out the windshield to the club door he could see at the end of the block. A handful of hopefuls still waited in line, though he had watched Rafi and Eliza skip the line and enter almost a half hour before.

He hadn't agreed with Rafi's plan when he and Eliza strolled back into her apartment—their linked hands evidence that *his* Eliza had picked up yet another lover.

Not my Eliza, he corrected himself.

Rafi looked more relaxed than Jack had ever seen the man, his "secret" adoration of Eliza fully bloomed now into obvious affection. Jack had to bite his tongue and let him finish explaining how tonight would go down.

"Eliza and I will go inside," Rafi announced, giving both Hak and Jack an appraising look. "You two both scream security and military. No way Valdano will let you in—and if he did, he'd watch you like a hawk the entire time." He frowned but added, "We want his attention, but not like that. He needs to see us as independent parties interested in seeing one of his possessions—not trained security there to force his hand, intimidate him, or steal from him."

Jack had wanted to argue, but he saw the acceptance on Hak's face, and he knew Rafi was right—though it galled him to admit it.

One Mummy to Go, Please!

"So you're going to take Eliza into a gangster's lair without any protection at all?" Jack tried, knowing it was useless.

"She will not be unprotected," Rafi insisted. "I may not be trained in the same way you are, but I have other skills—some that will be useful when we speak to Valdano."

"What's the plan, then? You just ask him nicely to give over a valuable book in his collection?" he asked, leaning back against the couch cushions and giving them his best judgmental stare.

"We're not keeping it," Eliza said, glancing at Rafi. "Right?" As she spoke, she moved her hand, and Jack noticed she wore a new bracelet, a scarab connected to silver links on each side. There was an empty circle dangling from the top of the scarab, designed to connect to another chain that would eventually connect to a ring on her finger. Jack had seen those bracelets before—on married women.

What the actual fuck? He wanted to say something, but he bit his tongue, not wanting to let anyone know how much he hated being part of a harem.

Rafi shrugged at the question, seeming not to notice Jack's shifting mood. "If the ceremony in the book frees the creature, we should be able to return it as soon as we finish using it."

"Do you think Valdano knows what's in the book?" Hak asked then. "Is he interested in the occult?"

"Not that I know of," Rafi explained. "Valdano collects all manner of things—books seem to be something he gathers on behalf of his wife Beatrice."

"Will she be willing to let it go?" Eliza asked with a frown, her other hand idly rubbing the new bracelet the same way Jack would spin a new ring if he wore jewelry.

"Valdano isn't the type of man who cares what his wife thinks," Rafi said. "He's a powerful, dangerous man who takes what he wants. He will respond to power."

"And you don't want us to come with you?" Jack asked, his meaning clear, unable to stop the judgment in his tone. Eliza narrowed her eyes at him but said nothing.

Rafi shook his head, the insult sliding off him, still seemingly riding the high from being in Eliza's arms. "There are different kinds of power," Rafi had said.

Hak gave Jack a look, a superior telling his subordinate to stand down.

Fine, Jack thought. Hak may not be his direct employer, but he ran Shogun Security, and Jack didn't want to risk his future there. Charles *wouldn't always be there to bankroll him. He needed to have something lined up when this contract ended.*

So now he found himself sitting in Rafi's boring car that lacked air conditioning, windows cracked just enough to let in the hot night air, waiting for them to come outside. Hak had taken his motorcycle (which didn't blend in at all, Jack had argued, to no avail) and parked around the back in the alley, able to catch them if something went wrong, and they had to flee through a back door.

Killing time, Jack pulled out his phone, opening up his photos to stare at a picture he had taken of Eliza. She was smiling at him through the window of her food truck, the breeze blowing the tendrils back and her blue eyes shining in the afternoon sun. His Eliza, he thought, before ... everyone else.

Jack knew that he was deluding himself, that a girl who had so quickly taken on multiple lovers was no stranger to the practice. She had never truly been his alone.

And now that she wore that bracelet...

He had to find out what it meant. She hadn't said anything about cutting the rest of them off. She still smiled prettily at all three men, eyes ever eager for the next tryst.

She still wants me. Yeah, he answered himself, *because you're convenient. And easy.* Jack had never thought he'd mind being thought of as easy, but here he was, pining over a girl who needed more than he alone could give her.

In fact, the more he thought about it, he wondered how much of her reason for hooking up with him at all was because of the damn mummy. That night in the tomb had frightened her, and he'd been a very convenient distraction.

Now he was just one distraction among many.

Frowning, he decided he still had one way to get her attention. Glancing around to make sure no one was near the car, he reached down and slid the seat back, giving himself more room between his body and the steering wheel. His hands found his belt, and he quickly opened his pants, freeing his cock. A few pumps and the thought of Eliza made him hard, and he fumbled one-handed with the phone, opening the camera app. It took a few different shots to find the angle he wanted, but he finally had the picture he wanted. He tucked his cock away, though it still tented his pants, then put both hands on the phone, opening the messaging app.

One Mummy to Go, Please!

[Jack: Thinking of you, sweetheart.]

[Jack: <dick pic.png>]

    He set the phone aside, giving her time to reply, knowing she was probably helping Rafi get the book. No doubt her contribution was looking adorably empty as her mind catalogued every detail of the encounter. Eliza knew how to play dumb when it suited her, but Jack knew she was far from it.
    The phone buzzed, and Jack snatched it from the seat.

[Eliza: Ooh, baby. Mama wants more!]

    Jack laughed, unzipping his pants and taking a few more pictures, sending them to Eliza in a row. Another minute passed, and then his phone buzzed again.

[Eliza: More, more!]

    Jack chuckled, the sound escaping as he continued to take more pictures.
    I knew it, he thought. *She's bored to tears being with Rafi. She's my dirty girl—she loves my cock.*
    She misses me.
    Smiling, he glanced around again, seeing that the line had moved slightly—the three hot girls at the front replaced by two older, more sophisticated women. Biting his lip, he decided that a few minutes wouldn't hurt.
    His hand moved on his cock, imagining Eliza's face as she watched him, lips opening in a pout, eager to take him in her mouth.
    At least I still have this.

Chapter 40

It was easy to spot Giuseppe Valdano.
He didn't sit at a booth so much as occupy it. Despite signs in English and Arabic that banned smoking, Valdano openly smoked a cigar; purplish smoke wafted around his head like an aura. It was his club, after all. He was surrounded by a handful of men who would make even Jack Manning look waifish. Holsters bulged beneath their sport coats, and they wore mirrored sunglasses, reflecting the dark club and its shadowy patrons.

Rafi selected a booth kitty-corner to Valdano's, steering Eliza there with a firm hand upon the small of her back. It was difficult to talk over the music, so they coordinated by touch alone. On stage, a woman in a diamond-encrusted bra danced with scarves, the silk seeming to float around her. Pound notes, dollar bills, and other forms of foreign currency littered the stage, and she bent to pick it up, tucking it into her cleavage.

As Eliza slid into a booth, the vinyl sticking to her legs, she couldn't help but stare at their target. Valdano was a tall, thin man, a far cry from the mobsters she'd seen in movies. He couldn't have been older than mid-forties, with unblemished skin and thick, glossy hair. He wore a well-tailored tweed suit, the jacket folded neatly over the back of the booth. The sleeves were rolled up to his elbows, revealing ropy forearms. Despite the casual atmosphere, he wore a waistcoat, a thin gold chain dangling between his buttonhole and his pocket.

"Who wears a pocket watch in 2023?" Eliza murmured out of the corner of her mouth.

"People who can afford one." Rafi was on edge, his jaw a right angle. "That watch is probably worth 5,000 pounds."

"You think?" Eliza's eyebrows rose. "Five thousand?"

"Minimum."

Before Eliza could speculate about the cost of his suit, a man stepped out from behind the heavy velvet curtain on stage. "Next up," he said, raising his hands as if about to conduct an orchestra, "put your hands together for Miss Tiana!" He drew out the name until his face turned red: *Teeeeee-ana!*

The lights dimmed, save for a lone spotlight at center stage. As the first notes of a ballad played through the pitchy speaker, a long shapely leg slid through the gap between the curtains. Someone wolf-whistled.

The woman slinking on stage was tall and comely, her face covered with a gauzy veil. While the ballad was slow and moody, she was anything but subdued. Her belly rolled, making her belly button ring sparkle.

An overzealous man rose from his seat, waving a 100-pound note. She knelt so that he could tuck it between her breasts. *Wait*, Eliza thought. *Did she just take something out of that man's pocket?* Surely, Eliza had imagined it. That would be far too brazen, especially with all of the concealed weapons.

Tiana gyrated across the stage, and as the chorus swelled, she leaped from the stage onto the nearest table. She wobbled when she landed but didn't fall. She took short, mincing steps through the patrons' dinner spread, knocking over a platter of gibnah. *"Sor—asif jidana!"* she said huskily.

The belly dancer vaulted onto another table, nearly landing in an older gentleman's lap. She bent to pick up his drink, downing the last of it. With her crimson lipstick adorning the rim, she handed it to him. "A kiss," she mewled, "just for you."

Tiana set her sights on Rafi and Eliza's table. Rafi shook his head vigorously, but Tiana seemed to be a woman on a mission. She jumped, her chunky heels clattering like horses' hooves. Slack-jawed, Rafi stared up at her as she violently rotated her hips, making the gold coins on her belt jangle.

Eliza found herself staring at the belly dancer's hip. Her harem pants had slipped down, revealing a tattoo of a begonia. *Where have I seen that before?* A memory itched at the back of her mind, but she couldn't quite grab a hold of it.

Tiana accepted an Egyptian pound from Rafi and blew him a kiss. When she hopped over onto Valdano's table, Rafi grasped Eliza's arm. "She took my ring!"

Sure enough, the ring that had once been on Rafi's pointer finger was gone, leaving only a pale shadow on his skin. "She took that guy's wallet too!" Eliza whispered, pulling Rafi close so they didn't alert any other guests.

Giuseppe Valdano didn't seem to appreciate the belly dancer's attention. He scowled as Tiana crawled across the tabletop, her performance more burlesque than belly dance. As the song ended, she pressed her lips against Valdano's, and the crowd burst into frenzied applause.

A pop song pulsed through the speakers, and a new dancer took the stage. But Eliza and Rafi only had eyes for Tiana.

Valdano violently pushed the woman away, her cherry-red lipstick smeared across his mouth. "Not here," he snarled. "Are you fucking crazy?"

"It's just for the show, sweetheart," the belly dancer chuckled. "No one batted an eye." She slid off the table and readjusted her costume.

"Beatrice will rip your hair out," Valdano replied coolly.

"Take a number, honey," Tiana said haughtily. She flipped her long hair over her shoulder. "Are you still going to take me out later, Daddy? Baby needs a new Birkin."

Giuseppe scrubbed at his face with his hands. "Just get out of here, Tee."

"Yeah, yeah, I'm going. You're no fun when Beezus is in town.'" The belly dancer sashayed toward the stage door as she counted the bills in her brassiere.

Eliza rose to follow her.

"Where are you going?" Rafi asked, alarmed.

"I'm getting your ring. Stay here and watch Valdano," Eliza shot back.

In the busy club, Tiana didn't notice her pursuer, nor did she notice that the stage door stayed open for a hair longer than usual after she passed through it. The dancer hummed to herself, shuffling the sweat-dampened cash.

"Hey!" Eliza called. As she approached, Tiana's phone went off, a series of message notifications that echoed the one set on Eliza's phone.

"No autographs please!" Tiana's heels clicked on the poured cement floor as she moved away, tucking the phone against her boobs.

Eliza scoffed. "You took my friend's ring!"

Tiana whirled. "Listen, Linda, I didn't steal a goddamn thing from anyone! If your 'friend' lost anything, he should take it up with the bouncers."

Eliza froze. *Linda*. The nagging feeling that she knew Tiana became an alarm bell clanging inside her skull. "Teo?!"

Tiana's perfectly groomed eyebrow quirked. "Who's asking?" Her voice dropped an octave.

"It's me. Eliza. We met in Barcelona."

"You'll have to be more specific, honey. I jet set every weekend to all sorts of tropical locales. Punta Cana, the Maldives, Bali… Tampa."

"You stole my passport." Eliza still had nightmares about the meandering security line at El Prat Airport, drug-sniffing dogs flanking the travelers. She was a nervous flyer and had forgotten to take a Klonopin beforehand. She'd nearly made it to the x-ray scanner when she realized her passport wasn't in her jacket pocket. Instead, she'd found an empty condom wrapper.

Recognition spread across Tiana—Teo's—face. "Elizabeth Marie Cunningham, born April 24, 1995, birthplace—"

"Yeah," Eliza interrupted. "That's me." He rattled it off like a schoolyard rhyme, which somehow made it feel more invasive. It was to the same melody he'd hummed earlier when he thought no one had been around to overhear.

"And how's your friend, the little strumpet … Lily?"

Poppy and Teo had become fast friends and even faster enemies during their brief stay in Barcelona.

"Poppy." Exasperated, Eliza snatched off the belly dancer's wig, revealing damp dark hair beneath an opaque wig cap. "I see you are taking the grift to new heights."

Teo removed his veil, revealing a narrow nose and a broad grin. "There's only one way to go, and that's up, baby." There was a bit of lipstick on his teeth.

"Give me back my friend's ring, Teo Cardoza. Now."

Teo scooped a handful of items out of his brassiere: a wallet, Rafi's ring, and a nondescript keycard with a magnetic strip. "You can have the stupid ring. It looks like it came from a Cracker Jack box anyway. Tacky."

Eliza slipped it onto her thumb for safekeeping. It was still warm from Rafi's skin—or perhaps Teo's cleavage. "What's the keycard for?" she asked.

"Oh, someone is feeling congenial. Are we bosom buddies now, Linda?" Teo pulled off his wig cap, scratching at his scalp with his coffin-shaped talons. Eliza couldn't help but think of sneaking into the hotel pool after dark, running her fingers through that luscious curly hair.

"Why were you flirting with Valdano?" Eliza pressed. "C'mon Teo, this is really important. I'm working on something too."

That piqued Teo's interest. "Oh? When we met, you were such a prude. That is, 'til you had a few mojitos."

"He has something I want," Eliza offered, hoping the shark would take the bait. But the shark was far more familiar with the water they were swimming in.

"Giuseppe has something everyone wants. He's one of the richest and most well-connected men in Cairo. Not to mention his dick is this big." Teo held up his hands to demonstrate, but Eliza slapped them away.

"God, can you be serious for five minutes?" She glanced back toward the stage door, terrified that Rafi would get into trouble without her. Or worse, that he'd follow her, and she'd have to contend with another man she'd slept with, though it had been years. Eons.

"I am being deadly serious. I'd never joke about something like that. That's why I tell everyone how tight you—"

"I'm looking for a book," Eliza relented, if only to get him to shut up. "The Book of Heka. It's old, full of hieroglyphics…"

Teo raised an eyebrow, considering. "Giuseppe has a whole lot of old books. Some of the girls say he reads them passages after they screw, like he's some kind of… of… Casanova. I can't relate. He can't talk after I'm done with him."

Eliza couldn't help the laugh that escaped. *Same old Teo.* "I showed you mine, now you show me yours. What are you trying to get with that keycard?"

Teo licked his lips. "Since we're talking larceny, there's a diadem in Giuseppe's collection. It's worth millions on the black market. That's 'change your life' money, Linda."

Suddenly, gunfire erupted on the other side of the stage door. "Where is my fucking keycard?!" Valdano boomed. Someone screamed.

After a moment, Rafi burst through the door.

Eliza grabbed Teo's wrist. "Tee, listen to me: we can help each other. Besides, you owe me."

Teo sighed. "C'mon, I know a quicker way out of here…"

Chapter 41

Jack had sent another batch of salacious images, but Eliza hadn't responded. He assumed things were heating up inside the club, and she had to focus on the task on hand. Heaving a sigh, he put his clothing to bits, then got his head back in the game.

He could lure her away later that night and have his way with her. Based on the thirsty texts they'd exchanged, she had to be up for it. His girl was as eager as he was.

Jack shook his head, knowing he was way too distracted. This job had gone from bad to worse—and with his employer's new demands, Jack wasn't sure how he would work everything out.

I'll keep her safe, he reminded himself. *That's the primary mission. Everything else is secondary—even that damn book Charles is after.* He sighed. The focus had been on the artifacts—but ever since the book had come up, it seemed like everyone wanted to get their hands on a copy. *Maybe I should read this one before handing it over.* He debated, thinking of the timeframe. If there was time. His hieratic was definitely rusty.

Perhaps Eliza would read it with him.

He frowned, eyes scanning his surroundings again. The line had dwindled, and only a few people lingered near the door now, most casually chatting with the bouncer, accepting that they weren't getting in tonight but no doubt laying groundwork for a better reception next time. He had seen the

bouncer wander away from the door at least twice, replaced by a small stout body in the doorway, the beefy form disappearing down the nearby alley with a motivated clubgoer.

At least they didn't care about books tonight.

Jack was about to text Eliza again, this time on a serious note to see how things were going, but as he picked up his phone, a person came running out of the club.

For a second, Jack was sure it was Eliza, but then he focused, spotting a blonde in high heels awkwardly sprinting down the street, followed by a burst of bodies. He could hear yelling, the sound of unmistakable gunfire, and then screaming. The bouncer and his latest companion stumbled around the corner, the bouncer struggling to button his pants, and then he was pulling people away from the door, hustling them out of the way so more people could escape.

"Fuck," Jack grunted, jamming the car into reverse and then drive, jetting out into the street to park across from the door.

A fight at a Valdano club wasn't unheard of. There was no reason to assume Eliza had something to do with it. It could just be rotten timing.

Doubt it, though. Eliza is a trouble magnet.

A few more clubbers spilled out, aided by the bouncer, and small groups began running up and down the street. A few ran across the street in front of his car, one woman dragging what must be her drunk companion and the two of them bouncing off his hood before continuing to flee down the opposite side of the street.

"Where are you?" he hissed, keen eyes scanning the crowd, waiting for Eliza's blonde hair. He didn't hear the sirens yet, but with this much commotion, they couldn't be far away.

He picked up the phone again, not sure if Eliza would even hear it ring in the noise, but then a familiar body ran to the passenger door, flinging it open.

Jack stared at Rafi. "Where is Eliza?" he demanded.

"We were separated," Rafi told him. "Drive."

"I'm not leaving her here!" Jack insisted.

"Nor am I," Rafi said, still way too calm for the situation. "She went out the back with a friend. Hak is picking her up." Rafi put a comforting hand on Jack's shoulder. "She's fine."

"Another friend?" Jack spat, and he was already driving away before he realized he had said it out loud. Rafi had a hand recessed hard against the roof, holding himself in place as Jack took a corner way too fast, but the lawyer still managed to give him a long assessing look.

"Our Eliza has many friends," Rafi said, voice still calm despite the corded steel of his muscles bracing himself.

"That she does," Jack muttered. "You sure Hak has her?"

"If you would stop driving like an American, I could use my phone to call her," Rafi admonished, and Jack slowed his erratic pace. They were two blocks away now, the crowd and gunfire behind them.

"What happened?" Jack demanded as Rafi pulled out his phone and called Eliza. Jack could hear the ringing, but she didn't answer.

"An enterprising belly dancer decided to get too friendly with Valdano," Rafi explained, brow furrowing as the call went to voicemail. He hung up, about to redial, but then his phone pinged with a message. He cocked his head, clearly confused.

"What?" Jack asked, driving more normally now but still unable to quell the fear that Eliza was still in trouble. They approached a red light, and Jack stopped, turning to face Rafi. The lawyer held the phone out to Jack, who read the message with matching confusion.

[Eliza: New Phone. Who dis?]

"What game is she playing?" Rafi muttered.

Jack pulled his phone free, then thrust it at Rafi as the light changed. "Use mine."

"But she didn't answer—"

"She didn't answer you. Maybe she'll answer me," Jack suggested, and he didn't miss the dirty look the lawyer turned his way.

"Of course," Rafi said coolly, swiping up to turn Jack's phone on. His nimble fingers found Eliza's number, but again, the phone just rang. After another voicemail, Rafi opened Jack's messaging app and tapped Eliza's name.

"Oh my," he said, and his voice showed more emotion than he had during the escape, gunfire, and wild driving.

"Did she send something?" Jack asked, glancing over but not wanting to look away from the road too much.

"You've been busy," Rafi commented, tilting the phone so Jack could see the history of pictures he'd sent.

"It's boring in the car," Jack defended, voice quiet under the weight of Rafi's judgment.

"Clearly," Rafi said. He skimmed the pictures, frowned, then slid to the bottom, typing a quick message. The phone pinged back immediately, and

Rafi nodded. "She says she's fine." Another ping, and his brow furrowed. "And she's gagging for it," he read slowly. Another ping, and then, "And so are you?" The last was a question, and as they stopped at another red light, Jack snatched the phone, reading the last few exchanges.

"What the hell?" he asked. He gave Rafi a hard look. "Call Hak. Now."

"Already on it," Rafi told him, phone already ringing.

"I got her," Hak's voice answered on the first ring. Jack could hear the whine of the motorcycle in the background, the sound muffled by Hak's helmet. "Heading to the rendezvous point."

"Salem," Rafi said, then hung up. "See?" He turned to Jack. "She's fine."

Jack handed Rafi his phone when it pinged yet again. "How is she texting while on the back of Hak's bike?" he wondered.

Rafi opened the newest message, then a small chuckle escaped.

"What?" Jack demanded, hating to be driving when so many important things were happening. Yet another way he was on the outside, excluded.

They were nearing Eliza's street now, and Jack slowed down, pulling into an amazing spot literally outside her doorway. "What?" he repeated. "What's going on?"

"I feel like I should be asking you that," Rafi said, turning the phone so Jack could see the newest message: a close up shot of a large dick.

Jack blanched. "That's … not mine," he managed.

Rafi laughed. "I know." At Jack's embarrassed expression, Rafi added, "I've seen you and Hak with Eliza." He glanced at the phone again, considering the image. "I'd guess that someone has Eliza's phone and has been having some fun with us." He paused, then added, "Unless there have been dramatic changes I am unaware of in the last few hours."

Jack snatched the phone back, turning it off and jamming it in his pocket. Rafi chuckled again, the entire exchange striking the lawyer as funny. *Who knew the bastard had a sense of humor at all?*

Jack turned off the car and followed Rafi out, both of them waiting on the street for Hak and Eliza to arrive. Staring at the sidewalk, Jack felt like his phone was burning a hole in his pocket.

Whose fucking dick is that?

Chapter 42

In the bathtub, tempered by two locked doors, Teo could hardly hear the frantic banging of the hotel concierge outside of his suite. His credit card—or rather, the credit card he had been *borrowing*—must have declined. He'd expected it, of course, but he had hoped he would have time for skincare. Maybe a massage at the spa ("Just charge it to the room, honey!"). In retrospect, the Four Seasons—with its E£13,000 per night price tag—may have been a bad idea. In his experience, cheaper was better. A few pounds here and there may go unnoticed and keep the card from being reported stolen.

But he deserved it. He'd done a good deed getting Eliza and her friend out of the Lair of Isis.

He sank down until the bubbles tickled his chin and reached for the glass of complementary champagne. The flute sweated on the porcelain rim alongside Eliza's battered iPhone 11. Teo was no Steve Jobs, but he knew it wasn't worth more than a sneeze. Except this one belonged to his former flame.

Rather, a spark. They'd only shared a night together. She'd been a college student in an Oxford blue sweater, and he was a twenty-something, dressed head-to-toe in shoplifted items from the Passeig De Gracia. They ran into each other at the Case Mila, which he'd found ugly with its rugged gray exterior and chimneys that reminded him of a ram's horns. She and her friend had asked him where the nearest cafe was, mistaking him for a

local. That night, they'd partied at Macarena Club and fucked in her hotel, and he'd left with the contents of her purse as a souvenir.

Teo downed the glass of bubbly and set it aside just as the landline in the room started to ring. He ignored it, picking up Eliza's phone with damp hands. Teo didn't believe in coincidences, and her lock screen proved that. It was a photo of the various entry stamps in her passport, with SPAIN in the very center. "Barcelona," he murmured to himself.

None of this was coincidence—this was kismet.

Teo scrolled through the messages with the man called Jack M., admiring the photos of his manhood. It was a pretty cock, as far as cocks went, and Teo had seen plenty. Then, he typed.

[Teo: Where am I meeting you, Linda?]

It only took a few minutes for Eliza to respond. She had been waiting for him. Had she waited for him that morning in her hotel room, stretching beneath those silky sheets, her body sore from all of the positions he'd twisted her into? Had she and Poppy had a difficult time looking at one another afterward because he'd made sure to satisfy them both?

[Eliza: Java, 9 a.m.]

[Teo: See you there, *mi vida*. Make sure you come alone… your hunky friends will be a distraction.]

Reluctantly, Teo climbed out of the bath, dripping water onto the tile. The towels were plush, and there was a bathrobe besides, embroidered with the Four Seasons' logo. He put it on and cinched the waist, wiping the steam off the vanity. He'd gotten a pimple overnight, right in the crease between his nostril and cheek. Frowning, he squeezed it, but it didn't budge. It was probably because of all the stress.

He really could have used that massage.

Teo selected a table near the window, the sun warming his face. He ordered coffee and was disappointed to find it was served in the tiniest teacup he'd

ever seen. Gingerly pinching the delicate handle between his thumb and pointer finger, he took a measured sip.

"You look ridiculous," Eliza said, pulling up a chair. Her expression was sour, as though she'd sucked on a lemon. "Give me my phone." She plopped into the chair and the table rattled.

"In a minute," Teo said, "we should catch up first." Her frown deepened.

The waitress trotted over, unaware of the tension crackling between them. "Would you like some coffee too?" she asked brightly, her ponytail bobbing.

"Sure," Eliza relented. She clearly needed it, her eyes hollow and her cheeks sucked in. She was clearly under a lot of stress. Teo couldn't blame her—she was not cut out for the life it seemed she was leading, what with all the running and shootouts. She was a pampered girl, a silver spoon firmly jammed between her jaws. It was what made her an easy mark.

"Can I get any food for you?" the waitress pressed.

"Absolutely." Teo grinned. "Though, I can't decide between pancakes or waffles. How about a waffle for me and a stack of pancakes for my friend here?"

"My pleasure," the waitress said, scribbling on her pad. "I'll have that out to you in a few minutes."

As soon as she was out of earshot, Eliza held out her hand. "My phone."

Teo sighed and passed it over. "You know, that Jack guy is really into you. I sent his pics to my phone, so be sure to thank him for those."

"How did you get into my phone anyway?" Eliza tapped into and out of a few apps, presumably to see what he'd meddled in.

"Well, it's very easy when the password is your birthday."

"How do you know my birthd—oh, right. My passport." Her brow furrowed as she placed her phone face down on the table, right beside her silverware. "Do you know what a pain it was to get a replacement?"

Eliza's coffee came, served in an identical doll-sized cup. "This place is a little hoity-toity, even for you," Teo remarked. "I can't wait to see what doily my waffle is served on."

"It's close to my apartment." Eliza poured creamer into her cup, nearly causing the coffee to overflow into her saucer. "Can we talk about business?"

"Sure, if that's what you'd like. It just feels like sucking dick before learning someone's name."

"That doesn't seem like something you'd necessarily be opposed to."

Their food arrived, and Teo dug into his waffle. He made Eliza wait while he popped a wedge into his mouth and let out an exaggerated groan.

His eyes rolled in ecstasy. "Linda, you must try this. It's perfect: crispy on the outside, soft on the inside… the melted butter, my god!"

Eliza didn't touch her pancakes, her hands in her lap. The pat of butter seeped into the pancake, making it soggy. "What exactly does the keycard open?"

Teo put down his knife and fork. "God, you're no fun. Rumor has it, there's a safe onboard his superyacht—that's where the diadem is. Maybe that Book of Becca you're looking for too. This keycard is supposed to open it. In my opinion, that's not very secure. He should have used a retina scanner…"

"Book of *Heka*," she corrected him automatically. "If I help you, can you help me get the book?"

"What can you help me with? I work alone. Adding a partner makes things complicated and more conspicuous."

"I have a … team, I guess you could call them. Resources. This can't be your only target, right? The Teo I know wouldn't put all of his eggs in one basket."

Teo wasn't sure Eliza knew him all that well. She'd only met a version of him, and he couldn't quite recall which version that had been. "Is one of those resources Jack? I haven't seen his credentials, but his cock seems like resume enough."

"Please be serious."

"I am deadly serious. In truth, the diadem is my only job. Someone has been hitting all of the museums and the whole scene has been hot." At her quizzical expression, he clarified. "Police. Lots of them. But the police won't know about a theft on Giuseppe Valdano's yacht because he won't tell them. He doesn't want them sniffing around anymore than I do." Teo reached across the table to spear a pancake off the stack and folded the whole thing into his mouth.

Eliza averted her eyes as he chewed. "What if I told you that I knew the man who was robbing all of the museums? And what if I told you that helping me get that book would make him stop?"

That intrigued him. "Oh?"

"And what if I told you he was a reanimated mummy?"

"Now you have my attention, Linda."

Chapter 43

"Let me get this straight, Linda," Teo said, staring at each of Eliza's men in turn. He continued, lifting a finger as he made each point. "You accidentally summoned an ancient mummy with your mom's necklace, but now that mummy is your friend, and you want to use some book to free him from whoever is controlling him." He sighed, then gestured with the three fingers at Jack, Hak, and Rafi. "And this is your crew?"

"They're my ... friends," Eliza managed.

"I am one of your friends," Teo said, gaze dropping flirtatiously as he stared at Jack in particular. "Maybe we can all get better acquainted before we embark on this suicide mission." Jack's neck reddened, and he looked away.

"It's not a suicide mission," Eliza insisted yet again.

"You want to steal from Giuseppe Valdano with this motley crew." He rolled his eyes, then pointed at Rafi. "Government. Too clean." He moved to Hak. "Clearly mercenary. He'll never get on the dock." Finally, he gave Jack a smirk. "Now this one is definitely a good time but still too rough around the edges. Not that I would mind polishing some of those edges."

Jack cleared his throat and looked away, red continuing to creep up his neck. Eliza frowned, wondering what she had missed. She didn't have time to wonder about it at the moment.

"Look," she said, "we're all in this. We're going in there, with or without you."

Teo scoffed. "Without me, Linda, you will fail."

"Then help us. Help me." She hesitated then added, "Look, if we can use the book to free Milf, your competition goes away. You can go back to being top dog thief or whatever it is you're up to these days."

Teo pursed his lips. "I do need to get into that safe," he admitted. "And Beezus isn't my biggest fan." He paused, adding, "Well, she's not Tiana's biggest fan." He raised an eyebrow. "Teo, though, hasn't been spotted in these parts yet."

"Beezus?" Eliza echoed, then realization caught up. "You mean Valdano's girlfriend, Beatrice."

"Not girlfriend, Linda. Wife. A girlfriend would have left long ago. Many have come and gone."

"Why does she stay?" Eliza asked. "If he's unfaithful...?" She noticed Jack's expression as he looked at her, then quickly looked away.

"He wasn't always that way, especially not when they first got married," Rafi offered, joining the conversation. "I understand they were very much in love at the start."

"So he became an asshole over time?" Eliza asked.

"Beezus isn't a saint herself, Linda," Teo interjected. "She may be a bitch about Giuseppe, but she's far from the dutiful wife these days."

"I guess people really change," Eliza mused, wondering what she would do if the man she loved and married changed like that. Then she caught herself. *Ha! Married. As if I would ever do that and tie myself to one person.* She glanced around the room at all the men. *No way I am giving this up.*

Her gaze landed on Teo.

"And some people don't," she continued. "So what's it going to be, Teo? You in with us?"

Teo frowned, then tilted his head and gave Jack a direct stare that made Eliza recall those few hot nights in Barcelona. "I might be persuaded," he began, "but I have a little proposition for you first. Call it a ... test. " His gaze shifted, taking in Rafi and Hak as well. "For all of you."

"What?" Eliza asked.

"Well, you said these were your guys, right?"

Eliza flushed at the direct question. Sure, she had started thinking of them that way, but no one had said it outright. "I..."

One Mummy to Go, Please!

"I know that you're dedicated to this little cause of yours, obviously because this mummy must have an amazing cock if you are managing to fit him in here—"

Eliza laughed, but the sound came out as a cough, and Rafi cleared his throat. Hak simply stared at Teo, waiting for the punchline he must be expecting, and Jack's red face grew even redder as he tried to pretend his pants weren't tenting.

"It's your little harem here that I'm not sure of, Linda. How dedicated are they to freeing your pharaoh? If I'm going up against Valdano all bold like this, I need assurances that they won't cut and run at the first sign of trouble." He glanced at Rafi. "I mean, he did leave you at the club."

"He left me with Hak!" Eliza defended, recalling Rafi shoving her into Teo's arms as the hallway flooded with bodies. She could see Hak waiting on the street beyond the fire exit. Teo made it sound like Rafi abandoned her to save himself. "I was perfectly safe."

"With me," Teo snapped.

"I had her," Hak said quietly. His voice was soft, no inflection to show how he felt about the conversation at all. Hak did that sometimes, reverted to a near machine when he was absorbed by his work or focused on something specific. Eliza assumed it was the mercenary in him—and as much as it should be disturbing that he could shut himself off like that, it only turned her on more. She liked to see him abandon that flat surface, break free as he lost himself inside her.

"You did," Teo admitted, considering the merc, "and it's not you I'm worried about. You'll finish the job because you don't know how not to." His gaze drifted to Rafi. "And you're so in love with her you can't see straight, so there's no doubt there." He finally made his way back to Jack sitting awkwardly on her couch. "You, though, you're the weak link."

"What—" Jack sputtered, but Teo cut him off.

"Boy, you got issues." He smiled, and Eliza knew that look; she had been on the receiving end of it more than once, but this time his eyes never left Jack as he continued, "I'm not saying I have a problem with issues, but Texas over here has some demons in need of exorcism. I offer my services, of course."

"Uhh," Eliza said, not sure how to respond to that.

He said Rafi loves me!

She forced herself to focus, leaving the observation for another time.

"Not sure where you're going with this, Teo," she said after a silent beat. "What's your proposition?"

"Hey, Texas," Teo said, addressing Jack directly, "why are you here?"

"I'm here for Eliza," Jack said neutrally, but the red flush of his skin had not gone away.

"Aren't we all?" Teo asked. "But you want her all to yourself, no?"

Jack shrugged. "I'm happy with whatever she is willing to share." Eliza wanted to believe him, but deep down, she knew she couldn't.

Teo laughed, a full belly sound that Eliza recalled from those wild days in Barcelona. "No doubt. Keep telling yourself that," he said, then gave Jack a sly smile. "You ever been with another man, Texas?"

Jack's eyes slid to Hak, no doubt recalling the threesome they had shared while Rafi watched. "I mean…" He looked at Eliza next as if asking permission to answer the question.

Teo chuckled as if such things were cute but not to be taken seriously. "I mean with another man, Tex, not just shared a woman. What is this—high school?" He nodded his head, decision made, and he clapped his hands together, standing up and tugging off his shirt, revealing a wiry chest corded with muscles. "Okay, listen, Linda, here's my proposal. He's here because he thinks you're the best thing to ever happen to him. He's not thrilled about sharing you, but he will because he's convinced there's nothing better for him. How about I show him that's simply not true? Then he can feel free to go on his merry way and not put us all in danger when he does eventually bail."

"I'm not going to bail—" Jack began.

At the same time, Eliza asked, "How will you show him that's not true?"

"I'll give him the orgasm of his life," Teo said simply, a wicked grin on his lips. "Believe me, Tex, you've never had your cock sucked until you've had a man's mouth around you."

"I—" Jack stammered, at a loss for words.

"Don't worry," Teo told the others. "I expect he'll need a show to get him started." He glanced at Eliza. "Just take off your shirt already."

"Teo!" Eliza yelped.

"Come on," Teo said, rolling his eyes, "you're all eyefucking one another across the room. I get it—dangerous mission, imminent death—everyone here is dying to get it on before we leave." He pierced Jack with his gaze. "Besides, I know someone who's just *gagging* for it."

Jack bit his lip, recognition of something flashing across his face, and his eyes dropped to Teo's waist, the smooth plane of perfect abs covered in a small trail of dark hair that disappeared below his waistband.

"Yes, yes, darling," Teo said, catching the look, "I'll let you see in person soon enough. But let's start the way most of your porn probably does." He crooked a finger at Eliza. "Linda, your shirt, dear."

Eliza couldn't help herself—she smiled, taking a few lazy steps across the room to where Teo now stood, shirtless. The years hadn't changed that glorious chest. She wondered if he had any new tattoos, recalling the one on his inner thigh that had made her and Poppy howl with laughter. Meeting his gaze boldly, she pulled off her shirt and handed it to him. She heard a soft gasp, but she wasn't sure if it came from Rafi or Hak. Probably Rafi. He was still getting used to her wanton nature.

Teo's gaze dipped to her bare breasts. "Oh, Linda," he crooned, "how I missed these girls." Instead of leaning down to suck on a nipple as she expected, Teo closed his eyes, focusing like a man on a mission. "Today, however, they aren't for me." He looked over her shoulder to where Jack still sat on the couch. "Next time though…" He growled, then snapped his fingers. "Merc, time to report for duty."

Hak stepped forward, a slight grin on his face, clearly entertained by the situation.

"Let's see," Teo pondered, head tilted as he began pulling his long curly hair out of the ties. "First, she's still wearing too many clothes."

Hak stepped up at once, dropping to his knees before her and sliding her shorts down, revealing her bare skin. He wasted no time, leaning in to press his mouth to her core.

"Someone understands the assignment," Teo said, then shook his head, all that hair free and running riot over his shoulders.

Eliza moaned, then flailed, losing her balance for a moment in the rush of pleasure, but then Rafi was there, supporting her weight as he shifted her body so she faced the couch and Jack. Hak moved with her, never missing a beat, hands squeezing her ass.

She fought to keep her eyes open as she watched Jack. The tent in his pants was undeniable, and he met her eyes. Then Teo dropped to his knees and started a sexy crawl toward the couch. Eliza wanted to watch, but Rafi's mouth was on her neck, and she gasped, melting into his touch. When she next opened her eyes, Jack's pants were open, and Teo's delicate hands were fisting his cock. Jack was biting his lip, watching Eliza, still slightly uncertain about his place in this situation.

Then Teo moved forward, flipping his dark hair to one side as he took Jack in his mouth, and Jack made a sound that Eliza had never heard him

make in all their time together. Eliza smiled, and Teo winked at her, then bent to his work.

Eliza watched in fascination, her pleasure building as Hak and Rafi continued caressing her. The first time she came, Teo paused with a soft chuckle. "Oh no, Tex," he said. "You don't get off that easily." He gave Jack a lazy lick, then gestured for the threesome to continue. "You have to earn it this time. Linda, I know you know how to give a good show. Let's remind Tex here what he's in this for."

At Teo's words, Hak moved, sitting on the floor, and Eliza climbed eagerly atop him, chasing a different kind of pleasure. Hak held her steady as she gestured Rafi closer, tugging his pants down and stroking his cock in time with Hak's steady thrusts. Teo continued teasing Jack, pausing to offer encouragement here and there.

"Now, now, Linda, you have better rhythm than that. Focus, dear." Eliza obeyed, mimicking Teo's motion as she took Rafi in her mouth, both men moving her as one.

"Oh fuck," Jack growled. "You are so hot, sweetheart!"

"You want to come, Tex?" Teo crooned, then resumed his motion, bringing Jack even closer.

"Fuck yes!" Jack yelled, and they all followed him into sweet release.

Chapter 44

"I cannot believe I agreed to this," Eliza snarked, fingers adjusting her boobs in the ridiculous sequined dress yet again. Teo slapped her hand, his voice the high-pitched resonance of Tiana.

"Leave it alone!" he snapped. "Your girls aren't going anywhere in that thing. I won't let them," he promised then stepped ahead of her, confidently striding down the stairs to the boat dock. Eliza didn't reply, too focused on keeping her footing in the spiked high heels as she followed, schooling her expression into the RBF expected of the entertainment.

As they hit the bottom, she tried not to gawk at the jaw-dropping yacht tied at the end of the dock. She counted at least four levels, the white bulk lit by strings of lights, soft party music drifting over the dock. She could see the ship's name, the *Aluza*, painted in curling black letters across the back as they approached. Eliza shivered at the similarity to her own name.

Is Aluza another one of his girlfriends? Eliza wondered, then decided against it. Valdano was married, and it was one thing to fool around. It was quite another to host a party on a boat named after a side piece. Maybe Aluza was his mother's name or something. Besides, his wife was coming to this thing tonight. It was her birthday party.

"Relax," she heard Jack's voice in the borrowed earpiece. "You're doing fine, sweetheart. Just follow Teo."

Eliza

She obeyed, glad to have a target for her nervous energy. She knew it made sense for just her and Teo to go aboard. The guys were watching from a safe distance, monitoring them with binoculars and high-tech gadgets, but she was still all alone in there.

I'm not alone, she reminded herself. *Teo is with me.*
The way he was with you in Barcelona?

She scowled, recalling the endless days spent pacing the embassy, waiting for a new passport to arrive.

This time, she decided, he would be the one left pacing an office, if anyone was getting left behind.

I just hope I can swim in this thing, she thought again. Teo had insisted it wouldn't matter, and seeing the height of the boat, Eliza understood. She wasn't jumping off that thing. There was a small swimming platform at the back that jutted over the water, but it wasn't lit up. This wasn't a swimming party, after all.

This was Giuseppe Valdano showing off for his wife's birthday party. Teo had insisted they wouldn't have any trouble getting aboard—Tiana was a favorite of Valdano's.

Beatrice, on the other hand, was not a fan. But she was the key, he had insisted. "She's a woman scorned," he had said, "and she'll let us into his office. We just have to make it worth her while."

Looking down at the skimpy dress she wore, Eliza hoped Beatrice Valdano had similar ideas about what was worth her while.

They approached the gangplank where two burly men in suits stood on either side, dark glasses covering their eyes despite the night sky. "Invitation?" the one on the left asked, and the one on the right eyed Eliza.

"Oh please," Teo simped. "Tony, don't act like you don't know me." He lowered his voice, the words clearly meant for the guard but still loud enough for Eliza and the other guard to hear. "You certainly seemed to enjoy my company last time."

Tony moved his shoulders, adjusting his tie. "I know you, alright?" he snapped, but his gaze flicked to Eliza. "But who's your friend?"

"A little double trouble tonight," Teo crooned, leaning down to show his fake cleavage. "I know it's the Missus' birthday party, but we all know what the boss wants."

Tony nodded, then glanced at his friend. "Just a little pat down," he said as the right guard stepped forward, eager grin on his face. "You understand."

Eliza plastered a blank smile on her face, acting like she enjoyed the man's hands on her body, squeezing her boobs and ass with more force than was necessary.

He lingered, and Teo snapped, "Come on, Marcus. You know there's no room for a weapon in that dress." He winked. "Perhaps later tonight you can see what's under it, huh?"

Marcus turned his gaze to Eliza. "That right, baby? You up for some entertaining tonight?" Eliza blinked prettily at him.

"Of course," she trilled in a voice that matched Teo's. "You know I can't wait."

Marcus swatted her ass and shooed her down the gangplank, Teo close behind.

"The nerve of that asshole," Jack griped in her ear.

"Cut the chatter, Tex," Teo hissed, and the earpiece fell silent.

Eliza stepped onto the boat, expecting it to move slightly under her feet, but it didn't even budge. If she couldn't look down at the water below, splashing softly against the hull, she wouldn't guess she was even on a boat.

They entered the boat on the lower deck, an area festooned with lights and tasteful decorations. Another pair of goons gestured them up the stairs, but not before Eliza saw the small placard reading "Guest Rooms" to the left of a hallway. Teo had said Valdano's office would be on one of the levels with the guest rooms. They just had to figure out a way back down here when the party got into full swing.

She gave the guards a playful smile, knowing how to play her part, then followed Teo up the stairs and into an open area filled with scattered high tables, a smattering of white couches against the walls, and small tables with hors d'oeuvres spread throughout. About thirty people already occupied the space, drinking glasses of champagne and laughing as they spoke of whatever insanely rich people talked about.

"Listen, Linda," Teo said, accepting a glass of champagne from a passing waiter and handing it to Eliza. "You need to relax. Don't be so obvious."

"I'm wearing four-inch heels," Eliza griped. "How am I supposed to relax?"

"Oh, that's right," Teo mumbled. "You only relax when you have a leg thrown over a shoulder. My bad."

Eliza scowled at him, unable to stop herself from remembering Teo between her legs back in Barcelona, all that glorious hair sliding everywhere. Trying to ignore the heat the memory conjured, Eliza downed the champagne, quickly replacing it with another as a waiter passed with a tray.

"There's my Linda," Teo crooned, watching the people move around the room. "Now," he leaned closer, "Beezus will be fashionably late, and Valdano will fawn over her for a little while. Then he'll get distracted, and that's when we pounce. Well, you pounce. We know she doesn't love me."

"How do you know that's what will happen? This is his wife's party. Maybe he'll want to be with her tonight," Eliza said.

Teo titled his head, giving her a sympathetic look. "The Linda I remember wasn't such a simp," he observed. "Too much dick softening your edges, Linda?"

"It's not soft to think a husband might want to spend time with his wife," Eliza defended, not sure why. Maybe Teo was right. Too much dick was fucking with her head. It wasn't like marriage was ever a possibility for her. Why was she so determined that a mob boss be nice to his wife?

"Not this husband," Teo said, "but yes, I suppose there are satisfied couples somewhere in the world." He paused, then added, "I've just never met any."

"You wouldn't," Eliza snapped. "You're too busy fucking people over."

"C'mon," Teo crooned, leaning closer and pressing his hip against hers, "you know you missed me."

Eliza couldn't help the small smile on her lips as she took another sip of champagne, watching the people stroll into the party. Teo was right. She had missed him. He was a scoundrel, but he was wild and fun and definitely a good time.

Not that she was lacking in good times lately.

The party was in full swing by the time Beatrice and her husband arrived. There was the typical fanfare—toasts, cake, a slow dance, an obligatory kiss on the cheek. Eliza watched their body language carefully, and she was sad to see that Teo was right. Valdano was going through the motions with Beatrice, but he wasn't into it. During their dance to celebrate his wife's birthday, Valdano made eyes at Tiana twice, also eyeing other women who returned his winks with promising smiles. Valdano would be fucking someone in an alcove the first chance he got.

Men, Eliza sighed. *If only I could get him to agree to lend me the book instead.* She had suggested such a plan—for her to seduce Valdano and convince him to bring her to his office, but Teo had nixed the idea at once.

"He's not going to bring someone he just met to his office," Teo told her. "Beezus is the only way in there tonight."

The formalities concluded, Eliza and Teo split, mingling, and Eliza watched Beatrice from a safe distance, wondering how such a beautiful woman put up with such a man. The mobster's wife was lovely, all long limbs and dark hair, and she smiled graciously as people approached her, offering congratulations.

Eliza listened to the smattering of conversations here and there, mostly about who was wearing what designer, who was spotted with whom, and some quiet grumbling about the markets. Eliza assumed they meant money, but part of her wondered how many of these people would bid on the artifacts Teo wanted—the ones that Milf had been stealing instead. She wondered why they would want them, then decided it was likely just to possess them. No one on the boat was familiar to her, and she would recognize any experts in the area. They didn't want the book to read it, that was for sure. Only to say they owned it, or perhaps to sell it to someone else for a profit.

And this is why I got out of that field, she reminded herself. *Better to make food than to lie to myself that I'm actually affecting history in the brief moments I'd be allowed to study an artifact.* The thought made her wonder who Reese's new sponsor was, and she cursed. She'd totally forgotten to call him back and schedule their dinner.

Teo's right. So much dick is making me an idiot. Maybe I need a break.

Her eyes found Beatrice in the crowd again, the woman stunning in her blue dress, and Eliza was surprised to find the mobster's wife was watching her. She gave a slow sultry smile from across the room then turned her attention back to the couple in front of her, nodding politely.

Eliza scanned the crowd, seeking Valdano, and she caught a glimpse of movement into a smaller area at the back of the room. She moved nearer, seeing a cluster of bodyguards stepping into position to guard what must be Valdano behind them. On her high heels, Eliza could glimpse the gangster bending his head down to kiss a bleach blonde woman before they both disappeared into the shadowy space.

"Bastardo," a voice hissed near Eliza's ear, "no?"

Eliza whirled, nearly losing her balance to face Beatrice Valdano. "Uh..." she managed, not sure what the etiquette was for greeting a mob wife at her party after watching her husband making out with someone else.

"You are new here," Beatrice said.

"Is it that obvious?" Eliza asked with a laugh, deciding to just go with it and see what happened.

"I know all the women who come to these things," Beatrice said. "They all come with hidden agendas and hungry eyes for my husband." She lifted her chin in the direction of the room where Giuseppe had vanished. "But not you." Beatrice lifted an elegant eyebrow. "You only have eyes for me tonight."

"Is it that obvious?" Eliza repeated, a new plan forming immediately. She looked away, hoping Beatrice would see her as suddenly shy.

Beatrice slid her finger under Eliza's chin, forcing Eliza to look at her. "Oh, darling," Beatrice whispered, "you're too good for this place." She leaned close, her mouth next to Eliza's ear, her breath a warm puff of air. "Come with me somewhere more ... private."

Eliza nodded, a delicious shiver teasing her body, and she let Beatrice lead her to a staircase in the opposite corner. A suited guard moved to block the way, but Beatrice dismissed them with a wave of her fingers, leading Eliza down the spiral steps slowly, mindful of her heels. At the bottom, Beatrice paused, stepping close to Eliza and running a hand up her arm.

"What's your name, sweetheart?" Beatrice asked.

"El—Linda," Eliza breathed, the name coming to her in a rush as she remembered not to give her real name.

"Ellinda," Beatrice repeated, "what a lovely name. Clearly not from around here."

"Bristol," Eliza replied. She had a friend from Bristol back in college named Allison. It was close enough.

"What brings you to Cairo?" Beatrice asked, slowly moving closer, pressing her body to Eliza's now.

"You," Eliza said, then reached out to kiss her. Beatrice stiffened for a second, clearly not expecting Eliza to instigate, and then she relaxed into Eliza's embrace. After a long moment, they paused, and Eliza added, "Though I didn't know that until tonight."

Beatrice smiled, and her face was truly lovely to behold in the glow from the lights above. Eliza glanced around the small room they had entered. It was dim, but she could make out the outline of two couches along one wall and a hulking piece of furniture at the far end of the room. Eliza wondered what this room was used for when there wasn't a party upstairs.

"Beatrice," Eliza whispered, pushing the woman slowly back toward one of the couches.

Beatrice's smile grew even bigger as she let herself be pushed. As the woman's legs met the couch, Eliza kissed her again, slowly pushing them

ONE MUMMY TO GO, Please!

both down so that Beatrice sat on the couch. Eliza knelt between her knees, hands roving freely now.

"Oh yes," Beatrice moaned as Eliza moved lower, hands sliding up her thighs. It had been some time since she'd been with a woman, but she still remembered what to do. She relaxed into the moment, allowing herself to focus on giving Beatrice the pleasure the woman was sorely lacking. "Please!"

Eliza had completely forgotten the earpiece she wore until Jack's quiet voice whispered, "Uhh, am I hearing what I think I'm hearing?"

Eliza jolted, then caught herself, bending back to her work, hand scrambling to push the earpiece out of her ear and shoving it ruthlessly down the front of her dress. It scratched her skin as it fought with the tight material, but Eliza ignored it, bringing both hands back to business.

She was just about to bring Beatrice to her third orgasm when there was a soft beeping sound at the door, and lights flooded the room. Eliza sat up, tossing Beatrice's skirt back down as she turned to see who had entered.

Oh fuck, we're so busted!

Staring at them front the doorway, his face just as shocked as theirs must be, was Teo. He held the keycard in his hand. Hesitating only a second, he ducked into the room and shut the door behind him, pressing his back against it as he surveyed the scene.

"Well, well, well," Teo crooned in his Tiana voice. "What do we have here? A little private birthday celebration?"

Beatrice didn't even move, her lust-glazed eyes surveying him from where she lay back on the couch, legs still spread wide with Eliza between them. "Don't you think I deserve some fun of my own?" she asked.

"You deserve everything your heart desires, Birthday Girl," Teo agreed.

There was an awkward silence then. Eliza wondered when Beatrice was going to ask about the keycard.

Keycard. What the fuck? Now that her eyes had adjusted to the light, Eliza glanced around. The keycard to Valdano's office. The piece of furniture she had glimpsed in the dim light was actually a massive executive desk. Behind it on the wall was a painting of a ship. Eliza wasn't an art expert, but she'd taken enough art classes to recognize the lines of a Rembrant, though she wasn't familiar with this one in particular.

I bet the safe is behind that painting.

She glanced at Beatrice, who was watching Teo with calculating eyes, neither willing to give the advantage.

"Oh come on," Eliza said finally, breaking the silence. "This is weird."

"Weirder than walking in to find you fucking Valdano's wife?" Teo snapped.

"I'm not just Valdano's wife," Beatrice snapped. "You know better, Tiana."

Teo shrugged. "So what's the play here? You scream for the guards and drag me before Valdano?"

Beatrice chuckled. "Maybe if you had come in earlier." She relaxed a little, hand reaching out to cup Eliza's chin. "Before your little friend here made me remember why women are far superior lovers."

"I don't recall you complaining," Teo said boldly, and Beatrice sighed.

"You are a fun little distraction, darling, but this one is a hell of a good time." She pursed her lips. "Now, whatever am I to do with you?"

Eliza's hand rested on Beatrice's thigh, and she slowly moved it upward again, slipping beneath the edge of her skirt, the implication clear. Beatrice let her eyes slip closed for a second, a satisfied sigh escaping, and then she opened her eyes again. "Very well. Ellinda," she ordered, "stay where you are. I need more of that glorious tongue. You," her gaze pinned Teo, "get over here and show me what I'm missing."

Teo paused, calculating, his eyes flicking to the desk and back to Beatrice and Eliza on the couch. "And you won't just call for your guards?"

Beatrice cocked her head. "Make it worth my while, and I might forget I saw you here."

"As the lady commands," Teo agreed, then stepped forward to kneel behind Eliza. She started to move to the side so they could both rest between Beatrice's legs, but Beatrice stopped them.

"I want you to show her what I'm missing," she said again, then gave Eliza a grin. "You're game, right Ellinda? Tiana here is a delightful time."

Eliza glanced over her shoulder at Teo, recalling the last time he had been so close behind her. Poppy had been on the couch that time.

That was the last time we shared a guy, Eliza realized. She met Charles right after we got back from Spain. Biting her lip, she nodded, leaning back to let Teo kiss her. His smooth face was a shock—he'd had a beard back then—but his lips were familiar territory. His face was androgynous, both beautiful and handsome, and though he was stuffed into the dress with fake breasts filling the bodice, she could feel his length poking against her back as they kissed. His hands roved over the front of her dress, finding her hips and then moving down, sliding the dress up.

Eliza smiled, then bent down, pushing Beatrice's dress aside and eliciting a groan as her fingers and tongue found the right spots. Teo's cock was hard against her, sliding against her wetness, teasing her. When Beatrice

cried out her pleasure, Teo finally slid inside, and Eliza fought to concentrate on both tasks, thrusting back with her hips as she chased her own pleasure while still licking and sucking the mob boss's wife. When she could resist no longer, she lifted her head, eyes closed tight as her body shook, and then she was being lifted up, Beatrice kissing her hard as Teo continued to thrust.

"Oh yes," Beatrice moaned, "come for me, little Ellinda!"

Eliza obeyed, then slumped, the three of them panting across the couch.

A few moments later, Teo stirred, pulling back and setting his dress to rights. His breasts were crooked, and he straightened them primly, then raised an eyebrow in Beatrice's direction, clearly waiting for her decision.

Beatrice stretched, long and languid, then reached down to give Eliza a lingering kiss. "That was definitely a birthday present I will remember, Ellinda."

"Me too," Eliza said truthfully, stress gone now that she'd released her tension.

"Me three," Teo added, then glanced meaningfully at the painting behind the desk. Eliza stared at him, not getting it. *The book*, he mouthed.

Oh wow, dick really does make me an idiot. Of course, we need the book.

"So," Teo prompted as he got to his feet, chin gesturing at the staircase and the guard who stood at the top. The man had no doubt heard them, but with Beatrice down here, no one would disturb them. Not unless she called for them.

Beatrice sighed, then gestured at the painting. "As if I care what you're here for, little thief. Just take it and get out before anyone sees you."

Teo scampered over the painting, swinging it wide and swiping the keycard. The door to the safe inside opened, and Eliza tilted her head, trying to see what was inside. Teo jammed something into his fake cleavage, then turned around, a golden bangle held loose on his palm. Eliza gasped. She had seen that bangle on Milf's upper arm. She reached for it, fear gripping her. She hadn't seen Milf since promising him they'd help find the book. What if something had happened to him?

She held it out, seeing the careful design work, the lines she recognized. This was Milf's bangle. How the hell did it end up here in Valdano's safe?

She was still worrying about the mummy's safety when she realized that Teo hadn't moved. She glanced up, seeing that the safe still held a few bundles of cash, but that was it.

No book.

Fuck.

"Ellinda," Beatrice purred from where she sat on the couch, "you look disappointed. What was it you wanted from my husband?"

Eliza shook her head, chest heaving with a sigh. "A book," she admitted.

Beatrice snorted, the sound still somehow delicate, and she got to her feet, crossing the room to the small coffee table before the other couch. She slid aside a few hardcover picture books to reveal an old tome beneath. She held it out. "You mean this book?"

Eliza slid the bangle on her arm, something jolting through her as she did so, some awareness, but she ignored it, eyes scanning the cover.

Yes! The Book of Heka!

Her finger slid across the cover, taking in the inscriptions, and then she flipped it open, revealing pages of ancient Egyptian text. She closed it, holding it close, cursing herself for not bringing a bag. She had wanted to, but Teo had refused, saying that any self-respecting entertainer would never have a bag with her dress.

"Giuseppe just picked up a batch of Egyptian artifacts," Beatrice said dismissively. "He used to get books for me, but I don't want Egyptian tomes. We live in Cairo! I want books from other places." She shook her head. "He used to know that about me."

She surveyed both Eliza and Teo, eyes shifting from satisfied minx to bitter wife. "You know what? I think he deserves a little frustration this evening, don't you?" Without another word, she raised her voice, "Guards! Someone is stealing from Giuseppe's office!"

Eliza raised wide eyes to Teo, who snarled at Beatrice. "You bitch!"

"You know you love me, honey," she purred, blowing him a kiss. "Now get out of here."

The guard was stumbling down the staircase as Teo dragged Eliza to the door. They slipped out just as two shots rang out, one pinging into the wall beside Eliza's face. "Go!" Teo shouted, pushing Eliza ahead of him as they stumbled down the hallway.

"Where?" Eliza asked, seeing that the hallway they were in ended at a glass door.

"Anywhere but here!" Teo shouted, and Eliza managed to slide the door open with one hand, the other clutching the book to her chest. Teo stumbled out behind her onto a small balcony, shouting men close behind.

"Now what?" Eliza demanded, frantically looking for another escape.

"Over the rail!" Teo insisted.

"What?!" Eliza screeched. "You promised no swimming tonight!"

"I lied," Teo said, then shoved her over the railing.

Chapter 45

The safe house was tinier than Hak remembered with so many people inside. They huddled together in the living room, boxed in by cheap chipboard furniture that smelled faintly of wood glue. Eliza gripped the book to her chest. Her hair was still dripping, her feet bare.

Despite the space constraints, Sloan was spread out on the futon, his sock-clad heels propped up on the armrest. There was a hole in the heel, revealing a swath of skin made leathery by combat boots.

He hardly acknowledged them as they burst in, his eyes glued to the television with a glass ashtray balanced on his belly. Hak was fairly certain Sloan had been wearing the same tank top when he'd last seen him. If he took it off, it would surely stand up under its own strength.

Sloan took a long drag of his cigarette and tapped the ash into the ashtray. "Where've you been?" he asked. His gold wedding band reflected the smoldering cancer stick. Hak wondered whether Sloan's wife had to contend with that same chilly tone. Hak had never met her, but he couldn't help but picture a long-suffering Stepford wife with dead eyes.

"Sloan." Hak snapped his fingers. "Move." Exhausted, Eliza swayed beside him. He placed a steadying hand on her back.

"This is my fucking place," Sloan grumbled. "I've stayed here for a week—by myself, I might add—and you expect me to just jump up like a lapdog? What have you been doing, Hak? Hanging out with a bunch o' ... nerds?"

"Nerds!" Jack snorted. "C'mon, man. We've worked together."

"I stand by what I said, Manning." Sloan didn't bother to look up at the mercenary. He sniffed and wiped at his nose with the back of his hand.

"Move," Hak repeated, exasperated. He smacked Sloan's foot off of the armrest. "Can't you see that she needs to sit down?"

Sloan's eyes finally flicked from the television to an ashen-faced Eliza and back again. "My show is on."

His "show" was an infomercial for a blow dryer. Models with wide smiles demonstrated how the appliance could turn damp hair into a lustrous Brazilian blowout.

Rafi snatched the remote up off the coffee table and turned it off. "Hey!" Sloan protested. "That's—"

Hak grabbed a fistful of Sloan's shirtfront and hauled him to his feet. The ashtray fell with a hollow thud, littering the carpet with cigarette butts, tar, and ash. "Don't make me tell you again," he growled. They were so close that their noses touched. Sloan reeked of old sweat and body odor.

"Geez!" Sloan threw up his hands. "Fine." He brushed an imaginary piece of lint off his crusty shirt. "Where have you been all week anyway?"

Hak didn't bother to answer him. He urged Eliza to sit down and knelt in front of her. "Are you hurt?" he asked. He had thought the mission had gone off without a hitch, but he didn't have eyes on Eliza and Teo when they descended into the cabin.

When he touched her, her skin jumped. "No," she managed through trembling lips. "I've never done something that ... scary before. But I couldn't act scared, not right then. It just hit me all at once."

Her pupils were pinpoints, and sweat soaked through her clothes. She shivered, and Hak shrugged off his motorcycle jacket, draping it over her shoulders. He hoped its heaviness would ground her. As expected, her shoulders slumped beneath its weight, and she let out a shuddering sigh.

Hak rubbed away the goosebumps on her arms. "You're okay," he said soothingly. "We're all okay. You're the girl who stood toe-to-toe with a mummy. A little larceny is nothing."

Except Hak knew the danger of a greedy man—especially a greedy man who felt slighted. Giuseppe Valdano would hunt them tirelessly, and it would be only a matter of days before he knew exactly who they were.

The safe house was only as safe as they made it. Sure, the apartment was rented under an alias—Bruce Mellencamp because Sloan was a big fan of

One Mummy to Go, Please!

classic rock—but there were CCTV cameras all over Cairo. If they stepped outside, they were on camera. Hak wasn't sure if Valdano had people in the police force, but if he were the leader of a crime syndicate, he would. They couldn't trust anyone.

"This place is ... gross," Teo remarked, his lip curling in disgust. He lifted the hem of his sequined dress up as if afraid he would drag it in something damp. "I can feel the mold growing in my lungs."

"What are you trying to say, lady?" Sloan asked, scratching his unshaven jaw.

"You don't need to be here," Jack reminded Teo.

"Well," Teo drawled, mocking Jack's accent, "y'all haven't fulfilled your half o' this here bargain."

"I do not sound like that," Jack huffed. "I hardly have an accent."

"You do sound like that, you hillbilly," Sloan snickered.

"Hey Sloan, fuck you!" Jack snapped.

"You kiss your sister with that mouth?"

Hak stepped between the two so that they wouldn't come to blows—the dick measuring had to stop. Sloan relented, combing his hands through his grease-slick hair, but Jack's chest flexed beneath Hak's palm. His heart thudded.

"Jack," Hak murmured warningly. "Let it go."

Jack's jaw tightened. "Fine." Hak's hand dropped to his side as he gave the mercenary a reassuring nod.

"It's better if Teo stays," Rafi said firmly. "He's a target now."

"No," Teo corrected him, twisting a strand of synthetic blonde hair around his manicured fingers "Tiana may be a target—if Beezus rats us out, that is. Teo is not. No one sees me without a full face, not even Giuseppe Valdano."

"I thought you said you and Valdano…" Rafi trailed off, awkwardly shuffling his feet on the foul-smelling carpet.

"He screamed 'Oh Tiana!' as I plowed him, if that's what you're asking." Teo snickered. "He liked the dichotomy."

Eliza took a deep breath. "What do we do now?" she asked in a soft voice. She rested the book on her lap, brushing her fingers upon the cover like a lover's cheek.

"Now," Rafi said, rolling up his sleeves, "we read the book."

"Whoa!" Teo shuffled backward in his heels. "Absolutely fucking not." He crossed himself. "I'm not a religious guy, but my mama didn't raise a

222

fool. That's something you sell and wash your hands of—before you sage your fucking house. You don't read it."

"It's important, Teo," Eliza said. "We need it to help Milfonnos."

"You didn't say anything about dabbling in the fucking dark arts, Linda."

Rafi sat beside Eliza and slid the heavy tome onto his own lap. Eliza had worried that their brief swim might have damaged it, but the book seemed impervious to water. It wasn't even damp. Rafi opened it carefully though, mindful of its age. An odd smell wafted through the room as dust rose into the air, and Hak wrinkled his nose.

"What are the odds that's some ancient Egyptian anthrax? They booby-trapped tombs, you know." Hak kept a hand over his mouth and nose.

"You've seen too many movies," Rafi muttered. "It's just run-of-the-mill dust."

Eliza's eyes squeezed shut, and her lips silently moved. Her brow furrowed, and her fists shook, but when she opened them again, all hope had drained from her eyes. "He isn't answering." She kept rubbing the bangle on her arm through the jacket.

"Keep trying," Rafi encouraged her as he gingerly turned the book's pages.

"What … is she doing?" Sloan asked.

"Calling Milfonnos," Hak answered, crossing his arms over his chest. "The spell will free the mummy from whoever is pulling his strings."

"You mean that mummy from the television is coming here?"

"Yes. If we can get into contact with him."

Sloan grasped Hak's arm and steered him into the kitchen. "Are you out of your mind?" The broad-shouldered mercenary slapped his hand on the peeling laminate countertop. "I kept my mouth shut when we came here as a favor to your friend—it's a waste of company resources and time, but that's none of my business. I still get a paycheck either way. But magic and mummies?"

Hak sighed. "Maybe you should go home, Sloan. This has gone beyond company business. This is personal for me."

Sloan scoffed. "I can't leave you here while your brain is as smooth as a soft-boiled egg. I'm staying—someone has to watch your six."

"You're a good man, Sloan."

"Besides, who's going to sign my paychecks?"

Chapter 46

When Milfonnos finally appeared in the tiny apartment, Eliza ran to him, wrapping her arms around the pharaoh and holding him close, eyes closed. "I thought…" she began but was unable to finish. "I'm just so glad you're here."

She had changed out of her dress and was wearing one of Hak's t-shirts and a pair of his sleep shorts, both way too big for her. She still had the bangle on her arm, and she was surprised to see a matching one still on Milf's arm, right where she remembered it. He returned her embrace, then his hand found the bangle, and he pulled away just enough to look at her.

"What is this?" he asked, sliding his hand over it. "How?"

"It was with the book," Eliza explained.

"You have the Book of Heka?" Milf demanded, scanning the apartment. Sloan had gone, abandoning his place on the couch, and Jack and Hak sat there instead. Rafi sat on the floor atop a towel, the book open in his lap as he continued to study the spell they would need to free Milfonnos.

"Where have you been?" Eliza demanded, turning her frustration on the pharaoh. "I thought something terrible had happened to you!"

Milfonnos shrugged. "What could happen to me?"

Eliza frowned, realizing that she had worried about Milf since seeing what she thought was his bangle—but it wasn't like the mummy could die. *Could he?*

"You know, your priestess could have been killed tonight getting your little book," Jack drawled softly. "You could show a little gratitude."

"Nonsense," Milfonnos said, tugging Eliza close again. "My priestess is fierce. She would not let me down."

"We'll set you free," Eliza promised. "When Rafi performs the spell—"

"Rafi?" Milfonnos echoed, body going rigid at the name.

Eliza stared at him. "Yes, Rafi. He knows the spell."

"You think I would trust my freedom to the same bloodline who betrayed me?" Milfonnos whispered, and a chill ran across Eliza's arms at the menace in his voice. She ignored the fear, anger fueling her now.

"That same bloodline is here now helping you," she snapped at the mummy. "Maybe Jack is right, and you should show a little respect."

"Respect for the one who betrayed and cursed me?" Milfonnos pressed.

"Rafi didn't betray or curse you," Eliza reminded him. "All that was long ago." She gently touched his arm, and something slithered up her own arm, a zing of connection. She could sense Milfonnos' hesitation, his struggle, and underneath that, another presence, a voice of reason urging him to trust her. She touched the bangle, wanting to ask about it, but knowing it wasn't a good time.

"Can he do it?" Milfonnos asked after a moment. He looked at where Rafi sat on the floor. "Can you do it?"

Rafi nodded. "I can."

"Will you do it?" the pharaoh asked, the question heavy in the room.

"I will," Rafi replied without hesitation. "You should not be controlled by anyone but yourself."

"I ... thank you," Milfonnos said formally.

Rafi nodded.

"Great," Hak said. "Now what do we need for this ritual?"

An hour later, Rafi, Milfonnos, and Eliza sat in a triangle around the coffee table, several candles resting atop symbols drawn in salt casting soft shadows on the walls. Eliza shuffled, wishing she had agreed to the towel Rafi had offered when they dragged the coffee table to the center of the room. She could feel the crunchy rug beneath her upper thighs, and she wished she had some clothes that fit properly. At least a pair of pants between her skin and the floor.

Jack sat on the couch, body alert and obviously ready to move at the slightest sign of trouble. Hak stood by the window, also alert to any danger. They didn't think Giuseppe Valdano knew who had robbed him the previous night, but they were waiting. It was only a matter of time.

Teo, also dressed in Hak's extra clothes, stood by the door, clearly ready to make his own escape if things went poorly. He hadn't said anything else against using the book, but everything in his demeanor screamed that he didn't want any part of this ritual.

The sun was setting, the natural light slowly fading as the candlelight took over the room. Rafi was bathed in shadow, hair falling in his face as he leaned over the book. His voice was low and melodic as he began the ritual. Eliza loved watching him like this—the scholar at work in his element.

They'd spent the day studying the book together, Rafi explaining how the ritual worked. He'd also had her memorize a small protective spell, just in case, the magic designed to separate the soul from the body for a time—just long enough for her to escape, Rafi had insisted. It wouldn't kill the person, assuming nothing happened to their body when they weren't in it.

He wanted her to be protected, especially since she hadn't put his bracelet back on since the boat heist when Teo insisted she remove it since it clashed with her outfit. She hadn't quite worked up the courage to put it back on yet, not sure she was ready for what it meant.

Looking at Rafi now, she wondered why she was hesitating. She loved Rafi, and he loved her. The others were fun—a good time—but Rafi was the one she wanted to still be there when this mummy business was over.

And if this ritual frees Milf, what then? Where will he go if he's not bound to the bidding of someone nearby?

She shifted her gaze to the mummy. The pharaoh's hand was steady, fingers strong as they entwined with her own. She gave a reassuring squeeze, and his eyes flicked from Rafi to hers.

The bangle on her upper arm gave a short pulse, and for a second, she heard a voice in her mind.

<*She will not betray us.*>

I won't, she told that voice silently, suddenly sure she was hearing Kasmut. The bangle had connected them more closely than her awakening him had done, and when they touched, she sometimes caught errant thoughts from Milf's bodyguard passenger.

<*But the descendant of Sabbagh...*>

<*He is true.*> Kas insisted.

Eliza sensed something then, a tingling sensation that began in her fingers and crept up her arms. The ritual was taking effect.

The spell was simple enough, a stronger version of the small spell she had learned. It was designed to separate a soul from other tethers, including other spells. If successful, Milfonnos would be free from whoever was controlling him, able to make his own choices.

And what will he do with that freedom? Eliza had asked herself the question several times, but she had not asked Milf, assuming that his freedom was the most important thing. She hated the idea that he was being controlled. She had a brief flash of their first encounter, him still covered in moldy rags, his body not yet fully regenerated. Would that creature return?

She didn't think so. Since the day he had saved her inside her truck, Eliza knew that Milf wouldn't let any harm come to her. He was bossy and arrogant, a pharaoh, but he was also devoted to those he found worthy, like Kasmut—and her.

Eliza hoped this went well. Then maybe he would find Rafi worthy as well and stop blaming him for his ancestor's betrayal.

The tingling was growing stronger, and Eliza watched Milf's face, wondering if she would be able to tell.

<I feel ... something,> Kasmut said, voice quietly awed.

<Not enough,> Milfonnos said. <It's working, but it's not enough.> He raised his free hand to his face, staring at his palm as if sensing something. Rafi's voice continued to speak. He was at the end now, the same syllables pouring from his mouth. As Eliza turned to him, she saw his eyes had begun to glow, a soft amber light building on his face.

Milfonnos too had begun to glow, his red eye pulsing in time to Rafi's words, and the bangle on Eliza's arm grew warm and then uncomfortably hot.

"Wait—" she managed to say, but neither Rafi nor Milf seemed to notice her distress. She was aware of movement behind her, men scrambling to help, but it was Jack who reached her first. Sensing the cause of her distress, he pushed her sleeve up and gasped at the sight of the bangle glowing with magical energy, Eliza's skin reddening around it.

"Get it off!" she squealed, trying to let go of Milf's hand, but the pharaoh's grip was like stone. His whole body was glowing red now, matching Rafi's amber halo.

Jack touched the bangle, then jerked away with a curse, fingers red. Hak's attempt was more successful, the mercenary able to touch the glowing bangle seemingly without being bothered by the heat, but he couldn't make it slide down Eliza's arm. It was Teo who finally broke the connection,

sliding the keycard to Valdano's safe between the bangle and her skin. There was a small pop and a terrible tearing, and then Hak was pushing the bangle down her arm. It fell to the floor with a hollow clang.

All three men stared at it. It was just a bangle now, no more glowing. Jack reached out tentatively to poke it, but it was just an ornament again. Eliza kicked it away, just in case. She looked at her arm, not shocked to see a raised welt of angry red circling her arm. As she watched, her skin continued to puff up. She could see the tiny details of the bangle's engraving seared into her skin. Heat flooded her, followed by a wash of ice as her stomach soured. Certain she was going to be sick, she tried to cover her mouth with her other hand, but Milf still held tight. She turned her horrified face back to the ritual in time to see both magical lights—Milf's red and Rafi's yellow—blend into a perfect vermillion that seared her eyes, there was a final shout—she wasn't sure whose—and then silence.

Eliza sat on the couch, her arm wrapped in gauze. She had stopped shaking, but she still had Hak's jacket wrapped around her shoulders. The warmth was appreciated, despite the heat of the night, but his scent engulfing her was more soothing than anything else.

He was safe. She would be fine. The ritual was over.

Except they had no idea if it had worked properly or not. Eliza's incident with the bangle didn't seem to have affected Rafi and Milf, but they couldn't be sure.

"I should have told you I was wearing it," Eliza said, shaking her head. "That was stupid to put it on and perform a ritual."

"You didn't know," Rafi reassured her.

"Yeah, just like I didn't know my mother's necklace would wake a mummy," she mumbled. "My luck is terrible these days."

"Not terrible," Teo reminded her. "You have successfully acquired a book from Giuseppe Valdano, and we're all still alive. I call this a miracle."

"I don't feel any different," Milf murmured, disappointment in his voice.

"We won't know if it worked until you are called again," Rafi mused. "Until then, you should stay with us."

Milfonnos surveyed the small, filthy safe house. "This place is disgusting," he observed. "Well beneath what my priestess and *medjay* deserve."

Rafi looked up at the title of *medjay*, the ancient term for pharaoh's bodyguards. Milfonnos tilted his head slightly, a nod of appreciation, but that was it. The gesture of thanks was more than Eliza had ever expected. She never thought Milf would name Rafi as a guardian.

Since they both came out of the ritual, Rafi had been nothing but apologetic and attentive while Milf had been quietly withdrawn. He had peered at the bangle when Hak offered it to him but shook his head, eyes darting to where Rafi sat on the couch, rubbing the burn on Eliza's arm with ointment and wrapping it in a bandage.

"Not until I know I am truly free," the pharaoh had said. "I do not want to be under someone else's control while restored to my full strength—both human and god."

Hak had nodded, setting the bangle on the table where it still rested, only now Eliza's bracelet with the protective scarab sat coiled next to it.

Eliza eyed them both—powerful artifacts they were afraid to use.

"Sorry the accommodations aren't to your liking," Jack drawled, "but getting the book put us on the radar of some pretty powerful people, so now we get to lie low for a while."

"You should sleep," Hak told Eliza. "We all should. It's been … a rough few days."

Eliza nodded.

"Take the bed," Hak insisted. "It has clean sheets, I promise. I washed them myself." At her worried glance at the window, he reassured her, "We'll take watches. Just rest."

Getting to shaky feet, Eliza followed him to the bedroom, Rafi on her heels. She crawled into the bed, but as they both turned to go, she reached out a hand.

"Stay with me. I don't … want to be alone."

Hak and Rafi exchanged a long look, then both sat on the bed, Hak stretching out to lay behind her, Rafi sitting and taking her hand.

"You aren't alone, Eliza," Rafi soothed. "We are all with you."

Chapter 47

Milfonnos floated through the dark apartment, his toes dragging on the filthy carpet. The detritus of the possibly botched ritual littered the coffee table. No one had the heart to clean up; it felt too much like admitting defeat.

Soft snores rose from the couch, where Jack and Sloan slept, head to foot. Both men were far too large to share the couch, but neither wanted to sleep on the floor.

Rafi sat on the floor, poring through the Book of Heka as though he'd missed a crucial detail. He hunched like a scholar, his phone's flashlight acting as a book light. Rafi rubbed at his eyes as Milfonnos passed him by. "Why are you awake?"

"When I was alive, I was prone to insomnia. Now, I do not require sleep—when I close my eyes, I find that I have done things I cannot remember." Milfonnos scoffed. "I could not even stay dead."

"I'm sorry I asked," Rafi said dryly.

"I am sorry you are related to that Amun Henet scum, Rafi Sabbagh."

Rafi only shook his head and returned to the book, the signet ring catching the light as he turned the page.

<You should be nicer to him,> Kasmut said. <He tried to help us.>

Milfonnos pretended not to hear him.

Milfonnos

As was his custom, Milfonnos settled on a chair at the window to wait for sunrise. It was a comfort because no matter where—or when—he was, the sun always rose in just the same way.

Eliza's phone chirped. It rested on the windowsill, charging on the only working outlet. The screen came alive.

[Poppy: You will not believe what time nightclubs open in Paphos. ONE IN THE MORNING. How does the economy of Cyprus even FUNCTION?]

Cyprus.

Cyprus was where the cancer had first made itself known, though it was months before he realized it.

Milfonnos swam alongside the skiff, his muscular arms slicing through the foamy surf. He was tired; his joints felt gummy and every muscle burned. But he couldn't quit—Kasmut was three lengths ahead. While he knew Kasmut would slow to let him pass in the last kilometer, he would prefer to win from his own skills.

The spotter aboard the skiff whistled shrilly, and Milfonnos raised his head just enough to see a craggy swath of land. Nearly there. He was determined to reach shore first.

The day was overcast, the clouds hanging so low he thought for sure he could touch them. It made the waves choppier than he expected. For every stroke forward, he was dragged two strokes backward. Regret hounded him, but he pushed forward.

After all, a bet was a bet.

Suddenly, a cramp seized his calf. After the first brief surge of panic, Milfonnos forced himself to tread water one-handed, using the other to massage the offending muscle. The rowers aboard the skiff halted, pulling their oars onto their laps. "Go on!" Milfonnos shouted. "Keep with Kasmut!"

"But Pharaoh!" the spotter cried, flapping his arms like a harried seagull.

"Go!" Milfonnos urged. The thought of them lifting him out of the water, sodden and shivering, was unbearable. He imagined lying in the bottom of the skiff as the oarsman tried very hard not to meet his eyes. Worse, was the thought of his victorious bodyguard climbing aboard, preening like a rooster. Kasmut would try very hard to be humble as he looked down on his Pharaoh, but he'd smile just a little.

Thankfully, the skiff and its crew carried on. Milfonnos rubbed at his calf with his knuckles. When he tried to swim, every kick of his legs caused the muscle to scream.

"Kas!" he sputtered just before a gray wave closed over his head. Underwater, there was only stillness; even with the oars churning up the surface ahead, all Milfonnos could hear was the pounding of his own heartbeat.

It would be simple to just give in. All it would take was an inhale and water would flood his oxygen-starved lungs. His limbs grew warm and heavy. Was he still in the Red Sea, or had he fallen from the ferry that would carry him to the underworld?

If Kasmut were here, he'd give him a good shake. "One of your dark moods again?" he'd tease, tickling his ribs. Kasmut was the only one who could pull him out of it, wasn't he? Why had he never told him that he loved him like a brother? Regret snapped at his heels.

Dark motes danced in Milfonnos' vision, sunbursts following suit. His legs kicked feebly. He knew very little about the brain, but he suspected that it was dying and this was its death knell. His eyes eased closed, and the water embraced him like a lover.

"Milfonnos. Milfonnos!"

The Pharaoh awoke to the heels of Kasmut's hands violently driving into his chest. He vomited sea water from his mouth and nose, the taste of saline and bile intermingling unpleasantly on his tongue.

The rock and roll of the ocean beneath him was enough to make him puke again. Milfonnos propped himself up on his elbow to heave, unceremoniously vomiting what he thought was stifado onto the deck. The Cypriots had insisted he try it, even though the thought of eating octopus made his stomach turn. He imagined its suckers sticking to his stomach lining as he heaved.

Finally, he lay back on the deck, his stomach as empty as the day he was born. The clouds had parted somewhat, revealing a narrow beam of sunlight. A seagull cruising on a thermal screeched. Wait—where was he? Milfonnos' thoughts were soupy and sluggish, and exhaustion dragged at his eyelids.

"I looked back and you were gone. The skiff was slow to turn around, and I got to you first."

"I…"

"We're back in Cyprus. I knew it was foolhardy to race. You always talk me into the most ridiculous things," Kasmut babbled.

"I would have won if you hadn't cheated," Milfonnos said weakly.

"How did I do that?"

As the skiff bumped up against the dock, Milfonnos sat up. The port was busy, their little narrow boat hardly drawing any attention. Milfonnos hated the port: thick with people, odd smells, and mules—always mules—loaded with saddlebags.

"Help me up, Kas." Kasmut gripped his wrist and hauled him to his feet. Milfonnos' calf protested, and he leaned heavily on his bodyguard. "I thought it was a cramp—perhaps not."

"We should get you to a doctor," Kasmut murmured, his voice so low that only Milfonnos could hear. Milfonnos tested his leg, but he could hardly put any weight on it. Reluctantly, he nodded.

Kasmut's arm slipped around Milfonnos' waist and steered him toward the gangplank. "At least this means we'll get to spend an extra day or two in Cyprus. I love it here. You know why?"

Milfonnos only grunted, scowling at the traders hauling silk, amphoras filled with fragrant olive oil, and jewelry. A mule brayed, laying its ears back as they passed.

"Because here, outside of the governor's mansion, we don't know anyone. No one even looks at us because everyone is a stranger to everyone else. We're just Milfonnos and Kas, like when we were kids."

"You are sentimental," Milfonnos huffed.

"You'd think nearly drowning would make you sentimental too."

Chapter 48

Eliza woke with someone pressed behind her, and she turned, expecting Hak, but it was Teo's gorgeous hair she smelled. Even after their dip in the river, and a quick shower with Hak's minimalist hair care products, he still managed to look wonderful. She turned around to face him, surprised to see his very awake eyes watching her.

"When did you get here?" she mumbled, stretching, her body pressed to his.

"Hak's on watch," Teo said, "and Rafi is still reading that damn book." He winked at her. "My turn to snuggle with our girl."

"'Our girl'?" Eliza repeated, not sure what he meant.

"Come on, Linda." Teo rolled his eyes. "You are all of ours, and we all belong to you. You know that, don't you?" He paused, then added, "Except maybe Tex." He reached a hand out to her hip, holding her close, but his face was serious for a moment.

"I thought the other night reminded him that he could get good sex from anyone," Eliza said, biting her lip as she recalled the sight of Teo in Jack's lap as Rafi and Hak touched her.

"Don't trust him," Teo said.

It was Eliza's turn to roll her eyes. "You don't trust anyone, Teo."

"I'm serious, Eliza," he said, and his use of her name made her pause.

Eliza

Before she could speak, Eliza's stomach gave a loud growl, and Teo smiled. "Interrupted again," he groaned, then smacked her ass. "Move it, Linda. Let's get some food in you."

"I was maybe hoping for something else in me," she said, eyebrows raised, but then her stomach growled a second time, and her hunger faded, replaced by the need for food.

"Fine," she agreed, rolling over and sitting up. Teo padded after her to the kitchen, and she began opening and closing cabinets to see what was available.

"You want some help?" Hak called from where he sat next to Jack on the couch, the two of them engaged in a heated game on the PlayStation. Milf was sitting by the window, staring contemplatively at the night sky, and Rafi sat at the small table, still reading the Book of Heka.

"We got this," Eliza assured him as she and Teo began pulling out random containers from the fridge. Sloan may have been here alone all week long, but there was plenty of food. Eliza began mixing different leftovers, making a version of koshari without onions, a passable ful, and a selection of bread. She put the plates on the table, and the men wandered over to eat small bites here and there. Even Milf abandoned his stargazing to sample her ful, and he smiled at her as he chewed.

Life may have changed dramatically for her over the last few weeks, but Eliza could still cook. Sitting at the table, surrounded by her men, she was content.

More than content, she realized, looking around at each man in turn.

I'm happy. They make me happy.

Teo slapped her hand away when she tried to gather the dishes, insisting that she did the cooking, so she wasn't cleaning up. Rafi had closed the book to eat, setting it out of the way on the coffee table, and he followed Teo into the small kitchen, towel draped over his shoulder. Hak and Jack wiped down the table, straightening up the mess as much as possible. Eliza watched them move around the small apartment, working together. Milf lounged on the couch, watching everyone else. Eliza didn't expect he would participate in clean up. It didn't seem like something a pharaoh would know how to do.

If he was going to stay with them, she would have to teach him a few things.

Is he staying with me? Is this my life now? When we decide Valdano hasn't identified us—or if he finds us—will we all live together somewhere? Or is this the last time we'll all be in the same place together?

The thought made her sad, and she frowned, determined to make the most of the rest of the night. It was nearly midnight, but the night was still young, not that Eliza cared much about dawn. It wasn't like she had a job anymore.

The thought reminded her that Shawarma Warrior King was destroyed, the remains of her food truck towed to a garage near her apartment. She doubted they had done any repairs—or if it even could be repaired—especially since she had been too wrapped up in mummy hijinks to follow up on it.

"What is it, Priestess?" Eliza looked up into Milf's concerned gaze—one eye still red and the other a warm brown. "You are here, but you are not here."

"I'm here," she said. "And so are you?" She paused, then added, "No need to leave suddenly?"

Milfonnos shook his head. "I am with you … Eliza."

Eliza smiled as he used her name, seeing her as something more than a priestess, more than part of his entourage. "Yes, you are," she told him, leaning forward to kiss him. His mouth was warm, tasting faintly of fava beans and spices, and she leaned into him, losing herself in the feel of him. His hands were in her hair, then sliding down her body, tugging her shorts free.

She wiggled, allowing him to pull them down her legs, and then another set of hands was lifting her shirt over her head. She looked up to see Teo standing behind the couch. "Hey," she said in greeting, reaching out to pull him down to her, "you joining in?"

Teo chuckled, his breath warm. "I haven't gotten a taste of the new guy yet. You think I'm missing out on the chance to make it with a pharaoh?" Milf's hands found Eliza's waist and pulled her to the edge of the couch, settling himself between her legs. Teo followed her down, hopping onto her side of the couch to sit next to her, mouth barely leaving hers as their bodies readjusted. Her hand slid down to caress his length through the thin shorts, and then Milf's mouth found her core, and she moaned. Teo kissed his way down her jaw and neck to settle on one nipple. She opened her eyes when another mouth found hers, though she recognized Hak's kiss. She kept one hand on Teo while the other cupped Hak's chin, trying to focus on kissing him while sensations flooded her body.

"Come on, Tex," Teo called, and Eliza was vaguely aware of him patting the couch beside her. They exchanged places, Jack's hard length in her hand as he sucked on her nipples. She looked up to see Teo kneel behind

Milf. The pharaoh sat up, pressing his body back into Teo, their bare skin a lovely contrast. "I've never had a pharaoh before," Teo said, kissing the mummy's shoulder.

"And you will never have another," Milf replied, twisting his head to claim Teo's mouth. Jack took the moment to slide his hands between Eliza's legs, pressing into her the way she wanted, and she moaned again.

"Take her," Teo said, "while I take you."

Milf groaned, then shuffled forward, flipping up his linen kilt to reveal a hard cock. Jack grabbed one of Eliza's thighs while Hak held the other, and Milf slid into her in one move. Eliza closed her eyes, savoring the sensation of so many people touching her at once, but opened them again when Milf grunted, body tightening against hers. Teo's hands wrapped around him and grabbed Eliza's thighs, pushing all three of them together, and then he was moving, setting the pace, and Eliza let the pleasure shatter her.

When Milf grunted a few minutes later, emptying himself into her, she was vaguely aware of more bodies shifting before Jack was inside her.

"Yes!" she yelled, aware that someone had slid over the back of the couch to sit behind her. Fingers moved against her ass, and then she was being lifted, ever so gently, and another cock found her entrance. Rafi's hungry mouth found hers as Jack paused, waiting as Rafi slid inside, and then she shuddered, pausing at the fullness of her body before Jack began to move again, this time slow and steady. He began to shake almost at once, and she was vaguely aware that Milf was behind him, hands moving in a steady rhythm, and then Jack looked over his shoulder and kissed Teo.

Eliza's body was on fire with pleasure, and when Jack came, she yelled with him. Falling heavily into Rafi's arms, she let herself be kissed as Jack slowly pulled himself together and moved away. Teo was next, leaning down to throw one of her legs over his shoulder. He gave her a wicked grin, clearly remembering the last time he had done this, then sucked hard on her tender flesh. Eliza clenched, still tight around Rafi's length, and bucked under Teo's tongue, the orgasm shattering her yet again.

When Teo slid inside her, she reached out to fist his hair, yanking him close and demanding he move faster, harder, loving the feeling as he rubbed against Rafi inside her. Teo came with a shout, and then he was dragging Hak over her leg and pushing the merc between her thighs. Hak's hands continued to massage her breasts as he gently moved in her, mindful of her battered state. Still, he made her come once more before losing himself and collapsing atop her.

A long time later, Rafi lifted her off him, and he carried her to the small shower to clean her off. The men took their turns holding her, washing her, stroking her body gently as she touched their slowly hardening cocks again.

After the shower, Teo and Milf took Hak to the small bed, each taking a side and devouring one another. Rafi made a nest of blankets on the floor and laid Eliza down, gently making love to her as the cries of the men filled the room.

Jack didn't join in this round, instead lingering in the bedroom doorway, fisting his cock as he watched them all find their release.

As Eliza fell asleep for the second time that night, Rafi's arms tight around her, she felt herself relax, the tension she'd been holding for weeks finally unwinding.

Chapter 49

As had become his custom over the last few days, Jack woke to a foul smell. He expected to find Sloan's feet, baking—or, rather, curdling—in woolen socks just beneath his nose. But Sloan was gone, and the smell was less damp wool and raging fungal infection and more rotting eggs.

Gas.

The apartment was dark and oddly quiet. It took Jack a moment to realize what was missing: the hum of the air conditioner. The power was out. Cairo was no stranger to intermittent blackouts, especially in the summertime. Had a gas line burst in the neighborhood and caused an outage?

Jack reached for his phone on the coffee table, intending to check for any relevant news reports, but his fingers closed around something else altogether. It was Eliza's bracelet, still resting on the coffee table next to the abandoned bangle. He pocketed the bangle, knowing that Charles would want it, then lifted the bracelet. Jack turned it over in his hands, dragging his thumb over the scarab charm.

The night before, he had been glad to see her not wearing it. Jack would have hated to feel its metallic chill after Eliza's palm coasted up his thigh, knowing that it was a promise from another man, which she'd readily accepted. Anger chewed at his gut.

What Eliza did was a betrayal. While he unequivocally despised the current arrangement, at least he was in the running to have her. That is, until Rafi gave her the bracelet; the lawyer was steps ahead now. It wasn't fair.

But Jack Manning didn't fight fair. He scratched out eyes and twisted testicles and put knives in backs. Fights weren't meant to be fair; they were meant to be won.

Jack rose and headed into the kitchen. The clock on the microwave was dark, though it had only blinked 12:00, 12:00, 12:00 before. He stood before the basin sink with the bracelet, staring into the dark abyss of the garbage disposal. He imagined dropping it in, the spinning blades chewing up the links.

Jack turned on the faucet full-blast and flipped the switch that would cause the garbage disposal to hum. Nothing happened. "Shit," he murmured, remembering that the power was out. He closed his fist, the scarab cutting into his palm.

Movement out the window caught Jack's eye; it was hardly perceptible—a shifting shadow against an inky backdrop—but his eyes were keen and his hackles were up. Someone was outside, crouching on the rooftop of the shorter building opposite the apartment complex.

The pieces clicked into place as the laser sight skated across the windowsill and settled on his bare chest. The smell of gas, growing heavier with every passing moment.

Giuseppe Valdano planned to burn them out like gophers out of a burrow. Jack dropped to the ground and crawled through the apartment.

In the bedroom, he found Hak, Teo, and Milfonnos curled up on the bed like a pile of sated puppies. While the pharaoh didn't sleep, his eyes had the unfocused look of someone deep in thought—and he wasn't looking at Jack.

Jack didn't even consider waking them. He would never hem and haw over putting his own oxygen mask on first, never mind the screaming child sitting beside him.

Eliza was asleep on the floor atop a nest of blankets, Rafi's arm slung over her waist. As the airless apartment had grown hot and humid, she'd thrown off the quilt, revealing her long, naked limbs. She wore only a rumpled t-shirt several sizes too large for her.

It was one of Jack's: a screen-printed Big Bend National Park shirt, featuring a prickly pear and Boquillas canyon. He'd gotten it during a trip with his sister and his niece, a spunky little tow-headed creature, who liked to touch bugs, no matter how many legs they had.

"Eliza," Jack whispered as he shoved the bracelet into the pocket of his sweatpants. "Wake up." He shook her shoulder.

Eliza's sleep-wrinkled eyelids cracked open. "Hm?" She stretched like a cat on a windowsill.

"C'mon, I want to show you something." He tugged on her arm, pressing his finger to his lips.

"What… what's that smell?" Eliza propped herself up on her elbow. "Do you smell that?"

Her voice was a hair too loud, and Jack clapped his palm over her mouth. He tried to make the gesture seem lighthearted, but he was far too forceful. Her eyes widened.

"Jack, what's going on?" she mumbled, her petal-soft lips trembling against his palm. God, the image of her kissing someone else with those lips…

"It's a surprise," he pressed.

Whether it was trust or confusion that got her to follow him, Jack couldn't say. Together, they crept through the apartment. He stopped only to scoop up the Book of Heka—it might prove useful if the stupid mummy came looking for him. In the hallway, he helped her into her shorts and Converse sneakers as she rubbed her eyes with her knuckles.

"What time is it?" she asked.

Jack made a noncommittal noise. It was either early or late, and he wasn't sure which. He gripped her hand and led her down the hall and to the building's staircase, their footsteps echoing off the concrete. Most of the apartments were deserted, or the residents had the sense to never peek out when their neighbors were on the move. That's how a person became a witness, and that's when the trouble started, which was probably why Shogun Security chose this place for their more clandestine affairs.

The stairs terminated in a small alcove, wherein an old Coca-Cola machine hummed. It was so old that a glass bottle of Coke cost only an American dime. The building must have once been popular with expats and an enterprising landlord though he could make a few extra bucks when they grew homesick for artificial sweetener.

Jack hustled out of the alcove, his grip tight on Eliza's wrist. When he unlocked his truck, she balked, a hand on his arm. "What is going on?"

"We need to go," Jack urged, tossing the book inside. "Valdano found us." He cast his eyes skyward, scanning the surrounding rooftops for potential snipers.

Eliza wrenched her arm out of his grip. "We need to go back. Everyone is in danger. We can't leave them up there, asleep!"

One Mummy to Go, Please!

Suddenly, a small explosion made the building shudder. Eliza turned toward it, but Jack grabbed both of her shoulders, forcing her to look at him—and only him. "I'm the only one who can keep you safe, Eliza. They are the loose ends we will trip over if we don't move. Get in the truck."

Eliza's eyes brimmed with tears. "We need to help them."

Jack shook her. "You're not listening. We have to go. We have to drive out of Cairo and away from this mess. We have to go back to how it was in the beginning: just you and me."

"Jack… you're hurting me."

Jack released his grip on her arms, the angry red marks of his fingers in stark relief to her skin. "Get in the fucking truck, Eliza," he growled.

"No!" She raised her hands and an invisible force slugged him in the gut. Jack stumbled back. Anger jetted up his esophagus like hot bile. Yet another reminder of Rafi's inextricable hold on her. She wasn't even wearing the damn bracelet and still his magic protected her.

Someone in the building shouted. Three syllables: Ee-lie-za! He was running out of time. Jack grabbed Eliza's arm and dragged her to the passenger side, ignoring her feeble attempts to hit and kick him.

Before Jack could push her into the cabin, a bullet punched through the windshield, spiderwebbing the glass.

The man holding the gun wobbled, nearly dropping the pistol.

"You stupid British prick!" Jack groaned.

"Reese?!" Eliza exclaimed, twisting in Jack's grip.

Chapter 50

Reese Eldrin had been stalking Eliza for days. After their last conversation, he assumed she was after the Book of Heka, and when she didn't return his call or meet him for dinner, he knew she must have decided to go after the other existing copy in Cairo. In the possession of Giuseppe Valdano, a criminal and gangster known for his inventive ways of torturing those who crossed him.

Reese hadn't thought Eliza would be so foolish, but once she got an idea in her pretty little head, it was very hard to dislodge it.

It must be the mercenary, Reese had decided. Jack Manning was filling her head with all sorts of nonsense. He needed the Book of Heka for his employer, and from what Reese had learned about the man, Jack Manning never stopped until he fulfilled his contract.

Except that Eliza still thought his contract was to protect the dig site.

Reese knew better now. After the catastrophe at the site when Milfonnos showed up and nearly killed everyone, Reese had despaired of ever getting more time to study the artifacts in the tomb. Then, his new benefactor had reached out, and everything was looking up.

That is, until Reese had been in the lab late lingering over the books when no one could spy on him, when he overheard a phone call between his new boss, a Mr. Montgomery, Charles' assistant here in Cairo, and a voice Reese quickly recognized as Jack Manning's Texas drawl. He had suspected

One Mummy to Go, Please!

that Charles was responsible for hiring Shogun to oversee security—except he hadn't realized that Jack's focus wasn't actually the site itself, but the artifacts. Listening to the call, Reese learned that Jack's purpose had shifted.

He still had to get the Book of Heka and as many artifacts as he could back to Cyprus, only now he had an additional goal—find something to lure Milfonnos back as well. Charles had lost control of the creature, which Reese knew meant he'd lose the Book of Heka to his benefactor. He didn't mind—he'd scanned the pages already and could decipher them at his leisure, the images hidden on his personal phone, a device Charles didn't know about.

Hearing the confident promise in the mercenary's voice, Reese's blood had run cold.

"Of course, sir," he'd said. "You need the creature to go to Cyprus. I have just the thing to make him follow."

Reese wasn't stupid. He'd been moments away from death in that sandstorm, and he recalled everything with distinct clarity. He had seen the creature lift the car into the storm, and then stop it from crashing down—because Eliza had been inside. Just like everyone else in her life, the mummy had fallen for her.

If Jack Manning could lure her back to Cyprus with him, the creature would follow, and Jack's contract would be fulfilled.

Reese couldn't let that happen.

Reese knew he was a fool. He had a new sponsor, a shiny new lab, and endless financing. All he had to do was put his head down and study the artifacts they'd unearthed in the tomb—the only damn thing he'd wanted since he started school.

Well, the only thing he'd wanted—until Eliza Cunningham walked into his life.

As soon as he realized that Jack was going to use her as bait, he knew he had to act. To do something to make Eliza see that he was actually worthy of her affections. She had wanted him once. She could want him again. He could make her see that she belonged with him, perhaps back in England, him teaching at the university, her home raising their children...

It wasn't hard for Reese to hack into the computer at the new site, revealing the financial records linking his new sponsor to Jack Manning—and connecting Jack Manning back to Shogun Security. When he realized they weren't returning to Eliza's apartment, he knew they must have gone aground in one of Shogun's apartments. They wouldn't have gone far.

Finding Shogun Security hadn't been easy, but Reese had spent most of secondary school on his computer, and he still recalled a few tricks. Once he had a few possible names to track, the property records search had turned up twelve possible locations. Reese had staked out most of them over the last two days.

It was nearly dawn by the time he reached the one on Ezbet, and when he saw Eliza struggling with Jack in the street, he could hardly believe his luck.

"Stop!" he tried to say, but the words froze in his mouth. Instead, he fumbled the gun free from the back of his waistband. He hadn't shot much since his early university days, but he still knew how to hold the weapon.

An explosion in the building behind them startled him, and he jerked, the gun going off. A hole appeared in the windshield of Jack Manning's truck. Reese cursed, thanking the gods that he hadn't accidentally hit Eliza.

"You stupid British prick!" Jack yelled, seeing him at last.

"Reese?!" Eliza exclaimed, twisting in Manning's grip. "What are you doing here?"

"Rescuing you," Reese said, taking a step closer with the gun held out in both hands. He knew he wasn't a match for the trained mercenary, but he had to try. He had seen other men around Eliza before she vanished—perhaps one of them would arrive to help. His gaze flicked to the burning building behind them.

Or perhaps they were still inside when it blew up, and we're on our own here.

Reese swallowed, finding his courage as his voice steadied. This was Eliza. He had to rescue her.

"With a gun?" she squealed, still trying to break free of Jack's grip. Reese could see she had some kind of bandage around her upper arm, and with a grunt, she yanked hard, the gauze slipping loose as Jack lost his grip.

She practically ran the few steps to where Reese stood on the sidewalk, a hand to her arm, which Reese could see was bleeding now that the bandage had been torn free.

"Eliza!" The name was a shriek, a tornado of sound, and the window of the building across the street shattered, a man's shape visible in the flames. He was there for a second and then gone, no doubt finding a better escape route.

The mummy! Reese recognized the creature and could only hope it was coming to protect her. He only had to hold Jack off for another few precious seconds.

Jack glanced behind him, then held out his hand to Eliza.

"Last chance, sweetheart," he said, desperation clear in his voice. "Come with me."

Eliza stepped closer to Reese, eyes wide as she shook her head. "No," she said. "I'm not going anywhere with you."

"Fine," Jack said, hand reaching behind his back, "if you won't choose me, then I choose the money."

Reese didn't see the gun Jack pulled from the waistband of his pants, but he heard the shot. His only thought was to protect his Eliza, so it made perfect sense to step in front of her, turning her so his body was between her and that awful sound.

He didn't even feel it when the bullet hit, but he was aware of his face hitting the sidewalk and Eliza's panicked stare as she grew dim in his sight.

"You bastard," she growled, turning to face Jack.

Reese's last sight was a vengeful Eliza, power glowing all around her as she spoke words he vaguely recalled from the Book of Heka.

Jack Manning would pay.

Eliza would avenge him. Reese was finally worthy.

Chapter 51

Hot tears brimmed in Eliza's eyes, and the world blurred. It was a small mercy, reducing Reese's prone body to a smear on a dark canvas. A sob bubbled past her lips and, behind it, bile. She spit on the ground, her saliva diluting a droplet of blood spatter. It turned the pink of a Cairo sunset. She felt dizzy.

The nonchalant expression on Jack's face hurt far worse than looking down the barrel of his gun. Where once he'd looked at her with desire, now there was only indifference. It was as though they were strangers.

Had he ever actually cared, or was she merely a means to an end? How much had each kiss cost his unknown benefactor?

Magic lapped against her chest, the sensation not unlike unexpectedly stepping off a sandbar into deep water. She had expected it to be as warm and as pleasant as an embrace, but there was a bite to it. Her tongue rolled to accommodate the vowels that were so unlike her own language, pressing firmly against her hard palate. Magic arced between her fingers like static.

"Eliza..." Jack raised his hands, making a big show of taking his finger off the trigger. "I admit, that was a little rash. You just make me feel so crazy. I did this for—"

"You killed him!" Eliza screamed. She didn't care who heard—let Valdano's men come. "You were going to kill me. I thought you cared about me."

"It's only business, baby," Jack drawled. "Just like it is for you."

Eliza scoffed, balling her hands into fists. Her nails dug half-moons into her palms. The incomplete spell crawled up her arms, runes and hieroglyphs dappling her freckled skin. She would marvel at it if it weren't for Jack's self-satisfied smirk, backlit by fire.

"Isn't that why you're fucking five men?" he continued. "You're keeping us in your stable, just in case your first choice realizes what a loser you are. Rafi's a smart dude. Eventually, he'll realize that you're beneath him. Why would a high-powered lawyer want an oversexed food truck owner? Oh, my bad—former food truck owner. So then you'll settle for whichever idiot will have you."

"That's not true. I love them. I loved you." Eliza took a step toward him, but Jack coolly trained the gun on her. His expression was unchanged; he may as well have aimed at a tin can balancing on a fence post.

"You don't even know what love is," he said, his voice nearly drowned out by shouting in the apartment building. The growing fire punched out the windows on the ground floor, the flames licking at the windowsill. Eliza tried to catch a glimpse of her men beyond the windows, but there was only thick black smoke.

"Please don't make me hurt you," Eliza pleaded. She took another step, but her toes butted up against an obstacle. It was Reese. Carefully, she stepped over him, trying not to stare at the blood pooling beneath his plaid button-down. *Oh, Reese...*

If only she could have loved him in the way he wanted her to. If only she could have told him "no" more plainly so that he could have moved on. He could have been anywhere else but here, maybe teaching at Oxford in a tweed sport coat with a wife to come home to.

"You already hurt me," Jack said through gritted teeth, his finger curling around the trigger.

Afraid, Eliza whipped her hand up, and Jack flew backward, slamming into his truck's grill. He fell into a heap onto the asphalt and didn't move, the gun skittering a few feet away. It may have only been her imagination, but it seemed as though his shadow was slower to join him, slithering across the asphalt like a serpent. Hadn't Rafi told her the protection spell could forcibly separate a person from his soul, even for just a moment?

Eliza hurried to the truck's passenger side, leaning into the cabin to grab the Book of Heka on the center console. When she straightened, intending to head back toward the apartment, someone grabbed a fistful of her hair, pushing her against the doorframe. Jack's spicy cologne burned her nostrils as he leaned into her. "I thought I would do anything for you—even share—but you know what I'm realizing, sweetheart? You aren't worth it. Maybe the heat got to me…"

Eliza couldn't move, her cheek pressed hard against the doorframe, her forearms pinned by the book she held.

The cool metal of Jack's gun slipped beneath her shirt, tracing up her spine. She hated feeling his rough hands on her, hated remembering the way he worshiped her with those same hands. He touched her unabashedly, taking his time; he wanted her to wiggle and fight him.

"I'm going to make sure none of them make it out of that building alive. But I'll do you one last kindness because I am a kind man, even if you don't think so. I won't make you watch."

Eliza imagined Rafi, Hak, Teo, and Milf stumbling down the stairwell, their hair singed and their eyes streaming. The open air alcove with its Coca-Cola machine would allow them to swallow fresh air and catch their breath. But they would also be within Jack's sights. *Bang, bang, bang, bang!* They would be fish in a barrel.

No.

No! Eliza wouldn't let him do it. She struggled in his grip, trying to recall the words to the spell she'd only just uttered. But they slipped away from her, replaced only by panic. She managed to free one arm, her fingers tingling with pins and needles.

The cold gun barrel dimpled her flesh. Jack's dry lips pressed mockingly against her neck; she could feel the curve of his cruel smile. He was so close that she could feel the edge of his wallet in his pocket and something else—something familiar. She recognized the flat disk with its engraving of a scarab beetle, the braided links. Carefully, she slipped her hand inside his pocket, hooking a finger around the bracelet.

"Goodbye, Eliza," Jack said.

BANG.

Eliza flinched. Her ears rang terribly, but she felt no pain.

Jack's full weight fell upon her before he slid down onto the ground. His knees cracked on the asphalt, and he landed on his side in the gutter. Blood bloomed upon his shirt front.

His weapon had misfired, punching a hole through his chest. He may as well have placed the muzzle against a brick wall and pulled the trigger; in a sense, that was exactly what he'd done.

Eliza sank down onto the curb beside him, watching numbly as a trickle of blood edged down the drain. The bracelet in her fingers seemed to glow,

but she thought it might just be a trick of the light. Rafi had promised it would protect her, but she hadn't expected this.

Jack's bloodless lips parted, and he let out a pitiful sigh. Eliza brushed his hair off his forehead, unable to bring herself to leave him to die alone. "I did love you, you know," she murmured. "We all loved you."

Tears—god, she didn't think she would ever stop crying—dappled his t-shirt as she leaned over him. His breathing was noisy and seemed to take a great deal of effort. He seemed to look through her, the pupils so large his eyes look black.

"Eliza!"

Rafi barreled through the smoke, the rest of them on his heels. In the distance, sirens keened. Relief flooded her body but only made her cry harder.

When Eliza finally looked back at Jack, he was dead.

Epilogue

Eliza sat in the passenger seat of Rafi's car, working up the nerve to open the door. They had arrived at the morgue in the late afternoon, the parking lot as empty as it had been when they visited last time. It seemed no one in Cairo was eager to face death.

"You don't have to do this," Rafi said, a gentle hand on her thigh. Eliza glanced down, seeing his hand atop the new floral pattern dress she had on. They had gone to the store, buying enough clothes for a few days as well as small suitcases. They were leaving here and heading to Cyprus, following Milf's gut feeling that his answers would be found there.

The mummy had been distant the last day, following their instructions as they gathered clothes and travel items, smiling when Hak took his picture for the fake passport, but Eliza could sense something had shifted. She wondered if Milf was thinking about the future the way she was.

What happens now?

Milf thought answers lay in Cyprus, where he had found himself time and again after his moments of missing time, and they had decided to go there. Anything was better than Cairo at the moment. Even Rafi's Amun Henet couldn't protect them from another Valdano hit. The man was just too powerful.

Eliza thought he just wanted to face the man who had controlled him and exact revenge. Thinking about Jack's face in that final moment, anger twisting his features, she understood completely. She wouldn't mind getting some revenge either.

She had suggested giving the book back, but Rafi had decided to give it to the Amun Henet instead for safekeeping. Besides, Teo had reminded them, it wasn't about the book for Valdano. It was about revenge. Something Eliza now understood.

Cyprus was sounding better and better. Besides, Poppy was still there. Her friend had texted constantly over the last days, though it had taken Eliza a moment to untangle the mess that Teo had made of her phone after his impromptu borrowing. Most of her contacts had been renamed, and while she appreciated the now seven digit high score on Candy Crash, Eliza hated reorganizing her messages. Though, she couldn't help the chuckle that escaped as she found Poppy, now labeled "Lily" with a picture of a tattoo that Eliza recognized from Poppy's thigh. She had stared at it for a while, trying to figure out how Teo had managed to get a picture of Poppy onto her phone—a picture that certainly wasn't anything Eliza had taken. Staring at it, she wondered what pictures Teo had of her.

"You asshole," she had grouched at Teo as she sorted her numbers, but he only smirked at her as she fussed with her phone.

"You know you love me, Linda," he had said, blowing her a kiss.

Eliza had rolled her eyes at him but said nothing else, focusing on responding to the slew of messages. Apparently, the explosion had made the news, and while Poppy didn't know just how close Eliza had been to the gas leak, she was worried—insisting that Eliza get away from that crazy city with sandstorms and gas leaks and come to Cyprus. They had made plans to meet up after Eliza got settled in her hotel. Poppy had sworn the au pair would have the kids so they could have some girl time. Eliza hadn't mentioned the guys—that wasn't a conversation she wanted to have over text. Poppy would understand when she met them.

That morning, she had contemplated going back to her apartment to grab her things—but Hak and Rafi had insisted it was too dangerous. Eliza had been surprised to find she didn't even mind. There was nothing there that she wanted, nothing that couldn't be replaced.

Glancing around the car again, she knew that everything she valued was sitting there with her. She just had to do this one final thing, and they could leave.

"I have to," she said softly, knowing that she had to face Jack Manning one more time—to say goodbye.

Eliza

"Our priestess is fierce," Milf said from the back seat, and Eliza twisted around to see him. The mummy was dressed like Rafi now, wearing khaki pants and a white button down shirt, the businessman on vacation. Sitting in the middle seat, Teo wore cut off blue jeans and a belly shirt, his hair pulled up in a bun, dark glasses covering his eyes while Hak still wore his dark jeans and black t-shirt, the mercenary the only one who still had access to his wardrobe.

All three looked at her expectantly, waiting for her to decide.

It was her decision. After all, she had been the one to kill Jack Manning. If she needed to say goodbye, they would go with her.

"I need to," she said softly, sadly. "He was wrong, but he was still … one of us. For a time."

Rafi nodded, patting her leg. "We'll all go."

Eliza opened the car door, and they followed, walking quickly into the city morgue. Giuseppe Valdano might still be after them, so they didn't linger, taking the chance that he wouldn't expect them to visit the morgue on their way out of the city.

Samir greeted them inside, face suitably somber as he led them all into the back room. An assistant raised a hand as if to ask questions but fell silent at Samir's head shake. The man left the room, knowing better than to upset his boss, and they were alone. Eliza's hand found Milf's, recalling the last time she was here and the wreckage Milf had left behind.

Since the ritual, Milf had remained with them, a good sign that perhaps the magic had freed him. Eliza was glad to have him with her now.

Samir approached a drawer, opening it slowly. Eliza closed her eyes, slowing her breath and trying to control her racing heart.

I'm so sorry, Jack. I had to do it.

A round of gasps made her open her eyes, and she saw what the others had already seen.

An empty tray where a body ought to be.

"Where the fuck is the body?" Teo asked, breaking the silence.

Samir was already moving, heading to a screen across the room. He began typing quickly. Both Hak and Rafi followed him, Teo lingering with Eliza and Milf at the empty tray.

"Where is he?" Eliza asked. Teo shrugged, looking as confused as she felt. She could almost hear his thoughts. *This is what happens when you fuck with ancient magical books, Linda.* Seeming to sense the mood, though, he didn't say anything, only raised an eyebrow and turned to see what the guys were doing on the computer.

Standing next to her, Milf squeezed her hand, and she looked up at him. The mummy hadn't said much, and now his face was blank.

"I have a confession, Priestess," Milf whispered.

"Did you do this?" she hissed, and Teo moved in to overhear the whispered conversation.

Milf shook his head. "I do not know what has become of your Jack Manning."

"Then what?" She frowned. "And why would you think now it is a great time for confessions, anyway?"

"Priestess," Milf said, eyes sad, "I have lost Kasmut."

ELIZA AND THE BOYS WILL RETURN IN BOOK TWO!

Book Club Questions

1. Reese Eldin is introduced as an old mistake who never quite lets go of Eliza, but it is his tenacity that ends up saving her life—at the expense of his own. What do you think of his obsession and eventual sacrifice?

2. Jack's agenda originally involves protecting the dig site, but eventually, his alternate loyalties are revealed. At what point did you start to suspect his motives?

3. As the first of Eliza's lovers, Jack resents being part of the harem. Is he justified in his feelings?

4. Hak hesitates to get with Eliza at first due to loyalty to Rafi but eventually changes his mind because Rafi has never made a move. Knowing Rafi has a thing for Eliza, should he avoid a relationship with her? Why or why not?

5. Rafi and Eliza have been close friends since she moved in, but he has resisted his feelings for her, claiming his obligations to the Amun Henet make a relationship impossible. Is this a reasonable excuse to avoid pursuing Eliza romantically?

6. Rafi clearly has familial obligations and expectations—things he has chosen to ignore to pursue Eliza. What do you think will happen as a result of his choices, specifically related to his uncle and Naur Salem?

7. When Eliza first invites Rafi to join her, Hak, and Jack, he chooses to only watch. Do you think Rafi is only a part of the harem to make Eliza happy?

8. Eliza struggles with her decision to include Milfonnos in her harem, largely due to his seeming villain status. What do you think of his redemption arc in this story?

9. Milfonnos and Kasmut share a body and a complicated relationship. Given Kasmut's disappearance at the end of the story, what do you predict is next for this duo?

10. Teo is an unrepentant thief and conman. What do you think of his character? Why do you think he chooses to remain with the harem when they head to Cyprus?

11. Jack, Hak, Rafi, Milfonnos/Kasmut, and Teo: Who is your favorite of Eliza's partners?

Author Bios

Beau Lake is a blue-haired, tattooed cryptid lurking in the mountains of Virginia. She is very happily married and lives with a menagerie of children (3) and dogs (3). Her favorite hobbies include digital art and screaming into the void. Mostly the latter. Her other favorite activities include staring a blank Word documents, listening to true crime podcasts, and asking herself, "What would Stephen King do?"

She is the producer of the Eerie Travels podcast. Her written works include the *DC Pride* series (co-writtten with Tatum West), the paranormal/horror romance series *The Wolves of Wharton*, and the upcoming horror series *Allgood*.

Author of the Klauden's Ring Saga and the Conjuring Fascination series, JM Paquette writes fantasy and paranormal romance novels. When she isn't writing, she can be found teaching English to college students as Dr. Paquette or watching her favorite Russian shifter romance movie, *I Am Dragon*. Her areas of expertise include the history of the English language and the intricacies of grammatical rules, but her favorite class to teach is on *Lord of the Rings*. (If you've ever wondered why English is a crazy language, watch her video series on YouTube under Editor JMPaquette!) She enjoys editing manuscripts for academic and creative writers alike, and she adores tabletop roleplaying (THAC0, anyone?) where her halfling ranger/

Twi'lek adept/vampire wizard/[insert race and class here] is often underestimated. You can also find her guest co-hosting the podcast Drinking with Authors--even though she doesn't drink, she loves getting to know fellow authors! Check out JM Paquette at authorjmpaquette.com and 4horsemenpublications.com and as Author JM Paquette on Facebook and Instagram.

**Discover more at
4HorsemenPublications.com**

10% off using HORSEMEN10

Milton Keynes UK
Ingram Content Group UK Ltd.
UKHW040843201124
2976UKWH00015B/34/J